HIGH PR...

"Cotton Smith is ... ...ed of writers of the Am... ...smith

"Cotton Smith's is a significant voice in the development of the American Western."
—Spur Award-Winner Loren D. Estleman

"In just a few years on the scene, Cotton Smith has made a strong mark as a Western writer of the new breed, telling it like it was."
—Elmer Kelton, Seven-time Spur Award winning author of *The Day It Never Rained*

"Cotton Smith is another modern writer with cinematic potential. Grand themes, moral conflicts and courage are characteristic of his fiction."
—*True West Magazine*

"These days, the traditional Western doesn't get much better than Cotton Smith."
—*Roundup Magazine*

"Hats off to Cotton Smith for keeping the spirit of the West alive in today's fiction. His plots are as twisted as a gnarled juniper, his prose as solid as granite, and his characters ring as true as jinglebobs on a cowboy's spurs."
—Johnny D. Boggs, Wrangler and Spur Awards-winning author of *Camp Ford*

"When it came to literature, middle-age had only three good things to show me: Patrick O'Brian, Larry McMurtry and Cotton Smith."
—Jay Wolpert, screenwriter of *The Count Of Monte Cristo* and *Pirates Of The Caribbean*

PINNED DOWN

From his pouch, Bass retrieved a new cartridge, shoved it into the gun's breech and recocked it. The guttural click-click had its own dimension of authority. Two bullets sought the source of the noise ricocheting against the rocks and whining away.

Only then did he seek more information, removing his hat and peering around the far jagged edge of the closest rock. It was an even better move than he guessed, giving him a good view of his adversaries' position while letting him stretch out safely. A flicker of darker gray behind the trees told him where at least one of his would-be assailants was hiding.

"Got to be one there, Bass. Make him pay." Lying flat on the ground, he eased to his right and pushed the rifle stock against his shoulder. He squinted and cautioned patience for a clearer shot. "You want him alive. One of these boys is going to tell what happened—and why…."

COTTON SMITH

BLOOD OF BASS TILLMAN

LEISURE BOOKS NEW YORK CITY

For my newest little treasure, Margaret Ann.

A LEISURE BOOK®

September 2007

Published by

Dorchester Publishing Co., Inc.
200 Madison Avenue
New York, NY 10016

ISBN-10: 0-8439-5853-7
ISBN-13: 978-0-8439-5853-9

Visit us on the web at www.dorchesterpub.com.

BLOOD OF BASS TILLMAN

Chapter 1

Bass Tillman hadn't killed a man in years. Or even thought about it. That was about to change.

He had worked hard to become a respected lawyer in Longmont, Colorado, and leave his wild past behind. Now he was ready to kill again. It was all he could think about as he stared at the freshly dug graves of his son and daughter-in-law.

Behind their last resting place was a silent, split-log farmhouse and beside it ran a narrow creek favored by overgrown currant bushes, graying willows and aging cottonwoods. Bass stared at the house, then at the ocean of rippling waves of buffalo grass to the west with its faint outline of great mountains. His glazed stare took in the tree-teased ridge in the distance to the east that held carefully planted crops in place.

He saw none of them. A soft, hesitant whisper came from barely moving lips. " 'The Lord gave . . .

and the Lord . . . hath taken away; blessed be . . . the name of the Lord.' "

Agony ripped at Bass's soul and jerked him to his knees. Deepening pain tore at the older man's heart. Grief etched new wrinkles on his wolf-lean face and wetness burned at the corners of dark eyes. How could God let this happen? How could He? Was this God's revenge for his days as a gun for hire? Was it life's payment for a time when he didn't believe in anything except a gun, his own nerve—and the two men who rode at his side? Was it retribution for the lives the three gunfighters had taken years ago?

Only light frost-breath followed his questions in the early spring morning as he laid the shovel on the spring-wet ground beside his knee-length boots and staggered to his feet. Mule-ear straps fluttered with the movement. Handmade wooden crosses would have to do for now; he would seek proper masonry in town later. Kicking the shovel away to get closer, he stepped toward the cross above his daughter-in-law's grave and straightened it from a perceived slight tilt to the right.

His need for perfection had not left him even in his stunned sorrow; the graves themselves were squared off and neatly presented. Even in his young, unbridled days, his proficiency with a gun came more from being accurate than being quick.

"I should've been with you." His voice crackled with the declaration. "Together we would've crossed over. Settie would've been waiting for us all. Yeah, we would've gone down . . . fighting. Together." He stepped back, his legs not wanting to hold him.

The words rolled out almost gently from the hardened attorney. Like he was talking to a small boy who had lost a pet. Yet he knew the ache within him would never pass. Never heal. Ever. Not even after the murderers paid with their own blood. Not even after he pissed on their dead faces. He was a hard man. On that, most would agree. But his heart was breaking. At that, most would be surprised.

Running his tongue across his parched lips, he removed his short-brimmed black hat with the wide silk band. Long white hair shivered across his shoulders. He wiped his leathery brow with one end of the long silk scarf wrapped twice around his neck and returned the hat to his sweating head.

"Where are You right now, God? I've tried hard to believe in You. Yes, I damn well have. You know it, too. So, You hear me wherever You are, understand?" He straightened his slumped shoulders. "By my blessed Settie's soul, if it's the last thing I do on this land, I will find the bastards who did this—and I will kill them."

His lower lip trembled and he bit it to keep the agony from overpowering him. "Jacob, my dear son, and Mary Anne, his beautiful lady, you heard me swear it. So, you rest easy now. I'll settle this for you. I promise."

Jacob and Mary Anne Tillman smiled at him from memory. Abruptly, their countenances became wretched, bloody bodies, as he'd found them only two hours ago. He squeezed shut his eyes to hold back the roar of emotion. Some of it escaped and ran down his cheeks. His promise of a revenge quest seemed hollow in the reality of seeing his beloved family no more. Unable to restrain himself any longer, a wail burst from his mouth and tore into the morning air, more like the cry of a badly wounded animal than the sob of a distressed human.

When the sounds would no longer come, he stood shaking.

Most Colorado folks in 1880 thought an older man like Bass Tillman should be sitting on a porch, enjoying his pipe and a good rocking chair. Most likely, they would have thought it, not said it, at least not to his hard face. Too many knew of his reputation as a gunfighter from years before, as well as his intense presentations to juries as an attorney. So far, he had refused to close his law practice in town, especially since his son had accepted the duties of a part-time deputy.

The old attorney took a weak step backward, wobbling, his always-tanned cheeks awash in tears. "Bass, you stupid old man, you should've been here."

Using his own name when talking to himself was a habit that had become more pronounced after his wife's passing.

"Jacob said he had something important to share with you, Bass. You should've guessed it meant trouble." His mind slipped to yesterday when his son had told him that he couldn't have lunch with Bass and his business partner because Sheriff Babbit needed the young deputy's help, but Jacob had something to share when Bass joined him at the farm.

"Oh Jacob, did what you wanted to tell me bring this?" he roared into the morning air. "Why didn't I ask? Why didn't I ask?"

He hardly looked like the calm man of the gun who had faced down three members of the mysterious Hoodsmen just two years ago—alone—as they tried to leave the Longmont Bank after robbing it. Two were killed; the third escaped. The town's money was saved. Even though the gang itself continued to plunder the region, they gave the town a wide berth from that day on.

Bass Tillman grimaced, fighting for breath that wouldn't come. He gagged and staggered sideways. New air burst through his anxiety like water through a cracked dam. His entire body shook. Hardly a match for the tales, from newspaper accounts to dime novels, that many knew of Bass Tillman, man of the gun.

His gunfights and the hiring of this ability to cattlemen in need of protection were well known. His two close friends in those glory days, Frank Schafer and Emerson Holt, were nearly as wild and nearly as good with any weapon. Although some had tried to connect them to Jack Slade and his highwaymen out of the Virginia Dale stage station back then, there was no evidence. Only saloon stories. Stories that included his two friends being killed in a Kansas gun battle ten years ago. The details varied with the telling. Even the name of the town where it occurred. The only constant in those tales was that Bass Tillman rode away. Alone. And changed.

"My God, this cannot be," Bass shouted. "This

cannot be. Jacob. Mary Anne. You can't leave me. You can't." He staggered sideways and fell down. Reading glasses spun from his coat pocket.

In spite of his age, some businessmen had discussed asking him to step in and help with the rash of holdups that had been raping the region for the past three years. Mostly bank and stagecoach robberies. At least one town's bank had been hit while another town's posse was out chasing them. But there had also been raids on silver mine freight wagons and four train robberies. A county fair money box had been taken, too. And one Pinkerton agent had been murdered trying to track them, as well as a railroad engineer during a holdup of the Colorado Central.

Newspaper accounts were constant about a band of armed men appearing out of nowhere, their faces hidden by dyed-black burlap sacks with eye-cuts. Some were certain the gang was actually the infamous James gang, but that seemed unlikely as they were accused of being other places, and in other states, at the same time.

The Hoodsmen, as they were being called, seemed to know when and where to strike. The federal marshal in Denver had his deputies searching high and low for them, and had asked the district prosecutor to ride with his men when possible, so justice would be swift and thorough. Several members of the gang had been caught and hanged, but so far that hadn't slowed their criminal operation.

None had enough nerve to ask Bass Tillman to help, though. A few even wondered if he was involved. Many others pointed to his unselfish caring for the town's well-being, ready to contribute time and talents for its betterment. Although he never spoke of it, some were quite aware he had secured, in court, an overturn of the foreclosure of a farmer's land, when it had been obtained fraudulently. Bass had refused payment from the jubilant farmer, knowing the man had none to spare.

"You sons of bitches will pay with your blood. I'll kill every one of you bastards," he screamed into the morning air, slamming the ground with his fist to match the pounding ache in his head. He grabbed the open-top Merwin & Hubert revolver from his shoulder holster. He wore it every day, just like he wore underwear and socks. Even in the courtroom. Unless a judge noticed and told him to shed the weapon.

The familiar weight of the gun gave him a strange comfort. He held it, cocked the weapon and pointed at a tree. He wanted to shoot. At something. Anything.

"No, Bass. No."

He shook his head and returned the weapon to its holster. Age had already slightly bent his shoulders and time had changed his brown hair into iron and snow. But his eyes remained sharp for seeing into the distance; reading glasses were his primary submission to time. Trying to stand, he saw the glasses on the ground and didn't understand how they had gotten there. He grabbed them and shoved them back into his coat pocket.

Taking a deep breath, he stood. Trembling. "What do You want from me, Lord? You already took my Settie. And our sweet baby children."

His shoulders rose and fell. "Now you've let them take my son. My son! And his Mary Anne." He shook his head.

Pneumonia had taken his beloved wife, Settie, from him five years ago, leaving the fiery lawyer stunned and in denial. It was her love that had turned him from the gun and into respectability. Their first two children died as babies from whooping cough and their love for each other had kept them sane and helped them find peace.

"Frank . . . Emerson . . . if you had been here, we'd have taken the whole damn bunch. I don't care how many there were." Bass leaned over and slapped at his pants to clear away the loosened soil.

Bass had tried relaxing some at his permanent residence in Longmont's largest hotel and very much enjoyed reading and attending the occasional theater presentations that came through. In fact, he had been at the theater last night. Much of his recent time, however, had been consumed helping his son with their fledgling homestead, wedged between a large ranch and several blossoming farms. He wasn't much good at plowing and that had nothing to do with age. Even so, he could work all week and never be stiff or sore. And never seem to tire.

Of course, he would rest on Sunday, the Lord's Day. Reading nothing, except the Good Book. Those who knew him best realized Bass was a changed man; those who knew him by reputation only were leery of his recent interest in the church's ways. The intensity that guided his days with a gun guided his acceptance of the church and its teachings.

"Indeed, I have done many sins, and have more to come, I suppose," he had proclaimed to his son and daughter-in-law more than once, "but to wash up dishes on the Sabbath day has not been among them. Thank the Lord."

Indeed, there was no whiskey or tobacco for him either. Not since Settie put her foot down. Although a little Christmas brandy and a holiday cigar were tolerated. Their only ongoing disagreement had been about his carrying a gun. His lone submission to her wishes in this matter was to leave it in their buggy while in church.

"I remember the day you showed me your first crop." He walked a few steps to Jacob's grave and touched the small crossbar to straighten its imagined balance. He saw again the green fingers of new growth stretching through the black earth. It was a glorious sight.

"Oh, how I wished your mother could have been with us." He took a deep breath, searching for something that would give him emotional relief.

Today was going to be particularly special for Bass, because he hadn't really gotten to spend any time with his son this week. They usually met for lunch in town once a week, often with Bass's business partner, Lucius Henry. But yesterday, Jacob had to leave almost as soon as they gathered to quell a saloon disturbance. He returned only to tell him that he had to help Sheriff Babbit with a task, and that he had something to tell his father when he came out this morning.

That was the last time Bass had seen his son alive.

"Was this related to that saloon problem?" He bit his lower lip to hold back more wetness. "Bass, you must talk with Frank—and with Leonard—when you're back in town." He would see what the sheriff and the owner/manager of the Lorna Saloon could tell him about the saloon situation. Maybe it was related to this awfulness. Maybe it wasn't.

"Whoever did this, I will find you. I will hunt you down. I will kill you." His words were guttural, almost rhythmic, but, again, they gave him no comfort. A vacant pledge against unspeakable loss.

Right now, no sweet memory could find a place in his thoughts to resettle. Right now, his dark eyes told of a different time—he was a hunter again. Of men. Few were better. Those who savagely murdered his son and wife would pay. It was the only thing his mind would accept at this moment. Focusing on one thing at a time and not letting go until he was satisfied was a well-honed trait, like a mountain cat tracking its next victim. He had approached reading the Bible that way—after Settie died.

He leaned over, grabbed the shovel for leverage and turned away quickly toward the house. If time had taken away any skill with a gun, or any thoroughness in his manner, or any savvy in practicing law, it would be difficult to tell. His long black coat was streaked with dirt from burying his loved ones. His tanned fingers were crusted with the same earth. His fingernails were lined with the soil of their graves. A swipe of earth had mixed with the wetness of his right cheek and created an oblong circle, making him appear like a silver-haired Indian in war paint.

Scalped and bloody, the sight of Jacob and Mary Anne in death rushed into his mind once more, bringing new bile into his throat. He staggered and gulped air to help him shove the awful image back into the darkness of his consciousness. His mind was dulled by the agony. But his knees buckled and he fell to the ground once more. The shovel clanked in front of him. How long he was there, he didn't know. But the sun had finally gotten up enough nerve to tiptoe past the horizon and take its place in the sky, no longer afraid of this old gunfighter's rage.

A worried rooster hurried past him, strutting and looking for hens. The motion brought Bass around to an awareness heavy with mental drain, as if an unyielding fog lay across his mind.

"Well. There's no need of worry, friend. They didn't hurt your ladies." His own words punched at his stomach.

The revolver under his coat prompted his fevered mind once again. If only there was something to shoot at. To kill. His gaze took in the retreating rooster and, for an instant, came the black thought of shooting it.

"That's stupid, Bass." He shook his head and let his hand retreat from the weapon, shaking as it did.

Slowly standing once more, Bass rolled his neck to relieve the awful tension and knew he must concentrate. Feeling sorry for himself wasn't something he did. Ever. He leaned over and retrieved his shovel to return it to the toolshed.

The sinewy attorney forced himself to study the ground around the home. It was one thing to swear an oath; quite another to find the guilty. No one, except him, knew what had happened here so far. The nearest neighbor was over that closest rolling hill. A cantankerous Scot. Bass realized the killers had counted on that distance—and the closest ranch's preoccupation with their roundup—to grant them freedom.

Bass had ridden out early to help build a corral. Instinctively, he glanced in the direction of the open space. From here, he could see through the half-opened barn door. Two milk cows, his son's horse and a lame bay were mostly visible, although there appeared to be many tracks there. Tracks of men and horses. His son planned on seeking his neighbors' help for the harvesting, as he would help them in turn. Bass didn't know what would happen to their crops now. That concern would have to come later. Right now, he wanted to learn from the land close by. A story was waiting to be told. An evil story that might lead him to the killers.

"Pay attention, Bass. Look. Learn," he muttered as he began to methodically walk near the dark house. His spurs and boot flaps made the only sounds in the cool morning air. Fierce eyes examined the soft earth close to the front porch.

"Not the time to hurry. Not now, Bass," he reminded himself. This examination would be all he would get.

His strong frame gave a slight groan, as if feeling the agony of death, and Bass looked up. The same sets of moccasin footprints he had seen earlier marched in and out of the house. He couldn't tell how many for certain. Maybe six, but it could have been more. Not many more, though.

The number was clearer with horse tracks. Yes, six sets of hoofprints circled the house and came toward it; all but two were unshod. Six also gathered at the barn and went inside. Since they didn't take the animals, why did they go there? Someone rode a horse with a deep cut in its left rear shoe.

"That's enough to track a man, Bass. You've done it before." He knelt beside the tracks and measured the uneven mark with his finger.

Unshod ponies, moccasins and scalping. All signs of an Indian war party. There were reports of small bands of warriors leaving the reservation to raid and return. Deeded lands were being explored by white settlers again, so it was possible Indians had attacked the farm. Possible. He had even heard about some white men hanging an Arapaho over near Fort Collins last month.

He had often thought to himself that he would have been one of those wild ones if his land and ways had been taken away so brutally. He stood for a moment, staring at the swaying trees, lost in the idea of riding with painted warriors to right the wrongs of trespassers who sought to carve up Mother Earth.

"Bass, it sure looks like a war party." Thin, gauzy lines of breath-smoke accompanied his observation. "Why don't you think it's so?"

Why did he suspect this wasn't the work of Indians? Was it just a plainsman's natural tendency to be cautious? Or a defense attorney's distrust of evidence? It certainly looked like an Indian attack. Maybe that was part of his problem with the picture. It seemed based on the assumptions a white man would make about what an Indian attack should look like. In actuality, he was certain a war party would have sneaked up to the house, not ridden around it, providing good targets. There should be moccasin tracks all around, not just walking inside. Deliberately, he dragged his boot across one line of padded marks, obliterating them, the mule-ear flaps of his boots and old spurs becoming a sort of music.

"Smart to leave the house alone. Burning it would've brought neighbors fast, Bass," he assessed to himself. "Indians would've burned it, though, then hidden and ambushed anybody who came to help. Of course they would've."

Frowning, he forced himself to think about the possibility of a band of outlaws. Six men riding together would likely indicate that kind of trouble. The only such group around, that anyone knew of, were the Hoodsmen. They were bold, robbing banks, stages and trains, almost without fear. According to the newspaper reports, several arrests of individuals blamed for being Hoodsmen—at different times and places—had, indeed, been made. All had been found with black hoods in their possession. None had confessed, denying the masks were even theirs. All had been convicted anyway, and hanged. Bass remembered reading the U.S. Marshal in Denver had promised to soon have all of them behind bars. To that end, he had assigned three deputy marshals and a roving posse.

But there were no accounts of the Hoodsmen attacking farms or ranches. So who were these men who killed his family, if it wasn't Indians? His mind tiptoed once more to the main room of the small house. To see again the awful violence there. Bullet holes snarled from the walls. Mary Anne's prized yellow curtains ripped and barely hanging. Overturned chairs. A shattered vase that had been a wedding gift. Blood splatters soiled the bare wood floor. Almost unnoticed among them were dried tobacco juice stains. Another reason to suspect it wasn't Indians. Bass didn't know any who chewed tobacco; probably some did, but none he could recall. Jacob didn't chew; he didn't smoke. His mind saw again the vase pieces he had carefully gathered together, as if they might magically resume their pristine appearance. Finally he had left them in a pile and exited the house, vowing never to return until the murderers were destroyed.

Numb from the mental return, he let his weary eyes take in the land around him. This time really seeing it. A vast rug of waving buffalo grass was held in place by the distant ribbon of hills running parallel to the farm. Silhouettes of grazing cattle were framed against contrasting shades of brown and greening grass, yellow bluffs and jutting gray rock.

"What will happen to Jacob's fine place, Bass?"

At the question, his heart pounded inside his chest. This was their dream. A clump of dirt clinging to a spur caught his attention. He dug at it and flung the brown ball as hard as his swirling anger could hurl it. His boots were also blotched from digging, but he ignored them.

He forced himself to return to an assessment of the scene. Nowhere had he seen any spent cartridge shells. Strange, he thought. Neither these men nor his son had fired at each other. That meant the so-called Indians had ridden in a circle around the tidy farmhouse for nothing. No, it meant the men in the moccasins had walked up to the house and been invited in. Riding in a circle had come after their deaths. For effect, he thought. Likely the moccasins had, too. It had to be.

"Jacob knew these men. He trusted them," he muttered and rubbed his unshaved chin. "It was somebody who was expected—or accepted—by Jacob without concern."

That let out Indians, too. Jacob didn't distrust them; he just didn't know any. Not like Bass did anyway. The elder Tillman stood for a moment and wondered if he should ride for his friend, Nancy Spirit Bear, an Oglala holy woman and one of the few practitioners of Bear medicine left that he knew about. She might be able to guide him to the murderers by talking with the spirits. Long ago he had quit scoffing at such ideas. He had seen things that made him leery of being so sure about things like that. But she often spoke in what seemed like riddles to him. Talking with her would have to wait anyway; he might find them on his own. It would be quicker, he decided.

Even so, her mysterious words about him and his ways found their way once more in his mind. She had told him that the mark of The River was on him. *Kin Wakpa*. The River was a strong, independent, powerful force, as was he. Yet The River was as changeable as its brother, The Wind, while always finding a way to advance. So was he, she said. The River was always pulling others to it. Defiant at times. Grand at times. Destructive at times. Never to be ignored. Driven with a purpose others could not see or understand. Ah, but The River could also get caught in backwater, stagnant and churlish, and become very destructive to any who sought its touch.

The River was ever a mystery to others. Bass Tillman was like The River, she said. She had even hinted that Bass, like this natural force, would live forever. He never could figure out what the sign of The River was and had advised her so. She had told him a long-ago story of a young warrior taken by the force of The River, but his presence there had been beneficial to his tribe, and eventually he became an old man living beneath the waters. That hadn't helped him either. She added that while The River was the fountain of life on earth, the river of death was the Milky Way. All souls must pass through that sky river on their way to forever. It wasn't something he understood either and said so.

She simply asked him to think about his life. She also told him to leave a tribute upon any water he passed, because all streams led to The River. She told him that all water—rain, teardrops— were related to The River and that he should honor them as well. Since Grandmother Moon controlled The River and all its offspring, he was always to step around moonbeams and never on them. He was never to cross water at night, however.

To help him remember his life-force connection, she had given him a small piece of rainbow quartz, a piece of The River. Frozen. He wore it as an attachment to his watch chain.

He looked down at the reflective stone hanging from the silver chain stretched across his vest. He touched it and forced himself to focus. She had often told him that stones were the oldest—and wisest—of beings. In a quiet place in his heart, he knew his feelings for her weren't all about spirits or Bear medicine. She had looked at him in a way that he knew his feelings weren't alone. Guilt had driven that fledgling emotion into a corner of his heart and told to stay there.

"Bass, you don't know everything. She might be right," he muttered to himself. To that end, he had always left a tribute when passing a creek or a pond. And he never knowingly stepped on a moonbeam. In truth, they were tributes to Nancy Spirit Bear.

A snort broke into his reverie and he swung toward the sound. His gun in his fist. Cocked.

It was his mule, tied to a struggling cottonwood at the edge of the cleared ranch yard. When he rode up, no matter how much Bass encouraged the animal, nudging it with his spurs and reassuring it with soft words, his mule wouldn't get any closer to the house and the death within. Now his ten-year-old gray mule was annoyed by a calf searching for its mother.

"Othello, that's enough" he yelled in the direction of the mule, uncocking and reholstering his revolver. "I'm trying to concentrate. You wouldn't help, so just stand there, damn it. That calf isn't going to hurt you. He's hungry."

In response, the mule trembled in fear, brayed three times and yanked on its reins. Bass couldn't remember the animal behaving so much . . . like a mule.

"Damn it, it's all right, Othello. It's all right." He knew it wasn't and never would be again, but the animal needed reassurance. Bass walked over briskly to his mount, his long black coat floating behind him like an ill-conceived shadow.

Othello's ears remained on guard while the old man turned the calf toward the open land, pointed at several cattle dark in the distance and gave it a swat on the rump. With a jump, the little animal curled its tail and crow-hopped sideways. Bass waved his arms and the calf finally decided to seek milk elsewhere.

"Atta boy, mama's waiting for you out there somewhere."

He watched the young animal bounce gaily toward its own, most likely a few head that had wandered away from the ranch down the way. The sight made him wince and he turned away, swallowing hard to keep his stomach down. Shadows of his son as a boy skipped through his mind. Voices of yesterday whispered to him and he stood without seeing, only hearing. Settie whispered sweetly in his ear; a grown Jacob told him about his goal to build a fine farm; Mary Anne whispered about growing a family; a six-year-old Jacob told him about a frog he had just found.

Othello snorted again and Bass finally returned to his search.

Something glittered ahead of him and he sped up. A brass tomahawk lay in a clump of grass. It was either Northern Cheyenne or Sioux. The latter, he thought, with its use of red flannel strips and geometric patterns on the handle. Beside the weapon were two eagle feathers clinging to the edges of the grass. He didn't touch the items, but knelt beside them. His dark eyes were skeptical and the deep crow's-feet surrounding them sought each other as he squinted. Both had once been worn in a warrior's hair; the leather base was intact. Circles and cuts on the feathers represented coups won, but he couldn't determine the tribe.

He stood and walked on, then stopped and turned around. "No blood, Bass. No blood. Why would a warrior leave behind such a fine weapon or coup feathers unless he had been wounded or killed?"

Ahead were eight scattered arrows, roughly paralleling the circle of horse tracks for about ten feet. These markings were definitely Cheyenne. It was possible the two tribes were riding together; they often did when fighting white men. The arrows, though, created the same problem for him as the tomahawk: Why would a warrior drop them here if not wounded? On his knees, he examined the ground itself for even a single drop of blood.

"Wouldn't Utes be more likely, Bass?" the old

attorney mused. "I hear there's silver on their reservation. That means white men will be taking away their land. Again."

He shook his head and studied the signs of battle again.

"No blood. No, this cannot be."

Somebody wanted others to blame this on Indians. That much was clear to him. Just the signs of an attack would be enough to send most people into a frenzy, demanding that the army rid the world of these godless heathens. Once again, his mind required knowing when this tragedy had happened. Once again, his rational thought produced an answer of only a few hours ago. His son's body was not yet cold when he'd first caressed it. Only the life was gone.

"Jacob, who would you open the door for in the middle of the night? Why?" he asked. "An emergency, of course. That's it."

It had to be. Perhaps one of the riders pretended to be hurt or wounded. Jacob—and Mary Anne—would respond immediately to someone injured, whether they knew the men or not. It was deep within them. Such caring, as far as his son was concerned, would have been one of his late mother's gifts. Jacob would also have considered it a part of his duties as a part-time deputy, even though his jurisdiction was strictly town-bound.

Death would have been easier than this. Much easier. His mind sought one of the Shakespeare passages where he had found both solace and enjoyment for years. He wasn't even aware of his recital. " 'To die:—to sleep: No more; and, by a sleep to say we end the heartache and the thousand natural shocks that flesh is heir to, 'tis a con-summation devoutly to be wished.'" He made a fist of his left hand.

It was only a partial fist, not quite closed; thanks to bullet damage in his hand years before. Whenever he thought about it, he would say that the stiffness made it easier to hold a rifle—or, these days, a hoe.

"What's that?" His voice was gravelly, halting and eager to be distracted.

Chapter 2

His gaze glimpsed something small a few feet from the farthest arrow. Quickly, he scrambled to determine the extent of his interest. A gold stick-pin. A fancy one with tiny diamonds forming the letter L. He lifted the pin from its grassy location and placed it carefully in his shirt pocket with his left hand.

"Whoever you are, 'Mr. L,' I'm going to find you—an' you're going to die."

Continued search yielded three more arrows and two eagle feathers next to the house. His mind told him they had been thrown there. The tall man's shoulders rose and fell. Nothing more would be gained by staying. His left hand sought the silver watch in his black vest pocket and clicked it open. The piece of quartz waltzed on the chain. A smiling Settie stared back at him from the cracked image laid within its lid.

Not now. Not now. He slammed it shut without

even seeing what time it was. With spring frost-breath billowing around his aquiline nose and thin lips, he decided it was time to follow the trail of the marked horseshoe. Maybe he could catch up, especially if they were celebrating. Quickly, he completed his circle of the house, leading the reluctant mule by its reins.

His mind clicked. Something was missing. Of course. Their dog. Cutter was a large black-and-brown farm dog of unknown parentage. Jacob loved him and Mary Anne tolerated him. Bass looked around the untelling land. Cutter was likely dead as well; the dog would have have tried to defend his masters.

"Cutter! Where are you, boy?" he muttered. His mind held back a louder cry.

Squinting into the morning, he tried to concentrate. Where was the dog's body? Probably it had been dragged off by wild animals. He must find it, no matter how much of a hurry he was in, and bury the remains alongside Jacob and Mary Anne. They would want that.

A small square of white caught his eye, restrained by clutches of a wiry bush next to the house. Leaning over with his mule stepping close as if to see as well, he realized it was a folded piece of paper and grabbed it with his free hand. A telegram.

The words snarled at him from the small sheet:

J T KNOWS STOP COUNT ON IT STOP GET VC OUT OF THERE QUICK STOP YOU KNOW WHAT TO DO WITH JT STOP DO NOT HURT VC STOP HIDE HIM STOP H

" 'VC'? Who—or what—is 'VC'?" he asked aloud. "And who is 'H'?" He stared at the note. " 'JT,' that's you, son. That's you. Why?"

Without looking up, he caught movement among the cluster of cottonwood trees guarding the gateway to the farm. It wasn't a dog. It was men. Or rather, their shadows. Two, maybe three, men.

"How long have they been watching you, Bass?" he muttered and, instinctively, ducked behind the mule as if checking the cinch.

No one was around when he'd ridden up, of that he was certain. Hair curled along the back of his neck. His own concentration would have made it easy for them to sneak close. Now they were forty feet away and waiting. He had felt a sense of being watched earlier, but dismissed the sensation as part of his heartache.

Whoever was there had disappeared once more, most likely settling into position at the base of the trees and underbrush. His mind dismissed the possibility of neighbors; they would have ridden right up. These had to be some of the men who had come before to kill. Had to be.

"Bass, it seems this note has somebody a bit worried. Or this damn stickpin. Or both," he whispered to himself, keeping his body and head behind the quiet animal. "Why are they waiting to shoot? Maybe they were waiting for me to find this. That's it, Bass. Bad men are lazy men. Count on it."

Keeping behind his mule, he pursed his lips, refolded the paper with his left hand and shoved it into his shirt pocket, along with the stickpin.

The owners of the jewelry and the note must have realized they were missing and become worried about their being found. Why else would they return? They had obviously taken care to give the scene the look of an Indian attack, and that took time. And preparation. This was no casual confrontation. It was murder. Calculated murder.

With his right hand, he lifted the mule's right front hoof, continuing the appearance of his not knowing they were there, while remaining a difficult target. With his left, he retrieved his rifle from its saddle sheath, keeping the weapon against the mule so it wouldn't be seen. It was awkward for his stiffened hand to handle the powerful weapon without help from the other. He gritted his teeth to assist in the withdrawal of the single-shot Ballard with an S-and-ring lever, shotgun-style stock and steel buttplate. One of the .50-caliber versions, it could stop a buffalo and had, more than once. Although the gun hadn't been fired in several years, he always kept it freshly oiled. Perfection demanded such care. A leather pouch of cartridges waited in his saddlebags.

He let go of the hoof and sought the additional ammunition. Slipping the sack into his pocket, he kept the long gun parallel to the mule so it wouldn't be seen. The old attorney forced himself to move slowly, keeping his head and body behind Othello's thick frame. Nonchalantly, he flipped the reins over a low branch as he slipped behind the tree, bringing the gun into position as he landed.

Bass squinted along the rifle barrel, following a dark, bobbing shape in a gap between two trees.

Sunlight found a rifle and winked back at him. He cocked the heavy gun and fired in one motion; the gun stock punched hard against his shoulder. The Ballard's roar was a mountain lion in the morning and the shadow jerked backward away from the trees as if a giant hand had pulled it aside.

Two return shots slammed against the trunk, spitting shards of bark and wood. Othello snorted and bolted with her reins slapping the hard ground. A too-hurried shot spat dirt a foot from his boots. Without waiting to determine his accuracy, Bass dove to his right and rolled until he reached a cluster of large rocks some ten feet away. Bullets bit into the ground where he had been and one followed his movement, clipping the heel of his boot. His own visible wisps of breath gave away his stopping place, but he wasn't trying to fool anyone, only to give himself a better angle. He levered the gun and freed the smoking cartridge.

"Damn it, Bass, you shot high. Or were you aiming at his shoulder, not his heart?"

From his pouch, he retrieved a new cartridge, shoved it into the gun's breech and recocked it. The guttural click-click had its own dimension of authority. Two bullets sought the noise, ricocheting against the rocks and whining away.

Only then did he seek more information, removing his hat and peering around the far jagged edge of the closest rock. It was an even better move than he guessed, giving him a good view of his adversaries' position while letting him stretch out safely. A flicker of darker gray behind the trees told him where at least one of his would-be assailants was hiding.

"Got to be one there, Bass. Make him pay." Lying flat on the ground, he eased to his right and pushed the rifle stock against his shoulder. He squinted and cautioned patience for a clearer shot. "You want him alive. One of these boys is going to tell what happened—and why. Remember that, Bass."

To his far left, another man was crawling toward him. Thirty yards from the tree line. Closing slowly. The day held its breath as Bass watched him advance. The other ambusher would have to wait.

"That first boy's hurting bad, Bass, but you didn't kill him. He'll talk, if you can get to him soon enough. Going to lose a lot of blood, though." Bass watched the crawler get nearer, while keeping an eye on the third silhouette nestled within the trees.

"Maybe you ought to wing this one, too, just in case, old man." He could see the crawler clearly; he was pumpkin-faced, hatless and wore leather cuffs.

The long-barreled Colt in the man's fist was attached to a lanyard around his neck and tied to the embedded loop in the gun's butt. His bald head was on a swivel, moving back and forth, as he eased himself along the land, shortening the distance that separated him from Bass. It was obvious neither he nor the third ambusher thought Bass had seen the crawler.

Bass was also certain the advancing assailant

didn't know his exact location, only that he was somewhere behind the rocks. He drew his shoulder-holstered revolver and laid the rifle against the rocks, so just a bit of the barrel protruded. It was time to let the crawler know where he was. The old attorney's pistol roared twice like a night train in the still air.

Surprised, the pumpkin-faced man groaned and slumped where he crept. A bright red circle blossomed along the man's right shoulder.

A rifle shot from the trees followed Bass's assault, but too late to catch him. From behind the rocks, Bass retook his Ballard and shoved the revolver into his belt. Cupping his hand to his mouth, he yelled, "Johnny, get to the far side of that last one. Right. He's behind the trees there."

The false statement might make the remaining ambusher do something foolish.

The sickening thump of bullets striking the top of the rocks and whizzing into the air followed. From the darkness of the trees, an unknown voice shouted out a name as if it were a question. Bass assumed it was the name of the crawling man now sprawled moaning on the ground.

He waited, hoping for another view of the last ambusher. Nothing. He grinned. Nobody could be as patient as he could. It was a well-learned trait. Part of the quest for perfection; no warrior could be without it for long. Nancy Spirit Bear said The River was always patient, until it was riled. He was riled, but his eyes studied the trees and the surrounding area for movement. Or a stray shadow. Or a hint of gunmetal. Or a sound that shouldn't be there. The first sounds were from the wounded man lying twenty yards or so away.

The pumpkin-faced outlaw raised his head and called out weakly, "B-Bill, I'm hit. H-help me!"

Bass waited, watching the crawler squeeze his arm to ease the accelerating pain. He studied the outlaw's frightened eyes and was certain the man would talk, when this was over. The signs were there. He didn't know about the initial wounded man telling him what he wanted to know, but, physically, he should be able to do so as well. First, he must concentrate on the third ambusher.

"B-Bill, p-please. I—I can't m-move."

A lone shot rang out and the wounded man's head jerked, then slammed into the earth. Blood escaped from the black hole in his skull.

Bass saw the orange flash from between two far trees and fired at the light. For an instant, he saw the gun itself. A Pedersoli rifle with a scope.

"What the? Damn, he read my mind," Bass grumbled, reloaded and cocked the big gun.

Three shots danced along the top of the rocks; two ripping off flint edges of the outcropping itself and the third, whistling overhead. Bass lay against the ground, trying to decide on his next move. Could he dash out to the right and get a good angle? What if the third gunman decided to rush him? What would his would-be killer expect? The gunman had already proven smart enough to prevent Bass from learning anything from his companion. Would he do the same to the first man Bass wounded?

"Cold he is, that's for sure, killing his own friend," Bass muttered. "Remember that, Bass. Wonder if his name begins with an H—or an L."

He glanced again at the open ground farther to his right. It sloped slightly downward, like the curve of a voluptuous woman's hip. He smiled at the analogy and gathered his feet to make the dash. Even if the gunman was waiting for a move, and wounded him, Bass figured he would be able to fire back. It was risky. So was staying.

Another gunshot snarled in the stillness. It wasn't close, he realized. What was the man shooting at? He guessed the first wounded man. Hoofbeats caught his ear. A horse galloping. Away.

Everything in him wanted to jump up and follow the sound, for surely it was the third ambusher getting away. He took a deep breath and waited. What if the man had sent one of their horses running just for this reason, to get him to stand? It was a trick he would've tried—and had in the past.

"Wait, Bass," he spat. "Act your age. Waiting is a helluva lot smarter than jumping up." Out of habit, he made a partial fist of his stiffened left hand, holding his rifle in his right.

After a minute of continued silence, he removed his hat, placed it on the end of his rifle barrel and eased it above the rocks. Nothing. He decided to stay with his original strategy and dash for the open slope.

"Run, you old bastard!" he muttered as he crouched and ran from the rocks, leaning over and glancing at the dark trees for movement.

Reaching the deepest part of the land hump, he stopped, raised his Ballard toward the trees and waited. His breath jerked in response to the race.

"Come on! The first shot I will give you. It's the last I want."

No signs of movement gave him more confidence to advance. Soon he was among the cottonwoods themselves and it was evident the third man had escaped. The two remaining horses, tied to underbrush, grazed some fifteen feet away. He was not surprised to find the first outlaw he had wounded sprawled at the base of a tree. The man's face was scraped, from his forehead to his chin, where it had slid down the trunk. Bass pushed the unmoving body with his boot, his rifle pointed at the man's middle. A large black hole was heart high in his back, his coat rich with oozing crimson. That was the shot he had just heard. Obviously, the third man wanted no possibility of either companion talking. Unseeing eyes appeared as he rolled him over. Bass's shot had hit the man in his right shoulder as he thought. It was a nasty-looking wound, but not fatal. Unless the man bled too long. That didn't matter now.

He remembered the second ambusher and went over to him. Even from a distance, it was apparent that this outlaw was also dead. He'd expected as much. There was only one thing left to do that made any sense: Track down the third gunman. He looked around for his mule. Othello hadn't gone far; the mule was grazing contentedly twenty yards away.

"'Time shall unfold what plaited cunning hides.'" Bass whispered a favorite passage from

King Lear, one of his favorite Shakespeare plays. In an odd way it felt good to repeat such a familiar line, as if his world was normal, when it was not and never would be again.

"Keep telling yourself that, Bass. You've got nothing but time . . . now." He reminded himself that he could always return and see if the two dead men had any identification. Turning loose the remaining horses might lead him to the rest of the murderers. Depended on the animals, though, and whether it was a moving camp or not.

"Can't hurt, Bass. Let them go—and follow that third bastard's tracks while you're at it."

Faint hoofbeats from the northeast alerted him. The sound was growing louder. Someone was headed this way. He stepped behind a tree to wait.

Chapter 3

A silhouette appeared on the green ridge directly north of the ranch, paused briefly and raced down the hillside. Sunlight flicked from the barrel of a long gun, now visible in the rider's fist.

Bass took aim at the approaching rider. And waited. About fifty yards away, the rider lay against his horse's neck and continued his rapid advance.

"Smart man," Bass mumbled. "But ol' Ballard here can still separate his backside from that saddle." He squinted along the barrel, noticing a dark shape bouncing slightly in front of the rider's right leg. "He'll rue the day he came back."

"Damn! That's Timbel McKinsey!" he half shouted. "Good Lord, you almost shot him, Bass." The weary attorney looked up from the gun, shaking his head.

The incoming horseman was his son's closest

neighbor, Timbel McKinsey, an eccentric Scottish farmer who liked singing, playing the accordion and going to church.

Without making himself a target too soon, Bass yelled a welcome. "McKinsey! Timbel McKinsey! It's me, Bass Tillman. Jacob's pa. Come on in."

McKinsey waved his shotgun in recognition, raised himself upright in the saddle and raced down the hillside. He reined in ten feet from Bass and the burlap sack containing shotgun shells swung wildly back and forth from its tied position at his saddle horn. A square jaw was jutted forward in his intensity, demanding an explanation without stating so. Long sideburns narrowed his ruddy face and a sweated-through, short-brimmed hat topped it. A herringbone sack suit was reinforced with patches at the elbows, knees and a few other places. It was once his wedding suit. At present, it served as everyday wear, even when plowing and planting. A boiled white shirt with a paper collar showed signs of equal use. Coffeyville boots covered his lower trousers and the streaks of mud on both were mute testimony to a morning spent plowing.

"Ye'r a *sicht* fir *sair eyen*. I, be *tae* hearin' a *muckle* o' shootin', Mr. Tillman," McKinsey said in his clipped Scottish brogue as he straightened in the saddle; his double-barreled shotgun lay across his lap, as he presented his reason for being there. "I says *tae* meself, I says, who be foulin' *thae guid* day with *sech*? Be there *sae* much game about? 'Deed, it *canna* be. Too *muckle* o' shootin' for it *tae* be that, I says. Must be *thae* devil hisself at work. My Sarah, she's *aye* at me *tae* be *gaun tae* see. But I tell her *thae* field be needin' me plow. Sarah be sayin' it can wait, *sae* I *coom*."

His wide, oval eyes reminded Bass of a barn owl searching for food. Most of the Scots he knew greeted the morning with anger, full of bullish declaration. Bass didn't need to be slowed by this intrusion; the third ambusher had a big enough lead as it was. Hurrying to retrieve his mule, Bass explained the situation over his shoulder, and that he planned to catch the remaining gunman if he could.

McKinsey's initial response was either a Scottish blessing or a curse. Bass didn't know which and didn't care, followed by *"Out o' thocht."* He knew that was a statement about the murders being beyond belief. To himself, he agreed.

"Be ye thinkin' *yer* mule *thae* match for *guid* horseflesh?" McKinsey continued.

"Reckon I'm going to find out." Bass eased into the saddle, holding his rifle away from his body in his right hand and trying to hide his own anger at the interference.

McKinsey watched him. *"Wadna* ye be mindin' *soom* company? Your Jacob an' his *breagha* lady be *guid* neighbors *tae* meself an' Sarah."

"Might be gone overnight. Maybe more." Tillman squeezed his legs against the mule's sides. "Won't your wife be worried?"

"I *wull* tell her an' catch up with ye."

"He rode west—but I don't know where he's going."

"Weel, me farm be *tae thae* west."

Bass didn't like the insinuation that Othello couldn't run fast enough. He slapped the reins against the mule's backside and the animal jiggled its way into a lope. "I could use the extra gun, but I won't wait."

"*Nae* doubt. I *wadna* ask ye."

Tying the reins loosely around the saddle horns of the remaining ambusher horses, he slapped them into a gallop and followed. One was unshod; none had a marked shoe; neither did the third ambusher's horse. The animals stopped at the first sign of fresh grass and showed no inclination of moving again soon. Bass decided not to wait and pressed on, following the third ambusher's clear trail. After a half hour at a hard gallop, he eased his mule into a walk.

McKinsey admitted he was impressed with Bass's mule and pulled off to inform his wife of the situation and said he would catch up later, promising "Be seein' ye at *thae* back o' four."

The trail of the last ambusher was warm and headed due west; his hoofprints told a fairly easy story to follow. Bass continued alone, keeping his mule at a steady pace, but mindful of the animal's strength. He passed a farmer plowing his field and waved. The man was walking behind a single plow with two oxen.

"Jacob's way ahead of that boy, Bass," he muttered. "Jacob's got the latest equipment." He pictured his son's two-bottom sulky plow drawn by three horses with him riding. The memory quickly snarled into a vision of the young man in death.

Bass tried to concentrate on the sight before

him. Trailing the farmer and his plow was a solitary woman walking behind him. Both returned Bass's greeting with their own waves and returned to their tasks. Her hand corn planter was repeatedly jabbed into the freshly opened soil, depositing four or five kernels with each thrust.

"Too late for that, Bass," he muttered again. "Jacob did his planting months ago."

The thought almost made him vomit. Jacob and Mary Anne would have been working their field now to make it grow and strengthen. He shook his head to remove the distress and tried to concentrate on the tracks ahead.

The escaped gunman either didn't think he would be followed, or didn't care, for he was making no attempt to hide his trail. Bass urged his mule into a lope that led him past noon. He didn't expect to see the Scot again. Returning to his wife would remind him of the danger of trailing a killer likely joining others. He stopped once at a spring-lusty stream to let his mule drink and sip the coolness himself. After remounting, he withdrew a small sack from his coat pocket and poured a handful of tobacco shreds into his hand. He tossed them onto the still water, as Nancy Spirit Bear had directed, and continued. The trail slanted toward the west a hundred yards past the creek, toward a black stretch of trees covering a distant ridge.

A land-eating gallop resumed. His mind was black and half wished the gunman would double back to ambush him. A gunfight would give his soul some relief, either way. Curling in and out of a mile-long string of cottonwoods lining a struggling creek, he passed a spongy swale of slick wet grass and slipped over three broken hills. The ambusher's trail was unmistakable, even as the shadows of dusk began to gather strength. It was a hurried escape, but appeared to be a planned one. The rider's direction hadn't wavered since leaving the farm.

"How fast things change, Bass." He spoke barely above a hoarse whisper. "Yesterday, you were having a nice lunch with your business partner, talking about money and the making of it—then a fine night at the theater—and now you're chasing the man who killed your son and his wife." He shook his head. "Is this Your way of shoving me back into yesterday, God?" No, he decided silently, it was more likely the devil pushing him into hell.

After his declaration, Bass was aware of a far-away rider coming behind him, his shape a mere stick against the darkening horizon. It had to be McKinsey, but a smart man was always careful. He reined Othello to a welcomed stop, swung down and yanked his rifle free from its sheath.

If this wasn't Jacob's Scottish neighbor, he would assess the man's intentions. Shooting would be a last resort. The unusual shape of rider, horse and sack of ammunition soon became apparent. It looked like another sack, a larger one, bounced on the other side of the man's saddle.

Bass knew he had underestimated the Scotsman. He patted his sweating mule's neck and waited. To himself, he muttered, "It's good to have him with you, Bass. You need to see a friend. Your son's friend."

Pulling up beside Bass, McKinsey proudly announced, "Aye, Sarah *maude* me *tae* bring a wee supper fer us. Figured ye *wadna* be carryin' *sech*, ah, because o' *thae* . . . day."

"That's real thoughtful." Bass pushed his hat back on his forehead. "Been wondering if there might be a piece of hardtack in my gear. Probably nothin' but a hunk of hard candy, though." He had planned on eating dinner with his family.

McKinsey swung down and triumphantly presented a bulky flour sack that had been resting on the opposite side of his saddle from his shotgun shell sack. "Here. 'Tis a fine salted pork sandwich I *braught* for ye. Bread be just from *thae* oven. Got *soom* bacon and black coffee for *thae* morn. *Wull* ye *nae byde a wee* an' sup?"

Thanking the Scot, Bass wolfed the sandwich, praised his wife's cooking and washed it down with gulps from his canteen.

" 'Tis me thinkin' that our devil's lad be stopping at *thae* cabin deep within *thae* trees ahead o' us," McKinsey volunteered with a mouthful of sandwich. "Ay, built by a hermit name o' Lark, it were. *Weel*, a strange fellow, he *tae* be. Speakin' only *tae thae* redman. Be eatin' coyotes an' ravens an' *naethin' guid*. A lad *tae haud wide o'*."

"How do you know this?" Tillman glanced at his companion as he checked the cinch on his mule, tightening it slightly.

Wiping his mouth with the back of his hand, McKinsey grunted, "Aye, be findin' it once, I did, lookin' for me strayin' milk cows, I was."

"Strays? Didn't think your land went this far."

"*Na, doesna.* Me cows be herded there. By Lark hisself. Bent on makin' *thaim* his own, he was."

Bass nodded, but didn't ask more. That would have been impolite. By the look on McKinsey's face, he had not brought back any cows.

The attorney squeezed his left fist until it hurt, released its half closure and changed subjects. "You're probably right. Thought our man would head for town, but he's riding like he knows where he's going—and isn't worried about being followed." The statement was said more to himself than to the Scot. "Or, more likely, doesn't expect it by now."

"Either *sae* or he be *thae* devil hisself, leadin' us on." McKinsey shoved the last bit of sandwich into his mouth and peered into the thickening woods, trying to determine if any of the shadows belonged to a man.

"How about this Lark fella, he still live there?"

"*Na*, he be *taekin'* *thae* wrong man's cows—and be findin' hisself at *thae* end o' a fine rope." A flask from McKinsey's coat pocket appeared and he downed a long swallow, then held it out for the older man. "A wee touch o' courage fer ye? Cock *thae* wee finger?"

Bass declined and climbed back into the saddle. The Scot did the same, returning the small container to his pocket, relieved that his riding companion hadn't wanted any.

"How would a man know about this place if he didn't live close?" Bass asked himself, pushing aside a low-hanging branch and entering the forest. "Unless it was part of an agreed-upon meeting place?"

An advance guard of birds announced their entrance and his mule balked for a moment at the noise. His spurs convinced Othello that moving on was the thing to do.

"Me not be knowin' o' such reasonin'." McKinsey made no attempt to push away the same branch, letting his horse bull it aside. The branch popped up into his face and he swatted it so hard the wood cracked. "But 'tis surely a place where *thae* wee people be livin'."

"Do they ride fast horses?"

"Donna ye be takin' a len o' McKinsey, me friend. There be much in this *warld* that nonbelievers *donna* see. Aye, 'tis so."

Bass almost told him that his Indian friend had said men like him, men of The River, could see little people, if they concentrated. He decided against sharing the thought. What difference did it make right now? He had never seen any little people himself, so why discuss it? Nancy Spirit Bear had explained, much like McKinsey had just said, that faeries would only show themselves to those who believe, even The River people. Maybe that was the problem, he didn't believe in them.

They rode farther into the darkening forest and startled a resting deer and its fawn. The two animals slid to another retreat deeper in the woods. The two men worked their way along a path unseen from beyond the trees, but wide enough for them to pass side by side.

"Rein up," Bass said in a hushed voice.

"Wha'?" McKinsey reached for the shotgun across his lap.

"I'm thinking we'd better expect a guard along here somewhere." Bass stopped his mule, who appreciated the rest. "Or our man doubling back. Easy, Othello. Whoa."

The Scot frowned, but did the same, watching the old man return his rifle to its scabbard and draw his revolver.

"Me thought there *tae* be only one scoundrel."

"I'm guessing he's returning to the rest of them, whoever they are." Bass explained the note and stickpin he had found and that they should be alert for a sentry. "Meanwhile, you be thinking about any men you know whose names start with any of those letters." He knew the Scotsman needed some time to let his nerves calm; talking now would help. It might eliminate chatter from McKinsey later.

"Aye, there be a Logerstraum in town. A fine storekeeper, he *tae* be." McKinsey folded his arms and frowned.

"Yeah, he teaches Sunday school. Think of someone else."

"*Canna* be bringin' 'nother *tae* me mind, right off."

"How about the letters V C? Anybody with the first name of V and the last of C come to mind?"

"I *canna* bring such *tae* me thoughts." McKinsey frowned to help him concentrate. "Maybe I *wull* . . . make better o' me thinkin'."

For the first time, both men noticed the moon in the lower sky; slap-dark was an hour away, but it seemed almost upon them within the thick forest.

"*Muir* to be worryin' about with *thae* moon in its full, me friend, ye be knowin' that." McKinsey motioned with his head. "*Donna* be pointin' at it. *Thae* man up there gets angry at bein' pointed at."

"I can appreciate that. Don't like being pointed at either," Bass said with a grin, recalling his Indian friend's assertion of the moon's control over The River, all waters and people's minds. He shook his head, admitting to himself that he was always careful about not stepping on moonbeams. Nancy Spirit Bear had told him not to do so. He shook his head to rid the concern; if it came to needing to step on a moonbeam, he would decide then. Not now. If he had to cross water, he would just leave a few shreds of tobacco in tribute. He shook his head at his obedience to such thinking.

" 'Tis a *guid* time to be killin' *thae* pig." McKinsey rubbed his unshaven chin. "When *thae* moon is takin' on her full self, makes *thae* fryin' bigger." He took a long breath as if preparing himself for a most serious statement. "Course, *thae* moon in her full can make a man crazy, ye know. Best *naught* to be temptin' her."

An owl saluted as it glided through the trees in search of something to eat. The Scotsman watched the wide wings and tried not to think he had heard once that some Indians thought the bird was a ghost. His shotgun clanged against a tree as they passed. The noise made him jump. Glancing at McKinsey, Bass saw early moonlight had painted his craggy face into a Scottish savage. Bass wondered if that meant the moon was helping or warning them.

Either way, ready or not, it was time to move on. He nudged Othello into a walk and placed his finger against his lips to remind McKinsey of the need to be quiet. Bass's tracking skills were the result of too many years of knowing the danger of sound when it wasn't wanted. Age had taken some of his agility, but it gave experience back in full.

He returned his attention to studying the forest ahead, his focus moving from tree to tree, looking for shadows that shouldn't be there. Shards of dusty yellow knifed their way through openings in the branches, seeking gray rocks and downed branches lying across the trail. The old attorney told himself that he was avoiding these occasional puddles of light because he might be seen, not because of some Indian tale. Night sounds around them were reassuring, indicating no sentries were waiting.

Minutes later, they saw it. Smothered within this fortress of clustered trees and overgrown brush was a small cabin. Strings of smoke from the chimney were caught in the early night sky as if weaving the handful of stars together. Whoever was inside wasn't worried about giving away their presence. At least not now.

Tracks from the man they sought blurred with others ahead. Unspoken questions bounced around Bass's mind. Was the place simply a convenient sleepover—or was their man expecting others? The tracks were fresh, so it was likely several men were in the cabin now. Waiting. Would one of them have a name starting with one of the initials he sought? Could the names of the two dead ambushers start with either letter? He hadn't thought to check their clothes for any identification. He doubted there would be any, though. Only the man he tracked could likely tell him that.

Down through a shallow arroyo they eased their mounts. Othello brayed once, but obeyed Bass's insistence on being quiet. This appeared to be the only way into the cabin area from the north. Shadows within the ravine were twisted and angry, striking out at the riders as they traveled downward. Bass and McKinsey rose out of a dry creek bed that served as an open spoon inside the stretch of clustered trees. Bass reminded himself Nancy Spirit Bear had not mentioned any concern about crossing where water had once been, night or day.

Within the brief clearing before the trees retook command, moonlight cascaded across the opening. McKinsey was puzzled as Bass reined his mule to the left and trotted around the silver thrust. The Scotsman followed and volunteered they were no more than a quarter mile from the hideout. The observation came with a Scottish exclamation that rattled through the quiet trees.

At Bass's suggestion, they stopped beside a husky oak tree to study the cabin and decide on their strategy. Dismounting, they held their reins and sought canteens. After a swig, they poured water into the crowns of their doffed hats and offered the refreshing liquid to their mounts.

Bass wondered aloud, "How can we handle this, Bass? You better figure there'll be more. . . ."

"*Haud* a wee. *Wad* ye be *wullin' tae* listen *tae* a wee thought I be having?" McKinsey plopped his hat back on his head, letting several trickles of water drift downward on his craggy face.

"I always listen to a wise man."

"Aye, an' then be runnin' off *tae* take on *thae* Devil hisself, I hear."

Bass Tillman's eyes indicated there was some truth in the statement, but he said nothing. With that, McKinsey suggested that he go ahead alone, acting like he was lost in the woods. He thought Bass might be recognized by the man they tracked. It would be unlikely they would be able to sneak up on the cabin without being seen. After he was inside, Bass could close in as well. He didn't mention the scary thought that there might be too many men waiting. He couldn't bring those words to his mouth.

Bass frowned and ran his right boot toe in front of the other; McKinsey was right about the likelihood of his being recognized. At least to a point. The third gunman wouldn't have seen his face, only his black coat. And his long white hair.

"Is it me actin' skill ye be questionin' now?"

"No, my friend, you're right. The man we're after will be looking for a fellow with long white hair in a black coat," Bass said, "but I can't let you do that. It's too dangerous." He took a deep breath. "An' it's my kin they murdered." He squinted to push back the ache that wanted control.

"*Aff thae gieg*, me friend. We be talkin' how best *tae* get inside—not who be losin'*thae* most."

"You're right. Here's how we do it."

Bass proceeded to outline an alternative. Both would ride in, announcing as they neared that they were lost. They would say they had been chasing stray cattle as McKinsey had actually done before. Without waiting for McKinsey to respond, Bass removed his long coat and laid it across the log, then took off his hat and dropped it beside the black garment. After pulling his hair up with both hands, he held the locks in place with his right and shoved on his hat.

"What do you think?"

"*Staun guid* for it, 'tis a different man I see, for *thae* sure."

Bass adjusted his hat, reassuring himself that his hair was well contained. "Put your shotgun away." Retreating to his saddlebags, Bass handed him a backup revolver carried there. "Stick this in your pocket. Five cartridges. Fresh. Chamber under the hammer's empty."

"*Auld i the horn*, ye be. *Naught* be havin' a short gun like . . . ye."

Understanding the Scottish expression for "wise," Bass slipped a boot into his stirrup and started to mount, then stopped. "You know, our man might've seen my mule, too. I'd better leave Othello here and walk."

"*Weel*, what ye gonna be tellin' *thaim* about *sech?*" McKinsey's eyes were furrowed in concern.

"My horse stepped in a hole and went down. We had to shoot it. That'll make us look even less dangerous. More lost," Bass responded as he tied the reins to a tree, close enough that the mule would have to stand and not attempt to graze.

He considered leaving the animal on a longer stand, in case he didn't return, but decided against it. Othello needed the manners. If he didn't come back, the animal was smart enough to figure a way to get loose. It had before.

The evening's growing coolness felt good as

the two moved slowly toward the hideout cabin; McKinsey decided to walk beside Bass, leading his horse. Five horses could be seen in the attached stable even in the darkness. Whoever was inside would have seen them by now, so Bass told McKinsey to stop.

"What will you find there, Bass?" he asked himself. "Why would men wishing to hide build any kind of fire, even one nearly free of smoke?" He decided that only someone close would see it. "Now you're thinking too much, old man," he told himself. "They just want some comfort after hard riding. A nice fire's the way to get that."

Methodically, the habit of being prepared for any situation took over his mind. The trials of many battles, both with guns and his fists, had left him with a set of practiced instincts. He rehearsed his actions if a shot was fired, or hopefully, he spotted someone about to shoot first. He imagined the revolver in his hand as he dove to the ground. Would McKinsey react similarly?

"Timbel, if I tell you to get down, don't ask why, all right? Just do it."

"*Staun guid* for I'll be knowin' *thae* reason."

"Don't worry about the empty cylinder. When you cock the gun, you'll be loaded."

"Aye. A short gun I be usin' before."

Yellow light seeped through the edges of the closed window shutters and out of the small watch holes in the center of each shutter. Their hands were deliberately kept in sight. A trickle of sweat skidded down McKinsey's cheek, but left no mark.

"Hey, the cabin!" Bass yelled from fifty yards out, his hands still held away from his sides to further indicate his nonaggressive intentions.

No one answered.

From under his hat, a sweat trickle of his own betrayed his tension. He blotted it carefully with his shirtsleeve, and pushed on his hair to make certain its length was still hidden. "Hey, inside! We're lost—an' hungry. Got a horse down. Been lookin' for our beef. Wandered off. Can we come in?" he yelled and stepped around a narrow streak of moonlight crossing the edge of the trail.

"Got a wee whiskey *tae* be sharin'," McKinsey yelled, proud of his addition.

"Come ahead—an' keep your hands where I can see 'em."

Neither man recognized the voice, but hadn't expected to.

"We thank you. It's getting a chill on." Bass waved and continued walking.

"Only a fiddler's biddin' we *tae* seek." McKinsey rattled off his favorite expression about a last-minute invitation.

Bass Tillman glanced at him and decided it didn't matter if anyone understood or not. The statement was certainly nonthreatening. The door opened and a silhouette filled the space.

The shadowed man had to be at least six foot four and well over two hundred pounds. "We've got coffee on. Some beans, too."

"Jensen's my name," Bass volunteered. "This is my partner, McFarlin. We own a small spread south of here. Got lost trying to find some beeves. M-J's our brand."

"*Guid* day *tae* ye, sire." McKinsey touched the brim of his hat.

The big man nodded.

Bass walked toward the waiting silhouette, emphasizing his own limp, and held out his hand to shake. Not using his real name was important; not using McKinsey's was instinctive. He saw no signs of a rifle, only a belt gun, on the welcoming stranger who received Bass's hand with a strong grip and said, "Yah see any other riders?"

"Riders? Wish we did, wouldn't be so damn lost. Haven't seen our beeves all day either. Missin' twenty. Been figurin' they must've sprouted wings an' flew." Bass was aware the man hadn't given his name. Likely a sign of an outlaw or few manners.

The massive, bulldog-faced stranger laughed. He had a head that looked like it connected to his shoulders without benefit of a neck. A flat rock for a nose and a thick, droopy mustache added to his rather comical appearance. A cigar stub grew from the corner of his mouth, which was cocked in a smile that was part fear and part relief.

Coughing to rid his fear, McKinsey offered his hand as well. "Ye *naught* be seein' any o' our beeves, have ye now? Pleased *tae* be sharin' one for supper, if'n ye have."

"Nossir, ain't no cows round hyar. None I seed anyhow." Benson shook McKinsey's hand and tossed the cigar stub to the ground with his free hand, glancing down to assure himself it was too short to retrieve. His eyes slowly came up as he asked, "Ya real sure ya ain't law?"

Bass shook his head. "Law? Us? Hell no. But if

you'd rather, we'll just keep on a-goin'. These damn trees gotta end some time."

"No, no. That's fine," Benson said. "Just being careful."

"Oh, well, my partner an' me, we look real dangerous, I reckon."

The big man chuckled again. "My name's Benson. Joe Benson. Put your hosses in the corral." He realized only McKinsey had a horse. "What the hell happened to your'n?"

Chapter 4

Without being asked, McKinsey led his horse to the corral while Bass explained his horse had stepped in a hole, broken its leg and had to be put down. He said it happened just inside the forest.

Benson frowned. "Didn't hear no shot."

"Huh, sounded like a cannon to me." Bass licked his lips. "Guess it was the thought of having to walk. Banged up my knee when it went down. Damn it all—an' lost to boot. What a hell-va day."

"How far's your place from Highland ... Jensen, isn't it?" Benson stepped aside to allow the attorney to enter the cabin.

"Oh, two, three hours, I reckon. Don't go there very often," Bass said casually. "You got kin there? Nice little town from what I've seen. Lots of silver coming out of there."

Benson pushed his hat brim back on his forehead. "Ya hear 'bout the bank bein' robbed yesterday?"

Bass straightened himself as if in surprise. "Bank robbed? Mister, I swear we didn't have nothin' to do with it." He paused and rubbed his mouth. "Although, I've thought of it a time or two. A mite easier than chasing after stupid beeves."

Benson slapped him on the back. "Come on in. There's plenty to eat. Whiskey, if ya want." He couldn't help himself and told proudly of the robbery. "Don't worry. I were the one done robbed the bank. Me an' my friend, Truitt. Got away clean. Guess no posse dared to come after us. Hell, they couldn't find us here anyways. Not in here. I found this place a few years back. Knew it'd be a good hideout if'n I ever needed one."

"Well, I'll be. Good for you. Damn banks cheat us ranchers to beat hell," Bass said.

Inside the log-lined cabin, a blackened and cracked stone fireplace held a fat, crackling fire made mostly from smoke-free branches and a few logs. Around a long, gray table sat two men; one was skinny and sour-faced, wearing thick glasses; the other looked more like a misplaced schoolteacher. A third man, dressed in a black three-piece suit, relaxed in a rocking chair and appeared disinterested in the others.

Only one room, it reeked of fried food, urine and sweat. Setting on the fire's edge was a coffeepot and a large pot of beans, mixing their tantalizing aromas with the other smells. A single oil lamp was doing its best to push the shadows into the corners. Two unrolled bedrolls lay in the far corner of the packed clay floor. In the far northwest corner were three rifles leaning against the wall. One was a Pedersoli rifle with a scope and a sling. Bass had seen it before. This morning at his son's ranch. Lying next to the weapons were saddlebags thick with their contents. Bass guessed this was the money from the bank. Another set of saddlebags didn't appear to contain much.

Bass wanted to ask who owned the Pedersoli, but thought it was too soon, too direct.

As an introduction, Benson explained the reason for the appearance of Bass and McKinsey, chuckling as he did; then he introduced Bass first to the smallest of the three and the closest, calling him only Truitt.

Wearing a scruffy buffalo coat and fringed leather leggings, Harry Truitt appeared to be a gentle soul, a man given to following others without much thought of the consequences. He could have been a schoolteacher or a store clerk, Bass thought as he shook hands, and essentially harmless, unless a man's back was turned. Probably followed Benson in the robbery because he didn't dare object.

The man Bass sought was either the sour-faced stranger or the well-dressed gentleman in the rocking chair, reading a book of Tennyson. He was pretty sure it was the former, but the man in the rocking chair was dangerous. Very dangerous. An ivory-handled pistol held in a shoulder holster under the man's black swallowtail coat was easy to notice and intended so. Bass tried to avoid the man's questioning stare as he stepped

forward to shake hands with Truitt. Had he seen
the man in the rocking chair before? Where?
Would his name start with one of the initials he
sought?

A minute later, McKinsey entered the cabin
and bobbed his head as a greeting, standing just
inside the doorway. "*Guid* eve *tae* ye gentlemen."
His wave was a half jerk that ended almost as
quickly as it began in a self-conscious reaction.

"This here's . . . what were your name?"

Bass spoke quickly. "He's my ranch partner.
McFarlin's his name."

"Aye, McFarlin, I be." McKinsey cocked his
head, as if to tell Bass he would have remembered. He strode toward the table and held out
his hand for Truitt to shake.

The timid outlaw kept his eyes on the table as
they greeted.

After reintroducing Truitt, Benson pointed at
Bill Drucker, the sour-faced man with thick eyeglasses, giving his name and adding that Drucker
was headed for Denver City. Drucker didn't like
the mention of his travel intentions. Not noticing
the frown, the bulldog-faced outlaw couldn't resist teasing Drucker that he had almost worn out
his horse and wouldn't be going anywhere until it
rested some.

Drucker's response was a sneer. It seemed to
go with his haughty face and odd, yellowish skin.
He stared at Bass through his spectacles. His dark
coat and short-brimmed hat were streaked with
dust. Bass didn't need the big outlaw's remark to
know Drucker had traveled hard and fast. Although the bespectacled man was seated, Bass

could see a revolver, butt forward, at his waist, and the flat handle of a large knife.

Drucker's clenched-teeth greeting was barely audible; the expression spoke of distrust. He made no attempt to extend his hand to either Bass or McKinsey.

Bass acted like he didn't notice, as he turned to Benson. "Well, I reckon he can have mine. She's a mite slow now, though."

Benson roared at the response, slapping McKinsey on the back.

Unsettled by Druker's rudeness, the Scot forced himself to create an odd-sounding chortle and muttered, *"Thae shakkins o' thae poke."* His face was ashen as he spat out the expression about last remains. How could he have agreed to this? Was Bass Tillman actually going to take on four armed men? McKinsey studied the elder attorney for any sign of what he would do next, but saw none.

Drucker was definitely the third ambusher; Bass could feel it in his body. He had lived too long not to trust his gut instincts. Would Drucker recognize him? The room got smaller as silence slithered up its walls and surrounded the men inside. He tugged on his hat to ensure that his long hair was hidden.

"Don't I know you? From somewhere?" Drucker stared at Bass.

"Aye, a saloon most anywhere, that's where he likely *tae* be found. *Tak* a *guid* bucket, he does," McKinsey declared loudly and forced a more throaty laugh this time. It helped to talk and relieve some of the tension growing within him.

Benson and Bass laughed. So did Truitt; his was

a thin giggle. Drucker looked like he had eaten
something that didn't agree with him.

Savoring his newfound courage, McKinsey
didn't wait for Drucker's response. "*Guid eneuch*,
an' who be . . . this other fine gentleman we *tae* be
sharin' *thae* grand night with?" McKinsey returned Benson's backslap with one of his own.

It felt good to be active. It actually made him
feel more positive about the situation. After all, he
was with Bass Tillman, the gunfighter of dime
novel fame and who had taken on the three
Hoodsmen trying to rob the Longmont Bank and
lived to talk about it, although he never did, so
folks said.

Rocking in the rickety chair, the fourth man
was wide-shouldered with slicked-back brown
hair and a thin mustache, light blue eyes, probably close to six feet tall, with a definite eastern air
about him. Could be a college professor, although
the handgun belied that concept. His derby hat
lay on the floor beside the chair, resting on two
other books. A man out of place, it seemed, and
obviously one who enjoyed reading. He could
easily have been ready to enjoy a night in Denver
City with his black, broadcloth suit, fresh-rolled
collar and boiled white shirt. Only his green silk
cravat was a bit off-center at the neck. A gambler,
possibly, Bass guessed, and on the run. Or a
hired gun.

The well-dressed man's overall manner was
vain and condescending. His sparkling eyes, not
yet dulled by drink, were those of a man hiding a
secret and enjoying it. His high forehead was ac-
centuated with arching eyebrows that supported

his mysterious stare. He returned to his reading without saying a word.

Drucker ran his tongue along his dry lips. "Wasn't no saloon, I think. Was somewhere else."

"Sorry, mister, don't believe we've ever met," Bass Tillman finally acknowledged without looking at him. "I'm just an old man who's spent too much time walking in these damn woods."

Benson laughed again and told about Bass having to shoot his broken-legged horse.

"*A cader's curse.*" McKinsey forced a grunt along with his expression of something worthless.

"Gentlemen, this hyar's Easter Sontag." The big outlaw returned his attention to McKinsey's question about the stylish occupant of the cabin. He bobbed his head toward the man in the rocker.

The well-known name slammed into Bass's brain. He wasn't a gambler; his stated profession was a hangman. An executioner, both legally and, some whispered, otherwise as well. Recently he had heard talk of Sontag being in Cheyenne to conduct a hanging. He glanced at McKinsey, but his friend turned away, looking for a plate.

Bass bit his lower lip. *Not a bad move, McKinsey. Not a bad move at all.* He noticed McKinsey's right hand had settled into his coat pocket, the one holding the backup pistol. An innocent-appearing stance, Bass thought and returned his attention to Easter Sontag. What was he doing here? Was he part of the conspiracy to murder his son and his wife? "H" could stand for "Hangman." Could he be the one behind his family's murders? Why? Was Drucker intending to meet him here—and both were going on to Denver City?

He frowned to keep his mind alert. If the names given by the others were real, none contained the letters he sought. Of course, they could be false and there were always nicknames. He forced the concern from his mind; it wasn't helpful at the moment.

Bass knew the tales about Sontag. Four years ago, after two drinks, a clerk in Laramie had related to Bass one particularly disturbing story about how Sontag had supposedly decapitated a victim somewhere in Nebraska. The head had snapped off during the hanging and Sontag had walked around, showing it off and spouting Shakespeare. Bass hadn't asked the clerk how he had acquired this information. He knew similar accounts had also been told about him. They weren't true; probably this wasn't either.

But none of that mattered. Here was the infamous executioner from New Jersey. It wasn't what Bass would have chosen this night. Drucker would be enough trouble—and he had no idea of what Benson, or even Truitt, might do when he confronted Drucker.

"Mr. Sontag were here when we came ridin' in. Not sure where he's headed. Didn't say," Benson explained. "Did say he wandered onto our little place by pure chance. Like you-all did. Didn't ya, Mr. Sontag?"

Lowering his book to his lap, Sontag appeared unimpressed by Benson and to have no interest in responding to his question. But he was definitely interested in Bass Tillman, as the hard-faced attorney walked toward him with his hand extended. At the fire, McKinsey turned and waved with his left hand, leaving his right in his pocket. Sontag glanced at the gesture and dismissed him with his eyes. As he shook hands with Bass, Sontag's eyes measured him curiously, his mouth twisting into a half smile.

"'Press not a falling man too far,'" Sontag stated, raising his chin.

"Don't mind him, Jensen," Benson said. "He just likes to spout stuff every now an' then. Ain't that Shakespeare or somethin', Mr. Sontag?"

"*King Henry the Eighth*," Sontag snorted.

"Oh, thought it were Shakespeare."

Bass met the executioner's gaze. "'Heat not a furnace for your foe so hot that it do singe yourself.'"

"Very good, sir." Sontag released the handshake and rocked the chair vigorously, letting his opened book wiggle freely on his thighs.

After the introductions, Bass walked back to the fireplace and sought two tin cups and began filling them with hot coffee from the boiling pot. It gave him time to think. McKinsey slid beside him, holding a plate of beans, his eyes fierce but fearful.

As Bass poured, questions kept returning in his mind. Was this famed hangman, somehow, behind his family's murders? Did Sontag really discover this hideout by chance? Was Benson's statement about robbing a bank intended to disarm him? Were Benson and Truitt in this with Drucker? Drucker and Sontag? All of them?

As he handed the filled cup to McKinsey, Bass told him to sit at the table. The Scot did so, arranging his loaded plate, a fork and the filled cup across from Truitt. Bass was proud of his son's friend, who he knew was tingling with nerves.

Drucker's eyes bored down on the Scot. McKinsey scooped up a hearty spoonful of beans. It was better when he didn't look at the scary man. Drucker snorted and returned his attention to Bass without speaking.

Watching McKinsey with his coffee reminded Benson of the whiskey he had been interested in before the latest arrivals. Standing in front of the cupboard, he gingerly touched the one door barely hanging in place and grabbed one of the four bottles there. Next, his search yielded three glasses and two cups. Filled glasses and cups were quickly passed around.

Truitt started to say he didn't want any, yet smiled his acceptance.

Thanking Benson warmly, McKinsey took the offered glass and set it alongside his plate of beans, next to his coffee. Bass took his and leaned against the wall. Drucker downed his cupful in one swallow.

When Benson brought a glass to Sontag, the executioner said, "Bring the bottle."

"Ah, sure, Mr. Sontag, sure," the big outlaw responded and anxiously brought the whiskey bottle from the table.

Sontag took it and began pouring himself a second drink, having already downed the first.

"Keep it, Mr. Sontag. Keep it."

" 'But a lie which is part a truth is a harder matter to fight.' " The executioner quoted from Tennyson's "The Grandmother" as he finished refilling his glass.

Benson muttered, "Ain't no liars in hyar—if'n that's your meanin', Mr. Sontag."

Sontag smiled and took a long swallow of the whiskey.

If the big outlaw was concerned about Sontag's recitation about "lies," it didn't show in his face or manner.

Chapter 5

"Ye be sayin' *soom* about a posse, Mr. Benson. Said ye an' Mr. Truitt were running from *thaim*. 'Deed be safe we are here?" McKinsey asked as he pushed his fork into the beans; his eyes were wide and blinking.

It took all of his nerve to bring up the subject. He wasn't certain what Bass wanted him to do, but guessed the attorney would let him know if he didn't like the question.

Benson bit his lip. For an instant, the massive man looked frightened.

"You shouldn't question everything you hear, McFlail," Benson said, staring at the Scot and deliberately misstating his name. "It isn't healthy."

"*Weel*, I—I *jist* meant . . . we could *tae* ride on. I—I *donna* . . ." McKinsey put his hand over his mouth, breathed deeply and spouted a Scottish phrase no one understood.

Bass wasn't sure if it was an act or if his friend

was close to panicking. He massaged his stiff left hand with his right, more out of having something to do than any need.

Bass couldn't take his eyes off Sontag, who appeared not to be listening, just staring at the fire. The executioner was definitely in control of the bottle and already pouring himself another glassful of whiskey. His book lay on his lap, forgotten for the moment. Would the hangman soon be drunk enough to no longer be a threat? Bass wondered if he should wait for the whiskey to take full effect before challenging Drucker. Or would more drink make Sontag imagine some slight against him and bring his gun into play? Was the Tennyson quote aimed at him? Or just a convenient quotation?

Across the table, Truitt seemed genuinely distressed and whispered support that the cabin was safe. Drucker was growing impatient; the fingers of his right hand tapped the tabletop in a nervous cadence. Bass pretended not to notice. Benson gulped down his whiskey in syncopation with Drucker's tapping. He was concentrating too much on regaining control of the whiskey to pay attention to anything else.

"I'll have another," Drucker barked.

Benson motioned toward Sontag.

Drucker wrinkled his yellowish forehead, pushed his glasses back to the bridge of his nose and changed subjects. "I don't believe you, Jensen. You're no more a cattleman than I am."

Bass saw the haughty man's hands had already disappeared under the table. Sontag perked up at the challenge. Incensed, Benson slammed down his glass at the edge of the table, whiskey splattering across his hand and onto the table. His jerky movement was like an excited deer.

"Goddammit!" Benson screamed in an agitated voice. "This here's gentle folk, like Truitt. You've got no call to be saying that."

"That's all right, Joe." Bass strolled toward the table, setting down his cup and moving to a position just behind Truitt and to Drucker's immediate right.

His move appeared casual, but it wasn't. From this angle, it would be difficult for Drucker to fire at him from under the table. He would have to bring his gun above the table first or, at least, shift his body awkwardly.

Smiling broadly, Bass spoke in a low, even voice. "You're right, Drucker, I'm not a cattleman. I'm a father on the trail of a man who murdered my son and his wife. This morning. Three of the men who did it came back to find evidence they left behind. They didn't expect me. One got away. That man carries a Pedersoli rifle and wears a long black coat. Sound familiar?"

McKinsey's cheeks drained, his eyebrows arched; both hands clenched and opened at his side. His right hand slid again into his coat pocket, curled around the pistol and silently pulled it free of the cloth.

Like a whip's snap, Bill Drucker reached for his holstered gun. As his hand settled around the butt, Bass's revolver was staring at Drucker's nose six feet away. The room grew small, no bigger than the dark hole at the barrel's end of the old attorney's revolver.

"What the hell!" Benson spat, his own thick hand lying against the pistol at his hip.

McKinsey swung his pistol toward the big outlaw. "*Haud a wee*. This *naught* be about ye, me *freend*." He glanced in the direction of the frightened Truitt. "Ye neither, *freend*."

The diminutive, buffalo-coated man glanced at Bass, hoping for a return to the friendly banter. The veteran attorney was staring at Drucker, yet aware of Sontag in his peripheral vision. The black-suited man had returned to his reading, as if he was oblivious of the changed situation. His half-filled glass rested in his left hand; the bottle sat beside him on the floor.

Slugging down a glass of the fiery liquid, Sontag quoted from Shakespeare's "Timon of Athens." " 'The fire i' the flint shows not till it be struck.' "

McKinsey looked up at the confused Benson, his gun pointed at the big outlaw's belly. He wasn't convinced his older friend's preemptive challenge was a good idea, but there was no returning.

"Put your hands on the table, Drucker. Bring them up slow. Real slow," Bass demanded and again reminded the others, "This is between him and me, boys. Nobody else. I want answers, Drucker. Start with why. Then where you're going—and who you're going to see there. I want to know who H is. And L. And VC." He glanced at Sontag to see if there was any reaction at the mention of the letters.

There wasn't, although the executioner had stopped his reading to sip more of his whiskey.

Drucker's face was shattered yellow pastry as

he moved his right hand slowly up and away from the untouched gun. Gingerly both hands finally touched the tabletop; his right pushed his glasses into place, returning to lie beside the other. Hard eyes blinked twice, then averted Bass's glare. Sontag's stare caught Bass's attention and Sontag moved his gaze immediately behind Bass as a warning. A second later came McKinsey's command, "*Donna* ye!"

Bass spun and fired. Benson's chest blossomed with a crimson circle where his heart was. Bass's second shot was an eyeblink later, slamming a hole in the big man's forehead. Benson's half-drawn gun slid unhindered back into its holster.

McKinsey stared down at his own handgun, unsure of why he hadn't reacted.

Using the distraction as his incentive, Drucker reached again for his gun. The revolver was halfway out when Bass's bullet hit the haughty outlaw in the shoulder. McKinsey's following shot slammed into Drucker's heart. The combined impact tore the outlaw's body from the chair like giant, invisible hands had grabbed it and tossed the bloody shape onto the floor as if a child's doll. Drucker's revolver flipped into the air with a life of its own, followed by a low jerky flight of eyeglasses.

Bass groaned audibly. He wanted Drucker alive. Alive! The rapid gunfire brought acrid smoke that sucked all of the sound from the room. Agitated with the results of the brief gun battle, Bass hurried to the dying outlaw, knelt beside his heaving body.

"Drucker, who were you going to see? Where? Don't die, Drucker! Tell me . . ."

Drucker's body sagged. Life fled and blood seeped into the clay floor.

Instinctively, Bass's attention was split between Truitt and Sontag, even though it was the executioner who had warned him.

Truitt lay flat on the floor, next to where he had sat; his eyes closed, clutching the tin cup with both hands.

Sontag was the only one who hadn't reacted to the shots. His drinking continued as if nothing had happened, muttering some phrase about "a life of nothing" that Bass couldn't recall, but assumed it was from Tennyson. It didn't matter; his lone opportunity to find the man or men responsible for his family's death was beyond questioning now. Benson lay against the fireplace with a pistol in his fat fist, his bulldog face staring unseeing at the ceiling.

"Truitt, your friend didn't give me a choice." Bass stood slowly, holding his revolver ready but at his side. "I don't know why. I told him we weren't after you." His eyes studied the terrified outlaw.

"I—I know he didn't. He was sure a posse was comin'. Been sure of it all day. Guess he thought you were lawmen," Truitt muttered without looking up. "I—I'm n-not going to do anything. I—I promise."

"Get up and sit." Bass was angry at himself.

His search for the answers to his family's murders ended, for the moment, in the death of Bill

Drucker. His study of the man only revealed the fatal wounds. He tried not to blame Timbel McKinsey; the Scot had reacted as most would.

"Who the hell are you?" Sontag drawled, turning slowly in his chair to face Bass. The hangman's eyes were beginning to shine with drink.

"Not many men can handle a gun like that. You aren't John Wesley Hardin. I know him. Got drunk together once. Besides, he carries his iron in two holsters, sewn right into a vest. Real slick-like," Sontag continued, smacking his lips and taking another swallow of the brown liquid.

Bass cocked his head to listen but said nothing, trying to decide if he would ask Sontag if he was the "H" he sought.

"Don't know any Jensen." Sontag pursed his lips. "But you might be John Ringo. Don't know the man . . . know he's good with a gun, though. Down by the Texas border, last I heard, though. Naw, you're not Ringo. Let's see, you're not Time Carlow either. Too old. He's real good. And a lawman. A real lawman. Texas Ranger. You wouldn't find him in a pissant place this far from the Red." He cocked his head in contemplation. "You might be Bass Tillman. Or Emerson Holt, his riding partner. Thought he was dead, though." He sipped again. "I know you aren't the third gun the two used to ride with. He was German. Frank Schafer. Yeah, that was his name. Frank Schafer. He's dead, too, I heard. In Kansas. Some pissant town, wouldn't you know?"

Bass tried not to show his surprise at hearing his name or that of his two old friends as the professional hangman warmed to his self-decided task. But he paused long enough to pour another drink and down it in one gulp, letting his book slide between his legs to the floor.

Truitt was on his knees, slowly returning to his seat. McKinsey held his pistol on the frightened outlaw.

"Figure your real name isn't Jensen. A runnin' man usually likes a different brand. So who's that leave who can handle a gun like that?" Sontag mused, examining the brown liquid in his glass before downing it.

Bass listened, taking the opportunity to quickly eject the spent shells from his revolver and replace them with fresh loads from his coat pocket. He recocked the weapon, holding it at his side. What were Sontag's intentions?

Sontag stood, letting the rocker continue its own adventure, and poured another glass of whiskey. He emptied it, stared at the empty glass and at the bottle in his other hand. With a nod, he took a long swig from the bottle, instead of pouring some into his glass.

"Let's see . . . you aren't me." Sontag chuckled at his joke. "But I'm not a pistol fighter. Just a poor man of the rope."

McKinsey chuckled.

Sontag gave him a sour look and the Scot bit his lower lip to end his response.

Bass smiled nonchalantly, but his lean frame was coiled, expecting the executioner to explode into violence. Instead, Sontag seemed bent on figuring out who he was; his apparent growing drunken fog making that more difficult. Taking a step toward Bass, he weaved slightly and stopped. He shook his head to clear it.

"Well, you aren't Preacher Miller." Sontag pursed his lips. "You remind me of him some. Not in looks, somethin' about the way you handle yourself. He's one tough sonvabitch. Cold. No offense."

"None taken, 'H.'"

"'H'? What the hell's 'H'? You making fun of me?"

Bass shook his head. "My mistake. Thought I heard of these guys refer to you as that."

"Be the last day they ever did. What the hell's 'H'? Damn, you broke my thinking." The cold-eyed executioner brought the bottle again to his mouth, letting whiskey trickle down the corners as he swallowed. Wiping his mouth with his sleeve, he returned to his task. His boot shoved the Tennyson book toward the others.

He stared at Bass. "Well, you aren't Hickok. He's dead. An' they done hung old Bill Longley down San Antonio way. An' you aren't my good buddy, Luke Short." He rubbed his chin to aid in his recollection as the others watched mesmerized at his recital. "You aren't Clay Allison either. Ran into Clay three years back. Down in Las Animas. Him and his brother, John, got into a shooting fracas there with a deputy sheriff and two other men. John was shot up bad by the deputy's shotgun, but made it through. Clay killed the deputy and was arrested." He stopped to chuckle. "That smooth-talking sonvabitch convinced the grand jury he had shot the deputy in self-defense—and went free. Can you believe that?"

Sontag's face went from mirth to discovery in an eyeblink as he backed into his chair and sat once more. "So . . . you know what? I think you're King Fisher. How 'bout that? Yeah, John King Fisher. Never met you before, but I hear you're slick as all hell. Yeah, that's it. King Fisher. Did I get it, King?" Sontag said, waving his arms with a flourish of victory; then he hiccupped.

Bass grinned, before answering, "Well, one of those is right. How about Bass Tillman?" Inside, he was anxious to end this line of questioning. He still wasn't certain the hangman wasn't connected to the morning's murders.

Looking ill, McKinsey nodded enthusiastically. "Aye, Bass Tillman. That's who he be. *Thae richt way o't.*"

Bass was unsure of what to think of the dead Joe Benson. He was a thief, for sure, but was he really a cold-blooded murderer? He didn't think so. Likely, he was what his partner said, a jumpy outlaw who overreacted. And that brought him back to Bill Drucker, who would talk no more— and Truitt and Sontag.

For the moment, the hangman appeared to be satisfied with Bass's answer, or more likely, had lost interest in the subject. He picked up his book and finished reading the passage aloud as if he had never stopped. When he set that volume down with his other books, the top book flipped open briefly, revealing its contents were handwritten.

"I see you are a writer." Bass pointed toward

the leather-bound pages. It couldn't hurt to get Sontag on his side or, at least, comfortable.

"Oh yes, to read—and to write. Those are the greatest of gifts." Sontag's chin rose dramatically. "Listen to this." He reached down and picked up the book and began to recite. " 'Oh cometh the land . . . grand and beautiful, she be . . . she waits for me, oh mysterious lady. See? She waits for me . . . Her bosom rises to meet the sun . . .'Til they are one . . .' " He looked up and grinned self-consciously. "There's more, but I won't bore you. No match for Tennyson, that's for sure. Helps me relax."

"I like it. Presenting the land as a woman. Paints quite a picture," Bass responded.

McKinsey started to say something and thought better of it, choosing to just nod.

McKinsey and Bass watched Sontag rise from his chair and wobble over to Truitt, holding the handwritten book in his hand. Bass whispered for his friend to put his gun away and the Scot complied without looking at Bass. McKinsey's hands were shaking.

Stopping within a foot of the small outlaw, Sontag breathed into his face, and said, "Say, you-ish got a cigar? That-ish sure sounds good." He hiccupped.

Truitt frantically checked his pockets without success. "J-Joe had some . . . in his saddlebags. Outside. Those are mine. An' Drucker's." He pointed in the direction of the saddlebags.

The blurry-eyed executioner ordered, "Go get them. *Hiccup.* See if there's a deck of cards . . . *hiccup* . . . while you're at it." He felt his own coat pocket. "Never mind. I've got a deck." He immediately forgot the idea. "See if he has any books . . . *hiccup* . . . while you're at it."

As Truitt headed urgently for the door, Sontag roared, "Where the hell you goin'?"

Sontag's fourth hiccup bothered him, as if the reason for it were a force somewhere in the room, not inside his body. He looked around and hiccupped again.

Stopping in midstride, Truitt's entire body shook. "I—I was going to f-find c-cigars . . . l-like you asked. Joe didn't read none, though."

"Oh yeah . . . *hiccup* . . . get 'em."

Sontag stared at McKinsey as if seeing him for the first time. The Scot felt an urge to reach for the gun now back in his pocket, but decided against it. He forced himself to pick up a fork and slid it under the beans on his plate.

"You got any . . . *hiccup* . . . cigars?"

McKinsey held the fork in place. "*Nae*, Mr. Sontag. I *donna* be smokin'. Got a wee whiskey, though."

"Let's . . . have it, then. *Hiccup*."

With a glance at Bass, who nodded approval, McKinsey reached into his inside coat pocket, withdrew the silver flask and handed it to Sontag.

Snorting his disapproval at the smallness of the container, Sontag downed its contents in one long swallow and handed the empty flask back. "Good whiskey. *Hiccup*."

"Welcome ye be."

"Are there any more . . . *hiccup* . . . beans?" Sontag asked, pointing at McKinsey's plate with his held book.

By the time Truitt returned with a fistful of cigars, Sontag was at the table with a heaping plate of beans in front of him. The executioner ignored the meal and continued to drink. His book lay beside the plate. The bloody bodies on the floor were forgotten. Sontag was talking to Bass about Denver City and the excellent theater there. Having Sontag talk about anything was better than having him angry. No one attempted to interrupt him, although his speech was disintegrating. However, his hiccuping had apparently ended for the moment.

From the fire, McKinsey shoved beans into this mouth with his fork. As he ate, a Scottish prayer passed through his lips with each bite, barely audible.

Unsure of what to do, Truitt shuffled shyly over to Sontag and handed him a cigar.

"H-here, s-sir. A—a cigar . . . like you a-asked."

Taking a second to focus, Sontag snatched the fistful from Truitt's other hand, leaving the initial offered smoke. With his free hand, the executioner took the lone cigar as well, placed it in his mouth and shoved the others into his coat pocket. One slid out his hand to the floor. The drunken hangman stared at the fallen cigar, then upward, glassy-eyed, at the terrified Truitt.

The outlaw bent over and retrieved the cigar, offering it with a trembling hand. Sontag took it and placed it in his pocket with the rest.

Bass snapped a match on the tabletop and lit Sontag's cigar, returning the hangman's attention to the conversation. The mere pop of the match made McKinsey jump and almost drop his plate.

Biting his lower lip, Truitt turned around and

headed for the skillet and the rest of the beans. McKinsey stepped aside to let him pass.

"*A wad rather dae this as that.*" The Scotsman offered his thought that he would rather eat than talk to the hangman.

Truitt frowned and shrugged his shoulders. "Don't know what you're saying, mister."

"Aye, *fine a ken* ye donna." McKinsey smiled at his expression meaning "I know well you don't."

The buffalo-coated outlaw shrugged again and sought the skillet.

Abruptly, Sontag began talking about Cheyenne. "Yeah, had a hanging in Cheyenne. Three of them, actually. Town law's John Lewis. Always got a bunch of hard-cases with him. Never alone. He'll bust your head open if he gets the chance. But he's usually busy making deals, grabbin' money an' screwing. Watch him, though." Sontag nodded agreement with his own statements.

Bass was fairly certain Sontag wasn't connected with his family's murders, but there was still a grayness. If he kept talking, maybe the clarity would come.

As he sat down with a filled plate, Truitt found enough nerve to observe, "Lewis ain't much with a gun, I hear tell."

Sontag laughed sarcastically. "Who told y-y-you that, pissant?"

"Well, that's what I—I—I heard tell. Course I—"

"Yeah, Lewis's not much with a gun. That-ish right." Sontag dismissed his own interjection. "Beat ya to death with his fists or a gun butt. He's hard, King. Don't mess with him. If he's dealing, the house is crooked. Know that for a fact. Yes-ish."

Chapter 6

Sontag's drooping eyelids and bobbing head indicated he was fully feeling the effects of the liquor; his words were slurring more and more.

Without touching the beans in front of him, Sontag rose and returned to his rocking chair. After sitting down, he grabbed the whiskey bottle and took a long pull.

"So, you know any he-dog around here whose name starts with an H? Or L? VC?" Bass decided there was no reason to wait any longer to seek the information he cared about. Sontag was losing his battle with the liquor

"Well, it's . . . oh, wh-wh-what's hish name?" Sontag's upper lip flopped over his lower as he spoked. Drool ran down his chin unnoticed by the hangman. He frowned at not knowing the name immediately. "Oh, you know, the one in Denver City."

Sontag was struggling somewhat to find a

name. "Wait a minute. Wait jush a minute." He jumped to his feet, momentarily lost his balance and took a step backward, pushing on the chair. His arms flailed the gray air. Stable again, he looked from one man at the table to another, as if deciding to draw his gun. "Wh-wh-where ish it, goddamm it?"

Calmly, Bass asked, "Where be what?"

"You know, King. Wh-wh-whiskey. I need it-ish."

"It's in your hand," Bass said, steeling himself in case the drunken hangman might object to this observation.

"Cocking *thae* wee finger, he be," McKinsey muttered to himself and shivered.

"A-a-ah-h-h-h, there it ish!" the drunken Sontag roared, discovering the bottle as if his hand were some hidden location. He brought it so swiftly to his mouth that he hit his lower lip instead and the last of the whiskey ran down his chin and onto his shirt.

Both Truitt and McKinsey watched him with widened eyes.

Bass's jaw was set; his one hand held the pistol at his side, cocked. "Did you know this Bill Drucker fella?" he asked. Waiting any longer might result in the executioner either going for his gun or collapsing from his liquor.

Sontag drew himself up as if considering his next decision. It came after a long swallow. "That pissant rode in here—on a half-dead horse. No sonvabitch should do that to a horse. Shoulda shot him then." He nodded agreement at his statement. "But you boys did that up right, I reckon."

"Did he say where he was headed? Or who he was meeting?" Bass asked. "I need to know."

Sontag puffed on his cigar and Bass thought the man had lost his train of thought. Finally, the hangman proclaimed, "Believe he said something about meeting somebody in Denver City. Yeah, that's it, Denver City. Somebody important, he said. Hell, that pissant didn't know anybody important. Anywhere."

Truitt nodded agreement and swallowed his fear. McKinsey stepped to his right, separating himself more from the outlaw.

"What's your middle name, Easter?" Bass asked, focusing on Sontag's eyes. They would be the first indication he was going to draw a weapon.

"My what?"

"Your middle name. Mine's Griffin. Bass Griffin Tillman."

"Thought it was King. King Fisher."

"No, it's Bass Tillman. I told you that earlier." Bass shifted his feet to better face the drunken executioner.

Frowning, Sontag removed the cigar from his mouth. "It's Joslin. Easter Joslin Sontag. Joslin's my mother's maiden name. Why the hell did you want to know that? Kinda personal to be asking a stranger."

It was time to tell what really had happened. He told Sontag the story of the murder of his son and wife, wounding the returned gunmen, finding the note and stickpin and tracking Drucker, who killed his own men so they couldn't talk. He told of the clues he had found with the various initials.

"So you thought Drucker came to see me." Sontag grinned. " 'H' for 'hangman.' "

"I needed to know."

"And?" Sontag seemed alert.

"If you were, we'd be killing each other right now."

McKinsey dropped his plate. "Aye, sorry I be." He looked down at the spreading beans underneath the tin plate.

"Leave it, Timbel. It's all right," Bass said without looking away from the hangman.

Sontag frowned again as if thinking through Bass's need and shook his head negatively. "Can't think of anybody with a name that starts with those letters in Denver City. But I'm a little tired. Maybe in the morning." He looked around for the rocking chair, griping to himself that someone had moved it. Stopping, he cocked his head. " 'When devils will the blackest sins put on . . . they do suggest at first with heavenly . . . shows,' " Sontag muttered, waving his hands dramatically as he muttered a line from the second act of Shakespeare's *Othello*.

Bass tried to hide his irritation.

Sontag's whiskey-filled laugh followed. "Well, what do you know? It's my friend, King Fisher. What in the world are you doing here in this pissant hole, King? You coming or going?"

Bass smiled. "Going. And it's Bass. Bass Tillman."

Sontag looked around for the whiskey bottle and spotted the shattered remains with the bottle's jagged bottom lying on a small, dark stain. He frowned and rocked in his chair angrily.

"Damn, that's a shame." He saw the bodies of Drucker and Benson and quoted Shakespeare again. " 'Men should be what they seem.' " A long belch followed his surprising clarity.

"Shakespeare had a way with words, didn't he?" Bass responded. "*Othello*, I believe."

"Say, whenish you get to Denver City . . . look up a fella named Hautrese. A foxy one, he is. Has a bunch of hard-cases with him. Might be your man."

Hautrese? Bass felt like he had been slapped in the face. He knew the name, of course, but they had never met. Boston Hautrese was the United States Marshal for the district of Colorado. Sontag's remark was obviously whiskey driven and ludricous. Yet he was quite lucid at times.

From what Bass had heard, Hautrese received a substantial fee from the railroad and Wells Fargo—and the U.S. mail—for each Hoodsman brought to justice. Typical patronage approach for the office. Hautrese had been outspoken about bringing down the mysterious gang. According to the newspapers, three of his deputies were assigned to ending the Hoodsmen's terror. They had deputized a posse to help them and the district attorney was aggressively prosecuting any Hoodsman they arrested. The other deputy marshals were assigned elsewhere. There was no way a federal lawman was involved in his family's murders. Bass swallowed what he wanted to say.

"Mine's Weaver," Truitt interrupted. "Harold Weaver Truitt. Don't know where it came from, though. My folks, ah, they died when I was a kid."

McKinsey sipped his drink, stopped and started to announce his middle name.

"How about you, Harry? Did you hear where Drucker was headed?" Bass's questions ended McKinsey's pronouncement.

"Mr. Sontag's right. He said Denver City. An' something about an important man was waiting for him." Truitt licked his cracked lips and looked at the ceiling. "He didn't say any name. Not that I heard anyway." He looked down at Drucker's body. "Didn't like our being here, that's for sure. Said he thought he was the only one who knew about this place. Kinda dumb of him, I thought." The timid outlaw ran his finger along the table. "I know a fella whose name is Henson. That starts with an H. He lives in Wichita. Or he did. A rancher there."

"Don't think he's the one." Bass tried not to sound annoyed.

"Yeah, probably not."

"W-wh-whiskey! More whiskey!" Sontag's eyes flashed open and he threw the empty bottle at the wall. Glass shards exploded and flew in all directions.

"Timbel, there's another bottle in the cabinet. Please." Bass looked at McKinsey.

The Scot quickly selected another bottle. "Aye, there be *muir*."

"K-Kingish, you're a good . . . man. You are. Not like these pissants-ish," the hangman slobbered.

His cigar fell from his mouth and bounced on the clay floor, flipping an orange spark and spewing gray ash. Almost the instant he plopped into the rocker, his head dropped against his chin and his eyes closed. The liquor had finally won.

McKinsey walked toward him with the new bottle, realized the man was sleeping or appeared to be, and looked back at Bass for instructions. Bass motioned for him to leave the hangman alone.

Replacing the bottle in the cabinet, McKinsey said, "Me middle name be Gleason." His mind was swirling. He had killed a man. Killed a man! He avoided looking at the lifeless body. Did Bass feel like he did? His stomach was trying to match his mind. Was he going to vomit? He wanted to be home. Home with Sarah. Surely Bass wouldn't want to stay here tonight. Surely. He slipped both hands into his coat pockets. His right hand touched the gun there and recoiled. He yanked both hands free and folded his arms as his vision followed Truitt, who was looking through Drucker's saddlebags.

After finishing his search, Truitt walked over to the dead man, knelt and unstrapped the gun belt and the big knife. Like a farmer picking weeds, he went through the pockets of the dead man's vest, shirt and pants. He pulled out several coins, a watch, a small roll of paper currency and a small dark medicine bottle.

"These are yours, either of ya." He looked up with the treasures cupped in his hands and the gun belt draped over his shoulder. "The gun and knife, too." His eyes motioned toward Drucker's pistol resting on the floor.

"You keep them," Bass responded.

Truitt kept at it. "He don't have anything special to wear. Has a blue shirt in his war bag. An' some licorice. Socks." He shrugged. "Spurs are nice, though."

"They be lookin' fine on ye." McKinsey tried to make sense of Truitt's matter-of-fact disassembly of the dead man's things. He swallowed to force back the bile.

"You think so?" The outlaw bounded to the body and lifted one boot to examine the spurs more closely.

"He's got hisself a good roan. Worn down some, but a good runner," Truitt said as he yanked off the first spur. "You'll be needin' a horse. Joe's got a good bay, too. You want 'em both?"

"You keep them. I've got a mule. Left it on the trail," Bass declared and waved toward the stacked rifles in the corner. "That be Drucker's fancy rifle? The one with the scope."

Truitt finished taking off the second spur. "Yeah, you want it?"

"No. Just asking."

"You sure you boys don't want some of this stuff?" Truitt continued, now trying on one of Drucker's boots over his fringed leather leggings. "Any of it's yours, I reckon." He chuckled. "They ain't gonna use 'em none." The timid outlaw's eyes widened with realization. "Oh, I get it. You want the bank money, don't ya?" He swallowed to find some grit. "You gonna leave me some?"

"Truitt, I don't give a damn about that money." Bass's response was edged with irritation. "Timbel, are you ready? I'd just as soon head out now."

"Aye. I *hae nae brou o'* this." A deep sign of relief followed from the Scot.

Truitt appeared not to care, busy with putting on Drucker's second boot. Nearby were his removed shoes, both with large holes in the soles; the left was also worn through where the big toe rested. A loud snore from Sontag made Truitt jerk and the boot flew into the air.

"Don't take the time to saddle, Timbel. Just carry it and walk," Bass said as they backed into the darkness.

The fingernail of a moon slid around a cloud and gave Bass and McKinsey enough light to discern the trail. McKinsey was tense, finally realizing his friend was fearful of an attack even now. It seemed like hours before they reached Bass's mule. Othello's noisy welcome made McKinsey shiver; it sounded more like a woman in distress than a mule's braying.

It was McKinsey who next broke the quiet. "Me blood was on *thae* turn, 'tis glad I be that ye wanted to leave that awful place."

"Yeah, it wasn't exactly what I expected." Bass glanced at the Scot and settled into the saddle. He couldn't remember feeling so depressed, except when his Settie left this world and him behind. And years before, when their first children died.

McKinsey looked at the older man and proclaimed, "I *neffer* shot a man before, Bass Tillman. *Neffer. Naught* eve' a redman. It *steiks ane's hert* to think on it."

Bass realized McKinsey was suffering from the anguish of having taken someone's life. The Scotsman needed words to help him. Why wouldn't any come to Bass's mind? Why didn't he feel the same way? Why did he only sense a dullness? Was it just the fatigue of a long, hard day? Or had the loss of his loved ones taken away the last vestige of caring?

He stared ahead at the narrow trail ahead, winding its way toward the sweet prairie. He told himself that he didn't care if he rode over some silly moonbeam or not. The hell with such a stupid superstition. They rode without speaking, letting only the soft thud of their mounts' hooves fill the night. Gradually, the normal sounds of the darkness joined the rhythm.

Looking straight ahead, Bass finally said, "Taking a man's life should feel that way, Timbel. It's forever. Even when that man was bent on ending yours—like Drucker was. You had no choice." He didn't believe that last part and it hurt to express the idea, but McKinsey needed to hear those words.

McKinsey nodded and pushed away an overhanging branch. He looked at Bass and let his shoulders rise and fall. "I *wull* be tellin' me Sarah that I be *gaun tae thae* city of Denver."

"No, Timbel," Bass said softly. "You've done plenty—and I'll always be in your debt. But this fight is mine. Not yours."

"Sarah may *naught* be agreein.' She be settin' store by your young kin."

"I appreciate that. I really do." Bass rubbed his fingers across the top of the saddle horn. "But your place is with her."

"*Weel, guid eneuch.*" McKinsey couldn't quite hide the relief he felt. "What about your kin's farm? Young wheat, they be seekin' *thae* sun an' *wull* be needin' care."

Bass leaned on the horn and looked at the Scot. "I can't worry about that right now."

McKinsey nodded. "Aye. *Weel,* maybe ye *shouldna* go *tae thae* city of Denver. Maybe ye should stay with *thae* land." His mouth twisted as if something sour had passed through his lips. Had he overstepped his bounds with this dangerous man?

They rode again in silence for several moments before Bass responded.

"You know, I've thought of that, I really have. Stay on the farm and make it work." Bass rubbed his unshaven chin. "But . . . I can't. I just can't. They can't get away with . . ." His voice slipped away and he glanced at the cloudless black sky. The moon had taken position behind a tree, keeping its light to itself.

"Ye can be *sur* their crops *weel* be tended to, as if they were me own," McKinsey whispered. His horse yanked its head and the Scot pulled the reins hard, more out of emotion felt than for necessary control.

"I can't ask you to do that, Timbel. It's too much."

"Na, it is only a wee bit o' helpin', it be." McKinsey straightened himself in the saddle, half expecting his horse to bob its head again. " 'Tis where I be happy. Workin' *thae* land."

"Thank you. You're a good friend."

"Turn *thae* crack now, shall we?"

Bass chuckled in spite of himself. The expression meant McKinsey wanted to change the subject, that the matter was settled.

"Aye, I almost be forgetting!" McKinsey blurted. " 'Tis Vernon Copeland whose letters be matchin' *thae* ones ye seek. Me Sarah did *thae* remindin', she did."

"Vernon Copeland? Who's he?"

"*Weel*, Vernon Copeland, he be a storekeeper. Near Wichita, in Kansas."

Bass frowned. "Does he ever get this way?"

"Na, I be thinkin' he *donna*. We met him a while *syne*, ah, ten years ago, when we were moving to Colorado. *Havena* seen him since." McKinsey rubbed his chin. " 'Tis *thae* only name we know that fits *thae* letters ye be seekin'."

Bass's shoulders rose and fell. "Well, thanks. Keep thinking on it. You and Sarah."

"Aye."

"Before I head for Denver City," Bass said, "I'm going back to Jacob's. I'll take the two dead bastards to town. To Sheriff Babbit. Could be they're wanted."

Like the others in the region, McKinsey didn't know Frank Babbit's real name was Frank Schafer, or that Bass and Frank had once ridden together as hired guns. Their friendship endured, however—and their secrets. Babbit had hired Bass's son, Jacob, as one of his part-time deputies. Not even Jacob knew of the sheriff's past connection to his father. Babbit spoke highly of Jacob Tillman and his steady way with handling trouble. However, he didn't suggest Jacob was anywhere as good with a gun as his father had been.

Few were. Although Babbit was close. So was the third gunfighting friend, Emerson Holt. Maybe better even.

Changing names and starting over in a new town wasn't hard. No one asked about someone else's past. Not out here. That was a good way to start an argument. Or worse. Emerson Holt, Bass's other old friend from their gun days, had changed his name as well, but had headed farther west. The story of Emerson Holt and Frank Schafer being killed in Kansas had been planted by Bass himself. Bass hadn't seen Holt in years. He never second-guessed his own decision to change his life but keep his name.

"Ye *naught* be *pitten' thae* shovel to their souls?" McKinsey's question interrupted the attorney's thoughts.

"Somebody else can do that." Bass's voice grew hard. "They aren't going to blacken the land of my son."

"Aye, *thae shakkins o' thae poke* can rest *effer* elsewhere."

"They can rot in hell."

False dawn was trying to convince a sleeping world that it was time to wake up as the two tired riders cleared the forest line and headed for Mc-Kinsey's farm. Both had taken turns dozing in the saddle; McKinsey's loud snoring had quieted the normal night sounds as they passed. Bass would turn off when they got closer and head for his son's farm. McKinsey was still sleeping when they recrossed the stream. He shook off Nancy Spirit Bear's admonition that he wasn't ever to cross water at night. But he did toss a tribute of tobacco, the last in his small pouch. He told himself that it wasn't really night, it was almost daybreak, and shook his head at the ridiculousness of being drawn to the Indian woman's strange notions anyway.

"Bass, you're a foolish old man," he muttered to himself. "But it can't hurt, can it?" He took a deep breath to ease some of the weariness.

As they cleared an uneven ridge, a camp of riders was evident, nestled in a shallow, but wide, ravine. Bedrolls encircled a dead fire and as many horses were tied to a remuda rope strung between two trees. Bass immediately saw a group of rifles stacked against the closest tree. A night guard also leaned against it; his steadily heaving chest indicated he, too, was sleeping.

He nudged his companion awake and McKinsey jerked in the saddle, blurting out, "*Fine a ken . . . I naught be nappin'.*"

"Shhh. There's a camp just ahead. Ten or twelve armed men. Sleeping."

"Ah, 'tis *thae* gatherin' of beef," McKinsey said.

Bass held out his hand to stop his friend from advancing. "Don't think so, Timbel. That looks more like a posse to me. Probably the one Joe Benson was so worried about."

"'Deed I have seen *muckle* o' *thae* roundups near our land."

"Ever see one without a chuck wagon?"

Chapter 7

McKinsey stared again at the sleeping band as if seeing it for the first time. "Aye, 'tis the constables in pursuit. What are ye *gaun tae* tell them?"

Bass tugged on his hat brim. "That we came across the bank robbers in a cabin."

"Wha' about . . . your family? *Thae* murderin'?"

"We'll see. I reckon they're more interested in finding the bank's money." He nudged the mule, encouraging it to begin the descent of the hillside. "Ride careful. They'll be looking for bank robbers wherever they see riders."

"Ah . . . *shouldna* we just ride around *thaim* a wee?"

"No. If they wake up while we're passing, they might not wait to ask questions."

McKinsey swallowed and his tiredness disappeared. He slipped his hand into his pocket and wished the gun wasn't there. He considered giving it back to the old attorney, but decided that was foolish.

Twenty yards from the sleeping men, Bass halted and McKinsey pulled alongside him. "Aho, the camp!" Bass yelled. "Any coffee on?"

The night guard jerked awake; his rifle clattered on the exposed tree roots as it fell from his hands. "Hold it right there," he commanded, hurriedly reaching for the weapon.

"Easy, mister," Bass yelled back. "We're just two tired men heading home."

"Topper! Two riders!" The guard tried to sound official, but came off childish.

Three heads popped up, then two more. One barefoot man ran for the rifle stack. To one side, a short man with a sparrow face and shaggy black hair stood, pulling on his suspenders. His pants were already shoved into the tops of knee-high cavalry boots. A military-styled jacket lay at his feet, along with a black, short-brimmed hat and a gun belt.

Squinting to see better in the morning gray, Bass watched the short man, deciding he was the leader. He looked vaguely familiar, but it was difficult to tell for certain. From the appearance of the awakening group, they seemed like mostly townsmen riding with a few gunmen. It was an odd impression and he decided it was due to his lack of sleep.

Only two men apparently wore badges. A tall, slump-shouldered man headed toward them with a badge on his shirt, just inside his coat. The other badge wearer was the small man. A star shimmered from its place as he put on his dark jacket. From his right wrist hung a quirt; Bass thought the man had slept with it on.

"Johnny, take charge. Wright, you and Painted Crow go with him. Shoot them if they try to run," the short man announced, strapping on a pistol belt holding a holstered, pearl-handled Colt.

Two more riflemen broke from the scurrying camp and ran toward the waiting riders.

"I *naught* be likin' *thae* looks o' this," McKinsey muttered.

His horse jerked its head and the Scot yanked the reins to keep the animal standing quiet. Lack of sleep tugged at the corners of his mind. Minutes before, all he could think of was climbing into his own bed.

The short man grinned viciously at the effect of his orders and snapped the quirt with a quick flick of his wrist. McKinsey thought the expression reminded him of a mean gray cat he had owned once, and shivered

"No sudden moves," Bass whispered. "These boys want an excuse to shoot."

"Aye."

"I'll do the talking."

"Aye."

The first rifleman to reach them was a half-breed called John Painted Crow. Wearing a black cavalry hat with the front brim turned up, the thick-faced man stopped a few feet away and pointed his rifle. It looked like he had slept in his clothes. Around his waist was a dirty, once-blue sash that held a long knife and a short-barreled revolver.

Painted Crow snarled something that sounded Lakotan to Bass, followed by a guttural command in English. "Hands up. Hands up."

"Do what he says." Bass laid the reins across his saddle and raised his hands.

"Aye."

The second and third riflemen arrived out of breath, both brandishing Winchesters. The taller man with a long face smiled, revealing a mouth of missing teeth. "I'm U.S. Deputy Marshal John Cateson. Don't you boys know better than to rob a bank in Marshal Hautrese's territory? Where's the money?"

He was hatless, revealing a bald spot that was likely to take full control of his head soon; long stringy hair surrounded the emptiness. His voice was filled with the soft lilt of Texas. Not a drawl really, more like warm syrup. After he spoke, his mouth remained open, a habit long forgotten, Bass assumed. The man's elongated face looked like dough, when it's been stretched for a rolling pin.

The smaller man with the thick beard and crossed eyes grinned his agreement. Beaded cuffs with fringe fluttered as he swung his rifle toward Bass. His hat lay on his back, held by a stampede string. Bobby Joe Wright mumbled something neither Bass nor McKinsey understood, but the taller lawman laughed his appreciation for the statement.

A fourth gunman, short, stocky and hatless with a handlebar mustache, started toward the first three. His lumbering walk reminded Bass of a sailor, except for the wide-brimmed hat and brown-and-white cowhide vest. The old attorney saw him clearly, but didn't recognize the man. The small man in charge yelled at him to remain in camp. Shrugging his shoulders, the gunman returned and sat near the campfire as two others piled new wood upon the struggling ashes.

Bass pushed back the hat on his forehead and tried again. "Mornin', gentlemen. We were hoping to get some coffee. But it looks like you're running a cold camp."

Cateson snorted, "You might say that." The Winchester in his long fingers was cocked and casually pointed in Bass's direction.

Without further comment, the tall marshal looked back over his shoulder at his nearly dressed leader. "Looks like we've done caught up with 'em, Topper."

The short leader was tying a silken cravat, obviously not worried about the two strangers riding away. Bass finally realized who it was: U.S. Chief Deputy Marshal Topper Lowe. He had met the lawman briefly a year ago in a Longmont restaurant.

"*Nay*, we *haff* not been robberin' a bank." McKinsey remembered he was supposed to be silent and looked at Bass for forgiveness.

Bass nodded agreement. "No, we haven't robbed any bank. Who are you boys anyway?" He watched the short man advance from the corner of his eyes.

Topper Lowe pushed aside Wright and the half-breed to stand in front of the mounted riders. He folded his arms and the quirt dangled from his arm. "I'm United States Chief Deputy Marshal Topper Lowe. This is U.S. Deputy Marshal John

Cateson—and these two are our duly deputized officers." Even this pronouncement carried a cruel undertone. His manner was that of a man used to having others obey his commands.

"We met last year, Lowe, in a restaurant. In Longmont. You probably don't remember," Bass said. "We met Cateson just a minute ago." He leaned forward in the saddle. "I'm Bass Tillman. I'm an attorney in Longmont. This is my friend, Mr. McKinsey. He farms over the way." He leaned forward. "How can we help you?"

At the sound of the old attorney's name, Lowe's expression changed for an instant. Bass wasn't sure how to read it. Fear? Hate? Distrust? Did the lawman know something about his family's deaths? Surely not.

Obviously, these were two of U.S. Marshal Hautrese's deputy marshals. The others, Bass guessed, were an assembled posse. The remaining men around the cold campfire looked like townsmen; these three, like gunmen. He saw no badges on Wright or Painted Crow. That wasn't unusual; many such lawmen, or their posses, wore no identification. Their authority came in the form of written commissions, and their guns, and the empowered leader they rode with.

"Step back, men. You two, get down. Now!" Lowe growled; his eyes indicated he was enjoying this. He waved at the others to stay where they were, making his quirt dance in the air. "So, you're Bass Tillman. How appropriate."

The three riflemen stepped back, taking their cue from the short leader. Deputy Marshal Cateson glanced at his companion and grinned; the cross-eyed man mumbled again. Bass thought he repeated Lowe's command.

With Bass's nod, McKinsey grabbed his horse's mane and swung down.

The elder attorney leaned forward as if he were stiff from riding, slid his right boot slowly from its stirrup and lifted his leg across the saddle. His left hand held to the saddle horn, as tightly as his stiffened fingers would allow, while his right hand slipped unnoticed inside his coat. He was counting on Lowe and his men to relax with the apparent compliance. With his weight on his left leg still in its stirrup, Bass stopped his dismount and remained fully upright on the left side of his mule.

His revolver was pointed at Lowe. "I think we'll stay where we are." Bass's voice was low thunder; the cocking of his gun was louder. His right leg eased back into place.

"Resisting federal lawmen isn't real smart," Lowe said. Surprise and hate boiled in his face. "I say the word and my men will cut you into pieces. And you know it."

Bass's glare grabbed Lowe's eyes and held them. "You won't live to see it. I'll put three bullets in your belly before I'm down. *And you know it*. Is that what you want? Or are you are seeking information?"

Realizing what was happening, McKinsey bounced back into his saddle and pulled the gun from his pocket.

"Aye, an' this tall one *wouldna* be singin' in church neither," the Scot announced, pointing the weapon at the stunned Cateson.

The cross-eyed gunman swallowed and rammed

his words together as he often did, "Whatisthis? Ithoughtweweresupposedtogettheirguns."

None of them had expected the daring move. In similar circumstances, most men were too frightened to do anything, except surrender. Only Painted Crow slowly moved his lowered rifle toward Bass, hoping to be unnoticed.

"Lowe, you're a dead man, if the breed doesn't stop," Bass growled without taking his eyes from the federal officer.

Othello snorted, but stood quietly.

"Painted Crow, no. No!"

Frowning, the half-breed let the gun swing to his side, holding it only with his right hand. His quizzical stare never left Bass.

"Tell your men—in camp—to stand easy." Bass ordered. "This doesn't have to be this way. We can all ride away from this. We'll answer any questions you have—but not at gunpoint. We haven't done anything—except ride close to your camp."

A snarl crept across Lowe's tightened mouth. "Stand down. Everything's fine."

At the camp, the remaining men gathered in twos and threes, wondering what was going on. Several were struggling to put on coats and vests. Bass advised Lowe to order them to sit. He yelled over his shoulder and they complied like wooden toy soldiers knocked down by a boy's hand.

"Tell your boys here to lay down their guns."

Lowe nodded and grunted, "Put your damn guns on the ground. That's an order. You too, Johnny."

As if the weapon were suddenly hot pokers,

the taller Cateson dropped his Winchester, his mouth remaining locked open. The bearded gunman with the crossed eyes followed. This time, he mumbled to himself.

Painted Crow stared at Bass as if seeing him for the first time. His question came in halting words of English. "You . . . Nancy Spirit Bear call . . . The River?"

Without looking away from Lowe, Bass nodded affirmatively.

Painted Crow's chest rose and fell. He bent over and gently laid his rifle on the ground at his feet. Straightening, he turned around and walked toward the camp.

"That's better," Bass said, unsure of what the half-breed's exit meant.

Neither did Lowe from his puzzled expression. For the moment, it didn't matter.

"Now, Marshals, what do you want?" Bass asked, keeping an eye on the Indian to make certain he didn't return. "Or do you always act this way with innocent men?"

Pulling on his quirt with both hands, Chief Deputy U.S. Marshal Lowe snarled an explanation that he and his posse were after two outlaws who had robbed the Highland Bank. Their trail had led this way, but they had lost it at dusk.

Refinding his courage, he asked, "What are you two doing out here, so damn early?"

"Milk cows," Bass answered.

McKinsey bit his lower lip to keep from smiling.

"Milk cows?"

Bass repeated his friend's tale·of losing milk cows years before. He had decided to tell about finding the forest cabin and the bank robbers in it. Something kept him from telling about his family's murders. A hunch. Maybe nothing.

Lowe's face was a mixture of frustration, fear and disbelief. He swallowed the insecurities that had run through him since childhood. No one had shown him any respect until he killed a Chinese couple as a fifteen-year-old. That had brought fear, and fear was close enough to respect for him. Now he faced two men who neither respected nor feared him. If his men realized this, they would change their feelings toward him as well. Yet challenging either man was tantamount to dying. Not today.

His bottled-up emotions took the form of a glare at Wright, who suddenly asked if Jacob Tillman was related to Bass. If the old attorney understood the query, his expression didn't show it. Cateson told Wright to be quiet.

"Marshal Lowe, we had a run-in last night with two rannies bragging about robbing the Highland Bank," Bass said.

With that announcement, he explained the two bank robbers were holed up in a cabin within the forest ahead. He decided not to tell about Joe Benson being dead, or Bill Drucker, or even Easter Sontag. There was no reason to complicate the story.

"You're saying we'll find those bank-robbin' bastards there?" Lowe asked. He was pleased his voice had resumed its heavy growl.

"Depends on how fast you get there, and how much noise you make doin' it."

"They got the bank's money with 'em?" Lowe

said, glancing at his men to see if they were watching him or Bass. He tried not to show disappointment that they were still staring at the old attorney

"Don't know. Didn't see any money—and we didn't stay. Didn't look like a healthy place to spend the night." The statements were basically correct, he told himself.

Lowe rubbed his hands together, letting the quirt dangle free from his wrist.

Cateson finally spoke. "We're missing Deputy Marshal Drucker and two of his men. They were scouting for sign. You seen them?"

"I haven't seen any lawmen," Bass said. His mind was whirling. Bill Drucker, a U.S. Deputy Marshal? Couldn't be.

Dramatically, the short lawman turned around and yelled, "Saddle up, men, the bank robbers are in a cabin in those woods." He pointed toward the dark world of trees waiting in the distance.

One of the men from camp brought Lowe's snow-white horse saddled and bridled. Without being asked, the man led the horse alongside a large, mostly flat rock and stopped it there. Lowe stood on the rock, then climbed into the saddle; red appeared around his ears at the embarrassment of his need of the prop to mount.

"Thanks for the tip," he said loud enough for his men to hear. "Bass Tillman, you'd better be tellin' the truth." He pointed with the quirt and jabbed his horse with his spurs.

"I always do. Some people don't like to hear it, though." Bass's gaze and his gun followed Lowe's retreat.

The left rear shoe of the white horse made a mark in the land. Like the ones at the farm. How could that be? Bass didn't believe in coincidences; Topper Lowe had to have been at his son's place—or his horse had. Why? Was it possible the posse was there before the attack? Was that why the cross-eyed gunman asked if Jacob was related to him? He squinted and watched the deputy marshal wave his arms for his men to follow. Their camp was alive with urgent preparations.

"Let's ride on, Timbel."

Chapter 8

Bass Tillman and McKinsey circled wide to keep the posse in direct sight as they hurried to comply with Lowe's order. Finally, they cleared a low ridge and the attorney nudged his mule into a land-eating lope and the Scot followed.

One thought nagged at Bass: He had crossed water at night, even though he had told himself false dawn wasn't really night. Shortly after that, they had a run-in with Topper Lowe and his men. Coincidence? He wouldn't let his mind ponder it further.

An hour and two ridges later, Bass reined to a stop. "My Scottish friend, I believe your farm is just over there. It's time you saw it again. You're a brave man—and a good friend. I owe you much. And please thank your Sarah for her fine food and her caring. It meant a great deal."

With little reluctance, McKinsey rode away, grateful to be headed home and to safety. Bass

watched him leave and swung Othello toward his
son's farm. He would check things out once
more, before heading for town and packing to
leave for Denver City. The thought occurred that
he should tell his few clients of his plans. They
wouldn't like it, but that didn't matter. He didn't
like it either, but Denver City was his only clue.

Behind him, a familiar silhouette cleared the
far ridge.

Easter Sontag.

The famed executioner waved and kicked his
steel-gray horse into a lope toward him. Led by
Sontag, a saddled horse without a rider followed.

As he neared, Bass noticed that the saddlebags containing the bank money were tied on
the second horse. Had Sontag killed Truitt—or
just intimidated him? Drucker's Pedersoli rifle
was apparent in the trailing horse's rifle boot.
Sontag saw Bass's recognition of the animal and
winked at him. The older attorney couldn't help
smiling.

Chuckling, the executioner rubbed his chin.
"Morning, Bass. Thought I'd catch up with you,
figured you'd be headed for Denver City. Right?"

"I'd enjoy the company."

"Took a guess that you'd be going to your son's
farm first," Sontag continued. "Wasn't sure where
it was, but your trail wasn't hard to follow.
Couldn't remember you saying."

"No one asked."

Sontag's chuckle became a smile. "Saw a bunch
of pissants riding for the forest. You rode near
their camp, it looked like. They didn't see me.
Who were they?"

Bass explained about the two deputy marshals and their posse.

Sontag licked his lips, took a cigar from his inside coat pocket and shoved it into his mouth. "Tell them about the cabin?" He pulled a match from his vest pocket.

"Yes."

"Topper Lowe's a major pissant."

"Seems like it. That's the second time we've met."

"Cateson's a pissant, too. Always walking around with his mouth hanging open."

"Hadn't met him before. Looked like he was taking orders from Lowe."

"Yeah, most likely," Sontag said. "Was there a half-breed with them?"

Bass shifted his weight in the saddle. "Yes. And a cross-eyed fellow. Had a beard."

"Sounds like Bobby Joe Wright," Sontag observed. "One crazy bastard. Mumbles like he's got a mouthful of marbles." He chuckled and continued. "Guess I've met most of them. Lowe, Cateson and Drucker, they're full-fledged deputy marshals. The others are just gunmen they've hired as their special Hoodsmen posse."

Bass's face showed surprise at Sontag knowing Drucker was a federal deputy marshal.

The hangman's eyes sought Bass without turning his head. "Hard to imagine why a United States Marshal, like Hautrese, would choose them, isn't it?"

Bass rode without commenting for several minutes, then asked, "So, you knew Bill Drucker was a lawman?"

"Yeah. Just another pissant taking orders from Lowe."

"Why didn't you say something—in the cabin?" Bass challenged.

Waving his arm dramatically, Sontag declared, "What would that have changed? Would you have relaxed? The pissant would've still tried to back-shoot you."

"Yeah. The farm's this way." Bass turned Othello toward the west.

A defiant noon sun squatted against the land as Bass and Sontag arrived at the small Tillman farm.

"Funny how the mind works," Bass declared, studying the silent home. "A part of me expected to see, just for a moment . . . Jacob and Mary Anne . . . waiting to greet us. Damn." He shook his head.

Sontag watched him silently. His mouth twitched as if he was about to speak, but his vision registered movement in the tall grass near the southwest corner of the house.

"Bass, something's in that grass. There." He pointed.

Drucker's sorrel behind him stroked the ground with its foreleg and the executioner jerked the lead rope to quiet the animal.

"Probably a coyote," Bass said, not quite removed from his reverie.

Sontag squinted. "No, it's a dog. Looks all bloody."

"A dog? My God, it's Cutter! I forgot all about him!" Bass exclaimed and kicked his mule into a trot.

Jumping from the saddle while Othello was still moving, Bass ran the remaining few yards to the wounded dog. Dried blood was smeared along his back and sides. Wobbling to its feet as he neared, the weakened animal stood on three legs, holding his right foreleg from the ground. Bared teeth turned to meet the advancing man.

"Cutter, it's me, boy. It's me. It's all right."

The fighting stance became a whimper and the lowered tail wagged.

"Cutter, oh, Cutter, I forgot you." Bass knelt beside the dog. "I'm so sorry. So sorry." He stroked Cutter's head and the dog licked his hand.

Sontag was immediately beside him, holding the reins of his horse and Bass's mule. Drucker's horse stood next to Sontag's mount, pawing the ground again. Sontag slapped the animal with his handful of reins and the horse stood quietly. With his free hand, the executioner handed Bass a canteen and a folded handkerchief.

"Th-thanks, Easter."

Bass took off his hat, poured water into it and held the liquid offering under Cutter's muzzle. Slowly, the dog began to drink. Bass poured more until Cutter stopped. With the soaked handkerchief, Bass cleaned the dog, finally finding a bullet hole beneath the knot of fur, blood and soil. It was a nasty-looking wound, but appeared to have missed any vital organs.

"Looks like it went through without hitting anything real bad," Sontag observed, shifting his weight from his right foot to his left.

"Yeah, I think you're right. Lost a lot of blood, though," Bass replied. "Leg's broken. Probably from a kick. Damn. I'm sorry, Cutter. I should've looked for you yesterday."

"Yesterday you were a mite preoccupied, judging from those two lying out there." Sontag was surprised by the older man's tenderness, not the result of the gunfight.

"In my saddlebags, there's a small tin." Bass looked up. "Would you mind . . ."

"I'll get it." Sontag returned quickly with a tin container that had once held pipe tobacco.

Inside was packed a thick mixture smelling of turpentine, hog's lard, beeswax and, possibly, cedar. Sontag wasn't certain. It didn't look like any medicine he'd ever seen.

"My Indian friend, Nancy Spirit Bear, fixed this up for me. Best I've ever seen for cuts—or bullet holes." Bass lifted a glob with his two fingers and rubbed the salve onto the dog's side. The animal winced, but lay still.

Finishing with the medicine, Bass patted the dog's head with his stiffened left hand. "We'll take him along. I'll leave him with Nancy. She lives not far from town. It's on the way. Sort of. She'll have the right stuff to make him better. She's done it before."

"Sure," Sontag said, returning his attention to the farmyard gunfight. "Where did you shoot from? Behind that jagged rock? Over there?"

Ignoring Sontag's professional interest, Bass said, "See anything I can use for a splint? A stick or something?"

In less than a minute, Sontag returned with a downed tree limb. "Something here ought to work. This looks good." He grabbed a stout bough and broke it off from the major branch with a quick snap.

"That stuff any good for a hangover?" Sontag kidded.

Bass laughed as he took the foot-long bough. "I don't doubt it. Did you leave any whiskey in the cabin?"

"Only found two full bottles this morning. They're in my saddlebags." Sontag said. "Want some—for you . . . or the dog?"

"No, thanks." Bass untied the long scarf from his neck.

"All right, then, ask me if I want a drink."

"Sure. Do you?"

"Believe I'll have a short one." Sontag headed for his saddlebags.

Bass hesitated, then asked, "Was Truitt still there—this morning?"

Sontag withdrew the bottle from his gear, pulled the cork free and took a long swig. "Yeah. Made him bury Drucker and the big boy. Have a feeling he'll stay there for a while. Too scared to ride on." He took another short drink, recorked the bottle and returned it to his saddle gear, not mentioning the bank money or how he came by it.

Bass nodded as he tightly wrapped the splint-stick against the dog's right foreleg with his rolled neckerchief. He wasn't paying close attention to Sontag's comments, but assumed the executioner had simply picked up the saddlebags with the money and dared poor Truitt to stop him.

A half hour later, they rode away with Cutter lying across Bass's lap, the weakened dog chewing on a piece of jerky Sontag had found in his saddlebags. If Sontag was impressed by Bass's tender care for a dog, it was well hidden.

Behind them was Drucker's horse weighed down with the bodies of the two men who had tried to ambush Bass. One lay strapped over the saddle; the other was tied over the money-fattened saddlebags. Bass didn't check Drucker's own saddlebags, under the filled set, to see if they contained a badge. He didn't check his clothes either. It wasn't that he thought Sontag was wrong, just that Drucker was nothing but a killer. He did seem a fit with Lowe and Cateson, though, and that bothered him. Were all of them at his son's farm? Why? Bass returned his attention to Cutter and stroked the wounded animal's back.

Sontag's constant gaze took in the soft hills and flattened ridges as they passed. But the strange executioner was already proving himself to be an enjoyable companion, knowledgeable about many subjects, especially the theater. Exchanging thoughts about favorite stage presentations kept Bass from dwelling on the murders of his beloved Jacob and Mary Anne. In a strange way, having their dog in his lap helped, too.

A part of him, though, was not certain he should trust Sontag; the executioner was waiting at the cabin where Drucker headed and had purposely caught up with him.

"Saw *Macbeth*, oh, three months ago, I suppose. In Cheyenne. Best ever."

"I saw *Macbeth* two nights ago in Longmont. Probably the same troupe. They were good." It seemed like another lifetime to Bass.

Nodding, Sontag continued. "Really felt sorry

for Macbeth. 'To be or not to be.'" The hangman glanced at Bass on his right. "Ever had those feelings? Like Macbeth?"

Bass wasn't certain what the famous executioner was trying to say. Was he suggesting Bass was considering suicide? Or should? Or was he trying to assess the attorney's state of mind? "Can't say as I have, Easter. Sure been all black inside, though. Like now."

"I imagine so," Sontag observed. "Losing your son and his wife. I'm truly sorry."

Sontag immediately declared he had no family, no wife, no children. His parents had died when he was ten and he worked for a gunsmith, until he became more adept at using the weapons than fixing them. Paid better, too, he observed dryly. Learning the hangman's trade came later. After a few minutes of silence, Bass told about his family; his statements were simple, but filled with love, pride—and sadness. There was no mention of his own past life as a gunfighter.

Sontag listened without comment, seemingly studying a grouping of ridges and ravines that appeared to have been striped with magical paint from green rows of stunted bushes, lines of yellow gold and rose rock and white alkali. As if the colorful land itself reminded him of something Bass had said earlier, the executioner asked, "So you figure your son knew something about the Hoodsmen, something important?"

Bass's response was casual, although his mind was alertly reassessing Sontag's words and actions for clues. "Yeah, I'm sure of it." His teeth clenched to close out the memories that wanted to consume him.

"He didn't tell you anything . . . ah, before?"

Cutter shifted in front of Bass and wimpered. The attorney patted his head and was thankful for the distraction to think through his response. What had his Jacob known or thought he had known? His son was levelheaded and thorough, like his mother, so it wasn't idle guessing. The note, now in his coat pocket, confirmed that. So did the stickpin.

"Yeah, he told me quite a bit." Bass decided it wasn't a lie, not quite.

Sontag's smile cut across his face. "Bass, you don't have to tell me anything about this, but don't say that to me. I know better. You're a terrible liar. I knew you weren't who you said you were the minute you stepped into that cabin."

Looking up from his attention to the dog, Bass said, "You're right. Never was good at it. All I know is Jacob knew something about that bunch, enough to get him killed." He paused and stared at Sontag. "And some boy whose name starts with an H or an L is behind it all. There's a VC fellow involved somehow, too."

"And you're still not sure if I'm involved or not, right? 'H' for 'hangman'?"

Bass stiffened and the dog whimpered again in response to his movement.

"I'm not," Sontag said, "but I can ride on—and no hard feelings."

"No. Don't." Bass almost smiled. "Haven't had anybody to talk to about the theater in a long time."

Sontag laughed, long and loud. His belly rippled with the true mirth. The executioner noted to himself that it was the first time in a long while that he had laughed like that. He liked this tough old man.

Their trail took them past a string of small farms. Here and there, a farmer stopped his spring plowing to wave and receive the same from the two riders. It wasn't recognition from this distance, just traditional courtesy in passing. As their saddles creaked a leathery song, Sontag and Bass talked about the region and its potential, about the continued richness of silver mining in the Denver area, and gradually back to the Hoodsmen and the deaths of Bass's family.

Sontag purported to know nothing more about the mysterious gang, except he was scheduled to execute a convicted gang member in Denver City next week. He volunteered to probe what the man knew, if he got the chance.

After Bass thanked him, Sontag asked, "You ever see ghosts? Of the men you killed? Or have nightmares?"

The question startled Bass.

"I have. Lately," Sontag looked at Drucker's horse to assure himself that the bodies hadn't shifted. "Hanged a young drover last year. In Denver City, it was. Supposed to be a Hoodsman. Lowe and his bunch caught him. That pretty boy Grant was the prosecutor. Man, is he a piece of work! Vicious as a wild dog in court. Hell, he'd prosecute his mother if he thought it'd make him look good. Hear he wants to be governor in a few years."

Bass listened intently, shifting his weight to make more room for Cutter.

The well-dressed executioner inhaled through his teeth. "Have this awful feeling that young drover was innocent. You know, down in my gut. Won't go away." He exhaled slowly. "I was putting the hemp around his neck and he spoke to me. Real quietlike. I hear the words in my head still. 'I'm going to meet my maker with a clear conscience, Mr. Hangman. I ain't no Hoodsman. I ain't no bandit. I never killed nobody, except an Injun once.'" He turned to check on the trailing horse again, then coughed and refaced the trail. "Those were his exact words. I see him every now and then—in my dreams. Sawyer Clary. That was his name."

Bass shook his head. "Don't all of them say they're innocent?"

"Not that way," Sontag acknowledged, adjusting his coat so it didn't get creased against the back of his saddle. "Most tell me the truth—just before. Or they curse me. Or cry like a baby. Not this one."

The executioner stared at his left thumb and forefinger rubbing against the reins and explained that he had checked into the evidence against the man. A black hood had been found in the man's saddlebags. That was the extent of the evidence. That and the fact he had no alibi for his whereabouts when some Hoodsmen crimes were commited.

"Nightmares. That one comes back real regular," Sontag concluded. "He's not the only one that visits me. Drinking helps. Sometimes."

Bass couldn't help examining the shadows of twin cottonwoods as they neared them. A small pond lay at their roots; spring had filled it to the limit of its uneven banks. Ten yards ahead of them, a lean coyote shot across the trail and both men reached for their pistols.

"Looked a bit like Deputy Marshal Lowe, didn't he?" Sontag said, laughed again, reholstered his gun and continued his motion to seek a cigar from his inside pocket.

"Better alert than dead." Bass turned toward the hillside whence the animal had come.

Othello's tenseness told him there was something else there. A dark shape ambled into view from within the ravine. The old attorney pointed in the direction of a young grizzly. "Look there. A young one. Probably just shoved out by his mother."

"No wonder that coyote was running," Sontag mused. "This boy needs to put on about ninety pounds before winter—or he won't make it."

Bass nodded agreement. "Say, why did you think I should see U.S. Marshal Hautrese?"

Sontag bit off the end of his cheroot, placed it in his mouth and lit the thin cigar. White smoke sought his hat brim before vanishing.

"He's the only H I could think of. Right off." Sontag pursed his lips. "And one of his deputies has a name that starts with L. Lowe. How about that?"

"Sounds like a real stretch to me."

"Say, got any whiskey? Those two bottles may not last us till Longmont."

Bass grinned. "No. Only flask we had was the

Scotsman's. You drank it last night. Gave it up . . . a long time ago."

"Hell. Well, at least I don't have to share it." Sontag licked his lips and asked, "No offense, Bass, but I see your left hand is, ah, a bit stiff? Gunfight?"

"None taken. Yeah, still works, though." He held up his left hand and closed it into a fist as best he could.

As he turned his head slightly, a second question was close to exiting the executioner's mouth when he chose silence instead.

"How about somebody whose first name starts with a V and his second with a C?" Bass watched the executioner as he spoke.

"V and C, huh?" Sontag rolled the letters around his mind and mouth. "No. Can't say as I do. Give me some time. I know a lot of people. Lot of pissants, too."

They rode without talking until Sontag asked if Bass had ever met District Attorney Touren Grant. He described a double hanging he had handled for him; two more men accused of being Hoodsmen.

"A blond-haired pissant. Looks like an actor. Speaks like a preacher, which I hear he once was," Sontag described. "Handles mainly Hoodsmen cases. Right now, anyway. Hasn't lost one that I know of. Or any other for that matter." He took a deep breath.

Bass spotted a fat persimmon tree off the trail fifty feet. It reminded him of the persimmon pies Settie used to bake for Sunday dinners whenever the fruit was ripe. He blinked away the memory. This wasn't the time or the place.

"Kinda like a specialist myself." Sontag puffed contentedly on his cigar. "You know, a man who really knows his way around his job, whatever it is. Like Grant."

Immediately, he began to discuss the right rope for a hanging. Motioning toward his saddlebags, he informed Bass that he always brought his own. Carefully oiled so it was easy to handle, easy to knot smooth to slide tightly around a man's neck. No hesitation, like a new hemp rope could provide. A new rope meant the man would struggle for several minutes until death reached him.

"Must know a man's height and weight. Exactly. I do the checking myself," Sontag said. "It's the only way you're going to get a swift drop and a clean snap. Yessir, a struggling man is a sign of an amateur hangman."

"Never thought of it that way."

"Yeah, you have to check out the gallows and scaffold, too. Even if it's a permanent one, like they've got in Denver City—or Cheyenne," Sontag continued. "Weather can weaken it. So can too much use. Redwood's the best. Pine can disappoint you, even if it's been treated with pitch."

Bass nodded and studied the approaching bluff; nothing appeared out of order, but he couldn't help wondering if Lowe, Cateson and their men might double back. There was nothing in any of them that he found at all trustworthy, much less likeable. That was still a big jump to their being involved in his family's tragedy. Yet it was quite a coincidence Lowe's name started with one of the letters he sought—and his horse carried the mark he had seen at Jacob's farm.

"Why didn't you check his cravat, Bass?" he said softly to himself. "What if he was missing a stickpin?"

Sontag either didn't hear the questions or didn't care as he continued his assessment of the techniques of properly hanging a man. "Four feet. Yessir, exactly four feet." He held his hand against his chest to indicate the distance. "That's how far a man must fall. That's when you get that crisp crack of the neck."

Bass nodded and changed the subject back to the theater. Sontag quickly joined in, making their ride go fast. Before long, they entered a shallow spoon of land where a small pond proudly glistened in the later afternoon sun. A windmill set against its far bank whispered of loneliness. The two men decided to rest and water their mounts.

"Doesn't it seem to you like these Hoodsmen are growing recruits?" Sontag said as he dismounted and led both of his animals to water.

"Interesting question. Wondered why nobody has offered one of them clemency to get him to talk. Find out who their leader is. How they operate." Bass jerked on his reins to quiet the sudden braying of Othello, angry at seeing the horses drink first.

"Yeah, unless these boys they've caught are innocent and flat don't know anything about it." Sontag pursed his lips and looked at the cigar in his right fist, then pushed it back into his mouth.

Cradling the wounded dog in his arms, Bass eased out of the saddle, grasping the saddle horn with his hand for balance. He led his mule to the water as he carried Cutter and laid him beside the pond's gentle edge. His boot heel held Othello's reins, but the animal showed no signs of going anywhere. For the first time, he noticed the groove along his boot heel and knelt to run his finger along the cut, wondering when it had happened. Yesterday's shoot-out refilled his tired mind as he stood, filled his hat with water and placed it under the dog's muzzle for Cutter to drink. When the animal was satisfied, Bass applied another hatful onto his reddened wounds and more salve from the jar in his pocket.

"How's the hotel in town?" Sontag suddenly asked. "Good beds?"

"Well, I live there. Hotel Sutton, that is. Not the Empire."

"No boardinghouse?"

"Oh yeah, Martha Thomas's place. Too many widows there for my taste."

Sontag smiled. "All of them with an eye on a certain attorney, I'm sure."

"Don't know about that, but the Sutton folks do a good job—for me." Bass studied the dog's wound, wincing as he did.

"Lately, I wake up all sweaty and petrified. From that god-awful nightmare. It just won't let me go." Sontag squatted and ran his fingers along the pond's surface. "A good bed and whiskey help . . . sometimes." He poked his finger into the ripples and stood.

"I think you'll find their beds passable," Bass answered and studied his bullet-sliced heel again, gradually realizing how close he had come to being hit.

The return to the subject of bad dreams reminded Bass of the little sleep he'd had since the gruesome discovery at his son's farm. A good night's rest before starting for Denver City would be welcome. He realized the mysterious men behind the murders would be difficult to find with so little to go on. An idea had been stirring in his mind to make it well known that he was looking and wait for the guilty ones to come for him.

Sontag's mention of Hautrese and Lowe seemed typical of the hangman the more Bass knew about him. The shock value of bringing up the U.S. Marshal and his chief deputy, when being asked about possible murderers, was just that. For shock. He was beginning to see that the executioner had a highly tuned sense of the dramatic. Maybe that was a way to compensate for his job's goal—to kill. Maybe that's why he enjoyed the theater so much.

"Say, maybe we can drift on up to Central City, after a few days," Sontag volunteered. "They've got a brand-new opera house there. A real beauty, I hear."

"Heard that, too."

"You know they put some goddamn silver ingots right down on the street—so that asshole Ulysses Grant could walk on 'em." Sontag was getting warmed up. "Five or six years ago, that was. He was president then. Quite a sight, I reckon."

"Were you there?"

"No. Read about it."

Sontag looked over at Bass. "You getting any of that mineral?"

It was a very personal question few would ask.

Bass decided it was typical of the man. Curious without appearing to be. Or was it just nosy? Or was it something else? "My partner and I have an investment in a freight line. Does all right, I suppose."

"Good for you," Sontag responded. "Hellva lot better than drilling holes down in the rock. Doesn't seem right to me. It's one thing to pan for gold, something wrong about cutting up the good earth with shafts and tunnels and the like."

Bass noticed Othello trying to nip at Sontag's horse and slapped the mule's face with his reins. If the executioner noticed, he didn't say, instead shifted to a new topic.

"You know, Leadville's got that May Company Department Store. Really something to see," Sontag declared. "Everything to buy. If you got plenty of silver—or gold."

"Haven't been to Leadville."

"Oh. Hey, how about this talking wire stuff I heard about?" Sontag shook his head. "What do they call it? Telephone. Yeah, that's it, telephone. I hear it's really something. Got it in Leadville. Denver. Central City, too. All those rich towns."

Bass perked up at the topic. "Would like to see that myself. Got a friend who says you can hear somebody like he was right in the room with you. Only it's scratchy. Hard to believe."

"Ever been to one of those cities with electrical lights down the streets?" Sontag waved his arms excitedly. "And inside stores, too. Some got water boxes in homes, too. No need for going outside. Can you believe that?"

"Heard about those things. Guess I'll just have

to wait till they come to Longmont." Bass patted the dog. "Getting too old for all these confounded changes." He shook his head and white hair whispered on his shoulders. "Makes a man just want to ride away somewhere alone and die."

"You don't mean that."

"Guess I don't. Just tired. I miss . . ."

Sontag swung easily into his saddle, belying his weight. "So you're going to this Indian woman first. Right?" He pulled the reins toward him and led the horse away from the pond with the Drucker horse following. "What's so special about her?" His smirk indicated he suspected a sexual relationship.

"She's a Bear medicine woman. Like her grandfather. Not many around anymore. Since the reservation." Bass lifted the dog onto the saddle and climbed behind it.

"What do you mean?"

"Bear medicine men were mostly healers of battle wounds."

Sontag watched the attorney for a moment as they swung onto the trail. "Interesting. How old is she?"

"Hard to say. Could be late twenties. Could be forty," Bass replied, concentrating on making Cutter as comfortable as possible. "Long time ago, she helped me heal from some bullet holes. Been good to me—and my family." He hesitated and added, "Settie . . . my late wife . . . she thought Nancy was mighty fine, too."

Sontag smiled to himself, patted his coat pocket for a new cigar and pulled it free.

Remembering what Nancy had told him, Bass

reached into his own coat pocket and yanked free the small tobacco sack. It was empty. Not even a single shaving.

"Say, you don't have another, do you?" Bass asked. "I'm all out of tobacco."

Sontag handed over the cigar and reached into his coat for another. "Sure. Didn't think you smoked—or I'd've offered you one before."

"I don't." The old attorney held the cigar between his second finger and thumb and squeezed it into bits and pieces. Satisfied, he tossed the torn tobacco onto the water, creating a beautiful series of silent circles.

"Hey, that's a good cigar! What the hell?"

Bass smiled. "I'll buy you another in town."

Sontag stared at him for moment. "What's that all about? Some kind of ritual? Something you learned from that Injun gal?"

"It's a long story, Easter."

"Got nothing but time, Bass. Nothing but time," Sontag said. "Especially since we've only got two bottles."

Chapter 9

As Sontag and Bass cleared a low ridge, an isolated cabin came into view. The one-room structure sat in a long valley, surrounded by trees that understood the need to be alone. The nearest neighbor lived over a mile away, on the far side of a fat creek and not visible until one cleared the back side of the enveloping ridge.

They reined to a stop ten yards from the house and Bass climbed awkwardly out of the saddle, holding the dog.

"That a bear skull?" Sontag nodded toward a painted skull hanging over the door.

"Yeah. Nancy's vision was about a bear. Not many men have that. Much less a woman. The Bear Medicine Society were fierce folks—back when the Oglala were pretty much running things in their part of the country," Bass said.

"Thought they were . . . ah, healers."

"They were, but they were dangerous, too.

Acted like a grizzly when they attacked. Mean as hell. Dressed like them, too."

Bass explained that the bear was the only animal ever seen in an Oglala dream offering herbs to heal a man. Nancy's grandfather was a Bear medicine man. *Mat'o wap'iya.* He could heal just about anything, from a broken arm to a headache to a gunshot. He was greatly revered and his granddaughter had been given the same exceptional gift; her father had been a fine warrior, but not a Bear medicine man, and had died in battle against Union soldiers. She lived alone. No white person wanted to live next to an Indian anyway, yet some came to her for medical help. At night, of course, so they wouldn't be seen by their peers.

"But this looks like a white man's place." Sontag cocked his head to examine the quiet house. "Thought we were headed for a tipi." The look on the executioner's face was disbelief. "If you don't mind, I think I'll ride on to town. Get me a room. You take as long as you want. I'll either be in my room, or a saloon—or looking for a book at the general." He paused. "They do have books for sale there, don't they?"

"Geiger and Sons did as of a few days ago." Bass dismounted, holding the wounded dog, and looped his reins across a convenient bush. "Don't eat the bush, Othello."

He turned back to Sontag, who had removed the money saddlebags from Drucker's horse and held them in the crook of his arm.

"I'll see you in town, Easter."

"I look forward to it," the executioner responded. "If there's time, maybe we can take in the theater tonight. You said there was one. Right?"

"That would be good. If I don't go to sleep first."

Pulling on his horse's reins to keep it steady, Sontag said, "Just thought of three more that run with Lowe. Wilbur Hinds, Chester Morgan and Virgil Crimmler." He smiled. "The first two are draped over that horse. I'll leave them for you to bring in." He left Drucker's horse by the bush.

"And . . . Virgil Crimmler?"

"Well, he's got the initials you asked about," Sontag said. "Something to think about. He's no federal marshal, just somebody they say is deputized. Another pissant. Met him at the trial of . . . Sawyer Clary. All those pissants were there. Grinning and laughing. I see that in my dreams, too."

"Virgil Crimmler. That's something to think about. Thanks."

Sontag tipped his hat and spurred his horse into a lope.

Before Bass reached the door, it opened and a tall woman with the hint of a smile stood in the narrow door frame. Beside her stood a three-legged wolf. She wore a plain dress of faded blue with a high collar surrounding her smooth neck. The cloth had been purchased; the sewing was hers. An apron, once white, was tied around her waist.

Except for her long black hair, now in braids, and darker complexion, she looked like most plainswomen in the region. A leather-thonged necklace held a small polished black rock in a small buckskin pouch. It rested between her breasts, forcing them against the tired dress cloth.

"Nancy, I need your help," Bass declared.

The wolf's back bristled and his white fangs flashed a warning. She spoke quietly to the beast, in Lakotan, and the animal relaxed and walked past Bass without pausing to check out him or his dog and disappeared around the side of the cabin. Bass knew the gifted woman had healed many wild animals. Once, even a wounded grizzly.

"Come in, *Kin Wakpa*. Your eyes tell me there is more than this dog." Her greeting included her name for him, The River.

"Thank you."

Through a prolonged legal effort, Bass had seen that she was allowed to live here, instead of the reservation. The home had belonged to her uncle. Several years ago, the old attorney had stopped a band of white men from attempting to burn her out. The presence of his gun had been enough to convince them that they had better things to do. With their families. Safer things.

"Your friend is welcome."

Bass glanced back at Sontag already nearing the closest ridge. "He's going to ride on. Get a room in town. Not long on waiting." He couldn't think of anything to soften the reason, so he said nothing.

Smells of cooking reached his nostrils and settled there. He wasn't sure what was cooking, but it smelled like meat. Probably rabbit. Nothing had changed since the last time he had visited. The two-room building was sparse; a bed in the adjacent bedroom, an old dresser, a wood-burning stove and a rickety table with two mis-matched chairs.

"Bring dog here. On floor. Inside circle."

"Oh, sure."

"It is where the Great Spirit speaks to me—and brings the teachings of the Bear . . . and the heal-ing of the Great Warrior Beast."

Nodding, Bass laid Cutter on the bare, earthen floor inside a circle of reddish rocks that took in almost the entire room. In a handful of sentences, Bass told what had happened and what he in-tended to do.

"I know," she said softly. "Your son and his wife, their spirits are here. They are happy you brought their dog here. They are worried about you."

Bass wanted to ask if their spirits could tell him who their killers were, but knew that would not be received well by his friend. He knew she be-lieved the spirits of the departed hovered near af-ter death, and for a year, before they began the journey to the spirit world, moving along *wanagi tacanku*, the ghost road in the sky. She had shown the ghost road to him one night. It was the Milky Way. The glowing aura was caused by the camp-fires of the dead, she had explained. For a mo-ment, he wanted to ask if the spirit of his Settie was here, too, but decided against it.

"You sit. Beside dog. I get *cannunpa wakan*. When I am given pipe, Bear power comes. It is the way. You know this, *Kin Wapa*. From before." She pointed at a long buckskin bag distinctively deco-rated with quill and beadwork, lying on a scarred dresser.

He knew *cannunpa wakan* meant "sacred pipe."

Some pipes were, of course, for pleasure. Not this one. It was to connect with *Wakantanka*. Even the tobacco she used in it was old-style *cansasa*, made from dried bark from the red willow and mixed together with snakeroot scrapings. It was kept in a small separate pouch next to the pipe bag.

Sitting near Cutter, Bass patted the dog and told him to remain quiet. It wasn't necessary. He leaned forward to make certain the animal was still breathing.

"Easy, Cutter. She will make it better. I promise," he whispered.

He recognized the bear symbol presentation in the tiny pattern of beads of white, black, yellow and red on the pipe bag as she lifted the buckskin sheath. Beside it and the tobacco pouch was a massive French-made revolver. He'd seen the gun before as well. Here. It was her father's. The LeMat handgun had a nine-shot, .40-caliber cylinder with a separate eighteen-gauge grapeshot-loaded barrel underneath the main one. It seemed out of place in the otherwise peaceful house and she had never mentioned it, other than to say the weapon was her father's.

Also on the dresser top was a printed trade card from a cigarette package, bent at one corner. This one showed a picture of a bear, a circus bear. A Blair's Blackamoor lead pencil rested there as well, along with a partially used bar of J.S. Larkin & Co. soap and a Wedgwood china plate.

Carefully, she withdrew the long pipe stem made of ash wood and the separate bowl; both were wrapped in red cloth. The bowl and stem must always be kept separated when not in use, because the pipe was very powerful. Only a sacred person could join the bowl and the stem. She placed the tobacco pouch into her apron pocket, singing to herself. Looking up, she smiled at Bass. A comforting smile.

Before holding the bowl in her left hand, she laid small leaves of sage so that it would rest on them, and not on her hand. Her fingers went to her mouth and she touched the stem and bowl where they touched the moistness.

Although most medicine pipe bowls were made of red catlinite, this one was created from polished black slate. The pipe stem itself was decorated with porcupine quillwork extending along its base. A series of bear claws and eagle feathers hung from an extended buckskin thong. Although he couldn't see it from where he sat, he knew there were intricate carvings in the wood of a spider, a turtle and a bear, all signs of considerable power.

She returned to where he was sitting and squatted easily into a cross-legged position close to the dog, holding the pipe with both hands. The pieces of sage were barely visible where she held the bowl. With the right hand, she reached into her pocket and withdrew a pinch of the special tobacco between her thumb and index finger. Moving precisely, her right hand rose quickly, and lowered ceremoniously until the tocacco touched the mouth of the bowl. This was repeated seven times, and with each, a prayer was offered to the four Winds, to Mother Earth, to *Wakan-tanka* and to the great eagle, the only messenger between man and the Great Spirit.

When seven pinches of tobacco had been placed

in the bowl, she tamped the pipe with a special stick from her apron pocket and lit it. After drawing on it and taking four puffs, she lifted it above her head, offering the mouthpiece in all seven directions. She paused and muttered something he thought had to do with addressing the Bear, but he wasn't certain. He had seen this ceremony before, but didn't know if it was her own or one that most Oglala holy men used.

With solemnity, Bass received the pipe from her and Nancy began to sing as he repeated the presentation. It was a song he had heard only once before, when he was shot. To smoke or even touch a pipe was regarded as a sacred act and only men and women of integrity could do so. He felt honored—and slightly guilty.

In her right hand had appeared a rattle that she began to shake in rhythm with her singing. He hadn't seen the rattle before and wondered where she had kept it earlier. At his completion of the pipe ritual, he returned it to her and she cleaned out the residue with the same stick, separated the bowl from the stem and returned them to the pipe bag.

He watched as she withdrew a small black stone from her necklace pouch and laid it gently against the dog's greatest wound, continuing to sing her special chant. Next came small cedar sprigs to be placed over the other cuts to help disinfect them. Over the cedar was placed a tiny heart, a turtle's heart mixed with yucca pith for swelling, shreds of tobacco and something she called "yellow leaves" to control swelling. He hadn't noticed her gathering the leaves before, but remembered seeing them when he was wounded. He couldn't help thinking it was as if she knew he was coming.

She seemed far away to him; her eyes were open, seeing something he did not. He studied her face and knew she was a true friend, like Frank and Emerson. Or was she more than that? He felt himself relax for the first time in two days, a strange sense of comfort washing over him.

"You should stay, Bass Tillman. Stay and sleep and eat. It is well you do so."

He heard her voice before the message registered in his tired mind. She had completed the Bear medicine ritual. Cutter was resting quietly and she was standing. It took a few more minutes to realize she had called him by his Christian name; he couldn't recall her doing that before.

Scrambling awkwardly to his feet, Bass thanked her, but said he must ride on.

"Yes, a war journey calls. You go. I care for dog," she said. "You come back when done. To me." There was a hint of a smile. "*Wanagi yuhapi* must . . . be done."

Bass knew that such a ghost-keeping commitment, *wanagi yuhapi*, could last at least six months, perhaps a year. She promised to begin the ceremonies in his honor and to care for Cutter until he returned. He agreed; how could he say otherwise?

She reached for his stiffened left hand and held it gently in both of hers, whispering words he didn't know. A healing prayer, he guessed. After an awkward touch of her arm and a brief meeting of her sad eyes with his, he left.

"Wait, *Kin Wakpa*." Nancy's voice cleared the closed cabin door.

He took Othello's reins, complimented the animal for not eating the bush and stood as the Oglala holy woman appeared in her doorway.

"Please . . . I want you to carry this." She held out a dark, odd-shaped rock in her right hand. "Medicine stone. *Wasicun tunkan*. Keep you safe." She continued. "It comes from the belly of the great bear. When no one is watching, rub it over all of you. Very carefully, do this. Let your mind reach out. Crazy Horse did so, before every battle. He never hurt. In battle."

He accepted the stone in his left hand and it felt strangely heavy for being so small. His stiffened fingers folded around the rock without tightly holding it. Was it his imagination or did it feel like his fingers were more flexible than usual? Couldn't be.

He led the mule and Drucker's loaded horse toward the house and received the special bag. "Thank you, Nancy Spirit Bear. That is very kind."

"You come back—for dog. And *wanagi yuhapi*."

He pushed the medicine stone into his coat pocket, beside his empty tobacco sack, and swung into the saddle.

"The stone carries the *sicun* of my grandfather," she said, swallowing back an emotion he couldn't read.

"I'll keep it close to me. I promise." He couldn't imagine rubbing a rock all over himself.

Chapter 10

Dusk was settling around Longmont as Bass rode past the last remnants of the early settlement of tents, crude huts and hewed-pine cabins, and down the main street of commercial activity. A lonely windmill acted as a sentry at the outskirts of the settlement.

The original inhabitants had built some fifty buildings in three months in 1871 to get the town started. Longmont was one of the agricultural settlements, "colony towns," created by the railroad with their large tracts of land to sell, courtesy of the federal government's enticement. Longmont was settled mostly by Chicagoans and was referred to as the "Chicago-Colorado colony."

"Lord a-mercy, those boys knew how to work." Bass glanced at Drucker's horse behind him.

A high-walled freighter rumbled past him;

Othello didn't like the closeness and kicked one leg in the direction of the rickety vehicle.

Ahead were the later houses and buildings of wood, stone and brick standing proudly in the advancing evening. Along the long mercantile street, stores proclaimed their wares in painted signs. Bass liked the town and its spunk. So had Settie.

He glanced at a small stone house among a group as he passed. He swallowed back the feeling. It had been their home, Settie's and his, after years in other towns and other settlements in Kansas and Colorado. They had come to Longmont not long after the town was established. Settie was the reason he hadn't died in some forgotten gun battle. He knew that. She was the reason he changed. The only reason. And why he became a lawyer. To make her proud of him. To give them a respectable life together.

They had raised Jacob to adulthood in that house, their only child to live that long. After Settie passed, he couldn't stand to stay there anymore with the crowded memories. He sold it to a nice young couple and moved into the hotel.

The town itself swelled with busy people; only a few curious enough to stop and watch the rider and his trailing horse pass. A carriage rattled past and the woman in the vehicle studied Bass Tillman with obvious interest. A young boy ran across the street and turned into a young Jacob. Bass shook his head to drive the image away.

A steady ping of a blacksmith's shop blended with a saloon piano, the cursing of a mule skinner and the hearty laughter of idle men. The heavy-armed blacksmith stopped his hammer against his anvil and the orange-hot horseshoe on it. He knew the older man; everyone knew Bass Tillman in Longmont. But he couldn't recall anyone leading a horse down the street, with two bodies draped over it. Tillman waved and the blacksmith returned the greeting. Curiosity satisfied, the musical ping of his hammer resumed as the attorney passed.

Bass's eyes darted from one side to the other, studying briefly a businessman, before darting to a batwing-chapped cowboy stepping from the saloon into the fading sunlight. Laughter and piano music escaped from inside before the door swung shut again. A loaded freight wagon rumbled past Bass and the driver saluted with a nod of his head.

From Bass's left, a man hurried toward him. His dress indicated he was a townsman; his suit was a bit rumpled; his paper collar, slightly soiled. He held a hat in his hand as he moved. He owned a small men's tailoring shop.

"Mr. Tillman, Mr. Tillman, did you forget our meeting this morning?"

Bass's face answered the question.

Agitated, Hamilton Jallon stepped next to Bass as he reined his mule to a stop. The man's narrow face was a swirl of concern and frustration. "They're gonna take my place. Remember? Mr. Moulton says he's got no choice. What am I gonna do?"

Bass didn't like Milford Moulton, the town banker; he was one of those men who acted as if the money deposited in the bank were actually his.

"Look, Mr. Jallon, somebody murdered my son and his wife yesterday." Bass motioned behind him. "Two of them ride back there. Another lies in a cabin. There are more. I intend to find them. I'm headed out to Denver City tomorrow morning. Don't know how long I'll be gone."

Hamilton Jallon stared at the bodies as if seeing them for the first time. "B-but it's m-my place. I built it . . . myself! I . . ."

The townsman was close to tears; he made no attempt to ask why Bass Tillman would think he should go to Denver City.

Bass pulled on his hat brim. "I understand. Before I leave, I'll see Moulton and tell him that he better not take any action until I come back."

His eyes shifted toward the bank. Closed. Of course. He would also tell the banker about Jacob's death and that he would cover his son's loan. He should also see the undertaker about headstones. Benjamin Ringly was always helpful; he was also the town dentist. Bass would leave the burying of the two dead men up to him as well.

"What good will that do?" Jallon's response had turned harsh.

"Maybe nothing, but it's the best I can do right now, Mr. Jallon. If he thinks we're going to sue him—and that will affect bank profits—I think he'll wait."

His shoulders rising and falling, the townsman turned and walked away as Bass reined his horse toward the sheriff's office. He was tired. Very tired. It would be good to sleep in his own bed. A good steak and a drink with Sontag would be nice as well. He would pass on the theater; it just didn't appeal. Not tonight. The executioner was probably in the general store or, more likely, a saloon. Wherever, he wouldn't be hard to find after Bass left the two bodies with Sheriff Babbit or his other deputy, William Manchester, if he was on duty tonight. He choked back the thought that tomorrow night would have been Jacob's turn.

If he was lucky, the sheriff himself would still be there, before heading home for supper. He reminded himself that he needed to speak with his two other current clients before leaving, as well as the bank president. He didn't want to be bothered with any of it, but knew he must. His tired mind wouldn't relieve him of the responsibility.

His hand found the medicine stone in his pocket. There was a certain comfort in the touch. Unexplainable, but definitely there. Had Nancy Spirit Bear known of his coming? Or was it something she had simply set aside to give him on his next visit? That seemed more likely, although it seemed best not to rule out anything of the unseen world, when it concerned her. He looked down at the crystal hanging from his watch chain. Her gifts were at once simple and profound. Natural and supernatural.

Lack of significant sleep again crowded into his mind. Denver City was three days away, so he would be facing nights sleeping in the open. It was something he hadn't done in years and wasn't looking forward to. The stagecoach was an option, but he hated being cooped up in those things, even if they did provide hostelry services along the way. At least he would have company; Easter Sontag was an enjoyable companion. Bass was convinced the executioner's appearance at the forest cabin was mere coincidence. It had to be.

"Drop off these two, Bass," he advised himself, "then head to Geiger's for supplies. You can look for Sontag after that."

From the planked sidewalk, two townsmen waved and Bass responded with a tip of his hat. The townsmen followed his arrival with interest mainly focused on the two bodies behind him. If Sheriff Babbit had already left, Bass planned on turning the dead men over to the other part-time deputy, who would have the evening shift. He choked back the swell of angst as the reason for knowing the lawmen's shifts hit him.

"Hey, Bass!"

It was Lucius Henry, one of his business partners. Their partnership was doing fairly well with investments in a freighting company, some mining properties and real estate; initial loans had been paid off a year ago.

"Good to see you, Lucius."

"What's wrong?" Henry limped closer. His dark suit, freshly ironed white shirt and striped necktie were the typical attire of the gentle businessman.

Bass told him.

Henry was the bookkeeper in their partnership. He was good at numbers, not so good at relationships. He mumbled his sympathies and quickly related that dividend checks from their mining stocks hadn't yet arrived and were due. He wondered if he should send telegrams, requesting their status.

"Wait till tomorrow, Lucus. Wait for the stage,"

Bass advised. He understood the man and the pull into the routine of life was actually comforting.

"Thanks, Bass, I'll do that," Henry replied. "I'm sorry . . . about your loss."

Bass nodded and the businessman retreated toward his offices on the second floor above the general store.

After tying Othello and Drucker's horse to the hitching rail, Bass stepped onto the planked sidewalk and dodged a small boy running past to catch up with his friends. Bass smiled. It felt good to do that. A middle-aged woman, with her thinning hair hidden by a large hat that seemed to be growing feathers and silk ribbon, paused to greet him as they met on the sidewalk.

"Good afternoon to you, Mr. Tillman," Mrs. Lancaster said, tilting her head slightly to the side. A beckoning smile found her mouth and her eyes twinkled an invitation.

"And to you, ma'am."

She gave a stiff curtsey and continued. There was nothing in the encounter to suggest that she had invited him several times to have dinner at her cottage north of town. And breakfast. He had declined each time and, for him, graciously. Her walk became more exaggerated as she continued past him. A glance over her shoulder brought a disappointment as Bass concentrated on opening the city sheriff's office door.

The combined sheriff's office and city jail was well built of rough-cut logs and adobe with a sharply sloped roof. It had initially served as a small fort against Indian attacks and the town had essentially grown around it, and the nearby well. Bass was proud of his old friend's achievement as a lawman. Frank Babbit was firm—but fair. People were secure in his handling of the town's safety. Bass grinned when he thought of his friend in the old days. Days best left to memory, he told himself.

"Got some awful news, Frank. My boy and his wife have been murdered," Bass declared as he stepped inside.

"Afternoon, Bass Tillman. Been waiting for you."

Chief Deputy U.S. Marshal Topper Lowe's smirk covered his entire face.

"You're under arrest for the murder of two of my deputies," Lowe spat. "And I have a feeling it's actually three, soon as we find Bill Drucker— or what's left of him. That's his horse you've got."

U.S. Deputy Marshal Johnny Cateson and Bobby Joe Wright, from this morning's encounter, held rifles pointed at Bass's midsection. The half-breed wasn't there.

Lowe sat with his boots resting on top of the sheriff's desk. In his hands was a pearl-handled Colt; the quirt wiggled from his wrist. The heavily scratched desk held several stacks of papers apparently separated into some classification known only to Sheriff Babbit. Unseen from Bass's angle was a book propping up the one leg shorter than the others. Bass couldn't remember it ever being level, or Babbit ever attempting to fix it.

Standing back near the six jail cells was Bass's old friend, Sheriff Frank Babbit, looking every bit of his fifty-one years. His face had lost its usual ruddy color and his eyes met Bass's in a silent greeting. He held a double-barreled shotgun, but it wasn't aimed at Bass. It was aimed at Lowe. Babbit's back was against one of the closed cell doors, using it to help keep him standing. His double-breasted gray suit was completely buttoned and worn at the elbows and knees. A once-white shirt was missing a button and his paper collar had seen better days. He was a stern man, German born, with a wide streak of stubbornness, if pushed.

Although he wore a gun belt under his coat, the holstered .45 Colt was rarely needed these days. Bass couldn't recall Babbit using it since he and his friends decided to ride a different trail. Babbit had married almost the same time Bass and Settie did. The only major criminal attempt, since Babbit was the law in town, was the failed bank robbery three years ago. Bass was the one who stopped it. Babbit was out of town serving foreclosure papers on a debt-ridden farmer.

Bass realized his old friend was acting in Bass's best interests. The shotgun was the lawman's assurance that Lowe and his men wouldn't shoot Bass as he entered. Babbit was a tough man to intimidate; his stubbornness had probably saved Bass's life.

"You look surprised, Tillman. Did you think we were actually going to take you up on that silly story about bank robbers hiding out in some cabin in the woods?"

Bass inhaled and let some of the anxiety ease its way through clenched teeth. He cursed himself for being so casual. He should have expected something like this from Chief Deputy Marshal

Lowe. Bass knew a move toward his gun would bring instant death. Lowe would also be looking for a diversion after being fooled earlier. Even in his protracted grief, he didn't want to end his life this way.

Going down fighting beside his son was one thing; getting blown apart by some misguided gunmen, quite another. This situation could certainly be explained; he had done nothing wrong, except tell a little white lie about milk cows.

"What the hell is this?" Bass Tillman straightened his back. "Are you charging me with murder? Whose?"

"Hell yes, I am. You murderin' son of a bitch. You murdered Wilbur Hinds and Chester Morgan. They're outside, lyin' across Drucker's horse. They're two of my posse men. You murdered them."

Cateson and Wright chuckled as Lowe continued his presentation. Loudly, too loud for the small office, he proclaimed that the bodies outside were those of his special deputies on the trail of the secretive Hoodsmen.

Jerking his head to the side, the cross-eyed gunman, Bobby Joe Wright, repeated the claim, but it sounded like a rushed echo. "Youmurderingsonofabitch."

The office area was small and seemed smaller. Wall lamps worked hard to rid the room of the coming dusk, leaving a yellow glow on everyone's shoulders. A rack of rifles and two shotguns occupied the far south wall. An empty place indicated where the shotgun in Babbit's hands usually rested. In the north corner, a woodstove

belched a tiny string of smoke; a blackened coffeepot looked less friendly than it usually did
whenever Bass came to visit. On the wall behind
the sheriff's desk was a framed picture of President Rutherford B. Hayes, slightly off center. Details like that weren't Babbit's long suit. They
usually bothered Bass, but not this time.

Bass listened quietly, continuing to make certain no gesture could be misconstrued as an attempt to reach his gun. His mind raced around
for answers to questions that hadn't yet been
asked. Legal answers. Should he even admit
killing those men? Actually, he hadn't killed either; Bill Drucker had done that. What about
Drucker himself? Again, he had only wounded
the man; McKinsey had overreacted and actually
killed him. He wouldn't lie about it. He had defended himself. He had no choice.

"Cateson, take his gun. Lock him in that cell.
The far one." Lowe's command broke through
his thinking.

With a gaping mouth, the tall deputy marshal
with the long face stepped next to Bass, opened
the attorney's coat and ripped his Merwin & Hubert revolver from its holster. Cateson grinned
and shoved the weapon into his belt and stepped
back. If the man had any problem taking orders
from another deputy marshal, it never showed;
Lowe wore his "Chief Deputy" status with obvious pride and constant usage.

Bass stood quietly, his eyes on Lowe, who
didn't want to meet them. The elder attorney's
mind was whirring. How could these two dead
men—and Drucker—be involved in any law en-

forcement matter? A federal concern, no less. That's what Easter Sontag had told him, but he thought the executioner was kidding. Or had this all been a terrible mistake and they had opened fire thinking he was the murderer of a farmer and his wife? No, that made no sense at all; they couldn't have known of any violence done at that moment, unless they had been a part of it earlier, as he suspected. But what were they doing, then, as a part of the U.S. Marshal's enforcement?

"*Mein Gott*, Bass, Jacob vas killed? And his sweet *frau*, too?" Babbit's question broke into the attorney's assessment of the situation. His conversation was always sprinkled with his native language, more so when he was nervous or agitated.

"Yes, Frank, I came to tell you of some very sad news. About my Jacob. And his Mary Anne," Bass said, staring at the tense constable who was wiping his hands, one at a time, on his trousers. "They were murdered. Two days ago." His face contorted with the anger filling it, but he forced himself to remain motionless. "By the two dead men outside. And others that, so far, have eluded justice. I'm going to find them and make them pay."

"*Es tut mir sehr leid*. I mean, I'm *sehr* sorry, Bass. Jacob vas a fine man."

"That's a goddamn lie, Tillman," Lowe roared and raised his rifle.

"I may be a lot of things, Lowe, but I'm no liar. Got no stomach for it. Ask around." Bass never glanced at the federal deputy, keeping his gaze fixed on Babbit. "The clues the killers left behind are taking me to Denver City. One has a name that starts with an H. Another killer's name starts with an L and another, with the letters V and C."

Lowe's expression fell like a loaf of bread taken too fast from the oven. He swallowed hard and finally stammered, "P-put him in that cell like I said. You're goin' to Denver City all right, Tillman. None of this local magistrate crap. You're going to federal court there. And a hanging." He sat up and snapped the quirt for emphasis. A vicious leering expression lingered on his face.

Bass's returned glare ended it and Lowe brushed unseen dust from his shirt. A part of him wanted to fight—or argue as any good lawyer would. But his weary mind urged him to be quiet. If this was going the direction he thought it was, such arguments were better saved for the trial. He frowned, trying to focus. What was really going on here? Bass could see a small hole in Lowe's cravat where a stickpin had once held court. Could it be? Lowe. L. It's what Sontag had intimated. The old attorney's mind was now agreeing.

"That doesn't make sense, Bass. He's a federal officer." The murmur to himself was loud enough that both Cateson and Wright frowned.

Ignoring them, the attorney walked unaided toward the small, ten-by-ten cell, explaining the situation at his son's farm to Babbit.

The cross-eyed gunman opened the cell door, as if a gracious host. A haughty smirk destroyed any sense of courtesy and he burbled, "BassTillmanwegotyounow."

Bass's hard eyes made the smaller man hurriedly shut the cell and lock it.

Sheriff Babbit's face tightened and with it came even more of the courage Bass had seen his friend exhibit over the years. "U.S. Deputy Marshal Lowe *und* Deputy Marshal Cateson, as I said before, *Herr* Tillman *ist* an *gut* citizen of our *stadt*, ah, our town. Himself, an officer of *der* court even. *Ja*, his son vas *mein* deputy." His stern expression focused on Lowe. "I *bin* sure there *ist* reason for *das. Ja*, I *bin* sure."

Without answering, Lowe strode to the lawman's cluttered desk and grabbed a telegram resting there. He spun around and held up the shivering paper.

From his cell, Bass could read it almost as well as the bewildered lawman:

ARREST BASS TILLMAN FOR MURDER OF TWO FEDERAL OFFICERS STOP BRING HIM TO DENVER FOR TRIAL IN FEDERAL COURT STOP U S MARSHAL BOSTON HAUTRESE

Chapter 11

Nodding at the telegram, Babbit asked, "Bass, did *du* kill those men?" He braced for the answer, expecting the worst.

Grabbing the bars, Bass said, "No, but I wounded them. I had just finished burying Jacob and Mary Anne when three men sneaked up on me and opened fire. They had returned, it appears, to retrieve evidence they didn't mean to leave behind. Evidence that's going to lead me to the rest of them. A third man with them finished the job on those two outside, to be sure neither could talk. Then he rode off. I went after him."

With a wild flurry, Lowe slammed the telegram down against the desk. "Bullshit! You ambushed my men."

Feeling more secure, Wright repeated the claim, but forced himself to speak more slowly than he often did. "Bullshit. You-ambushed-them." The fringe on his beaded cuffs fluttered as he jerked his rifle toward Bass.

More calmly than he felt, Bass asked, "Why would I open fire on men I've never seen before? Unless they shot at me first—at my son's farm."

"*Ja*, that *ist gut* question," Babbit eagerly replied, cradling the shotgun in his left arm, his right hand remaining near the trigger guard.

Lowe was rigid; his face glowed crimson and his eyes bounced from Cateson to Wright, who appeared eager to repeat whatever his boss said.

Babbit was silent, waiting for more. His eyes were wide to absorb every nuance of Bass's statement. The arrival of the federal marshals had come as a total surprise, as well as their stated purpose. Lowe had demanded Babbit leave while they waited for Bass; he wouldn't say why they knew he was coming. The old German had refused, more out of a worry in his gut than anything else. He had been cleaning a shotgun when they burst into the office and it had immediately given him some control over the situation.

There was no way he was going to let them have his old friend. The law was one thing and he believed deeply in defending it; friendship was another. Bass Tillman had saved his life on more than one occasion—and Babbit would never forget that. Even if it cost him his badge—or his life.

Now he was glad he had stayed. Lowe and the others would have killed Bass when he stepped inside. That much was clear. What Bass's son had told him two days ago was true. He was certain of it now. In the back of his mind grew the thought that they still might kill Bass Tillman—and kill him as well, saying it had been done by the attorney trying to escape. He shook his head to rid himself of the thought, but kept the shotgun aimed in Lowe's direction. If necessary, his first shot would be at him.

"Because you knew they were on your trail," Cateson blurted without waiting for Lowe to determine his answer, "because you're the head of the Hoodsmen gang." His mouth gaped open at the end of the statement and stayed there.

Bass burst into laughter. It wasn't a funny situation, but he couldn't help it. This was getting more ridiculous by the minute. Babbit joined in, laughing heartily and blurting German expressions that no one understood. Wright snickered; Lowe's glare stopped the response.

Shaking his head, Bass said, "So, these three men were sent by you to arrest me on suspicion of being a member of the Hoodsmen."

"Damn right. The head of it," Cateson proclaimed and his jaw wiggled as it remained open.

"Why didn't they just come to my office down the street, instead of guessing that I might be at my son's farm?"

"We suspect he was in it, too." Cateson rubbed his chin; the questions were coming too fast. He glanced at Lowe for assistance.

Bass's temper exploded and his fist slammed against the cell door. "You sorry-ass excuse for a lawman. Don't ever say something like that about my son again or I'll . . ."

"You'll what? Kill us like you did my men?" Lowe smiled, glanced at Cateson and corrected himself. "Our men."

Cateson's response was immediate. "We've got the outlaw Bass Tillman dead to rights." His grin became wider. "Soon he'll just be dead."

Bass's eyes were fury and he demanded that Babbit release him.

"Wish that I could do so, Bass, but this *ist der* federal business—and *du* know it." The constable raised the shotgun in futility. "However, ve vill *nein* be going to *der* town of Denver. Too far. *Ja*, too far, it *ist*. Ve vill vait for *der* circuit judge. He be *hier* in *drei* . . . three . . . days. Ve vill vait. For *der* hearing." His chin punched forward to emphasize the point. "*Der* hearing. To see if a trial *ist* . . . necessary."

Lowe's chest expanded as crimson took control of his face. "The hell you say! I'll decide what we do with our prisoner."

"Ve vill vait for *der* judge. Ve vill vait *rit hier*."

Lowe whispered to Cateson and the gunman immediately headed for the door. After two steps, he turned and asked, "What if it's locked?"

"Get the hotel owner and open it. Go!"

Bass realized Lowe was sending Cateson to search his hotel room. Evidently, they had found out where he lived, which wouldn't have been difficult. Just ask the first person they met. He wondered if there would be an attempt to get a search warrant; such legal niceties weren't always used, but that didn't mean they weren't to be. It didn't matter. Nothing in his room would yield anything anyway. It was bare, except for a bed, an old dresser—and a photograph of Settie, and one of Jacob and Mary Anne.

Lowe watched his man leave, shutting the door

behind him, then turned to the cross-eyed gunman, patted him on the shoulder. "Stay here,
Wright. I'm going to wire Marshal Hautrese that
we got Tillman. I'll ask him about waiting for the
circuit judge. Maybe Grant's not far and can ride
over to handle the prosecution." His eyes
sparkled with satisfaction. "I don't want anyone
coming in here while I'm gone. Unless it's Deputy
Marshal Cateson. Got it?"

"*Mein* deputy vill be coming. He *ist* on *zoll*, ah,
duty, *hier* . . . this *nacht*," Babbit protested. "Deputy
Villiam Manchester. He *ist* hard worker. Has job at
der general store. And some for *Richter* . . . ah,
Judge Pierce. An' for me. He and Jacob . . ." He
didn't finish the statement.

Lowe listened and advised Wright to allow the
sheriff's deputy in, but no one else. With a triumphant glance at Bass, he snapped the quirt
against the floor and left.

Bass stared at the closed door for a moment.
The stickpin had to belong to Topper Lowe. Too
big of a coincidence not to. Especially with that
peculiar horse mark. If so, why had he been there,
except as part of the murders? Bass had to assume
this was the case. But there was no reason to give
Lowe any idea of what his defense might be. He
shouldn't have mentioned the initials, but he had.

Was Lowe somehow connected to the Hoodsmen? The question jolted him and he grabbed the
cell bars. Of course! What a perfect cover! If that
was so, did it mean H was, indeed, Hautrese?

"That would mean VC was—what was the
name Easter said?" Bass hissed through his teeth.
"Virgil Crimmler. Yeah, that was it." He consid-

ered the enormity of the conclusion he had just reached. "Good Lord!" The exclamation popped from his mouth, barely louder than his hissed question and answer.

His shoulders jerked and the medicine stone in his coat pocket thudded softly against the cell door as the garment swung against it. He glanced down and shoved his hand into his pocket. How quickly the serenity of Nancy Spirit Bear's healing ceremony evaporated into the harshness of his arrest. He looked at his left hand and remembered her soft caress and gentle healing prayer. He tried to form a fist with it, but it was little more than closed fingers.

For a brief moment, he considered the reality that there was a certain fairness at work: He had never been arrested for the bad deeds of days long gone, so now he was being charged with something he hadn't done. A grunt rejected the idea. He must stay free—and alive—long enough to find the men who destroyed his family. Nothing had changed to deter him from that objective. Not even this.

"Frank, I would appreciate it if you would see to my mule." Bass held the cell bars with both hands. "Maybe one of the stable hands would—"

"I *vill* take him over myself," Babbit interrupted. "Anything else—for *du*?" He looked over at Lowe's gunman now settling into the sheriff's own chair behind the desk. "I be *vehr* sorry about Jacob an' all. *Das*, too. I am sure it vill get handled." His last statement didn't carry the energy of the first.

"Do me one more favor, will you?"

"*Ja*, sure."

Bass motioned for him to come closer.

Wright's eyebrows rose in concern as Babbit hesitated moving toward the cell.

"Leave-your-guns-here, lawman." Wright pointed at the desk, proud of his more pronounced statement.

"Nein. I vill keep them."

Bass met the gunman's stare. "I've got some loose ends to tie up, Wright. Sheriff Babbit isn't about to do something illegal. Just relax."

"Oh-yeah. Well, be-quick-about-it." Wright dismissed the situation with a wave of his hand, making sure his words came as slowly as possible.

Babbit stopped in front of the cell and Bass asked him to check the bullets in the two bodies. Quietly, he reminded him that he carried a .36 Merwin & Hubert revolver and a single-shot .50 Ballard rifle. He said the shots in the back had come from a Pedersoli rifle that took a .45 cartridge and advised the city lawman that his testimony might be necessary to prove part of Bass's story. He also asked Babbit to see if the dead men's shirts showed signs of pinholes where badges might have been worn.

With his lower lip between his teeth, Babbit nodded agreement, then asked, "Think I should vait here till *mein* deputy comes? Ja?"

Bass's shoulders rose and fell. "That would be good. Thanks. I appreciate your staying—before I came. There's something strange going on here, Frank."

Babbit shook his head and whispered, "They surprised me. About an hour ago. Said they think *du* vould be coming." His eyebrows jumped with concern. "It *ist* about vhat your Jacob knew. I should've *bien vit* him. I thought ve had time. . . ." He swallowed and glanced back at Wright.

The cross-eyed gunman was fascinated with a paper resting on the top of a pile on the desk, so Babbit continued. "I vas *nein* certain till *du* tell me of his dying. Then I know." His voice lowered even more, becoming a hoarse murmur. "They are *der* Hoodsmen, these lawmen. *Ja*, it *ist* true. I know it sounds *nein* so. Your Jacob, he vas killed for *der* knowing." He looked back again. "I think they vant to get you on *der* trail—*und* shoot *du*. For *der* knowing. Me, too, I be thinking."

"Frank, I don't understand."

In a hushed voice, Babbit asked, "Bass, did *nein* Jacob tell *du* . . . vhat he found out about *der* Hoodsmen? Didn't he tell *du* about Virgil Crimmler?" His eyes expected positive responses to both. Or was it hope?

"Virgil Crimmler? That's the second time I've heard that name today," Bass said. "What's he got to do with my son?" He swallowed. "We were sitting down for lunch two days ago. Lucius Henry was with us. Somebody came running in and said there was a disturbance at the Lorna. Jacob left. Right away. He came back a while later, said he couldn't stay—but that he needed my advice on something we would talk about at the farm." He swallowed again. "It was clear he didn't want to talk where others might hear." He studied his old friend's sad face. "Looking back on it, I guess

I thought he wanted my advice on buying some more land. Or maybe Mary Anne was in a family way. Something like that. I—I n-never saw him . . . again."

"*Der* Hoodsmen go all *der* vay—to *der* U.S. Marshal Hautrese." Babbit stopped, alternately watching Wright and looking at Bass. Movement of his tightened jaw was the only visible sign of his apprehension.

Bass rubbed his unshaven chin, puzzled by his friend's apprehension. He didn't recall the sheriff ever being that way in battle or at his job before. Rather, he was steady and hard to ruffle. It was Emerson Holt, his third gunfighting buddy, who was the emotional one of the three.

"I was beginning to ride in that direction myself. How'd you find this out?"

Babbit quickly explained that three days ago a stranger got drunk in the Lorna Saloon and started cursing and waving a pistol around. Jacob arrested the man for disturbing the peace. On the way to the jail, the man warned him that he knew some powerful people who could get him fired or worse. He proclaimed to be a Hoodsman and that Lowe, Cateson, Drucker—and U.S. Marshal Boston Hautrese—were involved. Topper Lowe ran the gang, who pretended to be a special posse searching for the notorious Hoodsmen, but Lowe took his orders from Hautrese.

"I take it this was Virgil Crimmler," Bass said, blinking away his anger.

"*Ja.*"

"Where is Crimmler now?"

"I do *nein* know, Bass."

Taking a deep breath, Babbit accounted for his disappearance. After Jacob told the sheriff what he had learned, they decided it would be wise if Crimmler was taken to his farm. The young deputy would stay there with him, until they could decide what to do. Babbit wanted Jacob to get Bass's opinion. Working in the alley behind the jail where no one could see them, they put the tied Crimmler in the sheriff's buckboard, lying down, and Babbit drove out of town. He thought Jacob had gone to tell his father of the situation, before following him to the Tillman farm. Biting his lower lip, the Germanic constable concluded that he was unsure of how to proceed with no proof beyond the outlaw's confession. He didn't think that would be enough evidence for such a powder keg. He figured his old friend could guide him.

"I am so *sehr* sorry, Bass," Babbit finished. "I thought ve haff more time than . . . I should have *bien vit* him. I thought he told *du*. He said he did."

"Don't blame yourself, old friend," Bass said. "It's too easy to second-guess trouble, especially trouble no one sees coming so fast." He swallowed a further question about why the sheriff didn't come and tell him about the situation himself.

Shifting the shotgun in his sweating hands, Babbit filled in the rest of the strange day, Jacob and Mary Anne's last. He and Jacob had secured Crimmler in the Tillman barn and Babbit had returned to town after the young deputy had assured him everything was fine. He had returned to the Lorna and announced they had sent the stranger out of town, so there would be no more trouble from him. He thought that would end any curiosity about what happened to Crimmler; there weren't any federal officers around, or that he saw.

"I thought ve vere being so *sehr* careful." Babbit's lips trembled. "I never—"

"Jacob accepted the badge, my friend," Bass interrupted. "He knew the risks." His words surprised even him; the responsibility didn't include Mary Anne, though. What would he have advised Jacob if he had known?

Glancing in the direction of Wright at the desk, he held up his hand for Babbit to stop talking and said loudly, "Sheriff, I'm not a Hoodsman! I'm not!"

Wright grinned, scratched his chest through his shirt and began rolling a cigarette. Satisfied the gunman wasn't paying attention, Bass whispered for his friend to continue.

As if anticipating the unsaid question, Babbit shook his head. "I vent looking for *du*. Vhen I come back." He looked away for an instant. "I vent to your office. *Und* your room. I could not find *du*. Then I vas too busy."

Bass's response was more of a groan. "I went to see *Macbeth*."

"Oh. I should *haff* thought of *das*."

"Who else knew about Crimmler? Did you tell anybody about taking him to the farm?" Bass's gaze tightened on his friend.

Babbit frowned. "*Ja*. Just two."

He explained that he had talked with Judge Pierce to get his opinion and he had shared the news with his other part-time deputy, William

Manchester. Judge Pierce had agreed that more evidence was needed and that keeping the man out of sight made good sense. Manchester offered to take Jacob's regular duty until the matter was determined, so Jacob could remain at the farm.

The old attorney's mind was whirling with his friend's news. He admitted to himself that the strategy was sound. His teeth locked together to hold in the frustration. Bass told his friend about the evidence found at the farm, the matching horseshoe seen on Lowe's mount and the bizarre encounter at the hidden forest cabin.

"I thought *du* had gone to *der* farm. I should *nein* assumed this," Babbit sighed, then growled, "Maybe *ist der* time for us to use our guns."

"No, Frank, that's what I thought, too. At the farm. Yesterday. Standing at their graves," Bass said. "But that makes us into them." His eyes narrowed. "We have to use the law against them. We have to. That's what Jacob would have wanted."

Wright slammed his fist against the desktop and blurted, "There-is-no-damn-way-you-have-that-much-to-talk-about!" He jumped up and stomped toward the cell.

Babbit handed his shotgun to Bass. "Hold this, please. *Danke.*"

"Sure."

"Getawayfromourprisoner, youcrazyoldbastard!" Wright grabbed Babbit by the left shoulder.

The sheriff spun toward the gunman's grasp. Babbit's fist drove into Wright's stomach. All of the cross-eyed man's air exploded from his mouth. As Wright's hands rushed to the unexpected pain, Babbit's left cross jolted the gunman's chin and Wright flew backward.

"Damn, that must've felt good." Bass smiled.

"Actually, it hurt like *der* hell." Babbit shook both hands and began rubbing his knuckles. "Getting too old for *der* fistfight."

"I doubt it."

A groan slithered from Wright's lips and he slowly lifted himself to one elbow.

"Wh-what did you slip on, boy?" Babbit walked over to the dazed gunman.

"Wh-what? S-slip?"

"*Ja. Du* slipped. I vill help *du* to your chair." Babbit leaned over, lifted Wright's pistol from its holster, shoved it into his own gun belt, put his other hand under the man's armpit and helped him stand.

After Wright made it back to his desk chair, Babbit returned the gun to its holster and stepped away. Watching the dazed gunman, the German constable returned to the cell and Bass held out the shotgun for him.

"Ve vill vait for *der* circuit judge." Babbit accepted the weapon, as if nothing had happened. "*Herr* Honorable Orrick W. Nelene. He be fair. Tough, *ja*, but fair he *ist*."

"Yes, I know Nelene. Tried a case before him." Bass smiled. "Lost it."

Easter Sontag popped into Bass's mind. The executioner would be expecting him soon. "Frank, there's a man in town. Just rode in with him," Bass said. "We were planning on riding to Denver together."

"*Du* vant me to tell him vhat *ist* happened?"

"Well, he's supposed to check into the Sutton," Bass said, "but he likes his whiskey."

"Vhat *ist* his name? I vill find him."

Chapter 12

"I'd appreciate that. It's Easter Sontag."

"*Der* hangman? *Du* met him at *der* cabin, *ja*? An' *du* rode together?"

"Yeah, you know him?" Bass studied his friend's face.

"Heard of him, that *ist* all I know." Babbit rubbed his chin, holding back his observation of Sontag. "Vant some coffee? Bet *du* have had *nein* supper."

"Not much of an appetite. Coffee'd be good, though," Bass said.

"*Du* vant to give me your holster?" Babbit asked. "To keep *vit* your gun?"

"No, thanks. It's part of me, I guess."

Without another word, Babbit headed for the burping woodstove and the blackened coffeepot resting there, ignoring the still stunned Wright.

The old attorney was calm. As calm as he had been all this day. In fights, Bass had always found this inner quiet. It just seemed to take over, almost make things move in slow motion. Nancy Spirit Bear said it was the spirits working with him; The River often appeared tranquil when its currents were swirling underneath. He didn't know about the spirit stuff, but he definitely was able to function well in times of stress. Times when other men froze.

This was a battle of a different kind. There would be a trial, of that he was certain. He expected the hearing to be little more than a formality. Yet there was no evidence against him. He had defended himself when attacked. It was that simple. But something told him that this wasn't about truth; this was something else. In an odd way, he was getting close to the reason his son was killed. He was certain of it.

"Say . . . Wright, isn't it? Was it your idea to make it look like Indians had attacked the Tillman farm? Great idea," he said, almost indifferently, as he watched the sheriff look around for a rag to hold the hot coffeepot handle.

Without looking up, the cross-eyed gunman muttered, "Naw. That-was-Topper's. He-is-always . . ." Realization of what he was saying grabbed the rest of his words and held them hostage as he attempted to switch responses. His confused head ached from the earlier blow and his midsection pounded. "Imeanahwhatareyoutalkingabout?" He frowned at Bass as his excited brain returned him to mumbling.

"Oh, sorry, I wasn't paying any attention. Just thinking out loud. I do that sometimes. Old age."

Bass acted as if he hadn't heard Wright's initial response.

"Youbequietnow." Wright rubbed his reddened chin, then moved his rifle to the desk and laid it there.

"Sure."

A push on the door made Wright spring from his chair, grabbing the waiting gun. The movement made him dizzy and he stumbled backward, fighting to regain his balance. Grabbing the chair arm stabilized him and he looked again at the pounding.

Babbit twisted away from the stove with a filled cup in one hand, his shotgun in the other. "That vill be *mein* deputy. *Du* let him in."

"I-will-do-the-decidin'." Wright walked toward the door. "Who-is-there?"

There was a hesitation on the other side of the door. "Ah, is Marshal Babbit there? This is Deputy Manchester. William Manchester." Another hesitation. "Who's this talking?"

"I *haff* said to let him in." Babbit raised his shotgun in his hand, bracing the butt against his thigh and holding it with one hand and the coffee mug in the other. Hot coffee from the cup slithered over the edge onto his fingers and scraped knuckles. The sturdy German warrior didn't flinch.

Wright's answer was to shrug his shoulders, prop the gun against the wall and lift the heavy guard beam from its iron rests bracing the door. He opened it, retrieved his rifle and strolled back to the desk and sat without watching to see who would enter. Instead, he concentrated on the soreness in his stomach, rubbing it back and forth.

A nervous deputy stepped inside. His eyes fought to adjust to the darker environment. Deputy Manchester was young, in his early twenties, and of medium build with a pudgy face and small mouth that reminded some of a fish. A thinly populated mustache and short-cropped hair matched a trim suit and short-brimmed hat. Born in Ohio, he'd been brought to Colorado three years ago by his yearning for the mountains.

His only bad habit, so far, was a taste for chewing tobacco. The spittoon in the sheriff's office had been brought in for him. Babbit had reluctantly accepted the young man's vice; Manchester seemed such a disciplined man otherwise. It didn't hurt that Judge Pierce also chewed. The deputy's manner was always serious and his expression now was a question.

Babbit quickly went to him, explained the situation, filling the air with explosive German expressions as he did and spilling more of the coffee in the mug held for Bass. He made no attempt to wipe it up or remove the hot liquid from his fingers. After handing the shotgun to the young man, he walked over to Bass and gave him the mug, apologizing for its outside wetness.

Bass thanked him and took a sip of the dark liquid. It actually felt good.

With renewed intensity, Babbit returned to the front door. "I vill take care of vhat ve talked, Bass." He opened the door. "An' be bringing *du soom* supper." He stepped outside and closed it behind him.

Immediately, the deputy sauntered over to Wright. "That's not your chair, partner. Whoever's on duty gets that chair. I'm on duty." The young deputy's voice was thin and high-pitched with an occasional crack that sounded like a teenager's.

But his voice belied a confident attitude. Sure of himself now, he strode to the side of the desk and deposited a healthy stream of tobacco juice into the spittoon.

Licking his chapped lips, Wright cocked his head to the side and slurred, "Iamondutybuster. WatchyourselfforIwilltellTopper." He patted the rifle in his lap.

"What? I didn't get that."

Wright said, more slowly, "I-am-on-duty, buster. Watch-yourself-or-I-will-tell-Topper. Ah, Chief-Deputy-Marshal-Topper-Lowe."

The young constable's gaze studied the man behind the desk. He shoved the chaw to the other side of his mouth, creating a considerable protrusion in his cheek.

Wright seemed confused by the deputy's attitude. His right hand slid from the top of the desk to an unseen position near his holstered gun. "Remember? I'm-part-of-Deputy-Marshal-Lowe's-special-posse. We're-after-that-Hoodsmen-bunch." He tried not to roll his words together, motioning with his left hand toward Bass. "Just-caught-their-leader. He-ambushed-two-of-our-men, the-bastard."

"Did you say you just caught the leader of the Hoodsmen? You mean Mr. Tillman?" Manchester's eyes widened as he comprehended Wright's reiterated assertion, even though he had just been advised the same by Babbit. He shook his head and began to laugh. A chuckle at first, then a full guffaw. He choked on the tobacco, swallowed and tears came to the corners of his eyes.

"Well, now, that's one I didn't expect. Kinda like the time Mrs. Kensington yelled out in church about a man she was seeing." His voice cracked and he managed to spit again. This time it was a thin line of brown that didn't quite make it to the spittoon.

Wright began to laugh, too, but it hurt his stomach too much to continue. He forced a cough to stop his glee, then a stern look that accented his crossed eyes. "Better-not-laugh, boy. That-man's-gonna-hang." Wright snarled the words as clearly as he could.

"I understand." Manchester lowered his head for a moment, letting his body shed the mirth. Finally he looked up, staring at Wright, who smiled.

Without waiting for a response, he walked toward Bass. "I'm mighty sorry to hear about Jacob—an' Mary Anne. We were good friends, you know." He paused and continued. "Whatever I can do to help you find who did it, you can count on me."

Bass nodded his thanks. Lately, the young deputy had spent time with Bass as well as the municipal judge, eager to learn all he could of the law. His unabashed goal was to become the town sheriff, after Babbit retired. Jacob had told Bass that it was fine with him; he had no interest in the job. He was a farmer; part-time deputy duty simply brought needed income.

His face bright with righteous indignation, Manchester walked over to the cell and positioned himself next to it; his peripheral vision included Wright. He took a deep breath and massaged his sparse mustache. He lowered his chin as if hoping it would make a corresponding adjustment in his voice. Like a gun being fanned, the young deputy spat out legal suggestions, none appropriate because the federal aspect took it away from municipal or state jurisdiction. After listening to the well-intended thoughts, heightened by the young man's nervousness, Bass thanked him for his advice.

A thunderous knock on the bolted door brought the conversation to a halt and Wright to his feet again. Wright opened the door to a triumphant Cateson and Lowe. The taller man held up a black hood mask with his left hand as he entered. His Winchester was carried at his side in his right fist.

"Look what we found in your room, Tillman. You're a dead man."

"Whadda ya have to say about this, Bass Tillman? We've got ya now." U.S. Chief Deputy Marshal Topper Lowe grinned like a plump cat.

The diminutive lawman expected an angry denial.

Instead, Bass locked both fists around the bars and said evenly, "Cateson, you should've known better than to keep that thing in your saddlebags. Smells like horse and leather. Even from here. Who'd want to wear something like that? You?"

Standing beside the door, Wright snorted at the comment, nodded and mumbled something that sounded like agreement without realizing the significance.

U.S. Deputy Marshal Johnny Cateson's eyes widened and his mouth opened. His elongated head jerked toward the held mask as if to inspect its aroma.

"Shut up, Tillman," Lowe snapped. "You know it's yours. We got it from your room. Didn't we, Marshal Cateson?" He stepped halfway into the crowded room, pushing Cateson aside. The quirt at his wrist jiggled like a strung-out snake.

His glare warned the tall gunman to be quiet as he added, "As suggested by local law enforcement, we will wait for the circuit court judge." The response to his hurried telegram requesting direction rested in his pocket:

STAY THERE STOP GET RID OF PROBLEM BEFORE G COMES STOP H

Standing beside the cell, Manchester raised his chin defiantly. "Did you have a warrant? You can't just go busting into somebody's house, you know." He looked around for somewhere to spit, but the spittoon was on the far side of the desk. He settled for holding it. Swallowing had already proven a bitter step.

Slapping the quirt against his thigh, Lowe stalked toward the young deputy. Manchester responded by bringing his shotgun to a firing position. The movement surprised Lowe and made him tentative. He stopped. "You'd better learn your place, boy. This is federal business."

Wright repeated the assertion, shoving the words together.

"Search warrants are guaranteed, Lowe." He wiped his mouth with the back of his hand. "By the *federal* government. Or did you forget that? I can assure you, Mr. Tillman won't. He's a fine attorney."

"I said, shut up—or you'll be in that next cell, you dumb bastard."

From the cell, Bass commanded, "That's enough, Lowe. Save your act for somebody who believes you're tough."

Lowe sputtered, his face reddening. He reached for the holstered pistol at his hip.

"*Wie* ist going on *hier?*" Frank Babbit stood in the doorway, holding a tray with both hands. A covered plate was centered on it.

Cateson and Wright were startled by the lawman's arrival, glancing at Lowe for guidance. He shook his head slightly to indicate they shouldn't react.

"We just returned from searching Tillman's room," Lowe declared, "for more evidence." He didn't like the interruption, but there was nothing he could do about it. Babbit had already proved to be more of an obstacle than expected. Most local constables were eager to do whatever he asked. Not this stubborn German.

It didn't matter, though. They would stay in town as he requested. There would be plenty of time to kill Bass Tillman and make it look like a jailbreak. The rest of the telegram said District Attorney Touren Grant was on the way. Lowe smiled to himself; Grant was an exceptional trial lawyer, one without morals or mercy. Only ambition.

Manchester took a step forward, signaling out

Lowe with his shotgun. "They went into Mr. Tillman's room—without a search warrant, Sheriff Babbit." He didn't seem to notice that his voice cracked once and decided it was time to relieve his mouth of brown juice. Casually, he walked over and spat into the brass cuspidor.

Lowe was fuming. What was this upstart of a deputy doing?

Wright leaned over in his chair and nodded his approval of the spitting performance. Satisfied by the resulting clank, the young lawman repointed his shotgun at Lowe.

"*Ist das richtig*, Deputy Marshal Lowe?" Babbit held the tray in front of him, staring at the short lawman, who didn't like being questioned or Manchester's pointed gun.

A jerk of his head was the introduction to Lowe's explosive response. "Don't give me that shit. You two should concentrate on arresting drunk cowboys—an' leave the real law enforcement to us."

"*Du* did not answer *mein* question." Babbit motioned for Manchester to lower his weapon and the deputy slowly complied.

Taking advantage of the confrontation, Wright hurried back to the desk and triumphantly reclaimed the chair.

Lowe glanced at Cateson. "Go get that warrant, Marshal Cateson." He looked back at Babbit, now ignoring Manchester. "We've got a warrant. From a federal judge—in Denver City." His smile was forced as he delivered it at Manchester.

"That's better, for Mr. Tillman would definitely

object to such a search—at his hearing," Manchester said triumphantly.

Babbit nodded, unsure of why his deputy thought it was so important to tell the federal officers of this apparent gaffe and decided the young man thought he was helping.

Cateson's expression was a mixture of puzzlement and determination. He started to leave and Lowe's words stopped him.

"Never mind. I'll get it. Johnny, you're in charge. No visitors." Satisfaction filled his face and sparkled in his eyes. He held his quirt and pulled on it with his free hand and stared at Bass. "You don't look so tough now, you old wolfer. You look like some broken-down ol' nag. We'll be putting you out of your misery soon enough."

Wright pushed away from the desk. "Youoldwolfer . . . brokendownnag." He grinned at his declaration, but no one noticed. His sore jaw throbbed more.

"Looks can be deceiving, Lowe," Bass said, standing with his face peering through adjacent bars. "Take you, for instance. You don't look tough—with or without a gun. Or that quirt. You look like what you are—a spineless back-shooter trying to act tough."

Lowe's face darkened with hate; his lower lip trembled in readiness for an outburst.

"Go on, Deputy Marshal Lowe, I vould like to be seeing this varrant of yours." Babbit's voice was calming, in spite of the command.

"Yes, we want to see a warrant," Manchester added.

This time Lowe made no attempt to make eye contact with Babbit, Manchester or Bass. The slam of the door punctuated his exit.

As if nothing had happened, Babbit said, "I *haff* brought *soom* supper for *du*, Bass."

"How 'bout us? We're hungry, too," Cateson growled.

"We'rehungrytoo," Wright jabbered excidedly.

"Get your own supper. *Ist de*r restaurant across *der* street. *Ja*, Tiehl's."

Manchester chuckled and spat again, more forcefully this time, into the once-shiny container. This time brown spit wandered down the outside. The messy habit didn't match the young man's demeanor, Babbit thought. Wright looked over at the spittoon, intrigued by the near miss. Wright's center-focused eyes wandered up as far as the shotgun now held by Manchester's right hand at his side, then darted away.

"Let's take a look at that first," Cateson said, pointing at the tray in Babbit's hands.

Wright stood and mumbled, "Yeah, let'shavea-looksee." His statement sounded like a muffled echo with only the phrase "look-see" discernible. He was quickly distracted by the chair wiggling when he left it.

Without a word, Babbit lifted the lid for Cateson's inspection and closed it. Smells of cooked beef, potatoes and onions laced the air and made the gunman lick his lips.

"Man, that looks good. Go get us some, Bobby Joe," Cateson told his cross-eyed companion and tossed the black hood on the desk.

Wright jerked his head up and down to affirm

the idea, walked over to the door, propped his rifle again against the wall and hurried out.

Frowning, Manchester's eyes never left Cateson, except when he delivered a center strike into the spittoon. The tall gunman glared at him, his mouth resting open, but the young deputy appeared oblivious to the reaction and was definitely not interested in the mask. Cateson licked his lips and his mouth returned to its favored open position; his orders were clear: Kill Bass Tillman and make it look like he tried to break out.

Pushing back his hat, Cateson took control of the desk and settled himself into the sheriff's chair. "No need to put up that bar. Yet. Bobby Joe'll be comin' back."

"I didn't intend to." Manchester spat again. This time his voice didn't crack.

After the inspection, Babbit carried the tray over to his desk, set it down and retrieved keys from the center drawer. Cateson watched him without comment. The German constable opened the cell door, letting it swing open.

"Hey, you can't do that! Damn it, he'll get out!" Cateson yelled and pointed.

"*Das ist mein* jail—*und mein freund*," Babbit said evenly.

Manchester spat again into the brass container and the clank made Cateson chuckle.

Returning for the tray, Babbit walked into the cell, made no attempt to close the door and stood in front of the now-seated Bass. "*Du* eat *das*, Bass, *mein freund*. It *ist* beef stew from Tiehl's. Gerard said it vas *gut. Ausgezeichnet*. Ah, delicious."

"Thanks, Frank, that's most kind of you. Just set it there."

With his back to the office area itself, Babbit motioned with his head for Bass to stand next to him, near the cot. "Better *du* to stand before I put *das* down. Other-to-wise, it might fall off."

As Bass stood, Babbit shifted the weight of the tray to his left hand alone and quickly pulled a short-barreled Colt hidden from under his vest. He slid it under the tray with the gun held by his right hand, his thumb locked over the tray's edge for support.

Bass watched the movement. His eyes flickered in surprise. He knew Frank Babbit well. Such an action would not have been done without considerable thought. It also meant he was very worried about the intent of the federal lawmen.

"Better to hold *wit* both hands," Babbit advised loudly. "Heavier than it be looking. *Ja.* Can you use your left hand?"

"Ah, sure." Bass nodded. "That was a long time ago."

"*Ya*, I vere there."

"Yes, you were, old friend."

Bass took the tray with his left hand as well and extended his right to grasp the gun's handle. Carefully, he laid the combination on the cot with the gun beneath the tray while Babbit crowded next to him so neither Cateson nor Manchester could see the significant exchange that had taken place. Banter behind them indicated neither man was paying attention; their discussion was centered on Cateson's suggestion that Manchester put the shotgun back in the rack, that it wasn't needed.

"*Nein* for breaking out, *mein freund*, mind you. But they may be trying something this *nacht*," Babbit whispered, leaning over and patting the lid over the plated food as if discussing it. "I expect it back in *der morgen*."

"Sure."

"*Du* vant more coffee?" Babbit asked.

"No, thanks. Still got some." Bass pointed to the mug resting on the cell floor.

Straightening himself and pulling on his vest to make certain it was again covering his pants, Babbit quietly said he had the slugs from the bodies; Dr. Williams had helped. However, Bass's friend, Easter Sontag, was nowhere to be found. He was seen in the general store earlier and a few recalled a stranger riding hurriedly out of town

Bass accepted the news with a Shakespearean quote. " 'The soul of this man is his clothes.' "

"*Du* always did like *der* theater," Babbit said softly. "Even vhen ve vere young."

"Yeah, guess I have."

"*Ist gut*," Babbit acknowledged.

"Maybe. Wish I hadn't been there . . . the other night."

Babbit inhaled. "*Ja*. Lots of *das* thoughts I *haff*."

Chapter 13

Easing next to the cell door, Sheriff Babbit grabbed it as he spoke. His face was taut and filled with guilt. Leaving a gun for a prisoner, even a good friend, went against everything he stood for. Except justice. Something was pounding in his stomach that nothing about this arrest was fair, or likely to be so. Something else was there. If it came to it, he would help Bass escape.

Even if it meant killing federal marshals. He knew it without saying it.

Based on his sudden arrest, Bass couldn't help but wonder if his first suspicions about Easter Sontag were sound after all. He barely heard Babbit offer his intention to continue searching, even though Bass was certain the man wasn't in town. Why he had chosen to leave was a different matter. The old attorney guessed it had a lot to do with him being in this cell. Why hadn't he seen that coming?

"Ah, I almost to forget." The stern town lawman shook his head. "Your mule, he be at *der* stabling." He chuckled. "Did *nicht* like *mein* taking his reins. *Nein*."

"That'll be Othello. Thanks, Frank, for everything."

Babbit paused, then added, "I look for Lowe's horse. *Der* rear hoof *ist* as you say."

"Yeah. He was there. I'm sure of it now."

"I am going to supper *und* see *mein frau*. Vill be coming at *der mitternacht*." Babbit turned to observe Cateson dealing solitaire on the desktop.

The town sheriff's frown was a question about where the cards had come from. Certainly not from his desk. Babbit decided, to himself, that they belonged to the gunman.

"I'll be fine. Thanks to this supper," Bass said. "You know, those federal boys didn't do a very good job of checking me for weapons."

A glimmer of understanding reached Babbit's eyes as he realized the significance of the statement. "*Ja*. They miss things . . . some of *der* time." He stutter-stepped around the door and closed it. He fiddled with the key resting in the lock, but didn't turn it. "Just in case," he said softly, "that *du* must need . . . to leave. I vill understand."

"Thanks, Frank, but I figure to stay," Bass replied. "Say, ask ol' Judge Pierce to issue a restraining order against the bank to keep them from foreclosing on Hamilton Jallon's place, will you?" He explained the situation.

"*Ja. Das* I vill do." He pulled the key free of the door.

"Speaking of Moulton, will you tell him that I

will take care of Jacob's loan?" Bass added. "I'm sorry to ask, but I'm sorta tied up right now."

"*Ist nein* a problem, *du* know that," Babbit assured his old friend, tugged on the brim of his hat and asked, "Shall I vire Emerson about *das?*"

"No. Absolutely not." The old attorney's reaction was hard.

Babbit took a step backward. "Should *nein* he know?"

"Not till this is over, Frank. It'll only make him worry." Bass's voice was softer. "There's nothing he can do but get in trouble himself."

"Emerson vill be mad vhen he finds out, Bass."

"No, Frank. Please."

"Why? *Ist* it that *du* think he *ist* a Hoodsman?"

"Of course not." Bass smiled and changed the subject, signaling the end of the discussion about their old friend. "Oh, and I'll need a letter from Judge Pierce that nobody asked for a warrant from him today."

"If I know *der* Reichter, he vill be mad as all hell about all *das,*" Babbit blurted.

"What's that, law daig?" Cateson challenged from the sheriff's desk. His mouth seemed to rattle afterward from its unclosed pose.

Babbit turned slowly toward the seated gunman. "It *ist nicht* . . . nothing."

"Good. I like *nothing,*" Cateson said sarcastically. "You got anything to drink?"

"There *ist* coffee."

"Hell, I know that." Cateson lifted an ace of spades from the three turned-over cards and tossed it ahead of his row of seven piles. He snapped his mouth shut, but it drifted open again as he continued to play.

The conversation ended between prisoner and sheriff with Bass requesting copies of the town's newspapers about Hoodsmen crimes and Babbit accepting the task. Walking away, Babbit tossed the cell keys on the desk, sending the cards fleeing.

"Hey, goddammit!" Cateson jumped back.

Babbit continued walking toward the surprised Manchester, positioned against the wall closest to the door. The sheriff spoke briefly to his deputy and left without glancing in Bass's direction, or Cateson's. The gas lamp on the other side of the door flickered its reaction to the door closing. Office walls inched closer in the blossoming silence. After Babbit left, Bass tasted some of the supper, but found he had little appetite.

Manchester chewed on his tobacco and shifted the shotgun in his cradled arms. He looked at the guard bar leaning against the wall and decided not to put it in place against the door. Let Cateson do it if he wanted. Manchester looked around for somewhere to spit. He cursed himself for not bringing the spittoon closer.

"Say, Cateson, I need something to write on. Look in the desk for me, will you? A few sheets of paper—and that pencil would be fine."

Bass's request jolted Manchester from his musing and he watched the annoyed Cateson yank open the middle drawer and glance at its contents.

"Can't find any, Tillman. Guess you won't be able to write your will." Cateson's laugh was thick and guttural.

Spurred by this reason to advance, Manchester marched to the desk, spat a welcomed thick stream into the spittoon, opened the large right-hand drawer and withdrew three sheets of white paper and closed it. He picked up a stubby pencil that lay on the desk, next to an ink bottle and a scrawny pen that had seen better days, and headed to the cell.

The attorney held the jail bars firmly as the young man handed the writing materials to him; Bass didn't think Manchester realized the door hadn't been locked and didn't want to expose that fact unnecessarily. He thanked Manchester, holding the paper and pencil in his right hand, while keeping the door pulled shut with his left. So far, the young deputy hadn't touched the door.

"You be careful, William. You're the only thing between them and me right now," Bass cautioned.

"I can handle myself," Manchester assured him. "You think they want you dead?" He didn't like asking the question.

"I'm sure of it, thanks to Frank . . . sharing what he learned from Jacob," Bass responded. "They'll try to create a distraction so they can get a drop on you. Or shoot without fear you'll fire back. Don't go over to the desk again, no matter what they ask for. Don't take your eyes off them."

Manchester's eyes widened. "Sheriff Babbit told you . . . about Crimmler?"

The young deputy's face stiffened with Bass's affirmative response.

Bass started to see if the deputy knew about the sheriff leaving him a gun, but decided against it. Likely, Manchester did not. It was safer for him that way. Bass had already transferred the sher-iff's hidden gun to his belt in back with his coat covering it.

"Ah, Bass . . . Mr. Tilllman? What can I do to help?" Manchester blurted. His already high-pitched voice whined higher in his nervousness.

Quietly, Bass began to explain the idea that had come to him. The only way he was going to get these men—legally—was to get them into court. To do that, he was going to have to let them put him on trial, assuming it got that far. He expected the hearing to be a perfunctory one. In court, he would have the opportunity to lay open their Hoodsmen's treachery for all to see. It was a gam-ble, one that would be played with his life as the stakes. Jacob and Mary Anne were worth that. As he talked, the old attorney kept his vision on Cateson, who had returned to his card game.

Manchester listened, not quite believing what he was hearing. The old man in front of him was casually stating that he wanted to go to trial for murdering federal officers. This couldn't be the Bass Tillman he knew and respected. This had to be some kind of old-age silliness setting in. Or the stress of losing his family. It had to be. They in-tended to bring him to trial—and hang him! Didn't he get that? Try and hang him!

"Mr. Tillman, that's crazy talk!" Manchester blurted and was immediately sorry that he had. He glanced back at Cateson, who had decided to look at what was under one of the larger piles in front of him and wasn't paying attention to them.

Shaking his head, Manchester apologized. "I'm sorry, but I don't understand. . . ."

"That's all right, William," Bass said, then motioned for the young man to stay to his right so that he could keep Cateson in his vision. "I'm going to need your help, but it's the only way I can see to strip them bare—in public. It's our best chance to get these Hoodsmen out from under their masks."

"You're playing with your life." Manchester's voice cracked twice.

"I know the game, son." Bass watched Cateson check another pile of cards and remove one. "The key to winning—is to anticipate. Remember that. Whether it's a fight or a courtroom. Anticipate. That's what I'm trying to do."

Bass asked him to go over to his hotel room tomorrow when he was off duty, getting a warrant from Judge Pierce first, and take him along, if possible. He asked him to make notes of what was in his room, to look in the closet, drawers, under the bed and the like. He also wanted Manchester to develop a list of all of the suspected Hoodsmen crimes, where and when, as best he could. As an afterthought, Bass asked him to wire the Texas Ranger headquarters in Waco and see if any outlaws matching the description of Bobby Joe Wright or Johnny Cateson were wanted in that state.

The deputy looked puzzled. Bass explained both men had a Texas way of talking and he had a hunch they were from there.

"I'm going to prepare for my trial, looking for ways to prove these boys are involved in the Hoodsmen operation. I'm likely to need your testimony at some point, if you're willing," Bass said. "That mask didn't come from—"

"I know that." Manchester looked over at the seated gunman and shook his shoulders to relieve the sudden ripple of fear.

Bass said it would also be helpful if the deputy could locate Virgil Crimmler, if possible, and arrest him, assuming that was all right with the sheriff.

"If I can't find him, I can testify about what he said."

"Well, no, you can't, William. You know that's hearsay and no judge will allow it," Bass said. "But I appreciate the thought."

Manchester looked disappointed, then whispered, "They're talking about not knowing where that other deputy marshal is. You know, Bill Drucker. Do you know what happened to him?"

The question surprised the old attorney.

Manchester bit his lower lip and shifted his chaw to his other cheek.

"He's dead, William."

Neither man spoke.

"Did you . . ."

"No, I didn't, but I was there," Bass said and changed the subject. "Your testimony will be important. Knowing the dates of the Hoodsmen's crimes. Knowing details about my room. Don't know if Frank'll give you the time off." He knew as he said it that Babbit would. "I'll pay you for your time, of course."

Sputtering, Manchester waved his arms and cussed. Loudly. Agitated, he pushed the chaw from one side of his mouth to the other. "I'm not taking your money!"

"That's only fair, son. I'm going to need your help."

"I'll be there. It's my duty," Manchester declared.

Bass studied the young deputy. "Are you a tracker, William?"

"Well, good as the next, I guess." The young deputy didn't like the question.

The old attorney folded his arms. "Guess that depends on who you're standing next to." He smiled. "I had a good friend, Emerson Holt, who could track a man across rocks and water—in hard rain. Never saw anyone like him."

"He was one of your gunfighter friends, wasn't he? Years ago." Manchester leaned forward, interested. "Were you with him—when he died?"

Clearing his throat, Bass responded carefully, "I watched the end of Emerson Holt."

He immediately returned to tracking, asking Manchester to go out to his son's farm as soon as Babbit thought it was all right and study the horse prints there. Then he was to take a look at the rear left shoe of Lowe's horse.

Manchester's face was twisted with determination. "I'll do it, sir."

"Thanks. It'll come in handy—in court."

After Bobby Joe Wright returned with food, the evening turned quiet. Deputy Manchester remained on his feet, usually pacing with the shotgun cradled in his arms. Cateson and Wright assumed that Lowe had left to sleep in one of the hotels.

Cateson controlled the desk, making Wright

seek the floor. The cross-eyed gunman stretched out and had apparently gone to sleep with his hat over his face. His snoring filled the jail. Yet Bass was certain the man was awake. From his cell, he could see Wright's rifle was cocked and his hand lay over the trigger guard.

Cateson also looked asleep with his head against his left arm, lying on the desk. A few inches away were their empty dishes and ironware. Bass wasn't fooled, but thought Deputy Manchester was. The old attorney could see Cateson's right hand under the desk, grasping a revolver. Waiting.

On his back facing the office and pretending to sleep as well, Bass lay with his hands behind his head, giving him an angle to watch the room without appearing to do so. His dinner plate, utensils and empty coffee cup lay beside him on the floor. Little of the food was eaten, except for most of a hunk of bread.

For the first time, Manchester noticed the stove had finally succumbed to the evening and its belly held little more than dying coals. Spring had not yet brought consistent warmth to the land and the room was growing cold. After walking quietly around the snoring Wright, Manchester laid his shotgun on the floor in front of him and concentrated on the fire's reconstruction. Latent embers responded to his nudging and flames sprang to life. As he lifted a small log to add to the renewed fire, Babbit returned to the jail, identifying himself loudly without attempting to open the door. It was ten minutes before midnight. Cateson did not stir. Neither did Wright.

"Coming." Manchester shoved in the log and closed the iron gate. He grabbed his shotgun and walked past the seemingly groggy Wright, pausing again to spit in the cuspidor. After removing the support beam, the young deputy opened the door.

"Evening, Sheriff. Everything's quiet. The two federal boys are asleep."

Babbit gave a half smile and entered. "*Guten Abend*, William."

Unnoticed, Wright's hand slipped into the trigger guard of his rifle.

From the darkness of Bass's cell, orange flame snarled and Wright jerked his hand away from the gun. Splinters rushed at him as Bass's bullet drove into the floor inches from the rifle. Instinctively, Babbit dove for the floor, grabbing for his holstered pistol as he fell; Manchester swung his shotgun in Bass's direction.

"The next one's for you, Cateson. Drop the gun." Bass's unexpected challenge rattled through the room. "Lower the shotgun, William, or point it at the door."

His face painted in a mixture of disbelief and shadow, Cateson fired at Bass.

The old attorney had already dived against the cell door and the Colt in his hand roared its own response. Twice. Once as he hurled against it and the second as he hit the floor. The cell door swung wildly on its hinges. His plate of uneaten food slid across the floor and splattered against the bars separating the adjoining cell. A fork floated on its own before clinking against the same bars.

His coffee cup bounced three times and came to rest in the middle of the cell.

Johnny Cateson spun in the chair and flew backward. His own gun fired again, driving lead into the far wall of Bass's cell. He hit the floor and groaned.

Manchester screamed a high-pitched warning to Wright, "Don't touch that gun."

Babbit scrambled to his feet and hurried around the desk to Cateson. In the lawman's hand was a .45 Colt aimed at Cateson's head. The wounded deputy marshal attempted to rise and cock his gun once more. He froze when he saw Babbit's weapon.

"I do *nein* think it vould be a *gut* idea."

Cateson glanced at the Colt, groaned again and let the gun slide from his fingers. His upper left arm was ablaze with crimson and he grabbed at the wound to stop the pain.

Snarling, he growled, "Where'd that sonvabitch get a gun? He's trying to escape!"

"*Nein. Herr* Tillman *ist* keeping us alive. *Du* vanted to kill Deputy Manchester—*und* me."

"The hell I was. He was trying to escape." Cateson's mouth stayed open, trembling. "Tell him, Deputy. You saw it." He waved in Manchester's direction, then regrabbed his bleeding arm.

The young deputy was mute, lowering his shotgun to his side.

Sheriff Babbit turned toward the cell. "*Vielen Dank.* Thank you very much, Bass."

"Glad to help."

Manchester looked up, first at Babbit, then at

Bass. His lips curling into an embarrassed smile, he started to say something, then thought better of it and was silent.

Babbit ordered Wright to stand and enter the cell next to Bass. He told Manchester to disarm the cross-eyed gunman, who stuttered about it not being allowed. After taking Wright's belt gun, the young deputy tossed it on the floor and jammed his shotgun into the gunman's side to emphasize the command.

With his hands raised, Wright ambled into the cell next to Bass and sat down on the cot. Bass quietly returned to his own cell and closed the door. Manchester watched the performance; his face was a puzzle. He couldn't help staring at the gun in Bass's hand.

"Deputy Manchester, go bring *Herr Doktor* Williams," Sheriff Babbit said evenly.

Manchester cleared his throat. The sound was more like a bird than a man. "Ah, sure. Sure. You . . . be all right while I'm gone?" Manchester stepped away from Wright's cell, wondering if he should get the cell keys first.

"I'm dying! I'm dying!" Cateson groaned.

"Do not be to touch *der* gun." Babbit motioned at the gunman's free hand inching toward his pistol. "Or dying *du* vill be. *Du* are *nein* hurt bad."

Cateson stopped the encroachment and cursed.

Babbit kicked Cateson's weapon in the direction of the cells as Manchester hurried out. Bass announced the two gunmen hadn't searched him very closely. He made no attempt to explain the opened cell door. Babbit tried to hide the smile that sneaked onto his face. Cateson curled up his legs, writhing in pain.

"I could use some more coffee, Frank. How about you?" Bass sat down on his cot, laying the smoking Colt beside him.

"Ja. First, I vill check *der* cells."

"Good idea." Bass motioned that his cell door should be locked as well.

Wright watched the sheriff secure both doors without moving from his prone position on the cell cot. He mumbled, "Icouldusesomecoffeetoo."

Babbit didn't acknowledge the request.

Sitting up on the cot, Wright stared at Babbit and spoke more slowly this time. "You-gonna-let-him-keep-that-gun?" It still sounded more like "You gonna eat the gump?"

Babbit frowned and told Wright to be quiet. It was like a teacher reprimanding a student. Wright nodded and lay back on his cot. Bass stood, shoved the Colt into his waistband and picked up the cup from the middle of his cell. He glanced at the strewn plate and food, but made no attempt to gather the spilled meal.

Without comment, the town sheriff handed Bass a handful of cartridges. Bass accepted them in silence and handed him the empty cup. Babbit walked over to the stove, picked up the coffeepot and shook it to determine the content level.

"Lowe's gonna kill you, Tillman—an' get you fired, Babbit," Cateson yelled from the floor. Blood had trickled onto the floor, creating a small, oblong red sphere.

"Lowe's gonna kill you, Cateson, for not checking me for other weapons," Bass said. "He doesn't have any jurisdiction over Sheriff Babbit—or don't you know the law?"

Cateson squinted and slammed his right fist against the floor. The movement brought new pain into his wounded arm and he screamed.

Wright finally muttered, "Tillman, how-come-your-cell-was-open?"

Running his left hand through his long, white hair, Bass replied, "You must be seeing things, Wright."

"Thedoorwasopen. Isawitswing." The response was louder than usual, but the words ran together. "Thesheriffjustlockeditagain."

"If you're so good at seeing things, why didn't you see my other gun when you put me in here?" Bass asked, ejecting old shells and replacing them with fresh cartridges. He shoved the unused bullets into his coat pocket, next to the medicine stone and empty tobacco sack, and returned the reloaded gun to his waistband.

Wright mumbled something Bass couldn't make out.

Bass stared at him, waiting for Wright to repeat himself, but the cross-eyed gunman stared at his hands and was quiet. The old attorney accepted the coffee from Babbit, thanked him and volunteered to clean up the fallen food if the sheriff would get a rag.

A knock on the front door stopped further conversation. Babbit walked to the door, leaving his cup on the desk, and opened it, expecting to see Manchester and the doctor. Instead, U.S.

Chief Deputy Marshal Topper Lowe stood there, grinning.

"*Guten Abend, Herr* Marshal Lowe."

Lowe's smile vanished as his gaze took in the gun in the sheriff's hand, then the room, and returned to Babbit. "How come my man is in that cell? Marshal Cateson . . . are you hurt? What the hell is going on here?"

"Please to *kommen* in." Babbit motioned with the gun in his hand. "Your men attempted to kill me *und mein* deputy."

"What? That's crazy!"

"Ah, *ist* it now?" Babbit closed the door and stepped to the side. "I *haff* sent *mein* deputy to bring *der doktor*. Your wounded man vill be tended to, then he vill be jailed for attempted murder— like *der udder* one."

From the floor, the tall gunman gasped, "Tillman . . . had a gun I didn't . . . see."

Lowe spun and pointed his quirt at Babbit. "What's he mean? Tillman shot him?"

"He means I shot him." Bass pointed his finger at the deputy marshal, mimicking a gun; his thumb acted as the hammer. "Before he could kill the sheriff and his deputy. Like you ordered."

"Bullshit. This is more of your Hoodsmen's vendetta against federal marshals."

Lowe realized Cateson and Wright had failed miserably in their assignment to kill all three men. First and foremost, they hadn't even disarmed Bass Tillman, at least not completely. Why hadn't Bass used the hidden gun earlier? He could have escaped using it. Why didn't he?

"I assume you have now disarmed the prisoner," Lowe said. His fists tightened around the middle of the quirt.

"I *haff* done vhat I thought *vas richt*."

Wright said as slowly as he could manage, "Tillman's-cell-door-wasn't-locked-neither," and added that Bass still had a gun. It sounded like "he was going to run."

Lowe shook his head and strutted toward the cell. Even now, he could shoot Babbit, and complete the mission by killing Bass. His hand eased toward the holstered, pearl-handled Colt as he crossed the room. From the sound of Babbit's voice, the lawman was almost directly behind him, near the door. Exactly where he was when Lowe entered. A quick spin and two shots would end the sheriff's interference, another turn and he would kill Bass. That foolish deputy could be dealt with later.

Easing his hand toward his holstered pistol so the movement wouldn't be noticed by Babbit, Lowe was close to Bass's cell before he grasped the fact that the attorney was standing near the front bars with a Colt aimed at his midsection.

"Move any closer to that fancy gun of yours, I'll put a bullet in your gut," Bass said.

Lowe's eyes were saucers of swirling fear. His right hand jerked and stopped with a wide space between it and his waist. The quirt tangling from his wrist slithered and gradually was motionless.

"Unbuckle that gun belt and let it drop," Bass growled.

Shaking, the deputy marshal unbuckled the gun belt and let the weapon slide down his leg, until it thudded on the floor. He stood with both hands away from his side.

"Now the gun in your boot."

Lowe started to object, but thought better of it. A moment later, a short-barreled gun plopped on the floor from its hidden holster inside Lowe's high-topped boot.

"Now leave. You can pick these up in the morning," Bass said. "You have my word—and my word is good."

Chapter 14

The first rays of dawn slid through the bars of Bass Tillman's cell window. He was awake and had been most of the night, in spite of his weariness. Cleaning up the spilled food had been strangely satisfying, even though it hadn't taken long. The harder part had been lying on the cell cot with his coat rolled up for a pillow. Sleep had been fitful and in spurts. Attempts at praying for guidance had not come easy for him, but they had come and he felt a certain comfort.

At the moment, Deputy Manchester was standing at the front window, watching the first brushes of rose and yellow touch the horizon. The earlier evening's turn had made him anxious—and alert. He couldn't rest now, even if he wanted to do so. He had moved the cuspidor next to him, so he wouldn't have to go to the desk to spit.

The two federal guards, Cateson and Wright,

were asleep in separate cells. In exchange for not pressing charges, Lowe and both men had signed a statement that relieved the sheriff and his deputy from any responsibility in the matter. It was Bass's idea. Lowe had left shortly after the settlement.

Assuring himself of its readiness, Manchester looked down at the shotgun cradled in his folded arms. A glance toward the cell told him what he expected: Bass Tillman was awake, sitting quietly on the edge of his bunk. It looked like the attorney was talking to himself. Or was he praying? Could that be? Yes, the old gunfighter was praying. Manchester smiled to himself.

Rolling his shoulders to relieve the tiredness, Manchester returned to the window. But this time, noises in the street surprised him. He couldn't tell what was happening, but it sounded like some riders were gathering. His curiosity wouldn't let him stay inside. It wasn't prudent, but he removed the door bar and stepped outside.

He was immediately surprised and confused. Outside were six men in an animated discussion with a tired Sheriff Babbit in the middle. The blacksmith was there, angrily trying to make his point. So was the town mayor, Justin Evans; and Bass's business partner, Lucius Henry; the undertaker, Benjamin Ringly; and two other townsmen. Sitting in the seat of his freighter wagon was a red-faced teamster and beside the wagon was one of the saloon owners. Several more men were headed their way.

What was this about? It certainly was no lynch mob. A jailbreak? Were he and the sheriff going to have to fight to keep them from breaking Bass out of jail?

"*Guten Morgen, Herr* Deputy Manchester," Babbit said without moving. "Some of our good citizens are worried about our friend." His entire body sagged with fatigue, but his eyes sparkled with purpose.

Manchester jerked his head to the side. Of course. These people were trying to make sense of this arrest and expressing their feelings in no uncertain way. When he looked around, it seemed like the whole town was awake and stirring. The news had traveled fast, he thought, most likely due to Babbit making sure of it.

"How *ist der* prisoner doing?" Babbit asked.

"I think it's safe to say Mr. Tillman is doing better than his captors."

A murmur slid through the assembled group, mostly comments about freeing Bass now and getting this over with. Lucius Henry raised a fist into the morning air and shouted, "This is dead wrong and we all know it. Why not end this? Now."

"Because it *ist der jura, der* law." Babbit's voice was firm. He licked his lips. "I do not be to liking it any more than *du*, but *der* law *ist der* law. *Ja*, that *ist* so. We vill wait for *der* circuit judge to come. By *der* law, that *ist der* way *Herr* Tillman vants it, too. *Ja*."

Manchester stepped toward the front of the sidewalk and spat. He was pleased the fresh tobacco allowed for a thick stream. It wasn't intended as punctuation to the sheriff's statement, but it was accepted as such.

"Here comes that chief deputy marshal now—

and some more of his bunch," Lucius Henry proclaimed. "I can't believe he's got the guts to show himself." His chin jutted out in support of the statement.

Several others agreed loudly as Lowe advanced, telling his two men to remain with their horses at the hitching rail. The half-breed, Painted Crow, grunted his understanding while a boyish-looking gunman with a strange smile made a noise that sounded like a duck quacking. He adjusted the bullet bandoleer over his shoulder, tugged on the brim of his battered derby hat and said something that made the half-breed wince.

"What the hell is this?" Lowe stopped in the middle of the street. "Babbit, are you responsible for this mob?" A gun handle was noticeable above his waistband.

Before Babbit could respond, Henry answered, "We are trying to find out just what kind of a fool thing you're trying to pull. Bass Tillman is one of our leading citizens. He's no criminal." He took two steps forward, limping noticeably, but his manner was of a man who had fought before. That attitude wasn't lost on Lowe.

Bending his quirt like a leather noose, Lowe studied the group. Nothing was going as he had planned so far. Bass Tillman was supposed to be dead by now. Those were his orders. Kill the old attorney before he could tell what he knew about the Hoodsmen from talking to his son. If Lowe thought the other local lawmen knew, he was to kill them as well. He was to make it look like an escape attempt.

What had started out as a simple matter was becoming increasingly difficult. It didn't take a genius to know this group intended on making sure nothing happened to Tillman between now and a court hearing. All of a sudden he would have to present a case. He smiled. When was Touren Grant going to arrive?

That brought a more troubling question to his mind: Where was Bill Drucker? The third federal deputy marshal assigned to the Hoodsmen issue hadn't been seen since Lowe asked him to return to the Tillman farm with the two now-dead men and retrieve the evidence inadvertently left there. It wasn't like Drucker to disappear. Had Bass Tillman killed him, too? Why wouldn't the attorney bring his body in as well, if he did? He brought his horse. Prosecutor Grant would get that out of him at the hearing. He was certain of it.

He wasn't going to tell Grant—or his boss—about his missing cravat pin or the lost telegram. He had an idea of turning this whole thing around. In court. After a slight hesitation, he headed for the telegraph operator. The telegraph was situated in the railroad station ticket office. He heard someone yell, asking where he was going, but he ignored the taunt. He had already decided not to mention in his wire that the old attorney remained armed. It would make him look weak.

He didn't notice a sandy-bearded man in a gray morning coat, matching hat and double-breasted vest walking briskly along the planked sidewalk, headed for the sheriff's office. Several of the gathered men turned to greet a determined

GET
4 FREE BOOKS!

You can have the best Westerns delivered to your door for less than what you'd pay in a bookstore or online. Sign up for one of our book clubs today, and we'll send you **4 FREE* BOOKS**, worth $23.96, just for trying it out...**with no obligation to buy, ever!**

Authors include classic writers such as
LOUIS L'AMOUR, **MAX BRAND**, **ZANE GREY**
and more; PLUS new authors such as
COTTON SMITH, **TIM CHAMPLIN**, **JOHNNY D. BOGGS**
and others.

As a book club member you also receive the following special benefits:
- **30% OFF** all orders through our website & telecenter!
- **Exclusive access to** special discounts!
- **Convenient** home delivery **and 10 days to return any books you don't want to keep.**

There is no minimum number of books to buy,
and you may cancel membership at any time.
See back to sign up!

*Please include $2.00 for shipping and handling.

YES!

Sign me up for the Leisure Western Book Club
and send my FOUR FREE BOOKS! If I choose to stay
in the club, I will pay only $14.00* each month,
a savings of $9.96!

NAME: _____

ADDRESS: _____

_____

TELEPHONE: _____

E-MAIL: _____

☐ **I WANT TO PAY BY CREDIT CARD.**

☐ VISA ☐ MasterCard ☐ DISCOVER

ACCOUNT #: _____

EXPIRATION DATE: _____

SIGNATURE: _____

Send this card along with $2.00 shipping & handling to:

**Leisure Western Book Club
1 Mechanic Street
Norwalk, CT 06850-3431**

Or fax (must include credit card information!) to: 610.995.9274.
You can also sign up online at www.dorchesterpub.com.

*Plus $2.00 for shipping. Offer open to residents of the U.S. and Canada only.
Canadian residents please call 1.800.481.9191 for pricing information.
If under 18, a parent or guardian must sign. Terms, prices and conditions subject to change. Subscription subject
to acceptance. Dorchester Publishing reserves the right to reject any order or cancel any subscription.

Judge Winslow H. Pierce, who brushed past Deputy Manchester, barely grunting a morning greeting through clenched teeth.

"Glad you're here, Judge. Maybe you can put an end to this madness," Henry said.

Mayor Evans added his salutation. "Good morning, Judge Pierce. I was wondering if you might join us. Your counsel is always welcome."

The light-skinned magistrate was well known for his temper. He had just heard the news of Bass Tillman's arrest—first from Babbit and then, a few minutes later, from *Longmont Advocate* editor Wallace Denson—and was spitting mad. Literally. His brown tobacco stream blistered the corner of the planked sidewalk as he pulled open the door and stepped inside.

"What's this crap about you being arrested, Bass?" Judge Pierce declared. "How come I didn't know about it? How come I had to hear it from that scumbag Denson? What the hell's going on?" He slapped the leather gloves in his right hand against his thigh and looked for a spittoon.

Trailing him, Manchester pointed toward the container next to the wall where he had stood guard. Judge Pierce eyed him with contempt and strutted to the cuspidor, spat and folded his arms waiting for an answer.

Standing in his cell, Bass couldn't help but chuckle. He knew the municipal judge well and liked him. While he was known for his tantrums and occasional bad disposition, he was also recognized for his care for the law. He expected respect because he was a judge—and he usually got it. Even from Bass.

"Judge, we've been kinda busy here," Manchester tried to explain. "And it's a federal thing. We don't have a choice."

"Be quiet, son. I asked Tillman." Judge Pierce spat again.

From the adjacent cell, Cateson sat up, trying to ignore his throbbing arm. He knew he had been hurt far worse. Nevertheless, he wasn't in any humor to listen to anybody. Especially this damn rooster of a local judge.

"Shut the hell up, yourself," Cateson yelled, "and get outta here."

Judge Pierce looked like a man about to explode.

"Good morning, Winslow, it's good to see you," Bass said brightly.

"Good morning, my ass. I asked you a question. How come you're in there? I hear you killed two men," Judge Pierce hollered and pointed at Cateson. "Don't say another word, mister, or I'll haul your ass into my court. *My* court, you hear?"

Wright mumbled that they were federal lawmen. It sounded like they were fishermen and the magistrate frowned.

"I'm U.S. Deputy Marshal John Cateson and this is one of our special deputies," Cateson stated with more caution than earlier.

"Interesting place for federal officers," Judge Pierce commented. He spat again into the spittoon and it rang with an authority that matched the manner of its launcher. "Still haven't heard the why of it, Tillman. Speak to me."

"Didn't Frank talk with you?"

"Of course he did. So damn excited, he was talking more German than American!" Judge Pierce said. "And he told me about the Jallon thing. I'll take care of that. Now talk to me, damn it."

Bass explained the situation, leaving out only the disappearance of Easter Sontag since it didn't have any bearing on the events of the past afternoon and evening.

The young deputy stood to the side of the small room, watching in total amazement. Here were two men he had once worshipped as his heroes. Now one was in jail and apparently not interested in getting out. The other was angry, but apparently helpless. He shook his head to rid the images and sought a fresh chaw from his coat pocket.

"This is absolute nonsense, that's what it is." Judge Pierce waved his arms above his head and gritted his teeth. "You may be a mean son of a bitch, Bass Tillman—but you sure as hell ain't no Hoodsman. And anybody with any sense knows it." He looked at the two gunmen in their cells. "I reckon that excludes these two pecker heads."

"Thank you, Winslow. I appreciate that."

"I'm not the only one riled up about this, from what I saw outside." Judge Pierce cocked his head toward the window.

Bass frowned. "Don't know what you mean."

Manchester quickly explained and Bass shook his head in amazement.

"Marshal Lowe isn't gonna like that—an' neither do I," Cateson declared, standing but not attempting to move his stiffened arm. "They can't do that."

"Who the hell cares what you two like?" Judge Pierce declared. "This has got to stop some damn where. You-all wouldn't know a Hoodsman from a rutting hog."

Wright said, "Ohyeahwewould."

Judge Pierce glared at him, not understanding.

Cateson's dark stare forced Wright to retreat to his cell's cot where he sat, staring.

"Bass Tillman, I'm going to wire the federal magistrate in Denver about this mess," Judge Pierce declared, "and U.S. Marshal Hautrese. Hell, I'm gonna wire the attorney general!" His chin jutted in support of the statement. "I know Judge Nelene, too—and I plan to give him an earful when he gets here."

With a glance at Manchester, Bass asked the fiery magistrate to come closer to his cell. Hesitantly, Judge Pierce complied and stood with his face against the bars while Bass whispered in his ear. His shoulders rising and falling in agitated reaction to the news, Judge Pierce stepped back. His pale face was even whiter. It was essentially the same story the sheriff had outlined for him two days ago.

"I—I d-don't know what to say, Bass. Frank told me just . . . two days ago. Something about a fella named Crimmler. I—I c-can't—"

"I know it's hard to believe," Bass interrupted. "That's why I've got to go through with this. It's the only way."

Judge Pierce rubbed his thick, sandy beard and finally spoke. This time telling Bass that Wallace Denson was writing a story about the arrest—from Lowe's point of view. It would be the lead story in tomorrow's edition. Judge Pierce admitted that Denson was no friend of his either.

"Save me a copy, Winslow." Bass grinned.

"It isn't funny, Bass."

"No, it's not—but there's nothing I can do about it," Bass said.

"What can I do?"

"Well, you're a damn good attorney. Give me your thoughts on how I should handle my defense at the hearing," Bass said.

Judge Pierce glanced over at the two gunmen in their cells. The look on his face was one Bass couldn't read. He probably shouldn't have asked for that kind of favor. The magistrate straightened his shoulders and, without further comment, left the office.

Manchester tried to thank him on the way out, but Judge Pierce either didn't hear it or didn't care to respond.

Bass watched him leave and shook his head. He shouldn't have asked Pierce for help. It was like asking him to go against his own profession. He could hear questions coming at the magistrate from the crowd outside as the door closed.

Outside, the whole community was fully awake and watching. Most were unsure of what they expected to see, if anything. Mrs. Lancaster stood alone on the sidewalk with a handkerchief pressed against her mouth. Tears stained her cheeks. She was dressed for attention in a plaited walking suit of dark green cashmere with lighter green accents of velvet. Her matching hat topped the ensemble.

A few feet away, Wallace Denson was furiously writing notes on a pad of paper, unaware of her performance.

A range of emotions painted the faces of the gathered groups of people. By now, only a few in Longmont weren't aware of the arrest of Bass Tillman for murdering two federal officers; far fewer, however, knew of the murders of the town's deputy and his wife, Bass's son and daughter-in-law. Virtually all had an opinion, mostly kept to themselves, of the gunfighter-turned-attorney based on their personal exposure to him, and when that encounter first occurred.

After receiving new orders by telegraph, Topper Lowe headed for the sheriff's office. Most of the assembled townsmen had migrated to the restaurant and were eating breakfast. Sheriff Babbit had joined them. However, others remained near the jail, either on horseback or standing talking. He touched his coat pocket for the reassurance of the telegram confirming what he should do.

His new orders were to wait for Grant to reach town. The district attorney should be there in two or three days. Meanwhile, Lowe was to continue with the original plan of eliminating Bass Tillman, but if it came to a hearing and trial, Grant would take charge. A Pinkerton agent was also expected to join them; he would be coming by stage, likely too late for the hearing, but in time to testify at the trial itself. Lowe felt his boss was not overly concerned with the way things were turning out and had even complimented him on deciding to give an interview to the local newspaper editor.

The last sentence was still ringing in his ears: "No HM until ordered. H."

It made good sense. If they were going to frame Tillman for being the head of the Hoodsmen, there shouldn't be any robberies while he was being tried. It would underline the charge and the coincidence would be pointed out to the newspapers.

After Bass Tillman was out of the way permanently, one way or the other, they would remove any others who might have heard the secrets of the Hoodsmen. Luckily, Cateson had seen Virgil Crimmler leave with Jacob Tillman. The long-faced deputy marshal was leaving a prostitute's back room when they exited the saloon. Lowe had let the two of them come to town to pick up any telegrams.

Babbit would be next on the list. Something would happen to Bass's friend, the Scotsman, too. Maybe Judge Pierce would have to disappear as well. It paid to be careful.

Lowe smiled. He was good at this, he told himself. His boss knew that. Then he shivered at the thought of staring at Bass's gun in the jail. How close he had come to dying then. How close. How did that son of a bitch get that gun? Was it really due to his men being careless? He snapped the quirt at his wrist and reminded himself that this was no ordinary situation and that it didn't matter, not in the long run. There was no way these local clowns knew what was happening and wouldn't, until he was rich. Just like his boss. Really rich. Then everyone would look up to him. He smiled to himself.

When Lowe entered the jail, Manchester was seated behind the sheriff's desk drinking coffee.

"Your guns are right here, Marshal Lowe," Manchester said without moving.

Lowe's attention went to the gun belt and hideaway gun on the desk where they had been placed last night. He buckled on the bullet belt, adjusted the holster and returned the small weapon to his boot. The hood brought in by Cateson lay on the desk and he wadded and placed it in his coat pocket.

"Get us outta here, Topper!" Cateson yelled. "An' get me some whiskey. My arm's about to drop off."

"Open the cells, deputy."

Manchester slowly rose from the chair, brushing against the spittoon, which had been returned to its normal position, as he rounded the desk with the cell keys in his hand. He glanced down and attempted to spit. Brown juice dribbled down his chin. Quickly, he wiped it with the back of his hand and tried again. About half of the sputum hit the brass container; the floor received the remainder. Trying to act nonchalant, he walked over to their cells and opened them.

Lowe pursed his lips and said, "Get your asses outta there."

"Tillman, it's going to be a real pleasure watching you hang," Cateson snarled as he hurried from the cell. A victorious grin took over his thin face; then his jaw popped open. He grabbed his shoulder as the shouting jolted fresh pain into the wound.

"Be careful about your pleasures," Bass said. "They might be the death of you."

Cateson frowned, not understanding the statement, and Wright mumbled a long sentence that wasn't discernible. Both men retrieved their guns from the desk drawer.

"Look who's talking." Lowe snapped the quirt against the floor. It didn't sound as dramatic as he had wished. "The great gunfighter Bass Tillman. Wonder if you'll get a new rope, Tillman. Easter Sontag's supposed to be in Denver about now—for a hanging of one of your Hoodsmen. Maybe we can convince him to head this way for yours, too."

Cateson brushed past him and Lowe stopped the tall marshal. "I'm bringing in two other posse men to watch my prisoner. Marshal Cateson, you stay here and get them settled in. Wright, you come with me." Lowe turned and left with Wright following.

Manchester approached Bass's cell slowly. "You know they're bringing in Touren Grant. He's been the prosecutor—for all the Hoodsman trials. I hear he's never been beaten in court."

"Maybe he'll be overconfident."

Chapter 15

Behind them, John Painted Crow and a boyish-looking gunman entered the jail and took their positions next to the door. The young gunman grinned and made a quacking noise again, this time flapping his arms folded with his thumbs hooked under his armpits. Painted Crow said something that the other man didn't understand, but Bass caught the Lakota words for The River. Cateson briefed them on their assignment. When he was finished, Painted Crow told the younger man, "Do not get in the way of The River."

A lopsided smile crossed the boyish face as he adjusted the bandoleer on his filthy shirt. The handle of a Colt was visible in his waistband. A crazed look controlled his reddened eyes, something Bass thought had been there a long time. Probably since childhood.

Hearing the statement about "The River" made Bass remember the medicine stone in his coat pocket. He reached there and felt its presence. Next to it was the empty tobacco sack. How far away Nancy Spirit Bear and his son's injured dog seemed right now. How far away the awfulness of his family's deaths. How far away his Settie seemed. And the peacefulness of his son's farm. He took a deep breath. If he was wrong, he would die. An ugly death at the end of a rope, likely handled by Easter Sontag.

Morning sun soon took control of the day and the crowds slowly returned to their daily endeavors, except for a few. Deputy Marshal Cateson took over the sheriff's desk chair and began chatting with Painted Crow and the bizarre-acting young gunman.

Sitting on the cell cot, Bass let his mind wander back to clipped views of his son changing from a rambunctious boy to manhood. Shards of memory glittered in his thoughts. Scraped knees. Discoveries of a frog. A black dog that loved the boy and was loved in return. Mischievous, yet caring, Jacob was like his mother. Rebellious and cocky, too. Like his father had been. Yet much more determined. A young Jacob came running at his father with open arms after Bass returned from a long trail, one he would never take again. That greeting was the main reason and the woman standing just behind it. Bass watched his beloved son choose his own way of life, one much different than that of his own. Bass smiled as he saw again the smitten look on Jacob's face as he told him about Mary Anne for the first time.

Without warning, their faces came at him in wretched death. He straightened.

"What's the matter, Tillman?" Cateson asked, half in surprise, half taunting. "See yourself hanging?"

Bass turned toward him, without responding. His eyes glowed with the anger of his family's murderous end. His hate looked into the man's face and Cateson shivered and began fiddling in his pocket for cigarette makings. The half-breed kept watching the old attorney with unreadable eyes. Quacking like a duck, the young gunman added a little jig to his performance.

For a fleeting moment, Bass wondered again what had happened to Easter Sontag. The executioner had apparently lied about wanting to stay in Longmont and ride with him to Denver City. But why? He didn't seem like a man who had trouble telling it straight. Could something have happened to him? What? Why? Or had Bass simply misread the man's intentions because he liked talking about the theater?

To himself, Bass muttered, "Bass, you were right about him. Right from the first. He's one of them. Maybe there's more than one H."

That ended his reflection as Manchester returned from his breakfast. Taking a shotgun from the rack, he stopped halfway, cradling it in his arms, and glanced at Cateson. "Good morning, Mr. Tillman. Would you like to . . . go out back? Then we'll bring you some breakfast. Have you had any coffee?"

"All of that sounds good."

Cateson smiled as he licked and closed the paper end of his cigarette.

Painted Crow studied Bass, but said nothing,

then looked over at Cateson, who was lighting his new smoke. After a long pull, the long-faced federal marshal leaned forward in his chair with his arms outstretched across the desk. "You're going to have to put him in handcuffs—an' take his gun. You know that." White trails of smoke slipped from the corner of his mouth and trailed upward.

Manchester grabbed the keys and handcuffs from the desk, walked to the cell and apologized as he opened it. "I'm sorry, Bass, but he's right."

Bass handed him the pistol and held out his hands to be handcuffed. He decided not to mention that Sheriff Babbit wouldn't have thought this was necessary. Or prudent.

"I'll give it back when we return. I'm sorry." Manchester propped the shotgun against the cell bars. "It is a bit strange, you know, your having a weapon while in custody," he said, shoving the gun into his belt and retrieving his own weapon.

"This whole thing is. Stay alert, William."

"I know my job, Mr. Tillman."

Manchester led Bass out of the cell and slowed to allow Painted Crow to step beside Bass on the right and the boyish-looking gunman eased beside him on the left. They walked side by side toward the door in stride with Manchester ten feet behind them.

Watching from the desk, Cateson took the cigarette from his mouth. "Bass, I don't think you've met Ernie Dawson. He and the breed are gonna take you to the outhouse."

Bass squinted and growled, "I met your older brother, Floyd. He and Leitel Penn—and a third crook—tried to rob the bank. Two years ago. They were Hoodsmen."

"Ya done kilt my big brother, you bastird."

Cateson frowned; he didn't want Dawson to tip their hand. The unbalanced gunman was told to act meek until they got out back. Manchester would stay in the office with Cateson, while Dawson and Painted Crow would kill the older attorney when no one was looking. The plan was simple and sure.

"That's right, I did," Bass replied. "He was no good. A two-bit thief."

The young gunman's face transformed into something wild. He reached for the long-barreled Colt resting in his waistband. Moving more swiftly, Bass slammed his handcuffed hands, locked together in a double fist, against Dawson's gun hand as he pulled the weapon from its resting place.

Bam!

The partially drawn gun fired as Bass's unexpected blow sprang Dawson's thumb from the advancing hammer. Lead ripped into Dawson's stomach so close to his shirt that it flamed where the bullet entered. Only Bass was certain of what had happened. Dawson screamed and flopped to the floor, grabbing his bloody stomach.

A stunned Manchester dropped his shotgun.

"What the hell! Who shot Dawson?" Cateson's head swiveled first one way, then the other. His cigarette flew into the air. A piercing ache in his arm drove him to hold it as he grabbed for his own holstered pistol.

Frantically, Bass dove for the fallen shotgun.

Manchester watched, frozen in place. Sheriff Babbit and Lucius Henry burst through the door, brandishing handguns. Cateson frowned and his hand retreated from his gun. Bass took a deep breath and stood, leaving Manchester's weapon where it lay.

Painted Crow stepped back, concentrating on Dawson writhing on the floor. Magic! It was magic. The River had made Dawson shoot himself—with his own gun! Magic. He knew the spirits were with this strange man, Bass Tillman. He shook his head; his hands slowly followed in a half-raised surrender.

"Bass just shot another federal officer," Cateson declared, standing behind the desk.

"My ass, he's a federal officer," Lucius Henry spat, waving his gun for emphasis. "Dawson's crazy as a loon—and his brother, Floyd, was worse."

"Yeah, Bass killed him when he and two others tried to rob our bank. They were Hoodsmen and Bass stopped 'em cold." The third voice was the mayor's, only a few strides behind the first two.

Rubbing his tingling left hand with his other as best he could with the handcuff restraint, Bass watched the young gunman crying out for his mother.

"The fool just shot himself. In the gut," Henry observed.

With no emotion reaching his face, Bass looked over at Cateson. "You'd better tend to him, Deputy Marshal Cateson. He's your man, remember?" He looked up at Painted Crow and the attorney's eyes challenged the half-breed.

Licking his lips, Painted Crow muttered, *"Wanagi. Kin Wakpa."* His gaze pleaded for mercy.

Bass understood the words of "ghosts" and "The River" and his gaze transferred to Babbit with a gun pointed at the surprised Cateson. The old attorney nodded his thanks.

Just outside the opened door, a crowd was gathering. Behind them came Lowe's loud commands to make room. He cleared the group, expecting to see Bass Tillman dead. Maybe Dawson, too. Dawson wanted badly to kill Bass for shooting his brother—and he was unbalanced and expendable. In fact, it was best if he didn't have a chance to jabber afterward.

"Seems like lawmen have trouble staying alive around you, Tillman," Lowe proclaimed as he stepped beside Cateson, who was tending to Dawson. Inside, he was fuming. Couldn't anyone do anything right? Bass was supposed to be disarmed and handcuffed. Surely the old attorney didn't have another hidden gun.

"Not the real ones," Bass said.

Watching, Henry added, "You've got to be kidding, Marshal. Who the hell would give this idiot a badge—of any kind?"

Lowe gritted his teeth and asked, "How bad is it?"

"It's real bad. Gut shot," Cateson observed, patting the dying man on the shoulder.

Screaming again, Dawson thrashed his arms and legs in an attempt to quell the anguish eating at his torn insides. "H-help me, b-boss. It h-hurts somethin' awful. I—I can't stand it." Blood from his mouth followed Dawson's claim. "M-Ma, wh-where . . ."

Sheriff Babbit rolled his shoulders. "*Herr* Marshal Lowe *und* Marshal Cateson, vhat do you plan *vit* your man? *Du* vant us to bring *der doktor?*"

"No. It's too late for that." Lowe picked up Dawson's long-barreled gun, partially hidden by his bleeding body. He knelt beside the frantic man-boy, whispered in his ear, cocked the gun and handed it to him.

Trembling and bawling, Dawson lifted the gun to his head and fired. It happened so fast only Bass moved to stop him.

"My God!" Henry exclaimed as blood and brain matter splattered across the floor.

"Happy now, Tillman?" Lowe said, looking away from the dead man.

"He shot himself. Twice," Bass said. "Both times, by your doing. Just didn't work out the way you wanted."

"Cateson, get that damn undertaker," Lowe said and turned back to the doorway, shoving people aside as he walked away.

"I vill take *Herr* Tillman to *der* back," Babbit said quietly, holstering his pistol and picking up Manchester's shotgun. "Take *der* handcuffs off. *Ist* not needed, are they, *Herr* Tillman?"

Bass held out his hands and a trembling Manchester removed them quickly.

"Give him his gun," Babbit said, grabbing the weapon from his deputy and handing it to Bass. "*Haben sie gut geschlafen?*"

Bass smiled. It would be like the lawman to ask

how he had slept—and mean it. "It was a long night, Frank. How about you?" He returned the Colt to his waistband.

"*Ja*. Vas fer me, too." Babbit nodded, cradling the shotgun. "*Entschuldigen Sie bitte*, I almost forget. *Herr* Judge Pierce give me this for *du*. Something *du* asked for."

It was Bass's turn to look surprised.

Babbit smiled and handed him a sealed envelope. "It *ist* a letter about *nein* varrant—*und* another *wit* ideas about your trial, he said *du* would know vhat it vas."

"Well, I'll be."

Shaking even more, Manchester stepped closer to the two men and confessed his fright. "I—I w-was so scared. I—I've never been in anything like this." He bit his lower lip to fight back the anxiety swelling within him. "First, Jacob and h-his wife . . . then th-they tried to k-kill us . . . and n-now this. I—I d-don't . . ."

Bass put his hand on the young deputy's shoulder. "I'm scared, too, William. But don't let them see it." He glanced over at the still body. "Just remember, they aren't going to stop—just because you do. The only way we can stop them—is in the courtroom."

"B-but . . . they'll just come after us—even if you win." Manchester realized the significance of his statement and apologized, "I—I'm sorry, I didn't mean it that way."

"I know you didn't, William." Bass returned his hand to his side. "Why don't you go home and get some rest? I'll be all right. You're worn out. Sleep'll help a lot."

Babbit agreed. "*Ja, ist* a *gut* idea, Deputy Manchester. *Go und* sleep. It vill be *gut*."

His head lowering in a mixture of relief and fear, Manchester followed the two men out of the jail. Outside the hushed crowd separated to let them pass; some added chants of support and a few grumbled that Bass Tillman was getting what he deserved. Topper Lowe was nowhere in sight; neither was his cross-eyed henchman. As Babbit and the old attorney turned into the adjacent alley, Manchester walked on toward his apartment above one of the buildings.

"*Nein* so *gut*, Bass," Sheriff Babbit said, watching him leave.

"He'll be fine," Bass said. "This isn't a picnic for anybody." He shook his head and his long white hair danced along his shoulders.

"Vhere vas he when *der* trouble started?"

"Behind me. He dropped the shotgun." There was no need to explain that the young deputy was ineffective at the worst possible time.

From the edge of Bass's vision, he saw the same boy who had passed him earlier. The towheaded lad was standing against the far building. Watching. In his hands was a homemade ball.

Bass stopped and greeted him. "Good morning, son. Going to play base-ball?"

"Ah, yes, sir, soon as my friends get through with their chores." The boy tossed the ball in the air and caught it.

"I bet you're a good player."

"I'm the best striker."

"I'll bet you are. Have fun." Bass resumed his walk with the sheriff.

"Ah, sir?"

"Yes?" Bass stopped and turned back.

"Were you really a pistol fighter?" The boy's eyes sparkled with interest.

"Well, I guess so, son," Bass answered. "But that was a long time ago. I'm an attorney now. An old one."

"Oh." The boy's expression changed. "Ah, did you kill those two men everybody's talking about?"

"No, I didn't, son, but I did defend myself against some men who murdered my son and his wife—and tried to kill me." Bass's mouth tightened with the statement. Maybe he shouldn't be saying things like that to a boy.

He looked at Babbit, who was uneasy about the delay, watching the crowd around the jail for any signs of trouble. Most of the people gathered were now watching Cateson advance with the lanky undertaker. Babbit was glad for the distraction.

"Ve'd better get on *vit das*," Babbit said.

"Sure. See you later, son." Bass waved.

The boy spun and started to walk away, yelling, "Wait till I tell my friends! I met the gunfighter Bass Tillman!"

A lanky farmer heard the one-sided conversation and put out his hand to stop the boy. "Ya know'd, son, ol' Bass Tillman were one of the gun trio." He grinned a jack-o'-lantern smile that declared four missing teeth. "Read 'bout 'em in them *DeWitt Ten Cent Romance* books, ya know."

"Did you know . . . the gun trio?" the boy asked, stepping back to avoid the avalanche of whiskeyed breath.

The farmer leaned closer. "Don't tell nobody . . . but I met all three. A'fore two o' them boys were kilt in a range war down in Kansas. A few years back."

"Thanks, mister. I gotta go," the boy said and slipped around the farmer.

Watching the departure, the farmer said, "Ask your paw if'n he ever read the story about 'em in *Harper's New Monthly*. It's a good'un."

Upon returning to the sheriff's office, Bass and Sheriff Babbit found Dawson's body was gone and Bass's business partner was waiting. The crowd itself had returned to their daily endeavors. Wright had rejoined Cateson, who was seated behind the sheriff's desk. The two were drinking coffee and talking among themselves. Painted Crow stood silently against the far wall; his eyes widened as Bass and the sheriff entered.

Stepping away from the cell, Henry proclaimed loudly, "We'll have us a grand celebration when all this crap is over."

"Probably so, probably so," Bass mumbled. "Thanks to both of you."

"I vill get *du* some coffee," Babbit said. "Then I vill get your breakfast."

"Thanks, Frank. Sounds good."

While Bass sat on his cell cot, drinking coffee, Henry talked mostly business, and mostly without response from Bass. It was as if Dawson's attempted murder of Bass and his eventual suicide had never occurred. Even Bass's arrest and pending hearing were left alone for the moment. Henry's concerns, instead, centered on their Denver partner's recommendation that they sell their stock in the freighting company and invest their profits in a Denver bank being sold. The profits from the bank wouldn't be as great, but they would be longer lasting. Both liked the idea.

Using "Denver" as an opening, Henry said he knew a good attorney there. "He's slick and smooth—and well connected, if you know what I mean."

Bass sipped his coffee and smiled. "Guess you think I'm not good enough."

Henry pursed his lips and rubbed his cheek. "Come on, Bass. You know what I mean. You're straight-talking. You're . . . too honest." He waved his hand for emphasis. "Too damn honest for this bunch."

He proceeded to state his growing concern that some of these men seemed more like outlaws than lawmen, especially the ones guarding the jail now. Slamming his open hand against the cell bars, he said, "Damn it, Bass, they're bringing in that district attorney, the one who's been traveling with them. Mean as hell, I hear. Thinks he'll be governor if he can bring down the Hoodsmen."

"Touren Grant."

"You know him?" Henry's hand slid from the bars to his side.

"No. Just his reputation." Bass grinned. "He doesn't know me either. Just my reputation. It'll be fun to watch."

Henry frowned and whispered, "Say the word—an' we'll have you outta here tonight. Lots of folks in town waiting to help. I mean it, Bass. You know those guys can't let you go." He added, "Sheriff Babbit told me all about it."

"I wish he hadn't," Bass said. "That's just going to get him killed. And put you in danger."

"They can't kill all of us."

"Of course they can." Bass set down his empty cup on the cot. "An' they'll make it look like an Indian raid, or something no one can pin it on them." He shook his head. "The only way is to expose them in court." His shoulders rose and fell. "Besides, I don't know for sure who the head man is."

"Isn't it obvious U.S. Marshal Hautrese is behind all this?" Henry's voice quickened. "I've been hearing stories about his investments around Denver City. And a silver mine in Leadville. One of the big ones. Where'd he get that kind of money? Congress passed a law that a U.S. Marshal can't make more than six thousand dollars a year. Most of them don't make anywhere near that, so I've read."

Bass cocked his head to the side. "Course he was appointed by the president and recommended by Senator Tries. More likely, it was money that got him the appointment in the first place, Lucius."

"Yeah, you're right," Henry agreed. "Damn." He motioned toward Cateson. "Look who he hired for his deputies. Good Lord!" His chin jutted and his voice lowered. "Hell, maybe we should bribe them. They don't make much either, Bass. Just fees from bringing in criminals and serving warrants and stuff. What do they get for travel? Three dollars a day or something like that."

"Don't try it, Lucius," Bass said.

Henry returned to his original concern. "Bass, I can wire this lawyer friend and he can be here in time—for the trial. Stage wouldn't get here fast enough for the hearing."

Bass saw Babbit entering with a tray. "Hey, here comes my breakfast. Not everything's bad about being in jail, you know."

"Just say the word, Bass, and we'll get you out of here," Henry repeated.

Bass shook his head. "Then you'd be outlaws—like me." A faint smile crossed his tired face. "Hi, Frank. Whatever you've got sure smells good."

"*Ja. Das ist gut,*" Babbit responded to Bass's observation about the food as he walked across the jail without looking at Cateson, Wright or Painted Crow, who continued to stand alone in the far corner.

After accepting the tray, Bass studied the tired lawman. "Frank, you go get some rest. I'll be fine." He patted the handle of the Colt in his waistband.

Henry slid his hand into his coat pocket and felt the handgun resting there. He didn't normally carry a weapon, but had purchased the short-barreled Smith & Wesson this morning. It gave him the confidence to volunteer to stand guard while Babbit rested.

Bass was immediately against the idea, but appreciative of the thought. He removed the lid from his plate and absorbed the smells of ham, eggs and fried potatoes close up. For the first time since his arrest, he was hungry.

Finally, Babbit declared, "I vill return before *mittags.*"

"Don't hurry. This breakfast'll hold me all day," Bass said, sipping coffee, "and this fella here'll keep the wolves at bay." He patted the gun in his waistband.

Henry shuffled outside the cell, advising that he would check back later.

"You're a good friend, Lucius."

Agreeing, Babbit closed and locked the cell door and walked out with Henry at his side. Cateson's wisecracks trailed their exit. Silence crept through the jail while Bass concentrated on his breakfast. He kept his body slanted toward Cateson, Painted Crow and Wright so he could see all three of them all of the time.

"Howcomehestillhasagun?" Wright mumbled. "Heisaprisoner."

"You won't have that pistol with you in the courtroom, Tillman," Cateson snarled. "It'll be sweet to watch." His open jaw wavered. "Grant's a real lawyer, not an old goat like you." Waiting for Bass's response, he looked at his bandaged arm and ran his fingers over the dark bloodstain that had seeped through the cloth. He had been lucky; the wound hadn't torn any muscle or shattered bone, only ripped flesh.

Without commenting, Bass finished the last bite of potatoes, laid down the fork and finished the remainder of his coffee. After laying the mug on the floor beside his cot, he stood and stretched. It felt good. Weariness wanted control, but there was no way he could allow himself to rest.

"What's the matter, Tillman? You afraid to go to sleep? What are you worried about? Nightmares?" Cateson challenged, rubbing his hand over his unshaven chin. He, too, was tired. This was an arrest like no other he had experienced. The old man had proved far tougher to remove than anyone expected.

After a few minutes of continued silence, John Painted Crow inhaled deeply and began walking toward the cell. Cateson watched him, saying nothing. Wright mumbled something, but Cateson ignored him. Bass's right hand slid around the handle of the Colt as he watched. Was this the beginning of a three-way assault? Could he stop all three? Probably not without being shot himself.

A few feet from the cell, Painted Crow stopped. In a soft voice, he spoke in Lakotan. *"Hau. He kci wowaglaka wkpa."*

Bass understood that he wanted to speak to him, calling him The River as a term of honor and respect. In Lakotan, the attorney responded, asking him what he wanted, *"Taku ca yacin hwo?"*

Paint Crow straightened his shoulders and looked Bass directly in the eyes. "I am not the enemy of The River. I no kill your son, his squaw. I not there. I no longer a rider of the masks." He finished and stood quietly with his arms at his sides.

Only Bass understood his declaration in Lakotan. Raising his hand in salutation, the attorney responded in the same tongue as best he could, stating that he understood and that he had no quarrel with the half-breed.

Painted Crow grunted, spun around and headed for the door without looking at either Cateson or Wright.

"Hey, where do you think you're going?" Cateson yelled.

"Let him go, Cateson," Bass warned. "He's too good a man to ride with you."

Opening the door, Painted Crow hesitated and turned toward Bass and spoke once more in his native language. "The River must keep flowing, keep moving—or it will die." He closed the door behind him.

Chapter 16

In his Denver apartment, United States Marshal Boston Hautrese dismissed the young prostitute with some money and began to button his trousers. He smiled. Things were going well again and soon his concern about that damn old attorney, Bass Tillman, would only be a distasteful memory.

This day would be significant. He had a meeting in an hour with a senator. It was about a contribution to the senator's reelection campaign. Dinner was with several Denver Pacific Railroad executives; they were eager for details on the arrest of the dreaded Hoodsmen leader. He was eager to supply them.

"You aren't the dashing young gunfighter of old, Bass Tillman. You're just a piece of crap. You should've known better. Age does that, you know." He walked over to the oblong mirror above his French-styled dresser and smiled again.

A wide, toothy smile that always brought results. Such smiles came naturally to him. Always had. It was a politican's trained smile that, coupled with his confident manner, had taken him far. Of course, he had started ahead of most, thanks to learning everything the hard way as an orphan.

He stared in the mirror, admiring his tanned good looks and thick, wavy hair and adjusting his silk cravat. "You've come a long way, a long way."

With that, he studied his chiseled face, rubbed his chin with its fresh shave and pronounced himself quite handsome. Dressing properly was an important part of the statement he should make as a federal lawman. Striped breeches were carefully tucked into knee-high black boots. Well shined, of course. A silver U.S. Marshal's badge, of his own design, sparkled from his blue brocade vest. Across the front was a heavy silver chain holding a timepiece resting in his right vest pocket. A gray frock coat and matching narrow-brimmed hat would finish his wardrobe. Both lay on the bed, waiting.

"Soon, I can quit this crap and live the way I should," he proclaimed and glanced around the small room and its studied appearance.

But it was also important for his surroundings to look appropriate for a U.S. Marshal. Professional and tasteful, not ostentatious, but not poor either. Hence, his office was rented space in the Denver City Marshal's jail. But only a fool would try to live on the fees from serving warrants and the like. He had resisted subscribing to the new telephone system. It wouldn't look right. Maybe later. The idea of being able to manage Lowe and the others directly was appealing. Of course, telephone lines only went a few places. Mostly businesses. So far, their telegraph strategy had worked well, using codes to inform of stage and train opportunities.

"What was the government's new law—a maximum of six thousand a year? Yeah, that was it." He turned his head to the right, then the left, to make certain his sideburns were the same length on both sides. "Wonder who's a big enough fool to do that?"

His actual annual salary was a pittance, two hundred dollars, plus two percent of all the court funds that came through his office. He was paid a small fee for each court paper served by his men. Major fees and cash bonuses for key arrests were awarded from the U.S. mail, Wells Fargo, the railroads—and even the Pinkerton Agency. He and his men were happy to provide them. Of course, the big money wasn't outlined anywhere, or recorded—and that didn't count the rewards generated by the Hoodsmen's trail of crime.

In many ways, he ran the U.S. Marshal's offices like a general manager of a company with a large sales force would. He supervised his deputies, giving them assignments and keeping the books. Most of his time, though, was spent courting local and regional power brokers. He shook his head and chuckled. The U.S. Marshal's job was, without a doubt, the plum of patronage he had expected. And more. The more was of his own doing, his own craftiness. Pure genius, he mused.

Always good with appearances, as a twenty-two-year-old with little formal education, he had bluffed his way onto the teaching staff of a small Colorado college. However, he quickly tired of the academic life—and its meager compensation. A chance meeting with Topper Lowe, then a hired gun, found kinship immediately—and soon the "Hoodsmen" strategy was formed. Getting an appointment to the U.S. Marshal's vacant job for the district was secured by Hautrese's considerable contribution to Senator Tries's election; it had taken all his savings. Lowe provided the actual opportunity: the incumbent U.S. Marshal Amos Frese was mysteriously murdered in his own home. Indians were blamed; none were brought to justice.

"I'm forgetting something. What the hell is it?" he declared, half angry.

He looked around the room and saw the answer. A silver-plated, ivory-handled Smith & Wesson revolver, a gift from a satisfied patron, lay on a small bookcase. He chuckled at his forgetfulness. "Whoever heard of a lawman without a gun?"

Walking first to the bed, he put on his coat, working the left sleeve first along the withered arm that had come with birth. He could do some things with it, but there was little strength or dexterity. He had long ago quit cursing the disability, realizing his brilliant mind more than made up for the inconvenience. However, he never forgave his mother for the defect and many years later had killed the doctor who handled the operation. His mother had died on her own.

The arm hung at his side as he eased his good arm into the coat. After the coat was in place, he walked over to the table, lifted the weapon as if it were a prop of some kind and placed it in his coat pocket. He rarely wore a holster, shoulder or hip.

So far, his well-developed scheme of the Hoodsmen had worked perfectly. No one suspected him of being behind the raids, or some of his deputy marshals being the Hoodsmen themselves. Lowe, Drucker and Cateson—and their selected men—had never been close to being caught. Except that one time—when Cateson and two others tried to rob the Longmont Bank and Bass Tillman stopped them. Cateson was damn fortunate to escape.

"I'm a lucky man—and you're not, Bass Tillman," he declared. "I've turned your son's arrest of Virgil Crimmler into a hanging for you." He laughed. Loudly.

It was true. Even when one of Lowe's henchmen, Virgil Crimmler, babbled to the Longmont deputy about what was going on, his men had been able to quash the possible outbreak of the truth by killing Jacob Tillman and his wife and taking Crimmler away from their farm home where the part-time deputy was hiding him. Hautrese had insisted Crimmler not be mistreated; he might come in handy later.

Of course, U.S. Marshal Hautrese knew full well the limitations of his three "Hoodsmen" deputy marshals, Lowe, Drucker and Cateson. The former tried to lord it over the other two, but Topper Lowe had no more sense of tactical insight than did Johnny Cateson or Bill Drucker.

All three were loyal, though. He let them make their own decisions about which banks to rob and when; trains and stagecoaches were a different matter and he telegraphed these opportunities. In code, of course. At first, he had been disturbed to hear a local lawman was keeping him from getting Bass Tillman to Denver City for trial—or, at least, on the way so that he could be eliminated without watchful eyes. Luckily, District Attorney Touren Grant was not far from Longmont when Lowe's wire reached him.

"'Luckily,' there's that word again," he muttered. "Some men just have it." He touched the small mole on his cheek. "Then there are unlucky bastards—like Bass Tillman—who are always in the wrong place at the wrong time." He snorted a chuckle.

Four of his other deputy marshals were assigned to the western part of his district. As far as he knew, they were good, hardworking lawmen. He read their reports with little interest and kept them busy with real assignments. None had anything to do with the Hoodsmen or knew of their boss's involvement. Like other deputy marshals, they were compensated with fees from serving warrants, making arrests and handling prisoners. They received two dollars a day, if there wasn't an arrest—for their trouble—as well as reimbursement of expenses. But no more than three dollars a day for food when transporting a prisoner—and ten cents a mile, one way. Three of his four honest deputies were also sheriffs in their respective counties.

To help keep them happy, he had not kept any commissions from their fees, as was a U.S. Marshal's due. Of course, his Hoodsmen deputies were promised a percentage of their ill-gotten gain when the time was right. He wasn't about to have them running around with a lot of money until then. All of that was kept hidden. Only he and Lowe knew where.

One of the key elements of his Hoodsmen's success was an occasional arrest of a "gang member." A black hood found in the man's home was sufficient evidence to result in a hanging. Especially with Grant handling the prosecution's case. He wasn't a part of the scheme, though, simply an aggressive—and highly ambitious—lawyer with his eye on becoming governor or even senator someday. Hautrese had fueled his ambitions with the assignment, noting the high-profile opportunity would yield much publicity for him. He handled Grant carefully, like a chess master with his queen.

The occasional arrest and subsequent trial had been enough to keep the press from examining the situation more closely. It had also made him something of a hero to the railroads and post office. Their rewards were generous.

"Of course it's brilliant." He smiled into the mirror once more. "Of course."

Grabbing his hat from the bed, he placed it on his head, jauntily, and went back to the bookcase and took a handful of cigars from the humidor. Always smart to have cigars to distribute, he reminded himself as he shoved them into his inside coat pocket.

Not even Lowe realized the operation was set up so that Hautrese could deny any involvement with the Hoodsmen, if it ever came to that. Evidence of their duplicity was kept in a special file. He paid a whore to go to the telegraph office and send his messages about train and stagecoach schedules and their respective riches. She was pefect. Even her name, "Happy Harriet." No one paid attention to her and she could easily be eliminated without arousing suspicions about him.

He figured another year, two at the most, would do it. He would be rich. Really rich. So far, he had managed to transfer some of his recent gains into property as well as ownership of selected companies in the area. Some of the purchases were in his name; some had been done through a special trust. He owned a fine casino in Central City, although no one knew it. A large silver mine was his, too. Both holdings were thanks to the previous owners disappearing mysteriously. Lowe would also be wealthy. The others would receive a thousand dollars or so each. Although, in the back of his mind was floating the idea of having Lowe kill them. It was something to consider.

Placing his withered left hand in his coat pocket, U.S. Marshal Hautrese left his room, locking it behind him. The room was free to him, an ongoing gift from the apartment owner, in exchange for certain considerations. He walked down the hallway, greeted two traveling salesmen on their way to lunch and pulled the silver watch from his vest pocket. It was 11:25. Enough time for a drink before the lunch with the senator.

"Good day to you, Mr. Zimmerman," Hautrese hailed as he walked across the lobby. His detail-focused mind told him the carpet needed some vigorous sweeping, but he kept the thought to himself.

"Good day to you, too, Marshal Hautrese," the hotel clerk said, please to be greeted and by name.

Outside, Hautrese hesitated, then warmly addressed the teamster working his loaded wagon down the street. A hearty wave came back to him. He tipped his hat to a passing man and wife and let his gaze stay a moment on the woman's face. Her twinkling eyes invited more inspection some other time.

Everywhere he looked, Denver City was bustling, brimming with new people and new wealth. He estimated the town had doubled in the last year alone. Silver was becoming the sweet allure, as gold seemed more and more difficult to find. Central City might have the edge in social niceties, but Denver City wasn't far behind, he mused to himself. Tall buildings shoved their way into the cool air with the majesty of mountains in the distance. Men and women of every walk of life jammed the sidewalks. Miners, gamblers, teamsters, businessmen and sophisticated eastern salesmen mixed with women in fancy dress and common thread.

A six-horse Concord stage rumbled past and jogged his memory to remind his men not to rob any stage, or anything else, while Bass Tillman was being tried. In fact, the Hoodsmen would not come alive again after the old attorney was dead, shot or hanged. He had already decided that. Instead, after a month or so, a "new" gang would resume their selected string of holdups. There would be no hoods. In their place, his men would wear kerchiefs as masks, and long coats. Some would suspect they were a renewed version of the James Gang. He giggled.

From across the street came the telegraph operator's assistant, running and waving a paper in his hand. "Marshal Hautrese! Marshal Hautrese!"

Waiting for the young man to reach him, Hautrese nodded and greeted passing townspeople as the busy settlement swelled into a full day of business. He liked the activity; he liked people, he thought. "As long as they do what I want them to do," he told himself and smiled.

Handing the young messenger a coin for his trouble, he immediately focused on the paper:

WILL COME TO DENVER LATER STOP WILL BE A NEED FOR ME IN LONGMONT FIRST STOP EASTER

Hautrese laughed and slapped the paper against his thigh. "Perfect! Lowe, Grant—and Sontag. That's three to draw to," he proclaimed loudly. He wondered, to himself, if getting the noted executioner to stay was Lowe's idea. Probably, he decided. Probably.

"Congratulations on your arrest, Marshal Hautrese." The voice was brisk and behind him.

Turning around, Hautrese saw it was one of the bank's clerks. "Good morning to you, Jeffrey. How are you this day?"

"Doing fine." The pudgy banker held out his hand in greeting. "Since I heard the news about that old gunfighter being the head of that awful gang. I thought for sure you were going to have to ask the army to come in. Seemed to me, folks were expecting an awful lot from a handful of lawmen."

"Well, thank you," Hautrese said and told him that a year-old federal law, Posse Comitatus, prohibited a U.S. Marshal from calling in the army for help. The clerk expressed surprise, concluded the army wasn't needed anyway and said good-bye.

Walking on, Hautrese wondered to himself how often the clerk ever read the newspaper. He had made certain the fact had been well publicized that the army had turned down his request for troops, just as he expected. The federal hindrance had actually kept him from worrying about military interference with the Hoodsmen.

"Only the federal government could do something so stupid," he muttered.

Still smiling, he walked down the street and slipped into the Denver City Marshal's office where he rented space, basically a desk and chair in the corner.

"Good day, Deputy Walton, where's your boss?" Hautrese said.

"How are you, Marshal Hautrese?" the black-goateed deputy said, looking up from the main desk. "Not sure where he is right now. Ah, you might try the First National, though. He was making the rounds, usually starts there." His expression indicated he would rather be making the rounds than sitting behind a desk. "Say, that Pinkerton man was in here earlier looking for you."

"Davidson?"

"Yeah, that's him." Deputy Walton glanced down at the badge on his shirt and rubbed it with his cuff. "Said he wanted to know if you were going with him on the stage. For the Bass Tillman trial."

"Thought he was going today," Hautrese said, leaning against the door frame. "Where was he headed?"

"Ah, the Denver Pacific office, I think."

"Good." Hautrese turned to leave.

"Shall I tell the marshal you were looking for him?" Deputy Walton's eyes indicated he wanted very much to impress Hautrese.

"Sure, but tell him it isn't anything urgent. I was just going to brief him on the big arrest we made."

Licking his lips, the lanky deputy worked up his courage to ask, "Marshal, is Bass Tillman really the head of that gang?"

Hautrese couldn't have asked for a better question. His answer would be all over town by tomorrow. "Yes, he is. I guess once an outlaw always an outlaw."

"But I heard he was an attorney. Done some good things in Longmont. That's what I heard anyway." Deputy Walton's face was a study in seriousness.

"Can you think of any better way to hide what you're really up to?" Hautrese's gaze sparkled with triumph and his mouth glared with white teeth.

Returning the grin, the deputy chewed on the question a moment. "Reckon so, unless it's a lawman." He looked up, enjoying his observation.

For an instant, Hautrese thought the man was implying something about him, blinked and his mind reassured him it was nothing but a dumb joke. "Right," he said and squinted. "Say, you're not a Hoodsman, are you?"

The question slammed against Deputy Walton's expression, changing it instantly from mischievous to concerned.

"Oh—Oh no, Marshal Hautrese. I—I was just funnin'."

"So was I," Hautrese said, pointing at the worried deputy and laughing.

Walton burst into a loud bellow, full of relief. That helped him regain his sense of office and he said, "Say, there's a telegram here for you. On our desk after breakfast, instead of yours. It's from your deputy, E. J. Vorak." Walton stood and held out the folded sheet. "I read it—by mistake. Thought it was one of ours. Sorry."

"Not a problem. We're all in the same boat, aren't we?" Hautrese stepped farther into the office and took the outstretched offering with his right hand, leaving his left in his coat pocket.

Returning to his chair, Walton watched as the U.S. Marshal read the wire. It wasn't important to him; nothing from Vorak ever was. He was one of the honest officers who worked for him; he had been a deputy marshal when Hautrese was appointed. Hautrese was certain the man was too old for the job and would one day die from attempting a young man's task. Vorak had been to his office only twice; once when he agreed to stay on as deputy marshal working for him, and another time when he brought in some prisoners for trial. The rest of the year, the old deputy marshal worked the western region. Vorak carried a sawed-off shotgun in a shoulder quiver, along with a rifle and a handgun, and, according to the stories, wasn't shy about using any of them.

Vorak's terse note indicated that he was going after some men who had stolen army mules and would report when he found them. That would be Vorak, Hautrese mused. Protecting federal property. Yes, sir, straight as an arrow. A strange shiver passed through him as he lowered the note. Topper Lowe had warned him to keep Vorak as far away as possible. He remembered what Lowe had said, "That son of a bitch may be long in the tooth, but he's one fierce warrior. Seen him come at three men, taking lead and not feeling it. Stopped 'em cold, he did." Hautrese reminded himself that the story occurred years ago.

He pointed at the deputy again and left with the man's fawning response trailing him. On the sidewalk again, he passed two men deep in discussion. Hautrese paid little attention. His thoughts were on the Pinkerton man and the railroad executives. He should go see them and remind them of the generous reward they had offered for the capture of the Hoodsman leader himself.

The railroads had become a major factor in Colorado since the Denver Pacific linked with the Union Pacific in Cheyenne. That was almost ten years ago. A handful of years later, the Denver and Rio Grande joined the mix, followed by the Kansas and Pacific. Railroad people were vicious when it came to capturing and prosecuting anyone robbing them. So were the U.S. mail bureaucrats, for that matter. Of course, neither had been able to stop the James-Younger Gang—or the Hoodsmen.

"Except the great Marshal Byron Hautrese," he muttered under his breath and chuckled, deciding to take the stage to Longmont. It would make a grand entrance for him, as well as giving him a chance to talk firsthand with his "Hoodsmen" deputies Lowe, Cateson and Drucker.

Passing the Tarkinson Gunsmith Shop, he had an idea. The regional vice president of the Denver Pacific would be thrilled to have a souvenir of the Hoodsmen gang. A gun from the awful bandits would be something the executive would prize. He backed up two steps and went inside.

Chapter 17

The morning stage arrived only an hour late into Longmont and with it came District Attorney Touren Grant. A handsome man with flowing blond hair, a Roman nose and a proud bearing, he was tired of the coach's jostling and thumping. He was eager to get cleaned up and meet with Deputy Marshal Lowe to review the case with him.

This trial was too important for any slipups, any surprises, any mistakes.

Victory would propel him a long way, maybe all the way to the governor's seat. Over and over again on the stage ride, in rhythm with the churning wheels of the six-horse coach, he had told himself what an opportunity this trial would be. The leader of the Hoodsmen gang. Bass Tillman. Governor Grant. The leader of the Hoodsmen gang. Bass Tillman. Governor Grant. The leader of the Hoodsmen gang. Bass Tillman. Governor Grant. A soft chuckle to himself had followed, leaving the other three passengers wondering what had amused him.

He licked his dried lips, stepped from the still-wobbling coach and brushed off his tailored gray suit. It was wrinkled from travel and he needed a bath and a shave. The matching vest controlled the paunch that had become an unwelcome part of him. Too much French food and wine, he knew. It was a difficult habit to break. His gray-gloved hand touched his striped silk tie to ensure its proper placement against the paper collar and then adjusted the bowler that matched his suit. A slight tilt to the right.

Turning toward the driver, he asked for directions to the Empire Hotel. The weary man was busy helping a woman passenger from the coach, but stopped to point.

"I assume my luggage will be delivered to my room," Grant proclaimed as he strutted away.

The driver could only stammer agreement as he turned to assist the other passengers.

In Grant's gloved right hand was a leather satchel containing material for possible use at the hearing and subsequent trail. Newspaper clippings of Hoodsmen crimes made up much of the file. The most important story was a lurid account of a train holdup that resulted in a dead engineer and a dead Pinkerton agent. There were more yellowing stories of other train holdups with the Hoodsmen blamed, as well as multiple stagecoach holdups with the U.S. mail taken. And accounts of banks robbed. Even a front-page story about the Boulder County Fair being robbed. Details of each previous trial of an arrested Hoodsman were filed alphabetically, along with related case information. Additional pages outlined ideas of how to handle the Bass Tillman trial, and a lengthy list of questions for Lowe and his men.

A leather-bound Bible completed the valise's contents. It was a great courtroom device. Looking through the pages while the other attorney was making a point to the jury guaranteed distraction. Of course, as a onetime minister, he liked using this background when possible. Depending on the court timing, he would seek out the town minister and volunteer to give a Sunday sermon. It always helped the jury pool.

A boy darted from the sidewalk and spun to a stop in front of the advancing Grant. Annoyed, the district attorney shoved his left hand into his pocket and stuttered to a stop.

"Yes, my son, what is it?"

"Are you a salesman?" the boy asked. "My friend, Bobby, thinks you're a salesman. From New York."

Grant smoothed his groomed mustache. "Tell Bobby he's wrong. Now, please. I have important business to attend to."

The boy frowned, but didn't move. "So . . . are you here for the Bass Tillman trial?"

Grant allowed himself a slight smile. "Well, maybe so."

"I thought so. Wait till I tell Bobby I was right." The boy put his hands on his hips. "Mr. Tillman is a lawyer, ya know." He looked around to see if anyone was close. "And he's got a gun—in jail."

"What?"

"Mr. Tillman has a gun—and he's in jail," the

boy explained, unhappy to have to repeat the statement. "I didn't think you could do that."

"You can't." Grant slid past the boy and headed once more toward the hotel. Lowe would have some explaining to do about this, he fumed to himself.

Grant was surprised to see him waiting in his two-room suite; the federal deputy marshal lay on the bed with his knee-high cavalry boots propped over the side. His military-styled jacket was unbuttoned and his hat was pushed foreward on his forehead.

"Good morning, Grant, glad to have you aboard," Lowe said jovially as he sat up, but making no attempt to stand or shake the district attorney's hand.

"Good morning, my ass. What's this I hear about your prisoner being armed in jail?" Grant howled. "What the hell's going on?"

Looking peevish, Lowe wrestled with his quirt and tried to explain. He blamed the situation on the local sheriff who was a friend of Bass Tillman's. He said the sheriff would disarm the prisoner before the hearing.

"And you're satisfied with that?" Grant shook his head in disbelief. "Who's running this arrest— you or some hick lawman? I want that man disarmed. Right now."

Lowe stood and let the quirt dangle from his right hand now at his side. "That's not going to happen, Grant. You can rant and rave all you want, but it's not going to happen. Maybe your time would be better spent getting ready for the hearing." His face became an evil smirk. "I'd hate to see the newspapers talking about how you screwed up an important arrest."

"I'll bet you would."

Grant moved to the shiny table in the small adjacent room and began methodically emptying his briefcase, making piles of related material.

"How 'bout you an' me getting some breakfast downstairs—an' talking this thing over?" Lowe asked. "Or did they stop an' feed you?"

Grant spun around. "Do you know when the hearing is set? I'd like to meet with Judge Nelene first, if I can arrange it. Who's the opposing counsel? Is Tillman going to use another lawyer from around here? What's his name?"

"Nelene hasn't made it to town yet. Tillman's gonna defend himself."

Grant broke into laughter. Lowe joined him, snapping his quirt against the floor. With the tension between them broken, they soon decided to meet downstairs in fifteen minutes. Lowe would head there now and Grant would follow as soon as he washed up.

Downstairs in the adjoining restaurant, Lowe was already eating when Grant finally joined him, wearing a different outfit. His black broadcloth suit looked freshly pressed, although Lowe knew it couldn't be. Grant held a pair of black gloves in his left hand and adjusted his black bowler to a familiar tilt. He paused at the bottom of the stairway, letting his presence be seen by anyone in the hotel lobby, and proceeded to the restaurant.

"Wondered if you'd gotten lost up there," Lowe said, his mouth filled with scrambled eggs.

"First impressions count," Grant said curtly

and sat down across from the deputy marshal, "but you wouldn't understand."

"I understand that I'm the one who caught the leader of the Hoodsmen," Lowe said, between sips of his coffee. "And I understand that you'll be blamed if the sonvabitch goes free. How's that for understanding?" For emphasis, he jammed his fork into a previously cut piece of ham and shoved it into his mouth.

A tired waiter came to the table and began pouring a mug of coffee for Grant.

"I prefer hot tea."

"Ah, sure," the waiter said. "You having any breakfast?"

Grant studied Lowe's plate for an instant, then declared, "Bring me one egg. Poached. Well poached." He pointed in the direction of the plate and added, "Some of that ham, too. With no gristle." He rubbed his smooth chin and enjoyed the light scent of rum from shaving. "Oh, and I would like a small portion of potatoes. Crisp, but not too crisp."

"Sure." The waiter turned and retreated to the kitchen.

As Grant waited for his tea and breakfast, Lowe briefed him on the situation, starting with Bass Tillman's arrest for murdering two federal officers and for leading the Hoodsmen gang. Hautrese had decided their best case was to link Bass and Jacob Tillman to the Highland Bank robbery, along with Virgil Crimmler. The short deputy marshal talked smoothly about what he wanted Grant to think had taken place. After the federal marshals learned of the bank robbery, Lowe ex-

plained, their special posse tracked the two outlaws to a farm that belonged to Bass Tillman's son.
They had suspected both Tillmans of involvement
with the Hoodsmen for some time; the son had
been posing as a part-time deputy in Longmont
and the father, as an attorney.

He warmed to his task between swigs of coffee
and mouthfuls of egg and ham, liking the story
more and more as he told it. He said Jacob Tillman tried to shoot it out and was killed. They
managed to capture the other bank robber alive
and Virgil Crimmler told them about the Tillmans and their roles in the Hoodsmen gang.
Crimmler had also warned them Bass Tillman
was coming to take the bank money and hide it,
and tell the outlaws what their next holdup would
be. Bass Tillman arrived later and murdered the
two posse men waiting for him. Deputy Marshal
Drucker had evidently chased after him and was
probably killed as well.

Crimmler was being held in a safe place out of
town and had agreed to testify against Bass Tillman, if given clemency. As Lowe finished this reve-
lation, the waiter brought the mug of hot tea and set
it in front of Grant, who ignored the presentation.

"Good. Good," Grant said. "Has Bass Tillman
admitted to the killings?"

"Only to wounding them." Lowe snickered.
"He brought them in lyin' over Drucker's horse
with a long-winded story about being ambushed."

"That's convenient."

"Yeah, convenient." Lowe swallowed the last of
his eggs. "We don't know what happened to
Deputy Marshal Drucker. He went after Tillman

after the bastard shot our men—and we haven't heard from him since."

"So, you figure Tillman killed him, too."

"Yeah, can't prove it, though. Not yet, anyway."

Grant smiled and sipped his tea, then added a spoonful of sugar, stirred and tried it again. "Maybe he'll tell us that—at the hearing."

As he spread a large wad of jam on his biscuit, Lowe looked up. "Don't underrate Bass Tillman. He's already wounded Cateson—while in jail—and, somehow, managed to gut-shoot one of our posse men when he was going to take a leak."

"That takes us back to the gun," Grant said. "I still don't understand."

"Wait till you meet the local sheriff. A stubborn German. Then you will."

"Hmmm." Grant watched as his breakfast was served.

Lowe bit into his biscuit and jam, wiping his mouth with the back of his hand.

Grant pretended he didn't see. "What else have you got?"

"We found one of them black hoods in Tillman's hotel room."

"Really?"

"Yeah, really."

"That's excellent." Grant tasted his poached egg and immediately waved at the waiter to get his attention. "This is barely warm."

"Yeah, sometimes, that's so." Lowe drank deeply from his mug to assist swallowing the biscuit. "Pretend it's hot."

Immediately Grant waved again at the waiter, busy across the room at a table with four miners.

Annoyed, the bald-headed man returned and left with Grant's plate. The district attorney retrieved his list of notes and questions from his inside coat pocket. He glanced at them, looking up occasionally like a deer at a watering hole.

Amused by Grant's manner, Lowe motioned for more coffee and the same waiter complied, pouring a fresh mug, and asked, hesitantly, if Grant wanted more tea.

"I will. When I get my breakfast," Grant declared louder than necessary.

"I'll check on it right away, sir."

"Good for you," Grant said and returned to his trial preparation concerns. "I'll want to talk with this Virgil Crimmler fellow—before I agree to anything."

"Sure. He'll say whatever you want," Lowe said, then thought better of the statement and clarified, "He's a Hoodsman an' he'll identify Bass Tillman as the boss."

Grant nodded. "About this hood from Tillman's room. Did you get—"

"Got a damn warrant," Lowe interrupted. "Wired Judge Weicker in Denver and he gave me the go-ahead."

"By wire?"

"Yeah."

"You have it, I assume."

"Course."

The waiter returned with Grant's breakfast and the handsome attorney pronounced it satisfactory and dismissed the relieved man, who said he would bring more tea. Picking at the potatoes with his fork, Grant asked for details about Cateson being wounded by the jailed Tillman. Lowe explained it was an attempted jailbreak. He reinforced the story by saying the local deputy was there at the time and would support that position.

"What about this . . . sheriff?" Grant tasted his egg a second time and joined it with a small bite of potato.

"Stay away from him. Frank Babbit. Damn German. He's a friend of Tillman's."

Grant's eyebrows posed in discovery. "Is he involved in the Hoodsmen?"

Lowe smiled and took a drink of his own coffee. He winced at its boiling intensity, coughed and answered, "Don't know. Can't prove it one way or the other. Obviously, one of his deputies, Jacob Tillman, was." He pursed his lips to ease the discomfort of the searing liquid. "Makes sense, though."

"Yes, it's a perfect place to hide, posing as a lawman," Grant observed as he cut into his ham.

"True enough." Lowe stared at his coffee to help keep a straight face. Hautrese was right. Of course. The cocky district attorney was more useful not knowing about the organization than if he did. Lowe chuckled to himself.

"What do you have on this . . . bank robbery?" Grant asked and placed a piece of ham in his mouth.

"Well, we've got eyewitnesses that say there were two men that did it. And we tracked them to Jacob Tillman's farm," Lowe replied, sipping his coffee gingerly and finding it acceptable. "Crimmler has already admitted they did it. We can bring in the Highland lawman—an' the bank president, if you want."

"For the trial, maybe. Is that all you have?"

"Well, I guess. Seems pretty cut-an'-dried to me."

"What about the money? Were they wearing those stupid hoods?" Grant swirled his fork within the potatoes and brought up a mouthful.

"Haven't found it yet. Crimmler said they were trying to fool us into thinking it wasn't Hoodsmen, so they used their neckerchiefs—for masks. He said it was Bass Tillman's idea."

After savoring the potatoes and a spoonful of poached egg, Grant changed subjects. "What does this Crimmler say about the Colorado Central holdup? The one where the engineer and a Pinkerton agent were killed."

Lowe ran his finger around the edge of his mug. "He was there." He paused for effect. "Says Bass Tillman shot the Pinkerton man. After the man gave up his gun."

Grant beamed. "That's certainly good news. I mean, it's good we're going to get the murderer finally." He licked his lips. "What about the engineer? Who shot him?"

"Dunno. I'll have to ask him."

"If it was Crimmler, I don't think we can let him go."

"Reckon it wasn't."

Grant focused on his breakfast for several minutes while Lowe retraced the evidence they had against Bass Tillman. At first, he was going to skip over the death of Jacob Tillman's wife, then thought he shouldn't let the prosecutor be surprised by that fact. His simple statement about her being killed during the gunfight between the Hoodsmen and federal marshals drew little more than an arched eyebrow from Grant.

As he drank the rest of his coffee, Lowe decided there was no advantage in sharing the fact they had tried to make the scene appear as if Indians had attacked the farm. This was, by far, the better story. It eliminated much of what he thought Bass would bring up in court and buttoned up some awkward loose ends. Bass Tillman would have a difficult time using any of that evidence against them, especially with Grant attacking his credibility.

From the back of the restaurant, a bulky man in a wrinkled suit of cheap cloth and a shirt with two small ink stains rushed to their table. *Longmont Advocate* editor Wallace Denson was eager to talk with the newly arrived prosecuting attorney.

"Good morning, sirs." Denson stood beside the table with his hat and a pad of paper in his hands resting in front of his groin. "I am the editor of the town newspaper—and I believe you, sir, are District Prosecutor Touren Grant."

Glancing at Lowe, who nodded approval, Grant stood and held out his hand. "Always glad to meet the backbone of a community. How are you, Mr. Denson?"

"Fine, sir. Just fine. Please forgive my interrupting your breakfast, but I wonder if it would be possible to talk with you later, sir, about this Bass Tillman thing." He looked at Lowe and smiled. "Marshal Lowe has already been kind enough to give me some of the background of the arrest of this heinous Hoodsmen leader—and I hoped to get some of your thoughts, too. My readers are very concerned about justice."

"As am I, sir. As am I." Grant pulled a silver watch from his vest pocket and studied it. "Would ten o'clock be convenient for you? In your offices?"

"Excellent, sir. Excellent." Denson put his hat on his head, dropped the pad and knelt to retrieve it. He stood again, his face slightly reddening. "If it would be all right with you, I would like to photograph you as well." He smiled his best smile. "It's not often that Longmont receives such an important statesman."

"It would be my pleasure."

Lowe and Grant watched the editor work his way out of the restaurant, stopping twice to apparently tell diners of Grant's presence, as the two tables of men immediately turned toward him.

Returning to his seat, the blond prosecutor wiped his mouth with his napkin, laid it back on his lap and sought the rest of his tea. A frown preceded his next question. "Now, where were we?" He glanced at his own list. "Ah yes. Would Crimmler know what happened to Marshal Drucker?"

Lowe shook his head. "No. Remember, we took him away—to a safe place—while Bill and his two posse men waited for Bass Tillman to show up."

"And that's when Tillman killed . . . our officers?"

"Yeah. After Tillman shot our two posse men and got away, we figure, Marshal Drucker went after him alone." Lowe grimaced. "Wish he'd come for us, but . . ."

Grant laid down his fork carefully across his plate to symbolize the completion of his meal.

"You haven't looked for him? My God, man, he may be lying badly wounded, somewhere!"

Lowe didn't like the rebuke, but said they had already looked for him and would send out another search patrol as soon as possible, then brought up his own concern about the jury. "You know, this Tillman's pretty well liked around here." He drew a cigar from his shirt pocket and lit it. "You worried about getting a, ah, fair jury?"

Grant straightened his shoulders. "That hasn't been a problem before, Marshal Lowe. I find people want these awful Hoodsmen brought to justice—whoever they are." He allowed himself a smug moment of silence and continued. "But we'll have to watch the sympathy factor at the trial. It's a card I'd play if I were Tillman."

Pushing back his chair, Lowe couldn't resist a smile as a circle of white smoke cleared his head. Grant had never noticed that certain key jurymen in the past had been motivated to vote correctly, either with a bribe or a threat. Obviously, he was as naive and egotistical, to think he was the magic, as Hautrese had said.

Both men stood. Grant advised that he wanted to interview Cateson and Wright so he would have a sense of their testimony, as well as the outlaw Crimmler. He also wanted to talk with the local deputy Lowe had mentioned. Lowe reinforced that the young man was eager to testify, adding it was the deputy's desire to become sheriff. He didn't mention William Manchester had already shared what he had learned from his conversations with Bass Tillman.

"Hmm, maybe we can help him along on that," Grant said.

"Yeah, I thought so, too. I'll have him come to your hotel room," Lowe said. "I'll take you to see Crimmler. Don't want to take a chance on anyone seeing him in town." He cocked his head. "You paying for this or am I?"

Grant blinked. "Well, thank you, Marshal Lowe. That's very generous of you." He placed his hat on his head carefully. "I'm going to see the town minister."

Lowe laid two coins on the table. "Don't forget Denson."

"Of course. Of course."

"You wanna meet Bass Tillman?"

"Should I?"

Lowe curled the quirt on his wrist into a ball, examining its leather bindings. "Well, you'd hear quite a tale. Might help you be ready."

"Of course. We'll let the fool tell his tale—to me. He's probably foolish enough to do it." Grant looked up at Lowe. "Is this the best place to eat? If it is, this is going to be a hard time."

"Yeah, it's the best. Have a good stew. At night."

His chest rose and fell. "Ah, the sacrifices one must make for public service."

Lowe ran the closed fingers of his free hand along the quirt.

Grant led their way out of the room, pausing at first at one table, then another, to introduce himself.

Lowe continued without stopping and snapped the quirt on the boardwalk as he stepped outside. He liked its abrupt bark and the way passersby turned to see what had happened.

Chapter 18

The shock of his arrest had finally dissipated in Bass's mind, leaving a residue of both depression and determination. The bright spots in waiting had been the visits from Lucius Henry and Benjamin Ringly. Sheriff Babbit had brought over clean clothes from his hotel room and offered reports on Othello's condition. He also shared the bad news that Lowe's horse had been reshod and the cut shoe had disappeared. So had all of the Indian articles at the farm.

Time went slowly, helped some by reading through the newspapers Babbit had brought. Babbit told him Denson thought the back issues were being requested to help build the case against Bass. The old attorney forced himself to make notes of suspected Hoodsmen crimes, dates and locations, countering them, if possible, with where he had actually been and who could verify it.

Deputy Manchester advised that he had not been successful in locating Virgil Crimmler's whereabouts, nor had he found any evidence of wrongdoing in Cateson's or Wright's background. Neither man was wanted in Texas, he said. He had not had time to prepare a list of Hoodsmen crimes and Bass told him it wasn't necessary. The young deputy seemed distant and preoccupied, spending time in the jail only when necessary.

Everything in Bass wanted the relief of being in court. Now. Now! He kept trying to remind himself of the need for patience—and the need to continue refining his own defense. But there was a point—in any battle, of any kind—when it was time to fight. Yet that timing was out of his hands. Judge Nelene would determine that—and he hadn't even arrived in town.

He had noticed the change in William Manchester, a change that seemed triggered by the death of the unstable Ernie Dawson. In some ways, it was understandable; a lot of violence had erupted in the young man's life very quickly. Especially the deaths of Jacob and Mary Anne. Yet Bass sensed something else was there.

It was late in the afternoon and the spring sun had decided it was time to act mature. A four o'clock sun poured into the barred windows of the jail. Sheriff Babbit and Bass were playing chess, with the attorney sitting on his cell bunk and the town constable seated in the desk chair pulled into the cell. Babbit's shotgun was propped against his left leg; Bass's Colt lay beside him.

U.S. Deputy Marshal John Cateson had opted to sit outside the jail and was dozing in a sidewalk chair; his associate Wright had left town with Lowe. Bass told Babbit he thought they were looking for the missing third deputy marshal, Bill Drucker. Quietly, he had shared that situation with his old friend and both wondered what Easter Sontag was up to. Bass had shared his thought that the celebrated hangman had decided it was best for his career to avoid Longmont until the trial was over. Babbit countered with the observation that Sontag was probably a part of the Hoodsmen operation and just biding his time to reappear.

"Vhen *ist der* first time ve played *der* chess?" Babbit asked, forcing a change of subject. He followed that by shoving his black bishop diagonally across the board, knocking aside Bass's white knight.

"The better question would be . . . when was the last time I beat you?" Bass studied the evolving assemblage of dark and light shapes before him, trying to keep his mind from retreating into black places within. "You'd think a fellow would show some courtesy to his guest." Finally, he moved his rook to a threatening position and Babbit immediately retreated with his bishop.

"I think ve vere *der* guns for *Herr* Sullivan. *Ja*, that *ist* vhen it vere."

Bass looked up at Babbit's strained face. He knew his friend was torn between his sworn duty and their long friendship. In some ways, this was harder on the German lawman than it was on him. Both men had outlived their gun-handling days and become respectable citizens with families. In Babbit's case, children now grown and on their own. Both, however, had lost children to sickness. Each had comforted the other during that darkness. Both had found comfort in discovering God and the discipline of churchgoing.

Bass had saved the sheriff's life in their younger gun days—and probably saved his job by stopping the bank robbery. Babbit had given Bass the will to live beyond Settie's death and saved his life now by his steadfast approach to the attorney's jail stay.

On the floor of the cell was today's edition of the *Longmont Advocate*. A lead story outlined the case against Bass Tillman, referring to him as a longtime gunman and outlaw leader. The piece featured the shoot-out at the Tillman farm between Hoodsmen and federal marshals after they tracked the outlaws from the Highland Bank holdup. In the top center of the story was a photograph of Touren Grant looking poised and confident. The cutline under the picture described him as an attractive candidate for the next governor's election. Bass had asked for a copy and made notes on his trial preparatory outline.

Babbit tried to make a joke of the story, saying that Bass had obviously offended Denson. Instead of laughing, Bass responded by saying that he had threatened the newspaperman once after Denson was caught by Bass trying to cheat an area farmer out of his land through a fraudulent deed the editor had printed himself. Babbit swallowed his own chuckle and returned his attention to the chess match.

"I vill be moving *der* knight *und* taking your pawn," Babbit said triumphantly.

"Well, if you do, you'll be in check." Bass motioned toward the board's situation.

"Damn. Vhy *ist* that so?"

"Kinda like life, I guess," Bass mused. "It just does to us what it's going to do."

Babbit made a less aggressive move. "In *der* old days, ve vould *nein haff bien* vaiting around for others to attack."

"In the old days, we didn't think much beyond our noses." Bass moved his once-endangered pawn forward one square. "Or, rather, the barrels of our guns."

"If *der* trial does *nein* go . . . so vell, I . . ."

"Don't say it, Frank."

"Bass, ve are *nein* going to let—"

A commotion outside the jail interrupted their game and discussion. A familiar Scottish brogue announced the intentions of one Timbel McKinsey. From beyond the jail door, Cateson declared his intention to keep the Scottish farmer from entering.

" 'Deed, it *canna* be. *Na. Na. Haud a wee.*" McKinsey's voice cleared the door. "Ye step aside now, laddie. I *wadna* be botherin' ye. *Raither* I be *gaun* inside *tae* see me friend, Bass Tillman."

"*Ja.* I best be looking at *das.*" Babbit grabbed his shotgun and headed for the door.

Before he was halfway across the room, the door swung open. It was Cateson doing the push, annoyed at being awakened.

He held his wounded arm close to his side as he said, "Here's a damn dirt farmer to see you, Bass. Tell him to quit jabberin'. An' no playing that damn squeeze box."

Standing in the doorway was McKinsey with an accordion on his hip, held there by a sling across his shoulder.

"*Wadna* ye be mindin' *soom* company?" McKinsey announced. "Sarah be doing our tradin' in *thae* store of Mr. Geiger and his fine son." He motioned over his shoulder. "She told me *tae* be seeing *tae* you."

Cateson grumbled something, but it was unintelligible as the Scotsman closed the heavy door with the deputy marshal outside.

"Come in, Timbel. Come in," Bass welcomed.

He wondered if the Scotsman had just heard the news when he and his wife came to town. His feelings about seeing the farmer were mixed; Bass had intended on not mentioning his being with him in the pursuit of Drucker. He hadn't quite decided about whether to mention Sontag or not. If he did, it would simply be to drop the name and provide some momentary confusion for the prosecution.

"*Thae* fine constable outside *hoes* not a love of music, I see." McKinsey patted the accordion as he walked toward Babbit. "Likely one o' those who be silent while *thae* rest o' us sing out *thae* Lord's praises on *thae* blessed Sabbath. *Weel, guid eneuch.* Lord pity his soul, I be sayin'."

"Probably so." Bass couldn't help chuckling. "Sheriff Frank Babbit, have you met Timbel McKinsey? He has the farm near . . . my Jacob's."

"It *ist gut* to meet *du*, sir." Babbit held out his hand, cradling the shotgun to his chest.

"Aye, and you, sir, indeed. I be bringin' me box.

It's always on me saddle." He raised his chin. "One ne'er be knowin' when a song be needed *Fine a ken*." He looked at Bass for the first time. "Ye'r a *sicht fir sair een*, Bass, me friend."

Unsure of how to respond, Babbit asked the Scotsman if he would like some coffee. He readily agreed and said his wife would be bringing over some homemade cookies later. She had insisted on baking them this morning. As Babbit headed for the coffeepot on the stove, McKinsey announced that he had learned of Bass's situation from Easter Sontag yesterday evening.

"Easter Sontag? Really?"

"*Weel*, it be *maire'n* of a surprise to Sarah an' me, I be tellin' ye." McKinsey waved his arms in support of his story. "There he be, sure as ye please, at me door. *Weill* into *thae* cups he be."

Bass stood and walked to the opened cell door, but not past it. "What did he say?"

"He be tellin' me o' your bein' here an' that ye be innocent, o' course," McKinsey said, dropping his voice toward the end of the statement. "Me Sarah, she asks him to be stayin' on for supper, but he says no. He *wull na byde a wee*. Polite, o' course. An' in a crack, he be gone. That's *thae richt way o't*."

"Wonder where he was going."

He accepted the hot mug from Babbit. "Thank ye. Steamin' *haut*, it be." He blew on the surface. "*Weel*, I know *naught* where he goes."

Babbit asked Bass if he wanted some coffee and he declined; then the sheriff moved next to the front of the desk and leaned against it. Bass invited the Scotsman to sit in the empty chair in the center of the cell and he accepted, setting his accordion in his lap and holding the mug with both hands.

Before Bass could say anything, McKinsey blurted that he intended to be at his hearing and his trial, and that he would testify about the bank robbers they ran into at the forest cabin—and about his shooting Drucker. His face was white, but his jaw was set.

"*Weel, guid eneuch,* if 'tis *thae* last thing I be doin', 'twill be *thae* tellin' o' *thae* truth. Swearin' *thae* oath to you, I be."

"Thank you, Timbel, but I don't want you to do that." Bass patted the Scotsman's knee. "There is no proof of Drucker being killed." He shook his head. "There's no reason for you to get mixed up in this. You shouldn't even be here."

"*Na, na,* me friend." McKinsey's jaw pushed even farther forward. "I tell me Sarah what *thae* doin' be—an' she tells me *tae* be clearin' me throat an' doin' *thae* tellin'. Aye, that she did." He swallowed. "Course, me wantin' *tae* do so . . . before."

Bass glanced at Babbit, who was listening and watching the door. In a few sentences, Bass explained the situation to McKinsey and what he hoped to prove in court. McKinsey's expressions kept changing as the situation became clearer to him.

"*Taen up wi this* trial *spiking,* are ye now?"

"It's the only way that makes any sense, Timbel."

McKinsey sipped his coffee, looked at Babbit for an instant, then back at Bass. "*Weel,* ye be a man o' *thae* gun, ar' ye *naught?*"

"That was a long time ago, my friend. A long time ago."

"*Naught* so long ago, I be seein' ye, remember?" McKinsey pointed his finger, resting the mug on his accordion with his other hand.

Bass shook his head again. "That's not the way. This time. Maybe it never was." He reiterated what he felt must be done in the courtroom. "If I don't, my Jacob and his Mary Anne died for no reason."

"Aye, it is out *o' thocht*. Out *o' thocht*."

Bass leaned forward. "Here's what I want you to do, Timbel. You are a brave man—and a fine friend to my family—and to me. It is for your sake—and your Sarah's." His shoulders rose and fell. "If they think you know anything at all, they will hunt you down and kill you. Do you understand?"

McKinsey was silent.

Bass rubbed his chin, searching for the words that would convince the Scotsman to stay away. "I want you to walk out of this jail—and as you leave, tell Cateson, the one outside, that you hope I swing from a tall rope. Say the only reason you came was to see for yourself that the leader of the Hoodsmen had finally been captured."

"I *canna* be sayin' such."

"Do it for Sarah. Believe me, if I thought there was a better way, I'd be asking you."

McKinsey was quiet again.

"Please, Timbel. You have to—and you have to convince Cateson. You have to."

Slowly, the Scotsman stood, shifting his accordion back to his hip. " '*Tis a muckle o*' a day when *guid* men must part so. I be prayin' for ye, Bass Tillman."

"I would like that."

"I *culd* be singing' an' playin the box a wee for ye a'fore I go."

"That's not necessary. Really."

Pursing his lips, McKinsey stood and lifted his accordion to his side. "*Thae* moon, I be lookin' at. Last night. Ready to be your friend, she be."

"I can use all the friends I can get." He was reminded of Nancy Spirit Bear's comment about Grandfather Moon guiding The River.

With that, McKinsey shook his hand, walked past Babbit, nodded his greeting and left. Outside, they could hear the Scotsman telling Cateson what Bass had asked.

"You think Cateson bought it?" Bass asked.

Babbit stood and took several steps from the desk. "Hard to tell. *Der* Scotsman did a full set o' swearin', it sounded like." He pushed his hat brim back on his head. "Not sure I know what all those words be meanin'."

"Now you know how we feel when you get going," Bass teased.

Babbit smiled, started to return to the cell and looked again out of the window. "Someone's coming, Bass. I think it's Judge Nelene. Did *nein* get a *gut* look, though. I think that Grant fellow *ist* with him."

"Quick. Take the chair out and close the door to my cell."

"*Ja. Ja.* I vill."

By the first knock on the jail door, Babbit had shut the door and sat down in the chair in the middle of the room. His appearance was one of someone on guard for intruders.

"This is Judge Orrick Nelene. Open up."

"I vill be coming."

Babbit opened the heavy door and stepped back. Following the heavily built magistrate into the office was the stylishly dressed Touren Grant, decked out in a blue suit with a deep crimson vest and a hat with a matching red band. The judge was a powerful-appearing man of fifty or so, with a sharp widow's peak centering his furrowed forehead. In his left hand was a wide-brimmed hat that had seen many days of travel and harsh weather, matching the stories in his face. A black cigar controlled the corner of his mouth. Uncombed hair was a mixture of gray, brown and sand color and creased heavily by his hat. A long coat was covered with trail dust and he looked like a man who had not slept well for some time.

For that matter, he looked more like a tough cattleman than a federal judge. His nickname of "Open Range Nelene" was appropriate for many reasons. Indeed, he was a transplanted Texan with family involved in the cattle business there. Bass had faced the ornery judge once before, defending a black man accused of robbing a white man's mule. The all-white jury decided in favor of the prosecution and the man was hanged. The white-haired attorney didn't like the judge's manner then and expected little change now, but he had no choice.

"Marshal Babbit, I have come to talk with the two lawyers who will try this case," Judge Nelene declared. "There are certain things I expect in my courtroom—and certain things I will not stand for." He took a hard swipe at the dust on his coat and looked up again. "What's this I hear about your prisoner being armed while in your custody?"

Bass was more than a little surprised at his old friend's response.

"Judge Nelene, it *ist mein* job to see *mein* prisoner *ist* getting his day in court." Babbit looked the judge in the face. "*Das* means I must see that he *ist* safe—from those who would *nein* vant him to have that day." Babbit pointed at Cateson, who was entering the room behind them. "*Der* federal lawmen do *nein* vant justice, they vant to make lies—*und* they vant to keep on robbing and stealing. They vant to kill Bass Tillman because he knows they are *der* Hoodsmen."

Both Grant's and Nelene's faces received the statement with shock.

Babbit wasn't finished. "They tried to kill me *und* my deputy," he said. "If *mein* prisoner *nein* had *der* gun, I vould not be here to tell you about it."

"Son of a bitch, that's quite a tale, Sheriff," Judge Nelene finally replied, removing the cigar from his mouth with his free hand.

"One of their posse men tried to kill *mein* prisoner vhen he vere unarmed *und* handcuffed. Handcuffed!"

Licking his lips, Grant declared, "Judge, it is clear we don't have an impartial local constable here. I must insist on federal marshals taking over completely."

"*Nein. Herr* Grant, I vill not do so." Babbit didn't wait for the judge to respond. "*Herr* Tillman vill give me his gun vhen ve go to *der* hearing. This he has promised. *Nein* before. I vill *nein* let him be vithout *der* gun until then."

"You accepted the promise of an outlaw killer? What kind of judgment is that?" Grant's questions were condescending.

"*Das ist der* promise of a *freund—und* an officer of *der* court." Babbit crossed his arms, reinforcing the presence of his shotgun. "*Das ist der* promise of an honest man. *Der* promise of a *gut* citizen taking stand against evil. *Ja, das ist* vhat it *ist*."

Clucking to himself, Judge Nelene waved off both men's further statements and strode toward the cell. Bass Tillman stood next to the bars. Silent. His eyes studying the advancing magistrate. He had been in the judge's court before; it had been a confrontational experience, with Bass ending up with a fee for contempt of court. Out of the corner of his eye, he saw Babbit move to his desk and stand behind it.

"Well, Bass Tillman," Judge Nelene said, "is it correct you intend to defend yourself as attorney of record in this matter?"

"I do, Your Honor."

"Why?"

"Don't know anybody better."

Judge Nelene's eyes became hooded as he concentrated on Bass's face. "Let's make sure you understand something. You're on trial for murdering two federal lawmen—and for complicity in a string of crimes commited by that damn Hoodsmen outfit. If convicted, you will hang."

Bass's eyes flashed and his fists took hold of the

bars. "Let's make sure you understand something, Judge, you and the flashy gent over there. My son and his wife were murdered by these so-called lawmen, because he knew they are the Hoodsmen. I defended myself against two men who tried to ambush me, while I was tending to their graves. If they're federal officers, this country has gone to hell in a handbasket."

Judge Nelene sucked on the thick cheroot and spoke through clenched teeth holding it in place, while white smoke slid out from the opposite side of his mouth. "Tillman, as I recall, the last time you were in my court, you were long on words an' short on facts."

"The last time I was in your court I defended an innocent man. Nothing's changed."

"I recall the jury didn't agree." Nelene's voice was thick with a growl as he moved the cigar to the other side of his mouth with his unseen tongue.

"That's because you let the prosecution present a whole lot of hearsay," Bass snapped. "No black man could have gotten a fair trial there."

Nelene's right eyebrow arched defiantly. "I reckon the job of the defense attorney is to challenge things like that."

"Hard to do when defense counsel gets censored—and found in contempt—and the judge asks the accused what he did with the mule—in front of the jury."

Nelene snorted, coughed, withdrew the cigar and scratched his butt. "Is that what happened? Forgot about that. Damn, you were a fiery bastard back then."

"I haven't changed."

Judge Nelene's eyes blinked. He replaced the cigar and spun around. "Gentlemen, unless there is more information I need to know, I'm headed for a stiff whiskey and a good steak. In that order. Good day."

Surprised, Grant began to babble about his intended list of witnesses and that he needed the same from Bass.

The judge opened the door and turned slightly toward the district attorney. "The hearing starts tomorrow. Eight o'clock." He slammed his hat back on his head. "Both of you better figure on cutting the fat from your talking. I'm a busy man."

He slammed the door behind him. The room was still and uncomfortable.

"You've still got time to get your picture taken, Grant," Bass said.

"I'm going to see you hang for your crimes." Grant's chin rose in declaration. " 'Thou art weighed in the balances, and art found wanting.' The book of Daniel, chapter five, verse twenty-seven."

Bass said, " 'Judge not, that ye be not judged.' Matthew, seven, one."

The blond-haired prosecutor squinted. He wasn't used to having Scripture played back to him. Was it a fluke? Bass Tillman was supposed to be this hard-bitten gunman. Grant didn't like surprises; no trial attorney did.

"Grant, for the moment, I'm going to give you the benefit of the doubt," Bass continued. "You may just be just an egotistical stooge for Hautrese and Lowe. If I find out different, you'll be going down with them. If not, you'll just be disgraced."

Grant hadn't expected this. He looked at Cateson, who was rubbing his wounded arm and avoiding his gaze. Not giving credence to an outlaw's bravado, the prosecutor turned slowly, a dramatic move, he told himself, and left the jail.

His mouth cocked open as usual, Cateson declared, "Tomorrow, boys. You won't be sounding so important come tomorrow. Judge Nelene's got your number, Tillman."

Without waiting for a response, he moved toward the door to resume his outside watch, stopped and looked at the stern sheriff.

"A smart man wouldn't stay too close to Bass Tillman," he snapped.

Babbit yanked opened a desk drawer and withdrew a handful of shells from the box. He straightened himself, kicked the drawer closed with his boot and placed the extra ammunition into his coat pocket.

As if just hearing Cateson, he looked up. "A smart man wouldn't mess with Bass Tillman."

Crimson took over Cateson's face. He opened his mouth to respond, then stomped out, slamming the door behind him. Babbit studied the closed door for a moment, shifting the shotgun cradled in his arms.

"Bass, I be praying that *du* are ready for *das*," he said softly.

"Me too, old friend."

Chapter 19

Bass watched his old friend mumbling in German, the shotgun shifting in his big hands back and forth, as if he was trying to decide whether to put it down or not. Sheriff Frank Babbit was never as stern as his Germanic appearance. Even when he was Frank Schafer, gunfighter. However, he was as steadfast as his steely gaze—and his word was a wall. He had given that word to the citizens of Longmont, to protect them to the best of his ability. Could the town best be served by having their constable challenge federal authorities? Was he helping them by helping his friend or was he breaking his promise?

"Frank, I don't want you to risk your job about this," Bass said quietly. "It's my doing, not yours."

"That *ist nein* your concern," Babbit said without looking at the cell. "What am I to say tomorrow—at *der* hearing?"

"The truth. Nothing more," Bass answered.

"*Ja.* I am ready."

Bass knew the subject of his friend's involvement wouldn't be discussed anymore. The German constable shared the latest rumor that U.S. Marshal Boston Hautrese himself was headed this way, along with a Pinkerton agent, for the trial.

"Some say *der* Pinkerton man coming *ist* Charlie Siringo himself," Babbit continued.

"I'd like that," Bass said. "Siringo's a straight shooter. I'd be very surprised if it's him, though. He's too likely to start backtracking on Lowe's tales."

"*Ja.*" Babbit twisted his face into a question. "Vhat about U.S. Deputy Marshal Vorak? *Du* think he be coming?"

"No. He's assigned a long way from here, Frank."

"*Ja,* but—"

"Frank, I could use some help on a couple more things for the hearing."

Babbit turned toward him, lowering the gun to his side. His expression was of a man who had made up his mind about something. His expression was one Bass had seen in their earlier fighting days. The expression of a warrior. A determined warrior.

"Did the Highland sheriff wire any description of the bank robbers?"

A frown preceded his eyes sparkling, Babbit declared, "*Ja.* It vere sent to all lawmen around, like always ve do. It *ist* somewhere in *mein* papers." Immediately, he went to his desk, yanked the wire statement free from a pile of papers and held it up.

"Good. May I see it?"

"Course. I do *nein verstehen* . . . I *nein* understand." Babbit hurried to the cell and handed it to Bass, who read it quickly and returned the sheet. "Better than I had hoped. Tomorrow, I will need you to testify. I'll ask you to read this and—"

"Vhat else *ist* needed?"

"How tall is this Virgil Crimmler?"

"He be short. About *der* height of Marshal Lowe," Babbit said and described the outlaw.

Nodding, Bass realized he had seen Crimmler at Lowe's morning camp, said so, and asked, "I need a Bible. Don't you have one in your desk? One in English?"

Babbit let a gentle smile creep onto his chiseled face. "It *ist* different than *der* old days, *mein freund*." He exhaled deeply. "I *haff zwei* of *der* Bibles. One *ist* in English."

Bass watched his friend retreat again to his desk, find the leather-bound book in the bottom drawer and return. Babbit handed it to him and asked what else was needed without questioning the need for the religious reference.

After thanking him for the Bible, Bass outlined the areas that he would like Babbit's testimony to cover and the sheriff quickly agreed. After several minutes of discussion, Babbit offered to get Bass some supper and the attorney agreed food would taste good.

Babbit looked away. "I vill not let them . . . hang *du*, Bass."

"Hey, you don't sound like you think much of me as a lawyer," Bass teased.

Frowning, the German lawman shrugged his

shoulders. "*Nein. Nein.* I think *du* are *der* best, but . . ." He struggled to find the right words and settled on a different reason. "Judge Nelene, I do *nein* think he be liking *du.*"

Bass rubbed his chin. "Probably not." He studied his old friend's tired face "When you testify, Grant's going to come after you, Frank. He's got to. You've got to figure he knows . . . your real name."

"Are *du* saying Frank Schafer can *nein* be handling *der* questions from *das* weasel?"

"No, I was—"

"Bass, I vant *du* to move to a new cell. *Der* one down there." Babbit motioned to the far end of the six cells, against the wall.

Bass's gaze followed the hand movement and he nodded agreement. It couldn't hurt. Clearly his friend felt there would be another attack on his life. A different location than the federal lawmen expected might be the difference. Especially during the night when the light was poor. After Bass was settled in the new cell, Babbit handed him in his own Merwin & Hubert revolver and a fistful of additional cartridges. Bass received the additional weapon without questioning his friend. Babbit's face was granite; no expression was allowed to reach the surface.

"*Du* keep them close," Babbit said. "*Vhen* I go, they may come. Fast."

"Fair enough. Thanks, old friend."

"I hope I be *vrong. Ja.*"

Bass spun the gun in his hand, liking its feel once more. "You be careful, too, Frank. They might figure it would be good to get you out of the way, too."

After bringing the attorney a gas lamp for his reading, Babbit waved the shotgun above his head. "That *ist* vhy I be taking *der* shotgun." Within minutes, he returned with Bass's supper, holding it with both hands. His shotgun was held in place squeezed under his left arm.

"It *ist gut. Var gud. Du* eat it all."

"I will, Frank. Thanks."

With that, Babbit retraced his steps across the room, opened the door and said, "Remember Apache Canyon." Without waiting for a comment, he left.

Smiling wistfully at the successful battle they had been involved in, one that took cunning, courage and determination, Bass sat on the cot and began eating and thumbing through the Bible.

"Bass, you're lucky it isn't in German," he muttered to himself.

He heard the scatching sounds of a chair moving outside and figured Cateson had left to get something to eat. Closing his eyes for just a minute seemed so good. So good. Just for a minute.

No! He forced his eyes open.

Sleep would continue to be a premium, he knew. The kind of rest he wanted could prove to be disastrous. In his younger days, he was known for his ability to catnap and remain fresh. It must be so now. It had to be. Even with Babbit or his deputy on duty.

"Bass, remember that stone? You're supposed to rub yourself with it," he muttered. "It'll keep you awake, if nothing else. Yeah, I know it's silly. Still . . ."

Even in the yellow light, he was embarrassed,

but did it anyway. Slowly and carefully, he passed the small stone over his arms, his legs, chest, stomach, head and back. It was difficult to hold the small item in his left hand, but keeping it against his body prevented the special rock from sliding away from the lessened grip.

"Don't forget your butt, you old goat," he said and chuckled. "I wonder if Crazy Horse ran it over his John Thomas." He rubbed the stone over both and finally returned it to his pocket and returned to his work for the hearing

The lamp was providing enough yellow light that he could read comfortably, even though dusk had given way to early evening. An hour passed quickly. Somewhere a dog barked and another answered. Someone was using a pump to get water and from the screeching, the pump didn't like it. A door slammed shut. The sounds of town settling in for the night. Then he heard the metallic sound of a key turning in the lock. It was a muffled sound, almost lost in the other noises of the street. Someone was entering and attempting to do it quietly. Attempting to catch him sleeping, perhaps?

After blowing out the lamp, he stood and stepped into the shadows next to the cell wall. Carefully, he assured himself that no moonbeams awaited his strides. His own revolver was in his fist, the Colt close at hand in his waistband. He inhaled and slowly let the new air ease its way out.

Was this what his friend was worrying about? It wouldn't be Babbit at the door; he would have said something. Bass pushed his back against the wall and slowly slid down the rough surface. A crouch would be a better position to shoot from, if necessary.

A shadowy figure slipped into the room and stood next to the door. Without moving. Three heartbeats. Four. Five. What was the man doing? What was he waiting for? More men? Bass realized the shadow was trying to let his eyes adjust to the darker room. Babbit had purposely left only the farthest wall lamp lit; its meager glow covered part of the desk, stove and a corner of the gun case. A long shape appeared from the shadow's bulk. A rifle or a shotgun, pointed in the direction of Bass's former cell.

The attorney watched the man slowly cross the room toward it. Dusky light from outside rushed across the man's face. It was William Manchester! In his hands was a double-barreled shotgun. Ten feet from the bars, he stopped, definitely puzzled by what he was seeing. Or not seeing.

"Good evening, Deputy. You can lower that shotgun now." Bass's words floated toward Manchester, seemingly unconnected to a body or a place.

The young deputy jumped and almost dropped the gun. He swung in a rapid semicircle, searching for the voice's location. The shotgun in his hands moved with his body. It certainly appeared that the deputy's silent entry was a prelude to catching him asleep. Of course, it could have been an attempt to be polite and not wake him. If that were the case, why wouldn't he just head for the desk?

Suddenly, it hit Bass. The reason his son had so readily opened the door to his home that awful night was that Manchester was the one at the door. That's why there were tobacco stains on the farmhouse floor. "Why didn't you see that before, Bass?" he muttered. "It had be Manchester. He would've known about Crimmler. Of course!"

"Wh-what? Wh-where are you . . . Bass?" Manchester stammered. "Oh, there. How come you . . . the sheriff . . . moved you?"

"Put the shotgun on the desk, William. Do it now."

Straightening his shoulders, Manchester didn't move. "Is that a threat?"

"Depends on what you do next."

Manchester shifted the chaw in his mouth to his left side. "I—I was trying to be quiet. Thought you were sleeping. I—I don't deserve this. I've been trying to help you."

"Really? Why don't I believe you?" Bass shifted his weight, keeping his gun aimed at the young man's midsection. "Is it because you were at Jacob's house the night he was murdered? Is it because you're working with Lowe and Cateson? Are you one of the Hoodsmen, William?"

Manchester's first instinct was to race toward the far cell and deny the charges, but his mind held him in check and he turned toward the desk and carefully placed the shotgun there, then eased around to face Bass.

"I think you've been in here too long," Manchester said and looked for the spittoon. "I was Jacob's best friend."

"Makes me wonder how you can sleep," Bass responded. "The spittoon's behind the desk, I think. Go ahead. I wouldn't want you to choke."

As Manchester hurried to the cuspidor, his right hand dropped to his gun belt.

"That would be very foolish, William. Very foolish."

His hand seeking air, Manchester spat into the brass container, wiped his hand across his mouth and declared, "My job is to keep you safe. That's why I'm here."

" 'When devils will the blackest sins put on, They do suggest at first with heavenly shows,' " Bass repeated one of his favorite passages from the second act of Shakespeare's *Othello*, standing and moving to the closer side of the cell, next to the cot. It was a small shift, but if the deputy tried something, it might make the difference.

"What did you say?" Manchester spat again.

"Tomorrow, you will be under oath to tell the truth." Bass motioned with his gun for the deputy to step clear of the desk. "Remember the truth? It's an interesting thing."

"Nobody has to tell me my duty."

Bass watched him clear the desk and stand beside it. If Manchester dove, he would have excellent cover. The attorney knew he shouldn't have been so smug to let him have a place to spit. A younger Bass wouldn't have been so careless. And those were the words that came out of his mouth. "As a younger man, Bass Tillman wouldn't have let an adversary get so close to a good firing position. Humor me and come closer, so I don't have to shoot you, just in case."

Manchester hesitated. The idea of dropping behind the desk had entered his mind; the courage to do so, hadn't. He licked his lips. Would Bass Tillman shoot him, really? His mind answered affirmatively and he stepped forward.

"Sit down on the floor. Right there. Yeah, that's fine," Bass ordered. "I'm going to share something with you. It might help you decide what's next for you." He knelt in front of the cot and turned the Bible toward him with his left hand. His stiff fingers began turning pages. "Ah, here it is. Listen. 'And ye shall know the truth, and the truth shall make you free.' John, eight, thirty-two."

"I reckon I know the Bible as well as you."

"The more I read it, the more answers I find, William. Hope you do." Bass stared at him. "What did Lowe promise you, William? Frank's job?" Shadows, emboldened by a solitary moonbeam, stretched themselves to paint his face into that of a warrior.

"Nobody promised me anything."

Manchester's face was crimson; he chewed vigorously on the tobacco, then wondered what he was going to do about spitting. His hand inadvertently came to rest on the butt of his holstered pistol and jumped away as if it were scalding hot.

"Be careful, William. Frank Babbit may seem old to you," Bass said, "but he's twice the man of Lowe, Cateson and Hautrese put together. Oh, and your hero, Grant, won't look so good after questioning him either."

"I'll be there."

Chapter 20

As ordered, Bass Tillman's hearing was convened the next morning. Judge Pierce's small municipal courtroom was packed with interested townspeople as well as out-of-town spectators eager to see the famous gunfighter, Bass Tillman. Journalists from as far away as Kansas City were also on hand. An electric atmosphere like that of anticipating a new performance at the theater was definitely in the air.

At the rear of the audience, the blacksmith was discussing horseshoes and horses with the mayor; Lucius Henry sat quietly near them. A pensive Hamilton Jallon was next to him, making an occasional comment about the weather. On an aisle seat on the fourth row, Timbel McKinsey and his wife appeared to be praying. In the back row, Wallace Denson sat with his pencil and pad of paper readied, an odd smile fixed to his face.

Next to him sat a smug Milford Moulton, the town's banker.

Standing at the back of the room was Sheriff Frank Babbit; Deputy Manchester wasn't in sight at the moment. Bass's eyes widened as he realized who was standing next to him. Nancy Spirit Bear! Seeing her brought a mixture of feelings. Her gaze sought his and brought him joy. For an instant. Then he was afraid for her safety; then he realized that was why Babbit was standing next to her. No one would bother her with him there.

The Lakotan woman's attire was a curious mixture of Indian and white man's garments. A well-worn buckskin dress was mostly covered by a long cattleman's coat, given her by Bass. Around her neck was a wide choker of elk bone, copper beads and reddish brown stones; in its center was a flat circular shell, featuring a single bear claw. The brim of an unshaped black hat barely cleared her forehead. Hanging from her shiny black-and-gray hair were two foot-long strands of beads and bone, attached to a circle-cross made of porcupine quilling.

A soft smile aimed at Bass did not match the worry in her eyes. Bass grimaced. How could she possibly understand what this was about? He wished she hadn't come and seen him like this. At the same time, her presence seemed to cleanse his soul of its black encasement. How did she know he was here? The question bolted into his mind like a runaway horse. Who would've sought her to tell the news? Frank Babbit didn't know about her and he was the only one who would have done so.

"All rise."

After taking his position behind the walnut bench, Judge Nelene opened the proceedings with a simple statement that the purpose of a preliminary hearing was to determine whether sufficient evidence existed for the accused to be bound over for formal trial.

Someone in one of the back rows yelled, "There ain't no evidence an' we'al know it. You're jes' a mite slow."

Across the room, a deep voice retorted, "Hang the gunfighter!"

"Another outburst of any kind and I will clear this courtroom." Judge Nelene's gavel slammed against the bench for emphasis.

Bass Tillman sat quietly at the defense table, having already declared that he would act as his own counsel. In front of him was a pile of papers and notes. Without fanfare, he had handed over his guns to Babbit before they entered the courtroom. Manchester had left the jail as soon as the sheriff returned with only a quiet good-bye. Bass shared with his old friend what had happened last night and of his confirmed suspicion that the young deputy had been involved in the Tillman farm violence. Bitterness showed in the German's tired face.

District Attorney Touren Grant was seated at the prosecution table along with smirking U.S. Deputy Marshal Topper Lowe. The federal lawman's quirt lay in his lap and he massaged the interlocked leather strips with his fingers. As the judge had ordered, he wore no gun. At least, none that could be seen; his Colt was shoved into his back waistband and hidden by his coat.

Witnesses for the prosecution were sequestered in a separate room in the courthouse. Tillman said he would be calling Sheriff Babbit to the stand and would reserve the right to call others as necessary.

"The issue before this court is the deaths of two federal officers and the exact nature of their demise," Judge Nelene declared, rolling his tongue across the inside of his upper lip. "Are both of you ready to proceed?" He stared at Grant, then at Bass.

"The prosecution is ready, Your Honor." Grant sat up straight, pulling on his coat lapels. He was dressed in a dark charcoal herringbone sack suit, rich red vest and a striped tie. His blond hair was carefully in place.

"I'm ready." Bass looked tired, but his clothes were fresh, thanks to the sheriff bringing them to the jail. His navy blue coat sleeves were frayed, but it was the suit he had worn at Settie's funeral. He had requested it. For the first time since being arrested, he had not worn his shoulder holster either. To help settle his nerves, he fingered the crystal hanging from his watch chain and wondered if Nancy Spirit Bear saw him.

"The burden of proof is on the prosecution to determine whether a trial is called for," Judge Nelene continued. "However, such a declaration is not an indication of guilt or innocence. It only means there is sufficient evidence for a jury to decide. A trial will then be held at the time I designate. A jury of the accused's peers will be selected to deliberate on the facts as presented to them as I direct. Any questions?"

Flashing his most confident, smile, Grant stood and declared, "Your Honor, we intend to show that the defendant, Bass Tillman, did knowingly and willingly murder two federal officers who were pursuing him, his son and another man after the robbery of the Highland Bank and that he is the leader of the infamous outlaw gang known in the newspapers as the 'Hoodsmen.'"

"Call your first witness—and quit preaching."

"I call U.S. Chief Deputy Marshal Topper Lowe to the stand."

Lowe stood, patted his hair with his right hand to ensure its proper combing and headed for the witness chair. After being sworn in by the bailiff, Lowe described the situation leading to the murders. He was heading up a posse of deputized men, a special force seeking to end the tyranny of the Hoodsmen gang, when he received word of the Highland Bank robbery. They had suspected Bass Tillman for some time, because of his reputation as a gunfighter and an outlaw. Their posse tracked two men to a farm outside Longmont and sought their arrest. In the ensuing gun battle, Jacob Tillman was killed and Virgil Crimmler arrested. Lowe's presentation was well rehearsed and eliminated the impropriety of the lost "L" stickpin and Lowe's hoofprint. It even set the stage for Deputy Manchester being present at the farm, if they choose to use it.

"A savvy strategy, Bass," the old attorney murmured.

"Were these the only two Hoodsmen at this farm hideout? Jacob Tillman and Virgil Crimmler?" Grant asked.

"Objection. No one has proven that Jacob Tillman was anything but an honest farmer and a dedicated lawman for this city," Bass said from his table. "Jacob Tillman was, indeed, holding the outlaw Virgil Crimmler until a safe transfer to a more secure jail could be established. Crimmler had admitted to being a Hoodsman and Jacob was afraid the man would be shot down before he could testify in court. Sheriff Babbit will verify this later."

"Your objection is sustained," Judge Nelene said. "You watch your language, Grant." He looked over at Bass. "And, Tillman, you lay off the sermons."

"Sorry, Your Honor." Grant pushed on his tie knot at his collar.

Bass stared at the judge. "Didn't think telling the truth was a sermon."

"That's enough, Tillman."

Grinning, Lowe said Crimmler told them of Bass Tillman's leadership of the Hoodsmen and that he was coming to the farm to take the bank money for safe hiding and to outline their next crimes. He killed the two posse men, Wilbur Hinds and Chester Morgan, waiting for him and escaped with Deputy Marshal Bill Drucker in pursuit. Lowe explained that they figured the old gunfighter had also killed Deputy Marshal Bill Drucker, but so far they hadn't found his body.

"Thank you, Marshal Lowe. Our state is thankful for your loyal and courageous service." Grant stepped back and sat down.

"Cross-examination, Tillman?" Judge Nelene waved his hand toward Lowe.

Tillman stood slowly, folded his arms and stared at Lowe, who pretended to be straightening his vest.

"So, you were in pursuit of the men who held up the Highland Bank. When did the robbery occur?" Bass said.

Lowe seemed pleased with the question. "Ah, it was Thursday. Last Thursday. Yeah. You know. You were there." He cocked his head to the side, waiting for the chuckling from the assembled crowd at his remark.

Some hesitant mirth followed and quickly silenced itself. This is just what Lowe thought would happen; the old attorney wasn't expecting this Highland Bank robbery approach at all. He would tell Grant to call William Manchester to the stand this afternoon and the old attorney would be through for good.

"And there were two robbers?"

"You know there were, Tillman." Lowe leaned forward in his chair, eager for the next question. This was easy; he had expected more from the old man.

Bass smiled. "How did you hear about this crime?"

Lowe explained that he had received a wire from the Highland sheriff alerting law officers in the area.

"Where were you when you got this information?" Bass walked around the far end of the table and stood, leaning back against it.

"Ah . . . where? Let me think." Lowe hadn't expected the question. "Ah, oh yeah. Actually, Deputy Marshal Drucker brought it to me. Think he was here, in Longmont, when it came in." He grinned and added, "Of course, Marshal Drucker is missing. Only you know where his body is. I'm hoping you'll do the right thing and tell us, so we can give him a proper burial."

Whispered response from the audience was stopped by the judge's gavel.

"You read the wire?" Bass ignored Lowe's comment; it was an awkward situation he hadn't quite decided how to treat. He wouldn't involve McKinsey; he would probably state, if asked under oath, he had killed Drucker when he tried to shoot him.

"Of course I read it. That's how I knew you bastards had robbed the bank."

The crowd murmured again and Judge Nelene warned Lowe to watch his language.

"I'm curious, Chief Deputy Marshal Lowe, which one—Crimmler or my son—was wearing a buffalo coat?" He paused and added, "Crimmler's no taller than you—and my son's my height, so which one was big, over six feet tall, as reported in that wire?"

Laughter popped and rolled through the courtroom, irritating Lowe, who looked out on the audience and glared.

"What the hell are you talkin' about?"

Bass turned back to the table and lifted a sheet of paper from his pile. "If it pleases the court, I'd like you, Marshal Lowe, to read aloud the wire you and other lawmen in the area received. This is a copy from Sheriff Babbit's office."

"You read it," Lowe snarled. "There's nothing new in it."

A nod from the judge preceded Bass's reading, which described the robbers: "Two armed men wearing kerchiefs over their faces robbed the Highland Bank today at ten o'clock. Escaped with three thousand dollars in gold and paper. One was a big man, over six feet. A second was thin, wearing a buffalo coat. Should be considered dangerous. They rode north. Am in pursuit with a posse." Finished, he walked over to the judge and handed him the copy of the wire.

"I never saw that!" Lowe's face reddened. "You're trying to trap me. I—I won't stand for it. What the hell's this?"

"Your Honor, I have never seen such a document before either," Grant said. "This is most irregular."

Bass spun toward the seated Lowe. "This is the wire you just said you had read, that told you about the robbery. Did you lie—under oath?"

"Of c-course n-not," Lowe stammered. "It . . . just sounded different . . . just now."

"All right, I'll ask the question again. Which one was which?"

"It doesn't take long to get rid of a coat," Lowe countered.

"I see. How long does it take to get tall?"

Laughter popped from throughout the courtroom. Even Nelene bit back a grin.

"Never mind, Lowe. My son—and I—weren't the men who robbed that bank and you know it," Bass said. "On that Thursday, if you had checked, you would have found I was in a restaurant here in Longmont, then at the theater." His eyes sought

Lowe's insecurity. "Come to think of it, my son, Jacob, was also in town, doing his duty as a deputy sheriff. He was arresting Virgil Crimmler for disturbing the peace in the Lorna Saloon. Lots of witnesses for both of us." The old attorney's chest rose and fell with the emotion racing through him. "Crimmler told Jacob about you, Cateson and Drucker and the others riding with you. He said you were the Hoodsmen—and that U.S. Marshal Hautrese runs the whole awful scheme."

Pausing to keep himself from physically attacking the man before him, Bass licked his lower lip, his eyes never leaving Lowe's reddening face.

"Jacob and Sheriff Babbit took Crimmler to the farm to keep him alive until they could bring in honest federal law or safely escort him to a bigger jail," he continued. "Of course, facts like that just get in the way, don't they, Lowe?"

Movement made Bass glance toward the back of the room. Painted Crow had just entered; he held up a sack for Bass to see, then pulled an arrow from it so he would understand the contents. Before Grant could object, Bass asked another question. "How did you track these two men?"

Lowe took a deep breath. "Got a half-breed scout. Can track a squirrel up his hole."

"How did you discover these two men of yours were dead?"

"You brought them to town. Real proud you were."

Bass walked across the room and asked if he had ever known an outlaw to bring two dead men into town. Lowe tried to explain away the situation, but ended up mumbling. The white-haired attorney glanced at his own notes and said, "Now that you've gotten that little fairy tale out of your system, let's talk about what really happened, Lowe." He went on to describe the scene of finding his dead son and daughter-in-law murdered and the signs of a supposed Indian attack left behind.

"Your Honor, the defense counsel is not asking questions, he's the one trying to build a fairy tale," Grant challenged from his seat.

"Get on with it, Tillman," Judge Nelene demanded. "Ask a question. Or shut up."

"Sure. Tell me, Lowe, whose idea was it to make the murder of my family look like an Indian attack? Yours—or Cateson's—or Drucker's? Or was it Hautrese's?"

"Don't know what you're talking about."

"Remember, you're under oath, Lowe. That means you are sworn to tell the truth. You do understand that word . . . truth?"

Judge Nelene leaned forward. "That's enough, Tillman."

Glaring at him, Bass said, "Do you or Hautrese decide where the Hoodsmen rob?"

Anger splattered across his face, Lowe looked up at the judge. "This is crap."

"I agree," the hard-faced magistrate said. "Tillman, I won't warn you again."

Tillman walked back to his table, picked up the stickpin and folded note and turned around. "Let's see if you've got an answer for this stickpin I found at my son's farm. A stickpin with your initial on it . . . and the cut hoofprint that belonged to your horse. That's the brilliance of this absurd bank robber strategy. Just a minute, Judge, I'm getting to it, but explain this note to me, will you? I found it at my son's farm." He held up the wire. "It's a telegram and it reads, 'J T knows. Count on it. Get VC out of there quick. You know what to do with JT. Do not hurt VC. Hide him.' It's signed H." He lowered the paper. "Would you like to tell this court what that message meant?"

"Never saw what you're talking about. Must be something you made up, Tillman." Lowe's eyes narrowed and he kept glancing at Grant, hoping he would stop the questioning, but the district attorney appeared mesmerized at the moment.

Bass strolled toward the short deputy marshal. "Now, Lowe, I'm going to give you a chance to answer again. Or would you like me to bring the telegraph operator to the stand to tell who this wire was directed to—and who it came from?"

He turned away from Lowe at the last moment as if preparing to call for the Longmont telegraph operator. Bass held his breath; he had no idea which telegraph office had received the message or if the message sender could be identified. Hautrese wouldn't have let himself be exposed so easily. Would Lowe challenge the bluff?

Deep furrows charging across his forehead, Lowe swallowed. "Wait! Yeah, it was to me. From Marshal Hautrese. We found out that you and your son were Hoodsmen—an' that your son, Jacob, knew it. I was supposed to arrest all of you."

"If you knew this before the bank robbery, why did you wait to come to the farm until your tracker led you there? Why did you need a tracker at all to find Jacob's farm?"

"You're a slick one, Tillman, trying to put words in my mouth," Lowe countered. "We headed to the farm as fast as we could. You outlaws have all the fast horses."

Finally, Grant stood. "My witness has answered the question about the telegram, Your Honor. Marshal Lowe is a loyal federal lawman with great responsibilities. Such timing is irrelevant. This is badgering."

"Move on, Tillman." Judge Nelene waved his hand as if shooing a dog.

Bass tried not to let his disappointment find his face.

Grant made a sweeping gesture with his arms to recapture the attention of the judge and the courtroom. "If it please the court, I would like to present an additional piece of information you should be aware of." He paused for effect, waiting for the murmuring in the audience behind him to silence itself, and for the judge to respond.

"It's irregular, but I'll allow it. Go ahead." Judge Nelene glanced at Bass.

"Marshal Lowe, I know this will be difficult for you," Grant said. "But I must ask you to tell us what you found when examining the bodies of your two dead associates. I'm sorry, but justice must be done." He motioned for Lowe to respond.

"Yeah, both had been shot in the back."

"In the back?" Grant liked the sound of the phrase and smiled.

"That's right."

Judge Nelene looked again at Bass. "Any cross?"

"Yes, as Mr. Grant said, justice must be done." Bass walked a few steps past his table toward the far wall, his back to Lowe. "Lowe, when you asked me if I had killed these two men, how did I answer?"

Lowe stared at his hands in his lap. "Ah, you said you shot them."

Several men in the courtroom laughed; a woman's weeping trailed the reaction.

"Not quite, Lowe, try again." Bass spun around and began walking toward Lowe. "I said I had wounded both men as they tried to attack me—just after I had buried my son and his wife. Isn't that right? Answer me, Lowe." Bass's face shimmered with anger.

"Ah, well, something like that, I guess."

"I also said one of your own men, Bill Drucker, shot both of them in the back, so they couldn't talk, and rode away—and that I went after him. Did I say that, Lowe?"

Lowe fidgeted. "Yeah. You said a lot of wild things."

"Did it ever occur to you to check the bullets in the two men?"

"What the hell for? I've seen slugs before."

Bass stopped and folded his arms. "Good. Then you should know the difference between a .50-caliber bullet that comes from the Ballard I carry—and a .45 slug from the Pedersoli rifle your man Drucker carried. Is that right?"

Lowe was silent.

"Your Honor, when it is time for the defense to present, I will show the court beyond a shadow of a doubt that the actual killing bullets did, indeed, come from the backs of these men, and they were not fired by me."

From the sixth row, a male voice yelled out, "That's tellin' 'em, Bass!"

Bass shrugged. "Lowe, you were in a big hurry to get me behind bars, weren't you? Too bad you didn't pay attention to details like bullets." He looked at the judge. "No further questions for him at this time, Your Honor. I reserve the right to call him back." He rubbed his chin. "But I'd like to hear from this scout. Think you would, too."

Judge Nelene frowned, but turned toward Grant. "Marshal Lowe, is this . . . ah, scout of yours here? We should hear from him."

"Well, Your Honor, he's . . ."

Bass pointed toward the back of the crowded room. "He's right back there."

Everyone turned to see Painted Crow standing beside Nancy Spirit Bear.

"Ah, Sheriff Babbit, please escort the man down here," the broad-shouldered magistrate barked. "Marshal Lowe, you are excused for now. Stay close. You may be called back."

"Wouldn't have it any other way."

Chapter 21

A townsman behind him leaned forward and patted Bass on the back as he sat down at the table. Bass nodded his appreciation and watched as Painted Crow came forward hesitantly, with Babbit at his side. The half-breed nodded his agreement to telling the truth when the bailiff held out the Bible and repeated the oath. Lowe urgently whispered in Grant's ear; the district attorney was clearly puzzled, as he watched Babbit return to the back of the courtroom. The handsome prosecutor stood and, speaking overly slow, asked Painted Crow if he could speak English.

"Me speak good."

Grant smiled and asked the half-breed to describe how he had helped the marshals find the three Hoodsmen. Painted Crow listened to the question, frowned and looked at the judge. Lowe whispered in Grant's ear and the district attorney changed his question.

"Ah, John, isn't it? John Painted Crow? Ah, good," Grant stammered. "Were you at the farm where the robbers were found?"

Lowe whispered again, this time frantic.

Grant's forehead showed signs of sweat. "Your Honor, the witness doesn't understand our language well. I think the court would be better served if we moved on. Deputy Marshal Lowe has stated the man served only as a scout and was not part of the actual party of marshals at the farm."

Bass stood at the table. "The problem isn't language, Grant. The problem is that he won't lie for you."

Judge Nelene slammed his gavel. "That's enough, Tillman."

"Really? I'm only getting started." Bass's gaze sought the judge's eyes and wouldn't release them. "I've put up with hell and I've had enough of this charade. Lowe and his men murdered my son and his wife because Jacob knew they were Hoodsmen. Jacob discovered this truth when he arrested and questioned their man, Virgil Crimmler."

He took a step closer to the judge's bench. "On the advice of Sheriff Frank Babbit, Jacob took Crimmler to his farm to keep him from being discovered by Lowe. Someone told Lowe and they murdered my family. The whole thing goes all the way to U.S. Marshal Hautrese." He pointed his finger at the judge. "I can prove it, Nelene— and I will, if you give me the chance. They want me dead before I do. That's why they tried to kill me when I was in jail. Twice. I will describe those attempts, too—and Sheriff Babbit will support those facts."

The crowd erupted into excited banter and Lucius Henry shouted, "He's right!"

"You're in contempt, Tillman. Don't point your finger at me again. I hereby fine you a hundred dollars. Another outburst and it's another hundred. Do it a third time—and you'll finish the rest of this hearing behind bars," Judge Nelene shouted above the noise and the banging of his own gavel.

Ignoring the judge's command, Bass walked toward Painted Crow, speaking to him in Lakotan. The half-breed grunted and replied in his native language.

"What is this, Judge?" Grant waved his arms. "No one knows what he's saying."

Bass swung toward Grant. "Be patient, boy. And listen. You're going to learn something you didn't know. At least, I don't think you did." He faced Painted Crow once more. "Did Deputy Marshal Lowe and his men try to make the murder of my family look like an Indian raid?"

"Yes. That is what they did."

Speaking in simple, slow English, Painted Crow described the placement of Indian weapons around the farmyard. Using sign language to support his testimony, he explained several men put on moccasins after Jacob and Mary Anne were dead to reinforce the appearance. He told of the group bringing in unshod ponies and running them in circles around the farmhouse to leave their tracks.

When Bass asked, Painted Crow snorted and described the weapons as a mixture of Cheyenne and Blackfoot, and that the only Indians even close to fighting around here were Utes. He said that he told Lowe the weapons weren't the right ones, but Lowe only laughed and said no one would know the difference.

"Do you know where those weapons are now?" Bass asked.

Painted Crow pointed to the back of the room and Nancy Spirit Bear began to walk forward holding a large sack. Arrows protruded from the top of the canvas bag. She laid them in front of him and walked back. Her glance at Bass was a worried look. Motioning toward the bag, Painted Crow explained they found Crimmler tied in the barn and took him away to another location. He said Lowe realized he had lost his stickpin and the note, and sent Drucker and two men back to get them. In response to Bass's question, he answered that he was not tracking any bank robbers at that time; that they met up with the Highland posse that night and made camp with them.

"Did you ever see me?" Bass asked.

"We see you next morning. You ride with the man of the Scots," Painted Crow said. "You tell us you found bank robbers in a cabin in woods."

Bass thanked him in Lakotan.

From the prosecution's table, Lowe howled, "That's a damn lie. I fired that no-good redskin for being drunk an' he's tryin' to get even, bringing that junk with him."

"Your Honor, after I discovered my son and his wife had been murdered, I buried them." Tillman's voice rose with the emotion climbing within him. "I searched the land for clues of who might have done this horrible thing. I found the 'L' stickpin . . . and the telegram. I knew the Indian things had been planted there. It was obvious to anyone who could read sign." He knew there was no use telling about Lowe's horse tracks.

Grant stood. "Your Honor, how much of this do we have to endure? This man is concocting a story beyond belief. Who would take the word of a red man anyway?"

Bass moved next to Painted Crow, standing to his left beside the chair's wooden arms. "John Painted Crow, do you know what will happen to you—if you are lying?"

His chest rising, the half-breed scout looked at the judge. "Yes, I will be hanged by the white man's rope." He glanced back at Tillman, then turned again to the judge. "The River . . . this man . . . is good man. You cannot hold him. He is not man of the hood." He swallowed, looked at Lowe and pointed. "He is man of the hood."

Reactions from the courtroom were instantaneous and intense.

Lowe whispered into Grant's ear and the district attorney announced loudly, "I would like to call Deputy Marshal John Cateson to the stand. We have heard enough of this nonsense." Grant's expression was tight frustration at the direction of the hearing and Bass Tillman's ability to force changes in courtroom procedure.

Cateson moved quickly to the stand, sat and grinned. Immediately, he produced the black hood he said had been found in Bass's room. Without being asked, he said they had a warrant from a Denver judge. After a deep breath, he described Bass's room in considerable detail. Obviously, Deputy Manchester had told them about expecting questions about his room to discredit their finding the hood there.

Grant looked at the seated Bass Tillman. Surely they had this old man now.

Without standing, Bass asked, "Mind if I put that hood on, Judge?"

Judge Nelene frowned. "It's your trial."

"That it is—for the moment." Bass stood, walked over to Cateson and took the mask from him. The outlaw chuckled. Bass slipped the hood over his head and dropped his hands to his sides. The room erupted in more laughter. The cut eyeholes in the mask rested against Bass's cheeks.

Bass pulled on the hood to make it clear he had done nothing special to create this appearance. "Sorry, Cateson, but if I was wearing this, I would've run into a bank, instead of robbing it."

Howls exploded and the judge hammered his gavel for quiet.

"That's enough, Tillman. You made your point." Judge Nelene pointed his gavel.

"Not quite." Bass yanked off the mask and tossed it at Cateson. "Put it on."

The long-faced gunman looked at Lowe, then Grant, who was stunned, then back at the judge. "What? I don't have to—"

"Put it on, Cateson," Bass growled and stepped next to him, "or I'll do it."

Reluctantly, the gunman slipped the hood over

his head. Bass grabbed the bottom and pulled it into place. Cateson's eyes were wide through the mask's holes.

"Marshal Cateson, this mask came from your saddlebags, not my room, didn't it? Are you the only one riding with Marshal Lowe who is a Hoodsman? Are you the only one who's going to hang for Hoodsmen crimes? Or is it all of you?" He stuck his finger into Cateson's chest. "Which one of you murdered my son and his wife?"

"I object. He's badgering the witness!" Grant stood, nearly screaming. His face was white with surprise. "What kind of hearing is this?"

"Objection sustained. Stop it, Tillman," Judge Nelene said.

Bass's glance at the judge was intense; his long white hair whisked across his shoulders as he retreated from Cateson, now pulling the mask from his face like it was filled with odor. Three steps from his table, Bass spun around.

"Why did you decide to make the murders look like an Indian raid?" he asked. "Was the idea yours—or was it Lowe's?"

Grant raised his arms and waved them, shouting, "This is ridiculous! Absolutely ridiculous. Judge, you're letting this hearing become . . . ah, a farce!"

"Never mind." Bass strolled over to the prosecution table. "We all know there is at least one Hoodsman in the room—and he's sitting in the witness chair."

"That's two hundred," Judge Nelene snapped. "One more and you're out of here."

Ignoring the warning, the white-haired attor-

ney ran at Cateson. "I said which one of you bastards killed Mary Anne, Jacob's sweet wife?
Which one shot their dog? Was it you, Cateson? It
was, wasn't it? Answer me, you no-good son of a
bitch!"

"That's it, Tillman. Sheriff Babbit, escort the
prisoner out of here!" Judge Nelene bellowed and
folded his arms.

Bass imitated the movement, folding his own.
"And what are you going to do with a federal
marshal who lied under oath and another who
manufactured false evidence?"

"I would like a half-hour recess, Your Honor."
Grant stood, color returning to his face. At the
corners of his eyes was wetness. The moisture of
tension.

"And I want my questions anwered." Bass
walked toward Grant. "This man and this man"—
he pointed at Cateson, then Lowe—"and Bill
Drucker, and those two dead killers, murdered my
family because my son knew they were Hoodsmen."

The audience gasped almost in unison. Whispers were manifest, both negative and positive.
The judge's pounding was barely heard over the
excited noise.

Judge Nelene banged and banged his gavel for
calm and finally declared, "This court is in recess
until one o'clock." He looked at the back of the
room where Sheriff Babbit waited, along with
Deputy Manchester, who had just entered. "Return this prisoner to his cell. In handcuffs. But I
will allow him to return to my court."

"*Nein*, Judge. He *ist nein* wearing *der* handcuffs," Babbit declared.

Manchester stared at him with a strange expression on his face.

"Are you challenging my authority?" Nelene bellowed.

"*Nein*. I just be telling *du* that he *ist nein* wearing handcuffs." Babbit's chin was set.

An exasperated Grant whined, "What is this, Judge? Who is in charge here?"

Nelene shook his head and waved away Grant's further comments. "Take the prisoner to his cell. Be back at one. Sharp."

Chapter 22

Immediately, Lowe called Cateson to him and the gunman nodded and left the courtroom by the back door. His quirt trailing from his hand at his side, Lowe joined an angry Grant in a small room adjoining the main courtroom. The handsome prosecutor was furious at the two deputy marshals for their selective testimony to him. He could not understand why their own scout had turned against them and why the old attorney had an apparently strong alibi, as well as one for his son.

"And what the hell is this about a fake Indian attack?" Grant bellowed.

Lowe explained that the Indian ruse was designed to try to fool Bass Tillman when he came to the farm. They didn't want the old attorney to know they were on to him—and the appearance of an attack would draw him to the farmhouse where they waited. He said there was plenty of time for Jacob and Crimmler to be seen in Longmont and ride to Highland; that was part of their strategy. The same with Bass Tillman. He assured Grant that Crimmler would blow a hole in that alibi a mile wide.

Writing a note to himself, Grant indicated that he would bring Lowe back to the stand to clarify both situations. He stopped writing and looked up. He was also upset about hearing about the possibility of there being two kinds of bullets in the dead officers, but decided he should deal with the timing issue first.

"Might be better if I have this young town deputy . . . what's his name? Yeah, Manchester. How about if I have him do this? He was there, right?" Grant's blond eyebrows arched.

Lowe rubbed his hand over his mouth. "I wouldn't do that. He's young and might rattle. There was nothing easy about this arrest, Grant. Tillman's a wily sonvabitch—and damn good with a gun."

"I can see the first part."

Pushing back his chair, Lowe reminded Grant that Crimmler would testify that the old attorney was the leader of the Hoodsmen. They had kept Crimmler out of sight, bringing him into town during the night. Right now, he was waiting in the witness room. He didn't mention Bobby Joe Wright had been told to stay in Lowe's hotel room until they came for him. The cross-eyed gunman would not do well on the stand.

"I haven't forgotten, Marshal Lowe," Grant said. "I've been a little busy putting out the brush fires your prisoner keeps starting." He stared at

Lowe. "Most of them because you didn't give me all the details." He raised his chin farther. "Nobody beats me in a courtroom if I have all the details. Especially not some old man. You have to trust me."

"I do," Lowe announced, curling the quirt in his hands. "Just didn't expect Tillman to come at us with such wild-ass stories. My God, me—an' Cateson—Hoodsmen! An' . . . an' Hautrese, too!" He shook his head vigorously, being careful not to look at Cateson for fear of laughing.

Grant straightened his vest. "Yes, that was wild. Nelene isn't going to let him get away with that stuff anymore. You could see that in his face. I won't either." He cocked his head to the side. "In a fistfight, it's good, sometimes, to let your opponent hit you to see what he wants to do." He liked his analogy and his eyes indicated it.

"Just so he doesn't coldcock you in the first round," Lowe chortled.

Grant gave him a stern look. "In the future, you need to explain your strategies fully to your men. We don't need another mess like this half-breed's testimony."

"Yeah, that won't happen again." Lowe twisted the quirt with both hands. There was a look in Grant's eyes that he didn't like.

The district attorney stood, more composed than when he'd entered the room. He held his position for a moment as if he expected someone to photograph him, then asked Lowe about the bullet details Bass had presented.

"Is it true there are different kinds of bullets in those bodies?" Grant asked. "Why?"

Lowe shook his head. "Tillman's trying to fool everybody. He used both guns. Both. A smart move. Crimmler will take care of that."

"He'd better." Grant inhaled and exhaled. "What about asking Tillman about Marshal Drucker?"

Lowe explained Deputy Manchester had told him that the old attorney said he hadn't killed Drucker, but knew he was dead. Wrapping the quirt around his right fist as he talked, Lowe thought Bass would simply deny killing him.

"Oh, really? Sounds rather convenient to me. How'd he know Drucker was dead, if he didn't kill him?" Grant's eyebrows rose to a haughty position before resettling.

"Don't know, but I wouldn't walk into that punch, if I were you." Lowe smiled at the repeated usage of the fistfighting analogy.

"What makes you think this Manchester is telling you the truth?" Grant's eyebrows arched again.

"He was with us at the farm. He wants to be sheriff," Lowe said. "And he wants the Hoodsmen put away."

Grant's expression was skeptical.

"Forget Manchester," Lowe said with growing force in his voice. "Crimmler'll also testify Tillman killed that Pinkerton man—on the Colorado Central. That'll nail him."

"Really?" Grant's face was painted with the skepticism that remained. "And what happened with that silly hood? You told me we had the old man dead to rights with it."

"Hell, I don't know. I wasn't with Cateson

when he went to Tillman's room," Lowe said. "Maybe he thought he was helping."

"By letting the judge see a hood that fit him— and not Tillman?"

Lowe smiled. "I never said Cateson was the smartest dog in the pack."

"Well, you'd better think of something," Grant said. "It sounds to me like we're going to be scrambling enough as it is, after that German sheriff testifies."

"Don't worry about Babbit."

"Are you a fool? You told me that he and Tillman were old friends!" Grant realized his stance wasn't impressing Lowe and returned to his seat.

"Yeah, more than that." Lowe picked at his ear with his forefinger. "I think Babbit's really Frank Schafer. It was Tillman, Holt and Schafer. Guns for hire. In the old days." He withdrew his finger and examined the earwax on his fingernail. "Bass Tillman was the best known. Street and Simmons even did some dime novels on 'em. No one seems to know for sure what happened to the other two." Lowe rubbed his finger on his pants. "Some say they were killed in a gunfight down in Kansas. But I heard two of them changed their names, but nobody knows to what. Lots of men do, you know."

Grant shrugged his shoulders. "So you think Sheriff Frank Babbit once rode with Tillman— under a different name."

"That's my guess. Hard to prove—unless you can find his mama."

Grant nodded and smiled softly. "Wonder if we could get some detail on them and use it to color

Babbit's testimony." He rubbed his chin. "Yes, the judge would have to wonder about his truthfulness, if we paint the picture right." His eyebrows preceded a question. "Do you think Babbit's a Hoodsman, too? You weren't sure before."

Lowe glanced away to control the beginnings of a smile. "Yeah, I do—but I can't prove nothin'. Not yet, anyway. We know one of his deputies was."

"Well, after we put Tillman away, you can concentrate on Babbit. That'll make this whole thing nothing more than a memory—and a platform for me to become governor."

"Sure will," Lowe said and added, "I'm going to go talk with Crimmler. Get him ready for you." He stood and grinned.

"Remember, I'm not promising him clemency until we see what he says."

In the courtroom, Babbit and Bass talked with each other beside the defense table, letting the audience clear. Several men walked over to them and patted the old attorney on the back and offered words of encouragement, which Bass warmly acknowledged. But Babbit was worried. Not about the way the hearing was going, but the fact that it was going well and that could spell another attempt on Bass's life.

Completing their discussion about the questions Bass would be asking him this afternoon, the German lawman handed Bass his revolver, with the admonition to be watchful on their stroll back to the jail. Shoving the gun into his waistband, Bass headed for the back of the room, explaining he needed to speak to Nancy Spirit Bear before leaving.

At the back of the courtroom, Babbit stepped away to talk with Henry, while Bass stopped to talk with the solemn Indian woman.

"Who told you I was here?" The question found form in Bass's words.

"The big man in black who rides with you. He came to my house yesterday as the sun found itself."

"Easter Sontag?"

She nodded. "I know not what he is called. He tells you are here and rides on."

Bass's face contorted into a frown.

She reached out and touched his shoulder. "*The People* would not have let this happen to such a great warrior as *Kin Wakpa*. Evil spirits are in this lodge, in this town." She paused and her eyes found Bass. "The River must not wait for new rains. Or he will be caught in stagnant backwash. The River must come out of its banks and seek a new way." She moved her hands to imitate the action of a stream changing course. "Grandmother Moon speaks to you. You must listen." She pointed skyward.

Bass nodded and returned to the stunning news about the famous hangman. "Did Easter say where he was going?"

"No. He rides away from the sun."

East? That was generally in the direction of the forest cabin where they had met. Why would he go there? Bass mentally challenged the statement. He thanked her for helping and tried to assure her that everything would work out. She told him that she and Painted Crow had gathered the Indian weaponry in a canvas sack, after he came to her lodge and explained the situation.

"Thank you, Nancy. Very much. Where did Painted Crow go? I wanted to thank him, too." He glanced over at Babbit, who was in an intense conversation with several townsmen.

"He left here not long ago. Said he must do something."

"Nancy, what do you think of the rider in black . . . my friend?" Bass returned to Sontag, eager to get her reaction.

Folding her arms over her bosom, she gazed skyward, as if recalling their recent encounter. "The spirits are in disagreement about him. He is a killer of men. He is of the white man's rope."

"I have killed men."

"Yes, and they are unsure of you, too." Her smile was just a bit mischievous.

He shook his head and started to respond, but she spoke first.

"*Kin Wakpa*, do you have the medicine stone I gave you?" Her gaze showed she expected a negative response.

"Yes, it is right here." He patted his coat pocket. "It gives me comfort." He smiled and added, "Got it right here, next to my tobacco sack. But it's empty. Had to borrow a cigar from my friend . . . to leave a tribute at the last water." He looked into her eyes, expecting praise for keeping her ritual.

"You will need it filled once more. Before you come to my home," she said, her eyes never leaving his. "There is a stream you must cross, remember, *Kin Wakpa?*" She smiled again and touched the bear claw at her neck. "Has The River protected himself with *wasicun tunkan?*"

"Yes, I did."

"It is well."

He suddenly remembered Jacob's dog. "How is Cutter doing?"

"Ah, he is doing well."

He shook his head in surprise and thanked her again, then said he needed to go.

"*Wowasi nitawa kin tanyan ecu wo,*" she said

Bass's shoulders rose and fell as he repeated her statement in English to himself, "Do your work well" as he sought Babbit to return to the jail. The sheriff's discussion had ended rather abruptly, from the expressions on the gathered men's faces.

Outside, Bass and Babbit stepped into the bright noon sun. Seeing Nancy Spirit Bear both lifted and depressed him. The old attorney pulled the small medicine rock from his pocket and began tossing and catching it as they walked. His only comment about the hearing was the observation that Bobby Joe Wright was absent. They agreed that Lowe, or Grant, had figured out the cross-eyed gunman was not a good choice to have available, in case Bass called him to the stand.

Babbit was quiet. His eyes were laced with worry, studying both sides of the street.

Behind them, Mrs. Lancaster exited; her eyes were focused on Bass, hoping he would look at her. Instead, the old attorney was concentrating his attention on another woman. Nancy Spirit Bear walked from the courthouse to the far end of the sidewalk, next to the alley, her warm eyes focused on his face. Bass looked over at her and tried to smile. It wasn't his best. He held up the rock for her to see. His eyes met hers for a moment; then he was distracted by Wallace Denson rushing up.

"Mr. Tillman . . . Mr. Tillman, do you have any remorse about the Colorado Central killings?" The editor's face was flushed with the courage of such a bold question.

Babbit started to shove him away, but Bass held him back.

"My only remorse is that the murderers of my family are hiding behind the law," Bass said, holding the medicine rock at his side, "and you are helping them."

Bass and Babbit continued their walk, leaving the editor speechless. Mrs. Lancaster harrumphed and marched on, snapping her parasol to life. A few steps behind the two friends, Timbel McKinsey hurried to catch up and immediately began arguing to let him testify, explaining that he saw the fake Indian raid setup and was the one who killed Drucker, not Bass.

"Thanks, Timbel, I told you before, there's no need for you to get involved. You've done plenty already. It only makes you a target," Bass said.

He transferred the stone from his right hand to his left, then returned it to his left coat pocket.

"*Wouldna thae* judge *wanna* know *thae* liars they all be?" McKinsey said loudly. "A *muckle* o' lies they be tellin'. Me Sarah says I *canna* sit. I must be tellin' that I did *thae* killin'. This *canna* be."

Babbit turned toward Bass, slowing his stride. "I think *der* Scotsman *ist richt*. *Du* need witnesses. *Du* can *nein* do this alone, *mein freund*."

"Look, my friends," Bass said. "They aren't going to ask me about Drucker. I'm sure of it. I told Deputy Manchester that I didn't kill him—and that news was passed on to Lowe. Grant won't walk into something he doesn't know where he'll land."

A homemade ball rolled between McKinsey and Babbit. Its sudden appearance startled the sheriff more than the Scotsman, who laughed and turned around to see a towheaded boy running toward them. Annoyed, the boy's friend pointed from the sidewalk. Scurrying between the men, the boy grabbed the ball and realized Bass was standing there.

"Hi, Mr. Tillman! 'Member me? Are you doin' all right?" It was the same youngster Bass had talked with after the Dawson shooting.

Smiling, Bass leaned over to ask the boy a question and a rifle shot sang past his ear.

With his shotgun in one hand, Babbit grabbed the boy and swung him forcefully to the side. As he was raising the gun to fire, dust popped from his vest and Babbit flew backward with two bullets in his chest. His body bounced on the street. Unmoving. His hat left his head to find its own path. His dropped shotgun danced on its barrels for an instant before flopping over.

Screaming a Scottish obscenity, McKinsey stumbled and fell.

"Run, son! Run!" Bass yelled, pulling his revolver from his belt and firing wildly in the direction of the attack. Bullets sought the old attorney as he knelt beside his downed friend, ignoring the bite of gunfire in the dirt around them.

"Mein freund, I vill *nein* be riding vit you . . ."
Blood slipped from Babbit's mouth.

Bass's upper thigh felt the sting of a bullet crease as he spun and sprinted for the far sidewalk, the side where the shots were coming from. Adrenaline kept him from feeling the wound as he snapped a quick shot in the general direction of the ambush. This bullet slammed into the hotel near the second-story window. His next tore into the sidewalk behind the adjacent water trough.

One rifleman was crouched behind that trough; the other in a second-story window of the Empire Hotel. More lead chased Bass onto the planked sidewalk and he stopped finally behind a post upholding an extended roof in front of a saloon. His breath was far behind his body, rushing to catch up in gulps. The gamble had paid off. So far. The window shooter wouldn't be able to shoot at him from this angle. So his only concern for the moment was the rifleman behind the trough. In the street, Babbit lay motionless. The Scotsman was moaning, but beginning to crawl. Neither boy was in sight.

Checking the remaining loads in his revolver, he noticed a cut along the top of the left shoulder of his coat and a black hole in the middle of his coat left-hand pocket. That bullet would have hurt him badly if it had struck. Why hadn't it? He felt with his left hand. The medicine rock from Nancy! Had the bullet hit it, instead of driving into him? It must've, but there was no time to look now. His eyes finally took in his blood-soaked thigh; whether it was just a crease or not didn't matter at the moment either. Pain from there caught up to his mind, before his wind reached his lungs again.

One bullet. Only one. His friend hadn't put a cartridge where the hammer could rest on it. Maybe he should try for the saloon. It was only ten feet away. Just ten feet. Inside, he would have a better defensive position—and, likely, find more ammunition. But it was an obvious choice. The shooter would have him wide open for several moments. His leg was tightening, making his lunge for the door's safety slower.

How did he know there wasn't another shooter inside? Waiting for him. He didn't.

"What do you say, Bass? Go for it—or see if you can stop him first?"

A bullet tore across the edge of the support beam and hurried into the sunlight. He looked at the street and knew his friend, Frank Babbit, was dead. A dark puddle spread under his unmoving frame; unseeing eyes sought what had been a nice day. Timbel McKinsey was struggling to his feet. All along the sidewalk, people had either darted into hiding places or run into stores. His mind told him the towheaded boy had escaped safely. So had his friend.

"Well, Bass, you shouldn't have tried to do this within the law," Bass muttered to himself. "You should've done what you wanted to do all along."

Two more shots sang past him, one on either side of the wood. At the moment, the post was the only thing that was keeping him alive. At the doorway of the saloon, a drunken cowboy stood, fascinated by the shooting. Bass looked at him and the cowboy drawled, "One o' them's behind that ol' trough over there." He disappeared again into the saloon before Bass could ask him for some bullets.

Bass shook his head. Did the cowboy think he didn't know that? Knowing where the shooters were—and getting to shoot at them were two different things. He was certain now that there were only two shooters. That was enough. Especially when he only had one bullet.

A moment later, the cowboy reappeared, hiccupped and held out a gun belt wrapped around a holstered Colt. "Here, ya gonna need this." He hiccupped again and added, "Ya might wanna come inside. When ya can. Hiccup. Nobody in here's gonna give ya a problem." He tossed the gun belt to Bass and disappeared again.

An empty buckboard pulled by two wild-eyed horses thundered down the street. Using the distraction to make his move, Bass slid down the pillar until he squatted on the sidewalk, shifted his gun to his left hand, pulled out the second gun and rolled over flat against the sidewalk to the right of the post. He first fired the remaining bullet from his own gun, then two more from the new weapon, directing them where he thought the street gunman might be hiding behind the trough. His shots ripped along the corner, sending slivers of wood into the air.

A fierce growl caught his attention. Cutter had come from the alley to Nancy's side and was now bounding toward the trough.

"No, Cutter!" Bass warned and fired twice more with his new gun to keep his hidden assailant from shooting at the charging dog. He didn't realize he cocked and dry-fired his own gun twice as well.

From the steps of the courthouse came a huge boom, followed by billowing smoke, and two more stout shots. A bullet bit the dirt a few feet from Cutter's front legs. Another shot from the courthouse sidewalk splintered the windowsill where the second gunman had been.

The man behind the trough stood, staggering backward. Bass fired twice more with his right-hand pistol and the man spun halfway around. Fleeing rays of sun identified him as Bobby Joe Wright. His beaded cuffs flickered as his arms lost control.

With his fangs flashing, Cutter hit Wright full force as the dying man crumpled to the ground. A Lakotan call finally stopped the dog's attack and Bass knew where the shots had come from, even before he looked. Nancy Spirit Bear hadn't moved. Both hands held the massive LeMat revolver. She had emptied the separate eighteen-gauge grapeshot-loaded barrel and two .40-caliber slugs into Wright and fired twice at the window.

From the courthouse doorway, Grant, Lowe and Judge Nelene watched the gunfight, stunned more by the presence of the gun-shooting Indian woman and her dog than by the sight of the dead sheriff and wounded Scotsman.

"What the hell's going on?" Judge Nelene asked, his voice deep with concern.

Lowe pointed to the dead sheriff in the middle of the street. "Some friends of Tillman's are trying to bust him free. They got the sheriff." He pointed toward the second-floor window of the hotel. "Marshal Cateson and one of my posse men are trying to stop it. They hit one of Tillman's friends." He pointed again, this time at McKinsey. "We suspect he's a Hoodsman, too." Shrugging his shoulders, he added, "They just murdered Wright, one of my deputies. There. Across the street."

"I thought you said Tillman and the sheriff were old friends," Grant said.

"Guess not," Lowe muttered. "Outlaws are hard to figure sometimes."

"Yeah, hard to figure," Judge Nelene observed without looking at either man.

Lowe raised his gun to fire. Judge Nelene's fist slammed down on the deputy marshal's arm, knocking his pistol to the floor. His quirt flipped in the air.

"What the . . . damn, that hurt," Lowe howled.

"Get your ass back inside, Marshal Lowe," Judge Nelene barked. "If I need you, I'll let you know."

Lowe rubbed his forearm. "That's a killer out there, Judge. He's trying to escape. He's killed three federal lawmen. An' that damn redskin, she's in it, too. Just like that no-good half-breed scout."

"I said to get your ass back inside. Do it now." The broad-shouldered judge turned his attention back to Bass.

Lowe leaned over to retrieve his gun, but made

no attempt to shoot again. Instead, he hurried inside to find Deputy Manchester.

Grant watched him disappear and declared dramatically, "Judge, I trust this attempt to escape will not need further exploration in the hearing. It should speak for itself."

"We'll see, Grant. We'll see."

A heavyset businessman with a gold chain dangling across an expanded vest stepped to the saloon doorway to observe the situation. He watched Bass return to his feet, keeping close to the wall and away from the second-floor shooter. Shoving the cowboy's gun into his waistband, the old attorney shoved new loads into his own revolver, from the gun belt loops. Finishing with that gun, he began reloading the second. The stiffened fingers of his left hand wouldn't work as fast as he wanted. The businessman turned away from the door and reported to the patrons inside.

From down the street, Lucius Henry came running. He was unarmed.

"This has gone on long enough," Judge Nelene asserted and stepped into the street.

"Don't do that, Judge! It's too dangerous," Grant pleaded.

"Oh, hell, Grant. Get inside."

"Bass Tillman, put down your guns," the big magistrate yelled, his robe swishing at his feet as he walked toward the wounded attorney. "Tell this Indian woman to do the same." He motioned toward Nancy Spirit Bear, who was watching the hotel window. Alerted by the shots and Lowe's plea to assist, Deputy Manchester hurried to catch up with the calm magistrate, a pistol in his hand. He cleared the doorway and spat in the direction of the street, but caught the edge of the sidewalk, and created a brown spray.

"Wh-what's going on, Judge? My God, that's Sheriff Babbit. Is he . . . ?" Manchester coughed and thought he was going to vomit.

"Dead. I'd say the other fella's going to make it, though."

Manchester stared at the wounded Scotsman. "That's Timbel McKinsey. He's a farmer. A neighbor of . . . Jacob's." He looked across the street. "And that's Bobby Joe Wright. He's one of Lowe's . . . posse men." He glanced over at the Indian woman standing quietly with the massive handgun cocked and held in both hands at her waist. Her gaze never left the hotel, in spite of Manchester's sudden interest and the judge's command.

Leaning against the wall, Bass yelled, "Why don't you tell that son of a bitch in the window to put his gun down first? They just murdered my friend."

Cutter wandered over to Bass and brushed his head against the wounded attorney's leg. With his own gun in his right hand and the second in his waistband, Bass leaned down to pet him and said softly, "My gosh, boy, you're just about healed. How'd Nancy manage that?" It was an honest reaction, for the courageous dog appeared quite healthy, except for the healing scabs.

Manchester glanced at the second-floor window of the hotel. A whisper of the curtains indicated someone had been there moments before. Without hesitating, he bolted across the street and bounded onto the sidewalk.

"Going inside to thank your buddy Cateson? Leastwise, I figure it's him. He just got you the sheriff's job," Bass said.

The deputy gave him a fleeting look and entered the hotel.

Judge Nelene walked closer, stopping to let a riderless horse pass in front of him. "Bass Tillman, this isn't the way, man. Listen to me."

Standing beside the doorway, Grant declared, "Does this mean the hearing is going to be delayed? I object. Or have you seen enough to get this killer to trial?" He ran his right hand through his hair to settle it.

"Shut up, Grant," Judge Nelene barked. "This is between the prisoner and me." He walked across the street, checking to make certain no breakaway horses or wagons were headed his way.

Breathing heavily, Bass lowered his gun to his side and growled, "I'm going to kill that bastard up there, Nelene. I'm sure it's Cateson—and I'm going to kill Lowe—and I'm going to kill Hautrese. It's gone too far. I don't give a damn what happens to me."

Nelene didn't respond as he whirled to the sound of footsteps behind him. From the doorway came a horrified Sarah McKinsey. She knelt beside her downed husband and told him to be still. Judge Nelene watched her and focused again on the old attorney.

"You don't mean that, Bass," he said. "It's never too far. Please. Let Deputy Manchester handle this. It's his duty."

Bass started to explain something about the young deputy, then felt too tired to say anything.

Stepping away from the wall, he eased into the street, headed for the McKinseys. Cutter followed at his side.

Grant yelled, "Judge, this is most irregular. I demand that you order Marshal Lowe to arrest this man."

"Take your demands and shove 'em up your ass," Judge Nelene barked. "I'm in charge here." Again he faced Bass. "Give me your guns, Bass. That's an order."

"Tillman will shoot you," Grant said.

"Then you have my permission to shoot him."

When Bass raised his eyes toward the judge, madness blinked for an instant, then disappeared. "Tell me first that no charges will be filed against her. Nancy Spirit Bear."

"You have my word."

"Then you have my word that you'll have my guns." Bass patted Timbel McKinsey on the arm and looked up at the hotel window. "Just as soon as I know the guy up there doesn't have his."

Cutter barked his reinforcement of the promise.

Chapter 23

From the hotel doorway, Manchester cleared the darkness. His puzzled look became a statement. "The only one up there—in that room—was Marshal Cateson. He's dead." His frown deepened. "His throat was cut." He spat to the side, but the new chaw wasn't ready to be relieved.

Bass mouthed "Painted Crow" as he looked at the Lakota holy woman. She nodded agreement and hurried into the street toward him. The white-haired attorney laid his guns on the ground and stood, watching her come. Cutter wagged his tail and hurried to meet her advance. No one heard the sigh of relief escaping from Nelene's tight mouth.

"Timbel McKinsey is a very good man," Bass said to Sarah McKinsey, "and very brave. I count myself lucky to have him as a friend."

Slowly, she raised her tear-washed face and took his hand. "Na. *Mae* Timbel, he *dinna* want *tae* be brave—but he *wad* be for you. He said ye were *thae* most brave he ever saw. *Thae richt* way o't, I be sayin'. Bless ye, Bass Tillman—and bless *mae* Timbel." She returned her attention to the bloody Scotsman, who was spitting out Scottish curses, and told him to be quiet.

From behind the white-haired attorney, Judge Nelene came slowly and stood. "Bass, I don't know why you did this—or if it was done to you. I honestly don't. But you have to come back inside. You are still under arrest. Do you need a doctor?"

"I'm not sure what I need, Judge." Bass looked up. "But it's probably nothing you can give."

Nancy Spirit Bear reached him, stopping a few feet away. She leaned over to return the happy greeting from Cutter.

"Nancy, you must leave," he said gently. "Now. Please."

"I will stand by The River." She hurried next to him and hugged him.

He hugged her back, kissing her cheek. "No. It is not safe. Take Cutter with you. Please."

She studied his face. "Will you come?"

"When I can." He touched the broken rock in his left coat pocket, then the empty tobacco sack in his right. "My medicine is strong, thanks to you." He patted Cutter on the head and awkwardly stepped away from her.

Waving his arms for attention, the judge commanded that Manchester go for the doctor. Lucius Henry finally reached Bass and asked him how badly he was hurt. Bass said he had been hurt worse and to see about Babbit and McKinsey.

"Marshal Cateson was trying to stop Tillman and his men from an escape attempt," Lowe said as he reappeared from inside the courthouse.

Grant hurried beside Nelene, spitting out legal phrases that didn't quite make sense. He was rattled, but managed to demand the hearing go on, that Bass Tillman was wanted by the federal government for murder and he could prove it.

"Looks like Longmont's gonna need a new sheriff." Lowe stood over the dead Frank Babbit; his boot toe nudged the still form.

Exploding with rage, Bass sprang at Lowe. "Get away from him, you son of a bitch!"

As Lowe reached for his holstered gun, Bass's right fist slammed into his face. Lowe staggered and collapsed, like a man sitting in a chair that wasn't there.

"My God, Judge, now he's assaulting a federal officer!" Grant whimpered.

Nelene held out his arm for Bass to stop, but the symbolic restraint had no significance to Bass. Cocking his head to the side, he said, "Want to see it again?" Without waiting for the answer, Bass grabbed the shirt of the dazed Lowe with his left hand; rage released its stiffness. He yanked Lowe to his feet and planted a second haymaker into Lowe's face. His nose splattered blood like an erupting volcano.

"That's enough, Tillman," Judge Nelene said, more softly than Grant expected.

"It's a long way from enough, Judge, but it's a start." Bass released Lowe's shirt and let him fall. He rubbed the reddened knuckles on his right hand. In an odd sort of way, the pain felt good.

Two hours later the hearing was resumed. A group of solemn townsmen had carried the body of Frank Babbit to the undertaker's office. Three Chinamen were paid to bring the bodies of Cateson and Wright there. Dr. Williams had tended to McKinsey's wounds and, reluctantly, to Lowe's damaged face. Bass refused attention, insisting he had only been creased. Judge Nelene told Manchester that he was acting sheriff until the Longmont City Council could meet; Judge Pierce concurred, adding a few fiery comments Nelene ignored. Nancy Spirit Bear and Cutter disappeared; no one saw Painted Crow anywhere. The cowboy asked for his gun from Nelene and the frowning judge returned it, then shoved Bass's revolver into his waistband under this robe.

When Grant returned to the courtroom after changing clothes, he was surprised to see Bass sitting at his table as if he had never left. Only a tear along the left shoulder of his coat indicated he had been in some kind of a scuffle. The prosecutor was greatly puzzled by the old man's behavior. Questions about the attempt to escape whirred through his mind.

Why hadn't the old man continued his flight? Did he lose his nerve? Surely that Indian woman had horses ready. Why had he given up so easily? Did he think the judge would view the surrender as negating the violent attempt itself? Why hadn't Nelene allowed Lowe to shoot the old man? Should he expand the federal charges to include the killing of Bobby Joe Wright? For that matter, why hadn't Nelene declared the need for a trial right then and there—and ended the hearing?

Wasn't it obvious Tillman was guilty? Was the judge envious of his growing reputation? Maybe Nelene wanted to be governor, too.

The handsome prosecutor shivered. It was the first time he had ever been so close to gunfire, to seeing someone die violently. Dealing with the other captured Hoodsmen had been so different than this, so controlled, so smooth. Bass Tillman was, indeed, a cold, calculating man, just as Lowe had described. But he had miscalculated this time. What kind of a man would have his friend gunned down so he could flee? Only a very desperate one. It was right Bass Tillman should hang. He was certain of it.

Grant studied Bass more closely and got a second surprise: Bass was reading a Bible. Next to the opened Scripture were two pieces of rock. Grant folded his arms. Was he trying to impress the judge? Well, he wasn't the only one who could use Scripture to his advantage—and anyone could grab a rock. Grant frowned; the old attorney must think he was losing to attempt such a wild escape and follow it with the appearance of abject penitence. Grant smiled; Lowe assured him Crimmler would end the wild hearing.

Unaware of Grant's arrival or attention, Bass looked at the broken medicine stone, then glanced at the crystal hanging from his watch chain. "Maybe it's all about believing in something, Bass, something bigger than yourself," he muttered. "Like a cross, maybe. Or a menorah." He told himself to concentrate, but his mind was frazzled. They had killed his son and daughter-in-law and now, one of his oldest friends. How much more could he take? Why had he laid down his guns? Was it because he was afraid of how Nancy Spirit Bear would react?

Kneeling next to him, Manchester waited for Bass to look at him. The young acting sheriff had no tobacco in his mouth. "Mr. Tillman, I would like to testify on your behalf," he said quietly. "You won't believe me, but I didn't know they were going . . . to kill them. Honest to God, I didn't. They said they just wanted to talk." He squeezed his eyes shut for a moment to keep from weeping. "I'll testify Cateson, Lowe, Drucker and their posse men are the Hoodsmen—and that Hautrese is behind it all. I'm ready for my punishment, too."

"Jacob and Mary Anne died because they trusted you. They opened their door to you, didn't they?" Bass's face was hard. "I don't want your help." He glanced away. "And if you testify for Grant, I'll see you hang with the rest of them." The old attorney's piercing eyes returned to the deputy's torn expression. "Now get out of my sight, William. When you hit your knees tonight, be thankful I didn't have a gun."

Manchester gulped, stood and walked to the back of the courtroom.

Bringing the session to order, Nelene declared, "Since the intent of the violence earlier is not clear to me, I will not consider it a part of this hearing one way or the other. My opinion is the only one that counts. Is that clear?"

Bass didn't look up; Grant exploded, demanding an explanation. Nelene told him the ruling was final and to be quiet. The handsome prosecutor whispered to Lowe, "Is he afraid of Tillman? Or his gang?"

Lowe answered softly, "Don't worry. Crimmler will finish that old bastard."

Nelene's glare stopped the whispering and he turned to Bass. "Mr Tillman, how does defense counsel respond?"

Bass raised his head. "I just lost a good friend to this murdering bunch. They've already killed my son and his wife. Just how the hell do you think I want to respond?" His shoulders rose and fell. "Give me back my guns and I'll show you."

"Tillman!"

"Go ahead." Bass waved his hand as if swatting a fly.

With Nelene's approval, Grant stood and proclaimed, "Your Honor, I call Mr. Virgil Crimmler to the stand." His toothy smile transformed into a victorious smirk.

A short, stocky man in a brown-and-white cowhide vest with a handlebar mustache lumbered through the side door. At the right corner of Crimmler's mouth, a nervous twitch performed regularly. Beside him was Lowe; the deputy marshal's swollen face was an aging pumpkin, his nose a purplish bulb. One eye was nearly closed, strands of red and yellow taking control of his cheek. Bass recognized the outlaw as being at Lowe's camp. He studied Crimmler as he was sworn in and heard the captured outlaw's response to Grant's initial query. It was like watching a boy recite in school. A nervous boy who didn't want to be there.

"Yes, I was a Hoodsman," Crimmler announced. "Marshal Lowe arrested me at Jacob Tillman's place. We, ah, were hidin' there after the Highland Bank . . . ah, robbery. We were supposed to wait there till Bass Tillman joined us. Had us, ya know, be seen here in town afore ridin' to Highland. Said it'd give us an alibi. Him, too." He exhaled, thankful the first answer had gone well. Now if he could just remember the rest of what he was supposed to say.

The somewhat thinned audience was painfully quiet. A man coughed and his wife chastised him for the interruption. The man next to him whispered Bass was guilty.

Grant strode toward the witness stand, like a mountain cat about to pounce. "You say you were at Jacob Tillman's farm . . . after the holdup. Who wore the buffalo coat?"

Shifting uneasily in his chair, Crimmler glanced at Lowe, nodded slightly and began to recite. "Jacob did. Yes, sir. Threw it away on the trail. Figured it was the only thing that could be tracked to us." He swallowed and tried to smile. "An' I reckon a feller looks a mite bigger holdin' a gun. Some folks think Jesse James is a giant."

A few uncomfortable chuckles followed from the audience and Crimmler grinned and looked at Lowe. The statement was Lowe's idea and it seemed to have played well. With Grant's prodding, Crimmler launched into a presentation about Bass Tillman being the head of the Hoodsmen. He repeated himself several times, inserting the same phrase in different sentences and got one entire thought backward. Grant completed his questioning and slid back into his chair, smiling broadly. Lowe patted him on the back.

Slowly, Bass rose. Cords on his neck gave away the tension. His voice was low and ominous. "I can forgive you lying about me, Crimmler. I can't, about my son. You, you lying bastard, are going to hang."

"I object. He can't threaten the witness like that," Grant declared.

Crimmler fidgeted in his seat and blurted, "You killed the Pinkerton man on the Central Colorado. An' . . . an' . . . Jacob killed the engineer. I was there. I saw you."

On the third row, a woman began to cry softly. A man's voice bellowed out that his son was on that train and died in the crash.

Amidst swelling whispers, Bass walked over to his table and held up a newspaper sheet. "There's something you might want to know. On the day of that awful crime, I was in this courtroom. This very courtroom. If Judge Nelene wishes, Judge Pierce can be brought in to verify that fact." He paused, trying to control his anger. "And Jacob was on duty—in the jail. We even had lunch together. There are witnesses to that, too."

The whispers stopped as Bass held the newspaper higher. "Had a feeling these boys would blame us for their crimes, so I got the dates of the suspected Hoodsmen from the *Longmont Advocate*'s back issues. Thank you, Mr. Denson, for your assistance." He couldn't hold back a smile.

Bass limped over to Grant's table and slammed the sheet down in front of him. "Grant, I've had enough of this. You want to drag out more hirelings to make more idiotic claims? Or do you want to save us some time—and admit this is all a bunch of nonsense to keep the truth from coming out? I find it increasingly hard to believe you don't really know Lowe and Hautrese are behind all this."

He spun away before the surprised Grant could respond. "Crimmler, the only honest thing you've said so far is that you were at the train holdup. You're going to hang for those murders, or didn't you realize that's what they set up?" He stepped closer to Crimmler, the old attorney's eyes cutting deep into the scared outlaw. "Unless you tell us right now who did kill them. Who was it, Crimmler?"

Terrified, Crimmler jumped to his feet and pointed at Lowe. "Look at me! You promised I'd go free if I said all this stuff." He shook his head, but stopped talking as the doors popped open and a loud voice from the back took control of the courtroom.

Easter Sontag strolled down the center aisle, holding an ivory-handled pistol and shoving the buffalo-coated Harry Truitt ahead of him. Over Sontag's shoulder were the full saddlebags from the robbery. The fat-bellied hangman was covered with trail dust and the timid man in front of him appeared tired and stunned.

Bass shook his head to clear it. What was the executioner doing here? Was this another trick by Grant and Lowe? To himself, he muttered, "Bass, old man, you'd better listen close. Easter Sontag's no fool like Grant."

"Pardon the court, I am Easter Sontag. We've met before, Nelene," the fat-bellied executioner boomed. "I've got some important facts you need to know."

Grant's head swiveled between Sontag, Bass, Nelene and Lowe. At Lowe's urging, he declared, "I can't imagine what a hangman can tell us that we don't already know, Your Honor. We've shown sufficient evidence to warrant a trail for murder." He coughed and tried to laugh. "We'll need Mr. Sontag at that time." His voice carried little of its usual conviction.

Sontag told Truitt to stop and he complied immediately, close to tears. Pushing his hat back on his head, Sontag stared at Grant and snarled, "You know, Grant, I don't think you know squat, I really don't. You're just an egotistical pissant being used by Lowe and Hautrese." He spun the gun in his hand and returned it to his shoulder holster.

"Watch your language, Mr. Sontag. This is a courtroom. My courtroom," Nelene said, rubbing the gavel in his hands.

"Sorry, Nelene. Meant no disrespect," Sontag said and glanced at Bass. "But I've been riding hard to get here. This Hoodsmen crap—sorry—has gone on long enough." He motioned toward the back of the courtroom. "Outside, you'll find two bodies. Aren't in very good shape. Truitt, here, just dug them up. One is a big fella named Joe Benson. He and this pissant robbed the Highland Bank. The money's here." He patted the saddlebags on his shoulder. "The other's that murdering bastard Bill Drucker."

"My God, Deputy Marshal Drucker?" Grant gasped. "Who killed him?"

Sontag smiled. "Somebody doing us all a favor and getting rid of a Hoodsman."

Nelene slammed his gavel. "Mr. Sontag, please come forward. If the two parties here agree, I would like your testimony. Under oath. Now." He looked at Grant, who licked his lips, then at Bass, who nodded his approval.

"Grant, what's the slowness here?" Nelene demanded.

"Ah, well, Your Honor, I'm just shocked," Grant said. "We were concerned about Marshal Drucker's safety since he disappeared in pursuit of the defendant. I was hoping he would be found alive." He looked over at Bass. "The tally of federal lawmen this man has killed keeps growing. He just killed a posse man outside, if you will recall, Your Honor, trying to escape."

"Yes or no to Mr. Sontag's testimony here and now. This is a hearing, not a trial. I will decide on protocol."

"Well, I guess . . . yes."

"Up here, Mr. Sontag," Nelene waved toward the witness chair. "Sheriff, please take this man into custody until his situation can be determined." He pointed at Truitt, then glanced again at Crimmler, who was trying to get Lowe's attention. "You are finished testifying, for the moment, Mr. Crimmler." He looked back at the advancing Sheriff Manchester. "Take Mr. Crimmler, too. The court will deal with him later."

The stocky outlaw rose from the witness chair without being asked and headed toward Man-

chester, who was hurrying forward. He looked
again at Lowe, who mouthed for him to be patient. Grant stared at Crimmler, then at Lowe.
Manchester ordered Truitt and Crimmler to the
back of the room and to sit down on the floor in
front of him.

After a few swipes at his coat to remove the
dust, Sontag dropped the saddlebags on the floor
in front of him and received the oath directly
from Nelene. Looking straight at Grant, he related
the details of the forest hideout, Benson and Truitt bragging about the bank robbery and his subsequent ride to the Tillman farm. Only Bass
seemed to notice the hangman remained armed.

Tepid cross-examination by Grant yielded only
that Drucker never identified himself as a deputy
marshal or was interested in the bank robbery.
Then the district attorney asked about Sontag's
interest in the case.

"Good question for once, Grant," Sontag said.
"I've had to hang three men you got convicted of
being Hoodsmen. You and that pissant Lowe over
there."

The handsome prosecutor inhaled deeply. "Justice must be served."

"'When devils will the blackest sins put on,
they do suggest at first with heavenly shows,'"
Sontag recited.

Only Bass recognized the line as coming from
Othello. He nodded and the executioner returned
the greeting. Grant frowned, trying to recall if
that was Scripture or not. He was jolted out of the
mental exercise as the hangman continued.

"Justice you say? Not hardly. I've been having

nightmares ever since," Sontag declared, shaking his head. "You boys set up those fellows, nice and sweet. Just like you're trying to do to the Tillmans here." He leaned forward with both hands tightly gripping the chair arms. "Not this time, Grant. Not this time. Bass Tillman is a damn good man—and everybody in this town knows it, or should." He stared at the crowd and every man there felt he was looking just at him.

Many heads bobbed in agreement; several people muttered support. The blacksmith stood and yelled, "You're right as can be, hangman! Bass Tillman ain't no Hoodsman—an' we all know it." From the other side of the room, another man stood and proclaimed, "Judge Nelene, I think you've heard enough. Let Bass go and arrest Topper Lowe."

Instead of banging his gavel for silence, Nelene looked down at Grant, who was ashen-faced. "Does prosecution wish to question the witness further?" Nelene asked.

Lowe leaned over to whisper in Grant's ear and the blond district attorney shrugged him away and stood. "I have some more questions, yes."

"Proceed and make it quick."

Grant walked from the table, his confidence seeping away from his eyes. "Were you personally aware of federal marshals seeking to arrest the Tillmans and Crimmler at the Tillman farm?"

"I am aware a murderous attack on an innocent man and his wife took place there."

Flustered, Grant looked at Judge Nelene. "Please inform the witness that he must answer my question with a yes or a no."

"I did answer it. You just didn't like my answer," Sontag huffed.

Grant licked his lower lip and tried again, "Yes or no? Were you there when federal marshals tried to arrest them?"

"That boat won't float, Grant. Can't answer a question that didn't happen," Sontag said. "Lowe and his bunch of pissants murdered an innocent family."

Holding back a grin, Nelene leaned toward the executioner. "You must answer the question with a simple yes or no." He knitted his brow. "And watch your language."

"No, I saw the fresh graves of this man's family. I saw the attempt to make it look like an Indian attack. Only a pissant would think it was." Sontag's eyes were hooded in anger, daring Grant to interrupt. "I saw what your boys tried to do to a dog on top of their murdering.

"A dog, Grant." He pointed his finger at the prosecutor. "Do you think a dog is a Hoodsman, Grant? Do you think this is a goddamn game you're playing with a brave man's life? Are you really so stupid to think Lowe, Cateson, Drucker—and Hautrese—are honest lawmen?" His temper made him stand with his fists doubled at his sides. "Don't you realize they're using you for the vain fool you are?"

The audience roared and Nelene was forced to bang his gavel for quiet.

Grant hesitated. He knew the executioner by reputation mostly. A man to be left alone, to be feared. It was obvious he had been a fool to believe in this Hoodsmen effort. How could he salvage his reputation from this? He stepped to his right and folded his arms. There was nothing to do now, but present himself as a thorough professional prosecutor, seeking truth. Afterward, he might be able to convince reporters that he was helping uncover the real Hoodsmen.

Realizing Grant was broken by Sontag's assessment, Lowe shifted in his chair, squinting his already half-closed eye, and growled, "Be careful, Grant. My first bullet goes to your head."

Grant swallowed, glanced at Lowe, then back to Sontag. "Tell me, Mr. Sontag," he asked in his best legal-sounding tone, "how did you—and all these others—just happen to be at this hideout cabin at the same time?"

Returning to his seat, Sontag explained the situation, emphasizing Bass was close on Drucker's trail for murdering his family, then noting that he, personally, was en route to Denver City to handle a hanging assignment of another convicted Hoodsman. As he finished, he faced the judge. "Nelene, that reminds me, when you get back to Denver City," Sontag said, "take a close look at the case against Charlie Arlman. I'll bet he's like the other men Lowe's brought in. He's no more a Hoodsman than you are."

Grant started to protest.

Sontag's glare silenced him and he resumed his demand of the judge. "You can't bring those other innocent boys back, but you can save Charlie Arlman. And you sure as hell can bring this pissant nightmare to an end."

His shoulders rising and falling, Nelene nodded slightly.

"Why did it take you so long to come forward, Mr. Sontag?" Grant's question brought the executioner's attention back to him. The handsome prosecutor was trying to think of something to salvage the day, even as he spoke. Should he simply ask the judge to release Bass Tillman and arrest Lowe? If he did that, Lowe would kill him, before anyone could save him. He could wait and tell reporters that he was part of the secret plan to bring to the real criminals to justice. His frantic mind assured him of the idea.

The famed executioner stared at Lowe, who looked away. "We were riding together, Bass Tillman and me. When we hit town, I went to the hotel to check in, while he turns the bodies of those two murderers over to the sheriff. Then I hear he's been arrested by Lowe and Cateson and that cross-eyed pissant who can't talk worth a damn."

He straightened his back and focused on Grant himself. "I knew what was happening. Lowe was going to try to get Bass Tillman hanged for something he didn't do. The only way to stop it was to do what I did." He licked his lips again. "Do you understand, Grant, or do I need to spell it out more? So far, you haven't shown much ability to understand much of anything."

"I believe you have answered my question." Grant's gaze pleaded with the judge for help.

"Well, I want to make sure of that," Sontag responded, then recited, " 'Truth is truth to the end of reckoning.' " He glanced at Bass again and nodded. "Five times now, I've been ordered by U.S. Marshal Hautrese to execute a man that I had a feeling wasn't guilty. All in all, I've executed twenty-two men, Grant. Twenty-two. That's my job and I'm damn good at it. Those were the first I ever suspected of being innocent."

"I said you answered my question."

"I'll tell you when I've answered your question." Sontag's face reddened and his voice deepened with anger again. "I don't like you, Grant. You're a reminder that I've been a party to this god-awful charade, too. Only I know it now—and you don't. You're a poor excuse for a man."

Firmly, Judge Nelene told Sontag that he was facing a fine if he swore again, and asked Grant if he had any more questions for the witness. The rattled prosecutor responded by returning to his chair and turning his back toward Lowe. Focusing his attention on Bass, the judge asked if he had any questions for the witness. Without standing, Bass said, "Easter, who did I suspect of being Drucker's contact, when I first trailed him to that cabin?"

Sontag laughed. "You suspected me, damn you. You had that wire signed by somebody 'H'— and you thought it might stand for 'hangman.' I told you it was Hautrese, didn't I?"

"Yes, you did. Who killed Drucker?" Bass stared at the table.

"That Scotsman with you did. Drucker was going to shoot you in the back. The Scotsman had no choice. You tried to keep Drucker alive," Sontag said.

"Why? Did I think he was a lawman?"

"Not hardly," Sontag answered. "You knew the pissant had been one of them who murdered your family, but you wanted to know who he was riding to see in Denver. You wanted the rest—and all you had were those damn initials." He glanced over at Nelene. "Is it a hundred apiece?"

Nelene smiled and said, "Yes."

"No more questions, Your Honor," Bass announced.

"Does the defense wish to call anyone to the stand at this time?" Nelene asked. "I believe the prosecution is finished. Is that correct, Grant?"

Lowe glared at Grant. Flustered, Grant whispered that he was and asked that the defendant be remanded for trial.

Nelene responded, "Call your witness, Tillman."

"I will take the stand myself," Bass declared. "Lowe's men murdered my other witness, Sheriff Frank Babbit."

Another disturbance drew everyone's attention to the back of the courtroom, where a flushed telegraph assistant rushed through the door. He said something to Manchester standing at the back with the two outlaws sitting on the floor at his feet. The young deputy unfolded the note, read it and motioned for him to go forward.

"Your Honor," Manchester called out. "There is a message here that you must see. Immediately, sir."

"I'm sorry, Judge, but Mr. Dickson said you'd want this right away," the pimple-faced assistant jabbered about the telegraph operator as he hurried down the aisle and handed the frowning magistrate a folded note.

"This had better be very important, young man. This is a courtroom you're interrupting. My courtroom."

"Yessir. I know, sir. It is, sir."

Judge Nelene opened and read the paper, cleared his throat and announced, "Seems we do have a change. I'll read this. You'll have to wait a minute, Tillman."

Bass frowned and touched the broken stones, then the Bible.

With a stern expression, Nelene faced the audience. "This wire is from Boston Hautrese, United States Marshal, Colorado District. It is directed to Sheriff Frank Babbit—and me. He says, and I quote, 'Critical facts have come to my attention. Bass Tillman is innocent of all charges against him. Release him immediately. Hold Topper Lowe, John Cateson and Bill Drucker for trial of all Hoodsmen crimes. Have evidence they are the leaders of the gang. I am grievously sorry to realize they held posts as my deputy marshals while endangering the good citizens of this state. Have evidence they killed Pinkerton Agent Simpson and the engineer of the Colorado Central. Hold Lowe also for the murder of late U.S. Marshal Amos Frese. En route to you now is Acting U.S. Marshal E. J. Vorak to take charge of their arrests and subsequent trials. He is bringing the evidence I have discovered. Because of a worsening health condition, I am resigning my post as U.S. Marshal effective immediately. Marshal Vorak assumes the responsibility until presidential appointment is made."

A sense of triumph crossed the judge's face as he finished reading and disappeared into a dour expression. "Is there anything else I need to know, son? I assume your employer had you come immediately."

The assistant started to speak, but was startled into silence as Lowe jumped to his feet. "Hautrese isn't gonna pin this on me. No damn way! He's behind it. All of it," he screamed. A revolver waved in the short deputy marshal's right fist with his quirt dangling below it. He glanced at a frightened woman seated on the front row behind the prosecution's table and pulled her in front of him. "I'm walking out of here. Her an' me. If anybody tries anything, she dies."

Holding the hysterical woman next to him with his left arm, Lowe began to back out of the courtroom. His pistol was pointed at her head. The telegraph assistant gulped and stepped into the third row, his trembling legs against an annoyed businessman. Lowe's gun moved from the woman's head to Bass and Sontag, then back to her head. Satisfied, he half turned toward Manchester standing rigid in the back of the room. "Don't try anything foolish, kid. You ain't Babbit."

The young deputy raised his hands as Lowe returned his attention to the front. Sontag sat nonchalantly, as if he were watching a play. Bass remained at the defense table, looking at a sheet of paper, his back to Lowe. Judge Nelene was stone-faced behind his podium. Grant sat with his elbows on the table, his face in his hands.

"Take me with you, Lowe," Crimmler said. "You owe me."

"Come on," Lowe growled. "Take the kid's gun."

Grinning, Crimmler jumped up, yanked Manchester's revolver from his holster and shoved the young lawman backward. "You're lucky I don't shoot you."

Truitt looked at Sontag and remained seated, while Crimmler pushed open the door, waving the revolver in the direction of the stunned audience.

Satisfied, Lowe shoved the blubbering woman to the floor. "I'll shoot the first man to clear this door."

The door slammed shut. Regaining his lost courage, Manchester headed to the door.

As Bass jumped up from his table, his words stopped Manchester. "No, William. It's my turn. Give me your gun, Easter."

"No, Bass, Lowe is mine." Sontag rose and brandished his pistol.

"Take this," Nelene declared and held out Bass's revolver for him to take it.

"W-wait, Mr. Tillman, sir. Ah, Mr. Sontag," the telegraph assistant blurted and stepped into the aisle. "I tried to tell the judge here. Ah, the mayor's outside with some men. A lot of them. They've got rifles and shotguns."

Outside, a muffled command barely reached inside. "You're under arrest. Both of you. Put down the guns."

"My employer hurried to find the mayor while I . . . I came here, sir," the assistant said. "Mr. Dickson said it was time the town stood up. That's what he said. Mr. Dickson did, sir." He permitted himself a smile.

"You can learn from your boss." Bass grabbed the judge's offered gun and headed for the door with Sontag beside him. The executioner patted Bass on the back. "My friend, let's get these sons of bitches. Together."

The courtroom door slammed back open. Lowe

and Crimmler stepped back inside with their hands up. Lowe's face was pale, except for growing purple around his swollen right eye and nose. Crimmler was furious, but his hands were held high. Following them were Mayor Evans, Judge Pierce, Lucius Henry, Dr. Williams, Benjamin Ringly, Arland Dickson and Jason Geiger Sr., all armed with various kinds of weapons. Geiger was carrying a brand-new Winchester from his store and still wearing his apron. It bore the blood of Sheriff Babbit. Henry's coat sleeve was similarly stained.

"Afternoon, Bass," Mayor Evans said brightly. "You too, Mr. Sontag. We've got two prisoners for you, Judge Nelene . . . and, ah, Sheriff Manchester."

"I see that." Nelene leaned forward from his podium. "I suppose you'll be wanting a ruling on this hearing first."

The fiery Judge Pierce stepped forward. "You damn better betcha we do, Nelene. You're way past due. Get at it."

Straightening himself to his full height, the magistrate declared, "I conclude the defendant, Bass Tillman, was fully justified in defending himself against the two dead men . . . and had no part in crimes attributed to the so-called Hoodsmen, or any other illegal act. This hearing is adjourned." He slammed his gavel down. "I hereby order Sheriff Manchester to arrest Topper Lowe and Virgil Crimmler for murder—and other crimes to be determined." He glanced down at the distraught Grant. "And you, Touren Grant, I shall talk with you in my chambers. There is a matter of disbarment."

He wasn't quite prepared for the happy outburst that followed. A wide-faced farmer yelled, "Good fer you, Judge. Didn't think ya was gonna figger it out fer a piece."

Henry eased next to Bass and held out his hand. "It's over, Bass. It's over."

"Yeah, guess so." Bass glanced at the gun in his fist and felt weak all over.

"I want a lawyer," Lowe shouted. "This is ridiculous! I am a United States Chief Deputy Marshal. I am the law."

Bass pointed his revolver at the surrendered man. "You're nothing but a pissant."

Sontag laughed.

For an instant, the old attorney was at his son's farm; then his mind took him further back in time, walking hand in hand with his beloved Settie. Across his memory, a small boy skipped in front of them and then he was riding with two companions, all three ready for anything and stepping aside for no man.

"P-please, don't. Don't shoot me," Lowe pleaded and dropped to his knees, his hands clasped together. "I—I didn't shoot your son. I-it was C-Cateson. H-honest."

Startled from his memories, Bass looked at the tense faces gathered close. He uncocked the gun and shoved it into his waistband. Relief on everyone's face followed.

Pushing to the front, the bespectacled Dr. Williams held his shotgun at his side and announced, "Timbel McKinsey's doing fine, Bass. That tough Scotsman won't stop talking, though. Even his wife can't stop him from jabbering about how good a man you are. Should make your ears burn."

Staring at him as if processing the information, Bass glanced upward, then back at the eager physician. "That's mighty good news, Doc. Thanks."

Still on his knees, Lowe refound his courage. "How'd you come to know Marshal Vorak? Why's he doing this—for you?"

"Don't know a Marshal Vorak," Bass said. "Get on your feet."

A brush against his side turned into Judge Nelene. The big-shouldered man stared at the cadre of armed men standing around Bass and asked them as a group, "What would've happened if my decision was different?"

"It wasn't going to be, Judge. It just wasn't," Henry said, turned and walked away.

Chapter 24

Three days later, Bass Tillman stood by himself beside the grave of his friend, Frank Babbit. He was trying to decide if the sheriff's headstone should bear his real name, Frank Schafer, or his adopted one. In his hand was a Bible. Babbit's. A few feet away, Othello hee-hawed and pawed the ground. Bass's clothes were the same he had worn at the funeral. Black and showing signs of having slept in them. The bulge of the refilled tobacco sack and two pieces of the medicine stone were visible in his coat pocket.

"Good-bye, Frank. Ah, *Auf Wiedersehen*. Reverend Masters did a good job . . . at your service, I thought. So did Ringly. Before. Wouldn't take a dime." Bass shifted the hat in his hands. "Whole town was here, you know, even Moulton. You were mighty well thought of, old friend."

A southern breeze danced along his sagging shoulders, choosing his white hair for a partner as the old attorney talked on about what had happened since the street gunfight. He stared at his boots, then at the temporary wood marker.

Biting his lower lip, he declared, "Going to get you a fine headstone, but I'm not sure how you want . . . the name. Thought maybe coming here would help me decide." He held up Babbit's German Bible. "Even brought this." He lowered it and patted his left coat pocket with his free hand. "Nancy tells me the spirits can talk . . . to worthy folks. So you're going to have to tell me what you want, Frank, whether I'm worthy or not."

A pheasant flapped its wings to escape the oncoming lone rider. Bass turned toward the intrusion. Sunlight was bright behind the silhouette as it cleared the low ridge and halted his tired horse.

"Morning, Emerson. Thanks for your help," Bass said without moving.

U.S. Deputy Marshal E. J. Vorak was short, no taller than Topper Lowe. But a thick chest and arms told of a physically powerful man. His flat face was sunburned permanently. A stub of a cigar was trying to quit on him, but he wouldn't let it. His long, double-breasted suit coat spoke of grueling days on the trail. A faded cravat was untied with its ends lying against his lapels. Across his back rested a quiver containing a sawed-off shotgun. A belt gun was hidden by his coat, as was his badge.

"No thanks to you. Had to hear about it from Frank. Sent me a wire," Vorak growled; his tired eyes studied Bass.

"I told him not to."

Vorak's shoulders shrugged in fatigue. His lathered roan horse looked ready to collapse.

"You'd better get off that horse before it falls down," Bass said.

"What's an old goat like you givin' advice for?" Vorak said without a smile, leaning forward in the saddle and yanking off his gloves.

Stepping away from the grave, Bass asked, "Have you eaten?"

"Not since last night," Vorak answered, shoving the gloves into his pocket. "Hardtack." He didn't need to say he had been pushing hard to get to Longmont and didn't. Bass knew the signs well.

"I take it you aren't any better at cooking than you used to be." A smile hinted on Bass's face.

"Look who's talkin'." Vorak swung down from the saddle, slow and stiff. "As I recall, neither you nor Frank could boil water." He led his mount toward the waiting attorney.

"Mighty good to see you, old friend." Bass held out his hand.

Dropping the reins, Vorak grabbed his hand and pulled Bass to him in a bear hug that was quickly returned by the old attorney.

"Been too long. Too damn long. I'm mighty sorry to hear about Frank." Vorak released him and looked around for the reins.

"Yeah, it was bad. Went down protecting me."

Vorak folded his arms, holding the reins with his left. "And you? Awful hard on you, I know. Losing your son an' all."

Bass didn't answer. The weary roan studied the spring grass and began to nibble. Othello bellowed a greeting and the horse's ears saluted.

"How'd you know where to find me?" Bass said, glancing at the fresh grave.

Vorak snorted and said, "Easter told me. He an' Nelene—an' Judge Pierce—were in the sheriff's office. Dropped off a saddlebag of papers against Lowe." He wiped his mouth with the back of his right hand. "You sure pick some strange friends, Bass."

"You mean Easter Sontag?" Bass chuckled. "Well, he came through for me. Real strong. He *is* a friend."

"Told me to tell you it's gonna cost you a steak dinner," Vorak said, "a bottle of whiskey and tickets to the theater."

Bass nodded and rubbed the toe of his boot in the dirt, while Vorak walked closer to the grave.

"Bass Tillman, Frank Schafer—and Emerson Holt. The gun trio. Lord, that seems like a long time ago." Vorak turned back to Bass. "How come you didn't change your name—like we did?"

"Settie wouldn't let me."

"Pretty little Settie. Man, she was somethin'." Vorak shook his head. "Wouldn't let you drink or smoke either, as I recall."

"Yeah, that's Settie. I didn't mind, though."

"Damn. Never thought I'd see Bass Tillman take orders from anyone." Vorak chuckled and ran his fingers along the top of the wooden cross. "Vorak was my maw's maiden name, you know. Same with Frank, I think."

"That's what he said."

Vorak studied the Bible in the old attorney's hand. "What ya got there? The Good Book?"

"It was Frank's." Bass held up the book with both hands.

"Can you read German?"

"No. Thought it might help. To bring it along."

"You know what I'd put on his headstone?" Vorak pushed his boot into the stirrup.

"What?"

Vorak swung back into the saddle. "I'd put Frank Schafer Babbit. Yessir, he'd like that. Frank Schafer Babbit. Has a nice ring to it."

Turning to get his impatient mule, Bass took several steps, stopped and looked up. "Thanks, I heard you." He gathered the reins, returned his attention to the waiting U.S. Marshal and asked, "What happened to Hautrese?"

"Oh, I had a talk with him. He decided it'd be good for his health to leave." Vorak smiled. "Last I saw, he was getting on a train. Headed for Chicago."

"He's getting off too easy."

Vorak nodded. "You going after him? Even if you found him, you'd play hell getting enough evidence to convict him."

"Wasn't thinking along those lines."

"Thought you gave up the gun a long time ago," Vorak said. "Reminds me, that young sheriff . . . what's his name, yeah, Manchester . . . he's already resigned. That rooster, Judge Pierce, wants you to take the job."

"Not interested. I told you what I was doing next." Bass cocked his head toward his old friend and eased into the saddle. "How about a drink in honor of our old friend? Settie wouldn't mind that. We'll get something to eat—and ask Easter to join us, if that's all right."

"You buying?"

"Don't I always?"

Vorak laughed and looked at his friend from the corner of tired eyes. "What's this I hear about an Indian gal taking a shine to you?"

BLOOD TRAIL TO KANSAS

ROBERT J. RANDISI

Ted Shea thinks he is a goner for sure. All the years he's worked to build his Montana spread and fine herd of prime beef means nothing if he can't sell them. And with a vicious rustler and his gang of cutthroats scaring all the hands, no one is willing to take to the trail. Until Dan Parmalee drifts into town. A gunman and gambler with a taste for long odds, he isn't about to let a little hot lead part him from some cold cash. But it doesn't take Dan long to realize this isn't just any run. This is a…*Blood Trail to Kansas*.

ISBN 10: 0-8439-5799-9
ISBN 13: 978-0-8439-5799-0 $5.99 US/$7.99 CAN

To order a book or to request a catalog call:
1-800-481-9191
This book is also available at your local bookstore, or you can check out our Web site **www.dorchesterpub.com** where you can look up your favorite authors, read excerpts, or glance at our discussion forum to see what people have to say about your favorite books.